THE ADVENTURES
OF
ROBINSON CRUSOE

At age fifty-nine, the British merchant and political writer Daniel Defoe first tried his hand at fiction writing. The result was *The Adventures of Robinson Crusoe,* published on April 25, 1719. The work became an immediate best seller and has remained one of the most popular books ever written. Defoe's realistic account of Crusoe's island life was based on several stories of actual shipwrecks, which had been widely circulated before the novel's publication. One of the best-known stories about castaways was that of the Scottish sailor Alexander Selkirk, who was put ashore at a deserted island four hundred miles off the west coast of Chile after a quarrel with the captain of the privateer on which he had served. Selkirk lived on the island more than four years before he was rescued by a passing ship. The currency of these stories convinced many that this book of the "Strange Surprizing Adventures of Robinson Crusoe, of York, Mariner: Who lived Eight and Twenty Years, all alone," as the 1719 title stated, was the narrative of an actual experience rather than a deftly wrought tale.

The impact of *Robinson Crusoe* extended over such diverse fields as literature, education, and travel. The novel's influence can be seen in the works of many eighteenth- and nineteenth-century writers, among them Samuel Taylor Coleridge, Sir Walter Scott, Robert Louis Stevenson, and Henry David Thoreau. Emphasizing practical experience in his educational philosophy, Jean-Jacques Rousseau admired the spirit of ingenuity evidenced by Crusoe in his island sojourn. In fact, Rousseau proclaimed that *Robinson Crusoe,* one of only two books comprising his library, would be the sole textbook he would use in the education of boys, personified by his character Émile. Defoe's tale also instilled readers with a desire to set off for foreign lands. René Caillié, an explorer who was the first European to travel to central Africa and return safely in the first half of the nineteenth century, remarked that "the History of Robinson Crusoe, in particular, inflamed my young imagination: I was impatient to encounter adventures like him; nay, I already felt an ambition to signalize myself by some important discovery springing up in my heart."

Unlike most Europeans of his day, Defoe himself was an inveterate traveler. He made his earliest journey—to Ipswich, near the site of Crusoe's first shipwreck—when he was eight years old. During his career as merchant and later as secret agent for King William III and Secretary of State Robert Harley, he traveled extensively throughout England, Scotland, Wales, and the Continent.

Defoe's religious background was also fundamental to the book's creation. Defoe was born a Protestant Dissenter and was educated for the ministry at the Reverend Charles Morton's academy at Newington Green, the leading college for Dissenters. Although Defoe eventually decided he was not called to the ministry, his religious instruction is evident in his depiction of Crusoe's story, and the book may be viewed as a moral guide. Robinson begins his travels ignorant of his relation to God, but at the end of his adventures, he undergoes a spiritual conversion and is able to live more peacefully with nature, his fellow beings, and himself.

The enthusiasm *Robinson Crusoe* inspired in Defoe's contemporaries was due to the portrayal of the main character as well as to the book's spiritual nature. Crusoe was an ordinary person, with heroic impulses and actions, but also with human flaws and failings. Readers could identify with Crusoe and imagine how they would act in his situation. Today, too, readers are fascinated by Crusoe's story. We are compelled by his "wandering dispositions," his adventures, his attempts to build a life for himself on his island, but most of all by his humanity.

The Editors

This Special Edition of

THE ADVENTURES OF ROBINSON CRUSOE

was prepared for
subscribers to
The Oxford Library of
the World's Great Books

THE OXFORD LIBRARY OF
THE WORLD'S GREAT BOOKS

THE ADVENTURES
— OF —
ROBINSON CRUSOE

Daniel Defoe

With the color woodcuts of Pierre Falké

OXFORD UNIVERSITY PRESS

THE FRANKLIN LIBRARY
has been selected by the
OXFORD UNIVERSITY PRESS
as publishers of
THE OXFORD LIBRARY OF THE WORLD'S GREAT BOOKS

The color woodcuts of Pierre Falké originally appeared in *La Vie et Les Adventures Étranges et Surprenantes de Robinson Crusoé de York, Marin,* published by Henri Jonquières et Compagnie, Paris, 1926, in an edition limited to 151 copies. They are reproduced courtesy of the late publisher's daughter, Madame Florence Jonquières, who graciously gave The Franklin Library access to one of these rare books.

The facsimile of the title page from the first edition (1719) of *The Adventures of Robinson Crusoe* was made available by the Rare Book Collections, Van Pelt Library, The University of Pennsylvania.

❖ ❖ ❖ ❖ ❖ ❖ ❖ ❖ ❖

THE
LIFE
AND
STRANGE SURPRIZING
ADVENTURES
OF
ROBINSON CRUSOE,
Of *YORK*, MARINER:

Who lived Eight and Twenty Years,
all alone in an un-inhabited Ifland on the
Coaft of AMERICA, near the Mouth of
the Great River of OROONOQUE;

Having been caft on Shore by Shipwreck, wherein all the Men perifhed but himfelf.

WITH

An Account how he was at laft as ftrangely deliver'd by PYRATES.

Written by Himfelf.

LONDON:
Printed for W. TAYLOR at the *Ship* in *Pater-Nofter-*
Row. MDCCXIX.

PREFACE

If ever the story of any private man's adventures in the world were worth making publick, and were acceptable when publish'd, the editor of this account thinks this will be so.

The wonders of this man's life exceed all that (he thinks) is to be found extant; the life of one man being scarce capable of a greater variety.

The story is told with modesty, with seriousness, and with a religious application of events to the uses to which wise men always apply them, viz., to the instruction of others by this example, and to justify and honour the wisdom of Providence in all the variety of our circumstances, let them happen how they will.

The editor believes the thing to be a just history of fact; neither is there any appearance of fiction in it. And whoever thinks, because all such things are dispatch'd, that the improvement of it, as well as to the diversion, as to the instruction of the reader, will be the same; and as such, he thinks, without further compliment to the world, he does them a great service in the publication.

THE ADVENTURES
OF
ROBINSON CRUSOE

I WAS BORN in the year 1632, in the city of York, of a good family, tho' not of that country, my father being a foreigner of Bremen, who settl'd first at Hull. He got a good estate by merchandize, and leaving off his trade, liv'd afterwards at York, whence he had marry'd my mother, whose relations were named Robinson, a very good family in that country, and from whom I was call'd Robinson Kreutznaer; but by the usual corruption of words in England, we are now call'd, nay, we call ourselves, and write our name Crusoe, and so my companions always call'd me.

I had two elder brothers, one of which was lieutenant colonel to an English regiment of foot in Flanders, formerly commanded by the famous Colonel Lockhart, and was kill'd at the battle near Dunkirk against the Spaniards. What became of my second brother I never knew, any more than my father or mother did know what was become of me.

Being the third son of the family, and not bred to any trade, my head began to be fill'd very early with rambling thoughts. My father, who was very ancient, had given me a competent share of learning, as far as house-education and a country free-school generally goes, and design'd me for the Law; but I would be satisfy'd with nothing but going to sea, and my inclination to this led me so strongly against the will, nay, the commands of my father, and against all the entreaties and persuasions of my mother and other friends, that there seem'd to be something fatal in that propension of nature tending directly to the life of misery which was to befell me.

My father, a wise and grave man, gave me serious and excellent counsel against what he foresaw was my design. He call'd me one morning into his chamber, where he was confin'd by the gout, and expostulated very warmly with me upon this subject. He ask'd me what reasons more than a meer wand'ring inclination I had for leaving my father's house and my native country, where I might be well introduc'd, and had a prospect of raising my fortunes by application and industry, with a life of ease and pleasure. He told me it was for men of desperate fortunes on one hand, or of aspiring, superior fortunes on the other, who went abroad upon adventures, to rize by enterprize, and make themselves famous in undertakings of a nature out of the common road; that these things were all either too far above me, or too far below me; that mine was the middle state, or what might be call'd the upper station of low life, which he had found by long experience was the best state in the world, the most suited to human happiness, not expos'd to the miseries and hardships, the labour and sufferings of the mechanick part of mankind, and not embarrass'd with the pride, luxury, ambition, and envy of the upper part of mankind. He told me I might judge of the happiness of this state by this one thing, viz., that this was the state of life which all other people envy'd; that kings have frequently lament'd the miserable consequences of being born to great things, and wish'd they had been plac'd in the middle of the two extremes, between the mean and the great; that the wise man gave his testimony to this as the just standard of true felicity, when he pray'd to have neither poverty or riches.

He bade me observe it, and I should always find that the calamities of life were shar'd among the upper and lower part of mankind; but that the middle station had the fewest disasters and was not expos'd to so many vicissitudes as the higher or lower part of mankind; nay, they were not subjected to so many distempers and uneasinesses either of body or mind as those were who, by vicious living, luxury and extravagancies on one hand, or by hard labour, want of necessaries, and mean or insufficient diet on the other hand, bring distempers upon themselves by the natural consequences of their way of living. That the middle station of life was calculated for all kind of virtues and all kinds of enjoyments; that peace and plenty were the handmaids of a middle fortune; that temperance, moderation, quietness, health, society, all agreeable diversions, and all desirable pleasures were the blessings attending the middle station of life; that this way men went silently and smoothly thro' the world, and comfortably out of it, not embarrass'd with the labours of the hands or of the head, not sold to the life of slavery for daily bread, or harrast with perplex'd circumstances which rob the soul of peace and the body of rest; not enrag'd with the passion of envy or secret burning lust of ambition for great things, but in easy circumstances sliding gently thro' the world and sensibly tasting the sweets of living, without the bitter, feeling that they are happy, and learning by every day's experience to know it more sensibly.

After this, he press'd me earnestly, and in the most affectionate manner, not to play the young man, not to precipitate myself into miseries which nature and the station of life I was born in seem'd to have provided against; that I was under no necessity of seeking my bread; that he would do well for me, and endeavour to enter me fairly into the station of life which he had been just recommending to me; and that if I was not very easy and happy in the world, it must be my meer fate or fault that must hinder it, and that he should have nothing to answer for, having thus discharg'd his duty in warning me against measures which he knew would be to my hurt. In a word, that he would do very kind things for me if I would stay and settle at home as he directed, so he would not have so much hand in my misfortunes as to give me any encouragement to go away. And to close all, he told me I had my elder brother for an example, to whom he had used the same earnest persuasions to keep him from going into the Low Country Wars, but could not prevail, his young desires prompting him to run into the Army where he was kill'd; and tho' he said he would not cease to pray for me, yet he would venture to say to me that if I did take this foolish step, God would not bless me, and I would have leisure hereafter to reflect upon having neglected his counsel when there might be none to assist in my recovery.

I observ'd in this last part of his discourse, which was truly prophetick, tho' I suppose my father did not know it to be so himself; I say, I observ'd the tears run down his face very plentifully, and especially when he spoke of my brother who was kill'd; and that when he spoke of my having leisure to repent, and none to assist me, he was so mov'd that he broke off the discourse, and told me his heart was so full he could say no more to me.

I was sincerely affected with this discourse, as indeed who could be otherwise; and I resolv'd not to think of going abroad any more, but to settle at home according to my father's desire. But alas! a few days wore it all off; and in short, to prevent any of my father's further importunities, in a few weeks after, I resolv'd to run quite away from him. However, I did not act so hastily neither as my first heat of resolution prompted, but I took my mother, at a time when I thought her a little pleasanter than ordinary, and told her that my thoughts were so entirely bent upon seeing the world, that I should never settle to any thing with resolution enough to go thro' with it, and my father had better give me his consent than force me to go without it; that I was now eighteen years old, which was too late to go apprentice to a trade, or clerk to an attorney; that I was sure if I did, I should never serve out my time, and I should certainly run away from my master before my time was out and go to sea; and if she would speak to my father to let me go but one voyage abroad, if I came home again and did not like it, I would go no more, and I would promise by a double diligence to recover that time I had lost.

This put my mother into a great passion. She told me she knew it would be to no purpose to speak to my father upon any such subject; that he knew too well what was my interest to give his consent to any thing so much for my hurt; and that she wonder'd how I could think of any such thing after such a discourse as I had had with my father, and such kind and tender expressions as she knew my father had used to me; and that in short, if I would ruine myself there was no help for me; but I might depend I should never have their consent to it. For her part she would not have so much hand in my destruction, and I should never have it to say that my mother was willing when my father was not.

Tho' my mother refus'd to move it to my father, yet as I have heard afterwards, she reported all the discourse to him, and that my father, after showing a great concern at it, said to her with a sigh, "That boy might be happy if he would stay at home, but if he goes abroad he will be the miserablest wretch that was ever born: I can give no consent to it."

It was not till almost a year after this that I broke loose, tho' in the meantime I continu'd obstinately deaf to all proposals of settling to business, and frequently expostulated with my father and mother about their being so positively determin'd against what they knew my inclinations prompted me to. But being one day at Hull, where I went casually, and without any purpose of making an elopement that time; but I say, being there, and one of my companions being going to sea to London, in his father's ship, and prompting me to go with them, with the common allurement of seafaring men, viz., that it should cost me nothing for my passage, I consulted neither father or mother anymore, nor so much as sent them word of it; but leaving them to hear of it as they might, without asking God's blessing, or my father's, without any consideration of circumstances or consequences, and in an ill hour, God knows. On the first of September, 1651, I went on board a ship bound for London; never any young adventurer's misfortunes, I believe, began sooner, or continu'd longer than mine. The ship was no sooner gotten out of the humber, but the wind began to blow, and the waves to rize in a most frightful manner; and as I had never been at sea before, I was most inexpressibly sick in body and terrify'd in my mind: I began now seriously to reflect upon what I had done, and how justly I was overtaken by the judgment of Heaven for my wicked leaving my father's house, and abandoning my duty; all the good counsel of my parents, my father's tears and my mother's entreaties, came now fresh into my mind, and my conscience, which was not yet come to the pitch of hardness which it has been since, reproach'd me with the contempt of advice and the breach of my duty to God and to my father.

All this while the storm encreas'd, and the sea, which I had never been upon before, went very high, tho' nothing like what I have seen many times since; no, nor like what I saw a few days after. But it was enough to affect me then, who was but a young sailor and had never known any thing of the matter. I expected every wave would have swallow'd us up, and that every time the ship fell down, as I thought, in the trough or hollow of the sea, we should never rize more; and in this agony of mind, I made many vows and resolutions, that if it would please God here to spare my life this one voyage, if ever I got once my foot upon dry land again, I would go directly home to my father, and never set it into a ship again while I liv'd; that I would take his advice, and never run myself into such miseries as these anymore. Now I saw plainly the goodness of his observations about the middle station of life, how easy, how comfortably he had liv'd all his days, and never had been expos'd to tempests at sea or troubles on shore;

and I resolv'd that I would, like a true repenting prodigal, go home to my father.

These wise and sober thoughts continu'd all the while the storm continu'd, and indeed sometime after; but the next day the wind was abated and the sea calmer, and I began to be a little inur'd to it. However, I was very grave for all that day, being also a little seasick still; but towards night the weather clear'd up, the wind was quite over, and a charming fine evening follow'd; the sun went down perfectly clear and riz'd so the next morning; and having little or no wind and a smooth sea, the sun shining upon it, the sight was, as I thought, the most delightful that ever I saw.

I had slept well in the night, and was now no more seasick but very cheerful, looking with wonder upon the sea that was so rough and terrible the day before and could be so calm and so pleasant in so little time after. And now lest my good resolutions should continue, my companion, who had indeed entic'd me away, comes to me, "Well, Bob," said he, clapping me on the shoulder, "how do you do after it? I warrant you were frighted, wa'n't you, last night, when it blew but a capful of wind." "Wind? A capful d'you call it?" said I. " 'Twas a terrible storm." "A storm, you fool you," reply'd he. "Do you call that a storm? Why it was nothing at all; give us but a good ship and sea room, and we think nothing of such a squall of wind as that; but you're but a fresh-water sailor, Bob. Come let us make a bowl of punch and we'll forget all that, d'ye see what charming weather 'tis now." To make short this sad part of my story, we went the old way of all sailors; the punch was made, and I was made drunk with it, and in that one night's wickedness I drown'd all my repentance, all my reflections upon my past conduct, and all my resolutions for my future. In a word, as the sea was return'd to its smoothness of surface and settl'd calmness by the abatement of that storm, so the hurry of my thoughts being over, my fears and apprehensions of being swallow'd up by the sea being forgotten, and the current of my former desires return'd, I entirely forgot the vows and promises that I had made in my distress. I found indeed some intervals of reflection, and the serious thoughts did, as it were, endeavour to return again sometimes, but I shook them off and rouz'd myself from them as it were from a distemper, and, applying myself to drink and company, soon master'd the return of those fits, for so I call'd them, and I had in five or six days got as compleat a victory over conscience as any young fellow that resolv'd not to be troubl'd with it could desire. But I was to have another trial for it still, and Providence, as in such cases generally it does, resolv'd to leave me entirely without excuse. For if I would not take this for a deliverance, the next was to be such a one as the worst and most harden'd wretch among us would confess both the danger and the mercy.

The sixth day of our being at sea we came into Yarmouth Roads; the wind having been contrary and the weather calm, we had made but little way since the storm. Here we were oblig'd to come to anchor, and here we lay, the wind continuing contrary, viz., at south-west for seven or eight days, during which time a great many ships from Newcastle came into the same roads, as the common harbour where the ships might wait for a wind for the river.

We had not however rid here so long, but should have tided it up the river, but that the wind blew too fresh and, after we had lay'd four or five days, blew very hard. However, the roads being reckon'd as good as a harbour, the anchorage good, and our ground-tackle very strong, our men were unconcern'd and not in the least apprehensive of danger, but spent the time in rest and mirth, after the manner of the sea. But the eighth day, in the morning, the wind encreas'd, and we had all hands at work to strike our topmasts and make everything snug and close that the ship might ride as easy as possible. By noon the sea went very high indeed, and our ship rid forecastle in, shipp'd several seas, and we thought once or twice our anchor had come home; upon which our master order'd out the sheet anchor, so that we rode with two anchors a-head, and the cable pay'd out to the bitter end.

By this time it blew a terrible storm indeed, and now I began to see terror and amazement in the faces even of the seamen themselves. The master, tho' vigilant to the business of preserving the ship, yet as he went in and out of his cabbin by me, I could hear him softly to himself say several times, "Lord, be merciful to us, we shall be all lost, we shall be all undone" and the like. During these first hurries, I was stupid, lying still in my cabbin, which was in the steerage, and cannot describe my temper. I could ill reassume the first penitence, which I had so apparently trampl'd upon and harden'd myself against; I thought the bitterness of death had been past and that this would be nothing too like the first. But when the master himself came by me, as I said just now, and said we should be all lost, I was dreadfully frighted. I got up out of my cabbin and look'd out, but such a dismal sight I never saw. The sea went mountains high and broke upon us every three or four minutes. When I could look about, I could see nothing but distress round us. Two ships that rid near us we found had cut their masts by the board, being deep-loaden; and our men cry'd out that a ship which rid about a mile a-head of us was founder'd. Two more ships, being driven from their anchors, were run out of the roads to sea at all adventures, and that with not a mast standing. The lightships far'd the best, as not so much labouring in the sea; but two or three of them drove and came close by us, running away with only their sprit-sail out before the wind.

Towards evening the mate and the boat-swain begg'd the master of our ship to let them cut away the foremast, which he was very unwilling to. But the boat-swain protesting to him that if he did not the ship would founder, he consented; and when they had cut away the foremast, the mainmast stood so loose, and shook the ship so much, they were oblig'd to cut her away also and make a clear deck.

Any one may judge what a condition I must be in at all this, who was but a young sailor, and who had been in such a fright before at but a little. But if I can express at this distance the thoughts I had about me at that time, I was in tenfold more horror of mind upon account of my former convictions, and having return'd from them to the resolutions I had wickedly taken at first, than I was at death itself; and these, added to the terror of the storm, put me into such a condition that I can by no words describe it. But the worst was not come yet; the storm continu'd with such fury that the seamen themselves acknowledg'd they had never known a worse. We had a good ship, but she was deep-loaden and wallow'd in the sea, that the seamen every now and then cry'd out she would founder. It was my advantage, in one respect, that I did not know what they meant by founder, till I enquir'd.

However, the storm was so violent, that I saw what is not often seen: the master, the boat-swain, and some others more sensible than the rest, at their prayers and expecting every moment that the ship would go to the bottom. In the middle of the night, and under all the rest of our distress, one of the men who had been down on purpose to see cry'd out we had sprung a leak; another said there was four foot water in the hold. Then all hands were call'd to the pump. At that very word my heart, as I thought, dy'd within me, and I fell backwards upon the side of my bed where I sat into the cabbin. However, the men rouz'd me and told me that I, who was able to do nothing before, was as well able to pump as another; at which I stirr'd up and went to the pump and work'd very heartily. While this was doing, the master, seeing some light colliers, which not able to ride out the storm were oblig'd to slip and run away to sea and would come near us, order'd us to fire a gun as a signal of distress. I, who knew nothing what that meant, was so surpriz'd that I thought the ship had broke or some dreadful thing had happen'd. In a word, I was so surpriz'd that I fell down in a swoon. As this was a time when every body had his own life to think of, no body minded me or what was become of me; but another man stepp'd up to the pump, and thrusting me a-side with his foot, let me lie, thinking I had been dead; and it was a great while before I came to myself.

We work'd on, but, the water encreasing in the hold, it was apparent that the ship would founder, and tho' the storm began to abate a little, yet as it was not possible she could swim till we might run into a port. So the master continu'd firing guns for help, and a lightship who had rid it out just a-head of us ventur'd a boat out to help us. It was with the utmost hazard the boat came near us, but it was impossible for us to get on board, or for the boat to lie near our shipside, till at last the men, rowing very heartily and venturing their lives to save ours, our men cast them a rope over the stern with a buoy to it and then ver'd it out a great length, which they after great labour and hazard took hold of and we hal'd them close under our stern and got all into their boat. It was to no purpose for them or for us after we were in the boat to think of reaching our own ship, so all agreed to let her drive and only to pull her in towards shore as much as we could, and our master promised them that if the boat was stav'd upon shore he would make it good to their master. So partly rowing and partly driving, our boat went away to the nor'ward, sloping towards the shore almost as far as Winterton Ness.

We were not much more than a quarter of an hour out of our ship but we saw her sink, and then I understood for the first time what was meant by a ship foundering in the sea; I must acknowledge I had hardly eyes to look up when the seamen told me she was sinking; for from that moment they rather put me into the boat than that I might be said to go in, my heart was, as it were, dead within me, partly with fright, partly with horror of mind and the thoughts of what was yet before me.

While we were in this condition, the men yet labouring at the oar to bring the boat near the shore, we could see, when our boat mounted the waves, a great many people running along the shore to assist us when we should come near, but we made but slow way, nor were we able to reach the shore, till being past the lighthouse at Winterton, the shore falls off to the westward towards Cromer, and so the land broke off a little the violence of the wind. Here we got in and, tho' not without much difficulty, got all safe on shore and walk'd afterwards on foot to Yarmouth where, as unfortunate men, we were used with great humanity, as well by the magistrates of the town, who assign'd us good quarters, as by particular merchants and owners of ships; and had money given us sufficient to carry us either to London or back to Hull, as we thought fit.

Had I now had the sense to have gone back to Hull and to have gone home, I had been happy; for my father, an emblem of our Blessed Saviour's parable, had even kill'd the fatted calf for me; for hearing the ship I went away in was cast away in Yarmouth Road, it was a great while before he had any assurance that I was not drown'd.

But my ill fate push'd me on now with an obstinacy that nothing could resist; and tho' I had several times loud calls from my reason and my more compos'd judgment to go home, yet I had no power to do it. I know not what to call this, nor will I urge that it is a secret overruling decree that hurries us on to be the instruments of our destruction, even tho' it be before us and that we rush upon it with our eyes open. Certainly nothing but some such decre'd unavoidable misery attending, and which it was impossible for me to escape, could have push'd me forward against the calm reasonings and persuasions of my most retir'd thoughts and against two such visible instructions as I had met with in my first attempt.

My comrade, who had help'd to harden me before, and who was the master's son, was now less forward than I. The first time he spoke to me after we were at Yarmouth, which was not till two or three days, for we were separated in the town to several quarters; I say, the first time he saw me, it appear'd his tone was alter'd and, looking very melancholy and shaking his head, ask'd me how I did and told his father who I was and how I had come this voyage only for a trial in order to go farther abroad. His father turn'd to me with a very grave and concern'd tone. "Young man," said he, "you ought never to go to sea anymore, you ought to take this for a plain and visible token that you are not to be a seafaring man." "Why, sir," said I, "will you go to sea no more?" "That is another case," said he. "It is my calling and therefore my duty; but as you made this voyage for a trial, you see what a taste Heaven has given you of what you are to expect if you persist; perhaps this is all befallen us on your account, like Jonah in the ship of Tarshish. Pray," continu'd he, "what are you? And on what account did you go to sea?" Upon that I told him some of my story, at the end of which he burst out with a strange kind of passion, "What have I done," said he, "that such an unhappy wretch should come into my ship? I would not set my foot in the same ship with thee again for a thousand pounds." This indeed was, as I said, an excursion of his spirits which were yet agitated by the sense of his loss, and was further than he could have authority to go. However, he afterwards talk'd very gravely to me, exhorted me to go back to my father and not tempt Providence to my ruine; told me I might see a visible hand of Heaven against me. "And, young man," said he, "depend upon it, if you do not go back, wherever you go, you will meet with nothing but disasters and disappointments till your father's words are fulfilled upon you."

We parted soon after, for I made him little answer, and I saw him no more; which way he went, I know not.

As for me, having some money in my pocket, I travell'd to London by land, and there, as well as on the road, had many struggles with myself; what course of life I should take and whether I should go home or go to sea.

As to going home, shame oppos'd the best motions that offer'd to my thoughts, and it immediately occurr'd to me how I should be laugh'd at among the neighbours and should be asham'd to see, not my father and mother only, but even every body else. I have since often observ'd how incongruous and irrational the common temper of mankind is, especially of youth, to that reason which ought to guide them, in such cases, viz., that they are not asham'd to sin, and yet are asham'd to repent; not asham'd of the action for which they ought justly to be esteem'd fools, but are asham'd of the returning, which only can make them be esteem'd wise men.

In this state of life however I remain'd some time, uncertain what measures to take and what course of life to lead. An irresistible reluctance continu'd to going home, and as I stay'd a while, the remembrance of the distress I had been in wore off. As that abated, the little motion I had in my desires to a return wore off with it, till at last I quite lay'd a-side the thoughts of it and look'd out for a voyage.

That evil influence which carry'd me first away from my father's house, that hurry'd me into the wild and indigested notion of raising my fortune; and that impress'd those conceits so forcibly upon me as to make me deaf to all good advice and to the entreaties and even commands of my father; I say, the same influence, whatever it was, presented the most unfortunate of all enterprizes to my view, and I went on board a vessel bound to the coast of Africa or, as our sailors vulgarly call'd it, a voyage to Guiney.

It was my great misfortune that in all these adventures I did not ship myself as a sailor, whereby, tho' I might indeed have work'd a little harder than ordinary, yet at the same time I had learn'd the duty and office of a fore-mast man and in time might have qualify'd myself for a mate or lieutenant, if not for a master. But as it was always my fate to choose for the worse, so I did here; for having money in my pocket and good cloaths upon my back, I would always go on board in the habit of a gentleman, and so I neither had any business in the ship or learn'd to do any.

It was my lot first of all to fall into pretty good company in London, which does not always happen to such loose and unguided young fellows as I then was; the Devil generally not omitting to lay some snare for them very early. But it was not so with me; I first fell acquainted with the master of a ship who had been on the coast of Guiney, and who having had very good success there, was resolv'd to go again, and who taking a fancy to my conversation, which was not at all disagreeable at that time, hearing me say I had a mind to see the world, told me if I would go the voyage with him I should be at no expence. I should be his messmate and his companion, and if I could carry any thing with me, I should have all the advantage of it that the trade would admit, and perhaps I might meet with some encouragement.

I embrac'd the offer, and ent'ring into a strict friendship with this captain, who was an honest and plain-dealing man, I went the voyage with him and carry'd a small ad-venture with me, which by the disinterested honesty of my friend the Captain, I encreas'd very considerably; for I carry'd about 40 pounds sterling in such toys and trifles as the captain directed me to buy. This 40 pounds I had muster'd together by the assistance of some of my relations whom I corresponded with, and who, I believe, got my father, or at least my mother, to contribute so much as that to my first adventure.

This was the only voyage which I may say was successful in all my adventures, and which I owe to the integrity and honesty of my friend the captain, under whom also I got a competent knowledge of the Mathematicks and the Rules of Navigation; learn'd how to keep an account of the ship's course, take an observation; and, in short, to understand some things that were needful to be understood by a sailor. For, as he took delight to introduce me, I took delight to learn; and, in a word, this voyage made me both a sailor and a merchant. I brought home five pounds and nine ounces of gold dust for my adventure, which yielded me in London at my return almost 300 pounds sterling, and this fill'd me with those aspiring thoughts which have since so compleated my ruine.

Yet even in this voyage I had my misfortunes too; particularly, that I was continually sick, being thrown into a violent calenture by the excessive heat of the climate; our principal trading being upon the coast, from the latitude of 15 degrees north even to the Line itself.

I was now set up for a Guiney trader; and my friend, to my great misfortune, dying soon after his arrival, I resolv'd to go the same voyage again, and I embark'd in the same vessel with one who was his mate in the former voyage, and had now got the command of the ship. This was the unhappiest voyage that ever man made; for tho' I did not carry quite 100 pounds of my new-gain'd wealth, so that I had 200 left, and which I lodg'd with my friend's widow, who was very just to me, yet I fell into terrible misfortunes on this voyage. The first was this, *viz.*, our ship making her course towards the Canary Islands, or rather between those islands and the African shore, was surpriz'd in the grey of the morning by a Turkish rover of Sallee, who gave chase to us with all the sail she could make. We crowded also as much canvass as our yards would spread, or our masts carry, to have got clear, but finding the pirate gain'd upon us, and would certainly come up with us in a few hours, we prepar'd to fight; our ship having twelve guns, and the rogue eighteen. About three in the afternoon she came up with us, and bringing to, by mistake just athwart our quarter, instead of athwart our stern as she intended, we brought eight of our guns to bear on that side and pour'd in a broadside upon her, which made her sheer off again, after returning our fire, and pouring in also her small-shot from near two hundred men which she had on board. However, we had not a man touch'd, all our men keeping close. She prepar'd to attack us again and we to defend ourselves; but laying us on board the next time upon our other quarter, she enter'd sixty men upon our decks, who immediately fell to cutting and hacking the decks and rigging. We ply'd them with small-shot, half-pikes, powder-chests, and such like, and clear'd our deck of them twice. However, to cut short this melancholy part of my story, our ship being disabl'd, and three of our men kill'd and eight wounded, we were oblig'd to yield and were carry'd all prisoners into Sallee, a port belonging to the Moors.

The usage I had there was not so dreadful as at first I apprehended, nor was I carry'd up the country to the emperor's court as the rest of our men were, but was kept by the captain of the rover, as his proper prize, and made his slave, being young and nimble and fit for his business. At this surprizing change of my circumstances from a merchant to a miserable slave, I was perfectly overwhelm'd; and now I look'd back upon my father's prophetick discourse to me, that I should be miserable and have none to relieve me, which I thought was now so effectually brought to pass that it could not be worse; that now the hand of Heaven had overtaken me, and I was undone without redemption. But alas! this was but a taste of the misery I was to go thro', as will appear in the sequel of this story.

As my new patron or master had taken me home to his house, so I was in hopes that he would take me with him when he went to sea again, believing that it would sometime or other be his fate to be taken by a Spanish or Portugueze man of war; and that then I should be set at liberty. But this hope of mine was soon taken away; for when he went to sea, he left me on shore to look after his little garden and do the common drudgery of a slave about his house; and when he came home again from his cruise, he order'd me to lie in the cabbin to look after the ship.

Here I meditated nothing but my escape and what method I might take to effect it, but found no way that had the least probability in it. Nothing presented to make the supposition of it rational, for I had no body to communicate it to that would embark with me; no fellow-slave, no Englishman, Irishman, or Scotsman there but myself; so that for two years, tho' I often pleas'd myself with the imagination, yet I never had the least encouraging prospect of putting it in practice.

After about two years an odd circumstance presented itself, which put the old thought of making some attempt for my liberty again in my head. My patron lying at home

20

longer than usual, without fitting out his ship (which, as I heard, was for want of money), used constantly, once or twice a week, sometimes oftener if the weather was fair, to take the ship's pinnace, and go out into the road a-fishing; and as he always took me and a young Maresco with him to row the boat, we made him very merry, and I prov'd very dextrous in catching fish, insomuch that sometimes he would send me with a Moor, one of his kinsmen, and the youth, the Maresco as they call'd him, to catch a dish of fish for him.

It happen'd one time, that going a-fishing in a stark calm morning, a fog rose so thick that tho' we were not half a league from the shore we lost sight of it; and rowing we knew not whither or which way, we labour'd all day and all the next night, and when the morning came we found we had pull'd off to sea instead of pulling in for the shore, and that we were at least two leagues from the shore. However, we got well in again, tho' with a great deal of labour and some danger, for the wind began to blow pretty fresh in the morning; but particularly we were all very hungry.

But our patron, warn'd by this disaster, resolv'd to take more care of himself for the future; and having lying by him the longboat of our English ship he had taken, he resolv'd he would not go a-fishing anymore without a compass and some provision. So he order'd the carpenter of his ship, who also was an English slave, to build a little stateroom or cabbin in the middle of the longboat, like that of a barge, with a place to stand behind it to steer and hale home the mainsheet, and room before for a hand or two to stand and work the sails. She sail'd with what we call'd a shoulder-of-mutton sail, and the boom gib'd over the top of the cabbin, which lay very snug and low, and had in it room for him to lie, with a slave or two, and a table to eat on, with some small lockers to put in some bottles of such liquor as he thought fit to drink and particularly, his bread, rice, and coffee.

We went frequently out with this boat a-fishing, and, as I was most dextrous to catch fish for him, he never went without me. It happen'd that he had appointed to go out in this boat, either for pleasure or for fish, two or three Moors of some distinction in that place, and for whom he had provided extraordinarily. He had therefore sent on board the boat over-night a larger store of provisions than ordinary and had order'd me to get ready three fuzees with powder and shot, which were on board his ship, for that they design'd some sport of fowling as well as fishing.

I got all things ready as he had directed and waited the next morning with the boat, wash'd clean, her antient and pendants out and every thing to accommodate his guests. By and by my patron came on board alone and told me his guests had put off going, upon some business that fell out, and order'd me with the man and the boy, as usual, to go out with the boat and catch them some fish, for that his friends were to sup at his house; and commanded that as soon as I had got some fish I should bring it home to his house; all which I prepar'd to do.

This moment my former notions of deliverance darted into my thoughts, for now I found I was like to have a little ship at my command; and my master being gone, I prepar'd to furnish myself, not for a-fishing business but for a voyage, tho' I knew not, neither did I so much as consider, whither I should steer, for anywhere to get out of that place was my way.

My first contrivance was to make a pretence to speak to the Moor, to get something for our subsistance on board, for I told him we must not presume to eat of our patron's bread. He said that was true, so he brought a large basket of rusk or bisket of their kind and three jarrs with fresh water into the boat. I knew where my patron's case of bottles stood, which it was evident by the make were taken out of some English prize, and I convey'd these into the boat while the Moor was on shore, as if they had been there before, for our master. I convey'd also a great lump of beeswax into the boat, which weigh'd above half a hundredweight, with a parcel of twine or thread, a hatchet, a saw, and a hammer, all of which were of great use to us afterwards; especially the wax to make candles. Another trick I try'd upon him, which he innocently came into also: his name was Ismael, but they call'd him Muly or Moely, so I call'd to him, "Moely," said I, "our patron's guns are on board the boat. Can you not get a little powder and shot, it may be we may kill some Alcamies [a fowl like our Curlieus] for ourselves, for I know he keeps the gunner's stores in the ship?" "Yes," said he, "I'll bring some," and accordingly he brought a great leather pouch, which held about a pound and a half of powder, or rather more; and another pouch which held five or six pounds of shot, with some bullets, and put all into the boat. At the same time I had found some powder of my master's in the great cabbin, with which I fill'd one of the large bottles in the case, which was almost empty, pouring what was in it into another. Thus furnish'd with every thing needful, we sail'd out of the port to fish. The castle, which is at the entrance of the port, knew who we were and took no notice of us; and we were not above a mile out of the port before we hal'd in our sail and set us down to fish. The wind blew from the NNE, which was contrary to my desire, for had it blown southerly I had been sure to have made the coast of Spain and at least reach'd to the Bay of Cadiz; but my resolutions were, blow which way it would, I would be gone from that horrid place where I was and leave the rest to fate.

After we had fish'd some time and catch'd nothing (for when I had fish on my hook I would not pull them up, that he might not see them), I said to the Moor, "This will not do, our master will not be thus serv'd, we must stand farther off." He, thinking no harm, agreed, and being in the head of the boat set the sails. As I had the helm, I ran the boat out near a league farther, and then brought her to as if I would fish. Then giving the boy the helm, I stepp'd forward to where the Moor was and, making as if I stoop'd for something behind him, I took him by surprize with my arm under his twist and toss'd him clear overboard into the sea. He riz'd immediately, for he swam like a cork, and call'd to me, begg'd to be taken in, and told me he would go all over the world with me. He swam so strong after the boat that he would have reach'd me very quickly, there being but little wind; upon which I stepp'd into the cabbin and fetching one of the fowling-pieces, presented it at him and told him I had done him no hurt, and if he would be quiet I would do him none. "But," said I, "you swim well enough to reach to the shore, and the sea is calm, so make the best of your way to shore and I will do you no harm, but if you come near the boat I'll shoot you thro' the head, for I am resolv'd to have my liberty." So he turn'd himself about and swam for the shore, and I make no doubt but he reach'd it with ease, for he was an excellent swimmer.

I could have been content to have taken this Moor with me, and drown'd the boy, but there was no venturing to trust him. When he was gone I turn'd to the boy, who they call'd Xury, and said to him, "Xury, if you will be faithful to me I'll make you a great man, but if you will not stroke your face to be true to me, that is, to swear by Mahomet and your father's beard, I must throw you into the sea too." The boy smil'd in my face and spoke so innocently that I could not mistrust him; he swore to be faithful to me, and go all over the world with me.

While I was in view of the Moor that was swimming, I stood out directly to sea with the boat, rather stretching to windward, that they might think me gone towards the straits-mouth (as indeed any one that had been in their wits must have been suppos'd to do) for who would have suppos'd we were sail'd on to the southward to the truly barbarian coast, where whole nations of Negroes were sure to surround us with their canoes and destroy us; where we could ne'er once go on shore but we should be devour'd by savage beasts or more merciless savages of human kind.

But as soon as it grew dusk in the evening, I chang'd my course and steer'd directly south by east, bending my course a little towards the east, that I might keep in with the shore; and having a fair fresh gale of wind, and a smooth quiet sea, I made such sail that I believe by the next day at three a-clock in the afternoon, when I first made the land, I could not be less than 150 miles south of Sallee, quite beyond the emperor of Morocco's dominions, or indeed of any other king thereabouts, for we saw no people.

Yet such was the fright I had taken at the Moors, and the dreadful apprehensions I had of falling into their hands, that I would not stop or go on shore or come to anchor (the wind continuing fair), till I had sail'd in that manner five days. Then the wind shifting to the southward, I concluded that if any of our vessels were in chase of me, they also would now give over, so I ventur'd to make to the coast and came to anchor in the mouth of a little river, I knew not what, or where; neither what latitude, what country, what nation, or what river. I neither saw or desir'd to see any people, the principal thing I wanted was fresh water. We came into this creek in the evening, resolving to swim to shore as soon as it was dark and discover the country. But as soon as it was quite dark we heard such dreadful noises of the barking, roaring, and howling of wild creatures, of we knew not what kinds, that the poor boy was ready to die with fear and begg'd of me not to go on shore till day. "Well, Xury," said I, "then I won't, but it may be we may see men by day, who will be as bad to us as those lyons." "Then we give them the shoot gun," said Xury, laughing. "Make them run wey." Such English Xury spoke by conversing among us slaves. However, I was glad to see the boy so cheerful, and I gave him a dram (out of our patron's case of bottles) to cheer him up. After all, Xury's advice was good, and I took it. We dropp'd our little anchor and lay still all night; I say still (for we slept none!), for in two or three hours we saw vast great creatures (we knew not what to call them) of many sorts come down to the seashore and run into the water, wallowing and washing themselves for the pleasure of cooling themselves, and they made such hideous howlings and yellings that I never indeed heard the like.

Xury was dreadfully frighted, and indeed so was I too; but we were both more frighted when we heard one of these mighty creatures come swimming towards our boat.

We could not see him, but we might hear him by his blowing to be a monstrous huge, and furious, beast. Xury said it was a lyon, and it might be so for ought I know, but poor Xury cry'd to me to weigh the anchor and row away. "No," said I. "Xury, we can slip our cable with the buoy to it and go off to sea; they cannot follow us far." I had no sooner said so, but I perceiv'd the creature (whatever it was) within two oars' length, which something surpriz'd me; however, I immediately stepp'd to the cabbin-door, and taking up my gun fir'd at him, upon which he immediately turn'd about and swam towards the shore again.

But it is impossible to describe the horrible noises and hideous cryes and howlings that were rais'd as well upon the edge of the shore as higher within the country, upon the noise or report of the gun, a thing I have some reason to believe those creatures had never heard before. This convinc'd me that there was no going on shore for us in the night upon that coast. But how to venture on shore in the day was another question too; for to have fallen into the hands of any of the savages had been as bad as to have fallen into the hands of lyons and tygers; at least we were equally apprehensive of the danger of it.

Be that as it would, we were oblig'd to go on shore somewhere or other for water, for we had not a pint left in the boat; when or where to get to it was the point. Xury said if I would let him go on shore with one of the jarrs, he would find if there was any water and bring some to me. I ask'd him why he would go, why I should not go and he stay in the boat. The boy answer'd with so much affection that made me love him ever after. Said he, "If wild mans come, they eat me, you go wey." "Well, Xury," said I, "we will both go, and if the wild mans come we will kill them; they shall eat neither of us." So I gave Xury a piece of rusk-bread to eat and a dram out of our patron's case of bottles, which I mentioned before, and we hal'd the boat in as near the shore as we thought was proper and so waded on shore, carrying nothing but our arms and two jarrs for water.

I did not care to go out of sight of the boat, fearing the coming of canoes with savages down the river, but the boy, seeing a low place about a mile up the country, rambl'd to it. By and by I saw him come running towards me; I thought he was pursu'd by some savage or frighted with some wild beast, and I ran forward towards him to help him. But when I came nearer to him, I saw something hanging over his shoulders, which was a creature that he had shot, like a hare but different in colour, and longer legs. However, we were very glad of it, and it was very good meat; but the great joy that poor Xury came with was to tell me he had found water and seen no wild mans.

We found afterwards that we need not take such pains for water, for a little higher up the creek from where we were we found the water fresh when the tide was out, which flow'd but a little way up. So we fill'd our jarrs and feasted on the hare he had kill'd, and prepar'd to go on our way, having seen no footsteps of any human creature in that part of the country.

As I had been one voyage to this coast before, I knew very well that the Islands of the Canaries, and the Cape de Verd Islands also, lay not far off from the coast. But as I had no instruments to take an observation to know what latitude we were in and did not exactly know, or even remember, what latitude they were in; I knew not where to look for them or when to stand off to sea towards them,

So we work'd at the oar towards the land, tho' with heavy
hearts, like men going to execution; for we all knew the boat
would be dash'd in a thousand pieces by the breach of the sea.

(page 49)

otherwise I might now easily have found some of these islands. But my hope was that, if I stood along this coast till I came to that part where the English traded, I should find some of their vessels upon their usual design of trade that would relieve and take us in.

By the best of my calculation that place where I now was must be that country which, lying between the Emperor of Morocco's dominions and the Negroes', lies vast and uninhabited, except by wild beasts; the Negroes having abandon'd it and gone farther south for fear of the Moors, and the Moors not thinking it worth inhabiting by reason of its barrenness. Indeed, both forsaking it because of the prodigious numbers of tygers, lyons, leopards, and other furious creatures which harbour there. The Moors use it for their hunting only, where they go like an army, two or three thousand men at a time; and indeed for near an hundred miles together upon this coast, we saw nothing but a vast uninhabited country by day, and heard nothing but howlings and roaring of wild beasts by night.

Once or twice in the day-time, I thought I saw the Pico of Teneriffe, being the high top of the Mountain Teneriffe in the Canaries, and had a great mind to venture out in hopes of reaching thither. But having try'd twice I was forc'd in again by contrary winds, the sea also going too high for my little vessel, so I resolv'd to pursue my first design and keep along the shore.

Several times I was oblig'd to land for fresh water, after we had left this place, and once in particular, being early in the morning, we came to anchor under a little point of land which was pretty high; and the tide beginning to flow, we lay still to go farther in. Xury, whose eyes were more about him than it seems mine were, call'd softly to me, and told me that we ha' best go farther off the shore. "For," said he, "look yonder lies a dreadful monster on the side of that hillock fast asleep!" I look'd where he pointed and saw a dreadful monster indeed, for it was a terrible great lyon that lay on the side of the shore, under the shade of a piece of the hill that hung as it were a little over him. "Xury," said I, "you shall go on shore and kill him." Xury look'd frighted, and said, "Me kill! He eat me at one mouth!" One mouthful he meant; however, I said no more to the boy, but bade him lie still, and I took our biggest gun, which was almost musquet-bore, and loaded it with a good charge of powder, and with two slugs, and lay'd it down. Then I loaded another gun with two bullets, and the third (for we had three pieces) I loaded with five smaller bullets. I took the best aim I could with the first piece to have shot him into the head, but he lay so with his leg rais'd a little above his nose, that the slugs hit his leg about the knee, and broke the bone. He started up growling at first, but finding his leg broke fell down again, and then got up upon three legs and gave the most hideous roar that ever I heard. I was a little surpriz'd that I had not hit him on the head; however I took up the second piece immediately, and tho' he began to move off, fir'd again, and shot him into the head, and had the pleasure to see him drop, and make but little noise, but lay struggling for life. Then Xury took heart and would have me let him go on shore. "Well, go," said I, so the boy jump'd into the water, and taking a little gun in one hand swam to shore with the other hand, and coming close to the creature, put the muzzle of the piece to his ear, and shot him into the head again which dispatch'd him quite.

This was game indeed to us, but no food, and I was

very sorry to lose three charges of powder and shot upon a creature that was good for nothing to us. However, Xury said he would have some of him, so he came on board and ask'd me to give him the hatchet. "For what, Xury?" said I. "Me cut off his head," said he. However, Xury could not cut off his head, but he cut off a foot and brought it with him, and it was a monstrous great one.

I bethought to myself however that perhaps the skin of him might one way or other be of some value to us, and I resolv'd to take off his skin if I could. So Xury and I went to work with him; but Xury was much the better workman at it, for I knew very ill how to do it. Indeed, it took us up both the whole day, but at last we got off the hide of him and, spreading it on the top of our cabbin, the sun effectually dry'd it in two days time, and it afterwards serv'd me to lie upon.

After this stop we made on to the southward continually for ten or twelve days, living very sparing on our provisions, which began to abate very much, and going no oftner onto the shore than we were oblig'd to for fresh water. My design in this was to make the River Gambia or Sennegall, that is to say, anywhere about the Cape de Verd, where I was in hopes to meet with some European ship, and if I did not, I knew not what course I had to take but to seek out for the islands or perish there among the Negroes. I knew that all the ships from Europe, which sail'd either to the coast of Guiney, or to the Brasils, or to the East Indies, made this cape or those islands and, in a word, I put the whole of my fortune upon this single point, either that I must meet with some ship or must perish.

When I had pursu'd this resolution about ten days longer, as I have said, I began to see that the land was inhabited, and in two or three places, as we sail'd by, we saw people stand upon the shore to look at us; we could also perceive they were quite black and stark-naked. I was once inclin'd to have gone on shore to them, but Xury was my better councellor and said to me, "No go, no go"; however I hal'd in nearer the shore that I might talk to them, and they ran along the shore by me a good way. I observ'd they had no weapons in their hands, except one who had a long slender stick, which Xury said was a lance, and that they could throw them a great way with good aim. So I kept at a distance, but talk'd with them by signs as well as I could, and particularly made signs for some thing to eat. They beckon'd to me to stop my boat, and that they would fetch me some meat. Upon this I lower'd the top of my sail and lay by, and two of them ran up into the country and in less than half an hour came back and brought with them two pieces of dry flesh and some corn, such as is the produce of their country; but we neither knew what the one or the other was. However, we were willing to accept it, but how to come at it was our next dispute, for I was not for venturing on shore to them, and they were as much afraid of us; but they took a safe way for us all, for they brought it to the shore and lay'd it down, and went and stood a great way off till we fetch'd it on board, and then came close to us again.

We made signs of thanks to them, for we had nothing to make them amends; but an opportunity offer'd that very instant to oblige them wonderfully, for while we were lying by the shore, came two mighty creatures, one pursuing the other (as we took it) with great fury, from the mountains towards the sea. Whether it was the male pursuing the female, or whether they were in sport or in rage, we could not tell, any more than we could tell whether it was usual or strange, but I believe it was the latter; because in the first place, those ravenous creatures seldom appear but in the night, and in the second place, we found the people terribly frighted, especially the women. The man that had the lance or dart did not fly from them, but the rest did; however, as the two creatures ran directly into the water, they did not seem to offer to fall upon any of the Negroes, but plung'd themselves into the sea and swam about as if they had come for their diversion. At last one of them began to come nearer our boat than at first I expected, but I lay ready for him, for I had loaded my gun with all possible expedition, and had Xury load both the others. As soon as he came fairly within my reach, I fir'd, and shot him directly into the head; immediately he sunk down into the water, but riz'd instantly and plung'd up and down as if he was struggling for life, and so indeed he was. He immediately made to the shore, but between the wound, which was his mortal hurt, and the strangling of the water, he dy'd just before he reach'd the shore.

It is impossible to express the astonishment of these poor creatures at the noise and the fire of my gun; some of them were even ready to die for fear, and fell down as dead with the very terror. But when they saw the creature dead and sunk in the water, and that I made signs to them to come to the shore, they took heart and came to the shore and began to search for the creature. I found him by his blood staining the water; and by the help of a rope, which I flung round him and gave the Negroes to hale, they dragg'd him on shore and found that it was a most curious leopard, spotted and fine to an admirable degree; and the Negroes held up their hands with admiration to think what it was I had kill'd him with.

The other creature, frighted with the flash of fire and the noise of the gun, swam on shore, and ran up directly to the mountains whence they came, nor could I at that distance know what it was. I found quickly the Negroes were for eating the flesh of this creature, so I was willing to have them take it as a favour from me, which when I made signs to them that they might take him, they were very thankful; for immediately they fell to work with him, and tho' they had no knife, yet with a sharpen'd piece of wood they took off his skin as readily, and much more readily, than we could have done with a knife. They offer'd me some of the flesh, which I declin'd, making as if I would give it them, but made signs for the skin, which they gave me very freely, and brought me a great deal more of their provision, which tho' I did not understand, yet I accepted. Then I made signs to them for some water and held out one of my jarrs to them, turning it bottom upward, to shew that it was empty and that I wanted to have it fill'd. They call'd immediately to some of their friends, and there came two women and brought a great vessel made of earth and burnt, as I suppose, in the sun. This they set down for me, as before, and I sent Xury on shore with my jarrs and fill'd them all three. The women were as stark-naked as the men.

I was now furnish'd with roots and corn, such as it was, and water, and leaving my friendly Negroes, I made forward for about eleven days more without offering to go near the shore, till I saw the land run out a great length into the sea, at about the distance of four or five leagues before me, and the sea being very calm I kept a large offing to make this point. At length, doubling the point at about two leagues from the land, I saw plainly land on the other side to seaward; then I concluded, as it was most certain indeed, that this was the Cape de Verd and those the islands, call'd thence Cape de Verd Islands. However, they were at a great distance, and I could not well tell what I had best to do, for if I should be taken with a fresh of wind I might neither reach one or the other.

In this dilemma, as I was very pensive, I stepp'd into the cabbin and sat me down, Xury having the helm, when on a sudden the boy cry'd out, "Master, Master, a ship with a sail!" The foolish boy was frighted out of his wits, thinking it must needs be some of his master's ships sent to pursue us, when I knew we were gotten far enough out of their reach. I jump'd out of the cabbin, and immediately saw not only the ship but what she was, *viz.*, that it was a Portugueze ship and, as I thought, bound to the coast of Guiney for Negroes. But when I observ'd the course she steer'd, I was soon convinc'd they were bound some other way and did not design to come any nearer to the shore; upon which I stretch'd out to sea as much as I could, resolving to speak with them if possible.

With all the sail I could make, I found I should not be able to come in their way, but that they would be gone by before I could make any signal to them. But after I had crowded to the utmost and began to despair, it seems they saw me by the help of their perspective-glasses, and that it was some European boat, which as they suppos'd must belong to some ship that was lost, so they shorten'd sail to let me come up. I was encourag'd with this and, as I had my patron's antient on board, I made a waft of it to them for a signal of distress, and fir'd a gun, both which they saw, for they told me they saw the smoke, tho' they did not hear the gun. Upon these signals they very kindly brought to and lay by for me, and in about three hours time I came up with them.

They ask'd me what I was, in Portugueze, and in Spanish, and in French, but I understood none of them; but at last a Scots sailor, who was on board, call'd to me, and I answer'd him and told him I was an Englishman, that I had made my escape out of slavery from the Moors at Sallee; then they bade me come on board, and very kindly took me in and all my goods.

It was an inexpressible joy to me, that any one will believe, that I was thus deliver'd, as I esteem'd it, from such a miserable and almost hopeless condition as I was in, and I immediately offer'd all I had to the captain of the ship, as a return for my deliverance. But he generously told me he would take nothing from me, but that all I had should be deliver'd safe to me when I came to the Brasils, "For," said he, "I have sav'd your life on no other terms than I would be glad to be sav'd myself, and it may one time or other be my lot to be taken up in the same condition. Besides, when I carry you to the Brasils, so great away from your own country, if I should take from you what you have, you will be starv'd there, and then I only take away that life I have given. No, no, *Seignor Inglese*, I will carry you thither in charity, and those things will help you to buy your subsistance there and your passage home again."

As he was charitable in his proposal, so he was just in the performance to a tittle, for he order'd the seamen that none should offer to touch any thing I had. Then he took every thing into his own possession and gave me back an exact inventory of them that I might have them, even so much as my three earthen jarrs.

As to my boat: it was a very good one, and that he saw, and told me he would buy it off me for the ship's use, and ask'd me what I would have for it. I told him he had been so generous to me in every thing, that I could not offer to make any price of the boat, but left it entirely to him, upon which he told me he would give me a note of his hand to pay me 80 pieces of eight for it at the Brasils, and when it came there, if any one offer'd to give more he would make it up; he offer'd me also 60 pieces of eight more for my boy, Xury, which I was loath to take, not that I was not willing to let the captain have him, but I was very loath to sell the poor boy's liberty, who had assisted me so faith-fully in procuring my own. However, when I let him know my reason, he own'd it to be just and offer'd me this medium; that he would give the boy an obligation to set him free in ten years, if he turn'd Christian; upon this, and Xury saying he was willing to go to him, I let the captain have him.

We had a very good voyage to the Brasils and arriv'd in the Bay de Todos los Santos, or All Saints' Bay, in about twenty-two days after. And now I was once more deliver'd from the most miserable of all conditions of life, but what to do next with myself I was now to consider.

The generous treatment the captain gave me I can never enough remember; he would take nothing of me for my passage; gave me 20 ducats for the leopard's skin, and 40 for the lyon's skin which I had in my boat, and caus'd every thing I had in the ship to be punctually deliver'd me, and what I was willing to sell he bought, such as the case of bottles, two of my guns, and a piece of the lump of beeswax, for I had made candles of the rest. In a word, I made about 220 pieces of eight of all my cargo, and with this stock I went on shore in the Brasils.

I had not been long here, but being recommended to the house of a good honest man like himself, who had an *ingeino* as they call it, that is, a plantation and a sugar house. I liv'd with him some time, and acquainted myself by that means with the manner of their planting and making of sugar; and seeing how well the planters liv'd, and how they grew rich suddenly, I resolv'd, if I could get licence to settle there, I would turn planter among them, resolving in the meantime to find out some way to get my money, which I had left in London, remitted to me. To this purpose, getting a kind of a letter of naturalization, I purchas'd as much land that was uncur'd as my money would reach and form'd a plan for my plantation and settlement, and such a one as might be suitable to the stock which I propos'd to myself to receive from England.

I had a neighbour, a Portugueze of Lisbon, but born of English parents, whose name was Wells, and in much such circumstances as I was. I call him my neighbour, because his plantation lay next to mine, and we went on very sociably together. My stock was but low as well as his, and we rather planted for food than any thing else, for about two years. However, we began to encrease, and our land began to come into order, so that in the third year we planted some tobacco and made each of us a large piece of ground ready for planting canes in the year to come; but we both wanted help, and now I found more than before I had done wrong in parting with my boy, Xury.

But alas! for me to do wrong that never did right was no great wonder. I had no remedy but to go on; I was gotten into an employment quite remote to my genius, and directly contrary to the life I delighted in, and for which I forsook my father's house, and broke thro' all his good advice; nay, I was coming into the very middle station, or upper degree of low life, which my father advis'd me to before, and which if I resolv'd to go on with, I might as well have stay'd at home and never have fatigu'd myself in the world as I had done. I used often to say to myself, I could have done this as well in England among my friends, as have gone 5,000 miles off to do it among strangers and savages in a wilderness, and at such a distance, as never to hear from any part of the world that had the least knowledge of me.

In this manner I used to look upon my condition with the utmost regret. I had no body to converse with but now and then this neighbour; no work to be done but by the labour of my hands; and I used to say, I liv'd just like a man cast away upon some desolate island, that had no body there but himself. But how just has it been, and how should all men reflect, that when they compare their present conditions with others that are worse, Heaven may oblige them to make the exchange, and be convinc'd of their former felicity by their experience. I say, how just has it been that the truly solitary life I reflected on in an island of meer desolation should be my lot, who had so often unjustly compar'd it with the life which I then led in which, had I continu'd, I had in all probability been exceeding prosp'rous and rich.

I was in some degree settl'd in my measures for carrying on the plantation before my kind friend, the captain of the ship that took me up at sea, went back; for the ship remain'd there, in providing his loading and preparing for his voyage, near three months; when telling him what little stock I had left behind me in London, he gave me this friendly and sincere advice. "*Seignor Inglese*," said he, for so he always call'd me, "if you will give me letters and a procuration here in form to me, with orders to the person who has your money in London to send your effects to Lisbon, to such persons as I shall direct and in such goods as are proper for this country, I will bring you the produce of them, God willing, at my return; but since human affairs are all subject to changes and disasters, I would have you give orders but for 100 pounds sterling, which you say is half your stock, and let the hazard be run for the first, so that if it come safe you may order the rest the same way, and if it miscarry you may have the other half to have recourse to for your supply."

This was so wholesome advice, and look'd so friendly, that I could not but be convinc'd it was the best course I could take. So I accordingly prepar'd letters to the gentlewoman with whom I had left my money and a procuration to the Portugueze captain, as he desir'd.

I wrote the English captain's widow a full account of all my adventures: my slavery, escape, and how I had met with the Portugueze captain at sea, the humanity of his behaviour, and in what condition I was now in, with all other necessary directions for my supply; and when this honest captain came to Lisbon, he found means by some of the English merchants there to send over not the order only, but a full account of my story to a merchant at London, who represented it effectually to her; whereupon, she not only deliver'd the money, but out of her own pocket sent the Portugueze captain a very handsome present for his humanity and charity to me.

The merchant in London vesting this 100 pounds in English goods, such as the captain had writ for, sent them directly to him at Lisbon, and he brought them all safe to me to the Brasils, among which, without my direction (for I was too young in my business to think of them) he had taken care to have all sorts of tools, ironwork, and utensils necessary for my plantation and which were of great use to me.

When this cargo arriv'd I thought my fortune made, for I was surpriz'd with the joy of it; and my good steward the captain had lay'd out the five pounds, which my friend had sent him for a present for himself, to purchase and bring me over a servant under bond for six years' service, and would not accept of any consideration except a little tobacco, which I would have him accept, being of my own produce.

Neither was this all; but my goods being all English manufactures, such as cloath, stuffs, bays, and things particularly valuable and desirable in the country, I found means to sell them to a very great advantage. So I might say I had more than four times the value of my first cargo and was now infinitely beyond my poor neighbour, I mean in the advancement of my plantation; for the first thing I did, I bought me a Negro slave and a European servant also; I mean another besides that which the captain brought me from Lisbon.

But as abus'd prosperity is ofttimes made the very means of our greatest adversity, so was it with me. I went on the next year with great success in my plantation. I rais'd fifty great rolls of tobacco on my own ground, more than I had dispos'd of for necessaries among my neighbours; and these fifty rolls, being each of above an hundredweight, were well cur'd and lay'd by against the return of the fleet from Lisbon. Now encreasing in business and in wealth, my head began to be full of projects and undertakings beyond my reach, such as are indeed often the ruine of the best heads in business.

Had I continu'd in the station I was now in, I had room for all the happy things to have yet befallen me, for which my father so earnestly recommended a quiet retir'd life, and of which he had so sensibly describ'd the middle station of life to be full of; but other things attended me, and I was still to be the willful agent of all my own miseries; and particularly to encrease my fault and double the reflections upon myself, which in my future sorrows I should have leisure to make. All these miscarriages were procur'd by my apparent obstinate adhering to my foolish inclination of wand'ring abroad and pursuing that inclination, in contradiction to the clearest views of doing myself good in a fair and plain pursuit of those prospects and those measures of life, which nature and providence concurr'd to present me with and to make my duty.

As I had once done thus in my breaking away from my parents, so I could not be content now, but I must go and leave the happy view I had of being a rich and thriving man in my new plantation, only to pursue a rash and immoderate desire of rizing faster than the nature of the thing admitted. Thus I cast myself down again into the deepest gulph of human misery that ever man fell into, or perhaps could be consistent with life and a state of health in the world.

To come then by the just degrees to the particulars of this part of my story. You may suppose that having now liv'd almost four years in the Brasils and beginning to thrive and prosper very well upon my plantation, I had not only learn'd the language, but had contracted acquaintance and friendship among my fellow-planters, as well as among the merchants of St. Salvadore, which was our port; and that in my discourse among them, I had frequently given them an account of my two voyages to the coast of Guiney, the manner of trading with the Negroes there, and how easy it was to purchase upon the coast, for trifles such as beads, toys, knives, scissars, hatchets, bits of glass, and the like, not only gold dust, Guiney grains, elephants' teeth, &c. but Negroes for the service of the Brasils in great numbers.

They listen'd always very attentively to my discourses on these heads, but especially to that part which related to the buying of Negroes, which was a trade at that time not only not far enter'd into, but, as far as it was, had been carry'd on by the *assiento*, or permission of the kings of Spain and Portugal, and engross'd in the publick, so that few Negroes were bought, and those excessive dear.

It happen'd, being in company with some merchants and planters of my acquaintance, and talking of those things very earnestly, three of them came to me the next morning and told me they had been musing very much upon what I had discours'd with them of the last night, and they came to make a secret proposal to me. After enjoining me to secrecy, they told me that they had a mind to fit out a ship to go to Guiney; that they had all plantations as well as I and were straiten'd for nothing so much as servants; that as it was a trade that could not be carry'd on, because they could not publickly sell the Negroes when they came home, so they desir'd to make but one voyage, to bring the Negroes on shore privately, and divide them among their own plantations. In a word, the question was whether I would go their super-cargo in the ship to manage the trading part upon the coast of Guiney. And they offer'd me that I should have my equal share of the Negroes without providing any part of the stock.

This was a fair proposal it must be confess'd, had it been made to any one that had not had a settlement and plantation of his own to look after, which was in a fair way of coming to be very considerable and with a good stock upon it. But for me that was thus enter'd and establish'd, and had nothing to do but go on as I had begun for three or four years more, and to have sent for the other 100 pounds from England, and who in that time and with that little addition could scarce have fail'd of being worth 3,000 or 4,000 pounds sterling, and that encreasing too; for me to think of such a voyage was the most prepostrous thing that ever man in such circumstances could be guilty of.

But I that was born to be my own destroyer could no more resist the offer than I could restrain my first rambling designs when my father's good counsel was lost upon me. In a word, I told them I would go with all my heart, if they would undertake to look after my plantation in my absence, and would dispose of it to such as I should direct if I miscarry'd. This they all engag'd to do and enter'd into writings or covenants to do so. I made a formal will, disposing of my plantation and effects in case of my death, making the captain of the ship that had sav'd my life as before my universal heir, but obliging him to dispose of my effects as I had directed in my will, one half of the produce being to himself, and the other to be shipp'd to England.

In short, I took all possible caution to preserve my effects and keep up my plantation; had I used half as much prudence to have look'd into my own interest and have made a judgment of what I ought to have done and not to have done, I had certainly never gone away from so prosp'rous an undertaking, leaving all the probable views of a thriving circumstance, and gone upon a voyage to sea, attended with all its common hazards; to say nothing of the reasons I had to expect particular misfortunes to myself.

But I was hurry'd on and obey'd blindly the dictates of my fancy rather than my reason; and accordingly, the ship fitted out and the cargo furnish'd, and all things done as by agreement by my partners in the voyage, I went on board in an evil hour, the 1st of September, being the same day eight year that I went from my father and mother at Hull, in order to act the rebel to their authority and the fool to my own interest.

Our ship was about 120 tun burthen, carried six guns and fourteen men, besides the master, his boy, and myself. We had on board no large cargo of goods, except of such toys as were fit for our trade with the Negroes, such as beads, bits of glass, shells, and odd trifles, especially little looking-glasses, knives, scissars, hatchets, and the like.

The same day I went on board we set sail, standing away to the nor'ward upon our own coast, with design to stretch over for the African coast, when they came about 10 or 12 degrees northern latitude, which it seems was the manner of their course in those days. We had very good weather, only excessive hot, all the way upon our own coast, till we came to the height of Cape St. Augustino, whence keeping farther off at sea we lost sight of land and steer'd as if we were bound for the Isle Fernand de Noronha, holding our course NE by N and leaving those isles on the east; in this course we pass'd the Line in about twelve days time and were by our last observation in 7 degrees 22 minutes northern latitude, when a violent tournado or hurricane took us quite out of our knowledge. It began from the SE, came about to the NW, and then settl'd into the NE, whence it blew in such a terrible manner that for twelve days together we could do nothing but drive, and, scudding away before it, let it carry us whither ever fate and the fury of the winds directed; and during these twelve days, I need not say, I expected every day to be swallow'd up, nor indeed did any in the ship expect to save their lives.

In this distress we had, besides the terror of the storm, one of our men dy'd of the calenture, and one man and the boy wash'd overboard; about the twelfth day, the weather abating a little, the master made an observation as well as he could and found that he was in about 11 degrees northern latitude, but that he was 22 degrees of longitude difference west from Cape St. Augustino; so that he found he was gotten upon the coast of Guiney, or the north part of the Brasils, beyond the River Amozones, towards that of the River Oronoque, commonly call'd the Great River, and began to consult with me what course he should take, for the ship was leaky and very much dis-abl'd, and he was going directly back to the coast of the Brasils.

I was positively against that and, looking over the charts of the seacoast of America with him, we concluded there was no inhabited country for us to have recourse to till we came within the circle of the Carib Islands, and therefore resolv'd to stand away for Barbadoes which, by keeping off at sea to avoid the indraft of the Bay or Gulph of Mexico, we might easily perform, as we hop'd, in about fifteen days' sail, whereas we could not possibly make our voyage to the coast of Africa without some assistance, both to our ship and to ourselves.

With this design we chang'd our course and steer'd away NW by W in order to reach some of our English islands, where I hop'd for relief; but our voyage was otherwise determin'd, for being in the latitude of 12 degrees 18 minutes, a second storm came upon us, which carry'd us away with the same impetuosity westward and drove us so out of the very way of all human commerce that had all our lives been sav'd, as to the sea, we were rather in danger of being devour'd by savages than ever returning to our own country.

In this distress, the wind still blowing very hard, one of our men early in the morning, cry'd out, "Land!" and we had no sooner run out of the cabbin to look out in hopes of seeing whereabouts in the world we were, but the ship struck upon a sand. In a moment, her motion being so stopp'd, the sea broke over her in such a manner that we expected we should all have perish'd immediately, and we were driven into our close quarters to shelter us from the very foam and sprye of the sea.

It is not easy for any one who has not been in the like condition to describe or conceive the consternation of men in such circumstances; we knew nothing where we were or upon what land it was we were driven, whether an island or the main, whether inhabited or not inhabited; and as the rage of the wind was still great, tho' rather less than at first, we could not so much as hope to have the ship hold many minutes without breaking in pieces, unless the winds by a kind of miracle should turn immediately about. In a word, we sat looking upon one another and expecting death every moment, and every man acting accordingly, as preparing for another world, for there was little or nothing more for us to do in this. That which was our present comfort, and all the comfort we had, was that, contrary to our expectation, the ship did not break yet and that the master said the wind began to abate.

Now tho' we thought that the wind did a little abate, yet the ship having thus struck upon the sand, and sticking too fast for us to expect her getting off, we were in a dreadful condition indeed and had nothing to do but to think of saving our lives as well as we could. We had a boat at our stern just before the storm, but she was first stav'd by dashing against the ship's rudder, and in the next place she broke away and either sunk or was driven off to sea, so there was no hope from her; we had another boat on board, but how to get her off into the sea was a doubtful thing. However, there was no room to debate, for we fancy'd the ship would break in pieces every minute, and some told us she was actually broken already.

In this distress the mate of our vessel lay'd hold of the boat and, with the help of the rest of the men, they got her slung over the ship's-side, and getting all into her, let go, and committed ourselves, being eleven in number, to God's mercy and the wild sea; for tho' the storm was abated considerably, yet the sea went dreadful high upon the shore and might well be call'd, *Den wild* Zee, as the Dutch call the sea in a storm.

And now our case was very dismal indeed; for we all saw plainly that the sea went so high that the boat could not live and that we should be inevitably drown'd. As to making sail, we had none, nor, if we had, could we have done any thing with it. So we work'd at the oar towards the land, tho' with heavy hearts, like men going to execution; for we all knew that when the boat came nearer the shore, she would be dash'd in a thousand pieces by the breach of the sea. However, we committed our souls to God in the most earnest manner and, the wind driving us towards the shore, we hasten'd our destruction with our own hands, pulling as well as we could towards land.

What the shore was, whether rock or sand, whether steep or shoal, we knew not; the only hope that could rationally give us the least shadow of expectation was if we might happen into some bay or gulph, or the mouth of some river, where by great chance we might have run our boat in, or got under the lee of the land, and perhaps made smooth water. But there was nothing of this appear'd, and as we made nearer and nearer the shore, the land look'd more frightful than the sea.

After we had row'd, or rather driven about a league and a half, as we reckon'd it, a raging wave, mountain-like, came rowling a-stern of us, and plainly bade us expect the *coup de grâce*. In a word, it took us with such a fury that it overset the boat at once and, separating us as well from the boat as from one another, gave us not time hardly to say, "O God!" for we were all swallow'd up in a moment.

Nothing can describe the confusion of thought which I felt when I sunk into the water; for tho' I swam very well, yet I could not deliver myself from the waves so as to draw breath, till that wave having driven me, or rather carry'd me a vast way on towards the shore, and having spent itself, went back, and left me upon the land almost dry, but half dead with the water I took in. I had so much presence of mind as well as breath left that, seeing myself nearer the main-land than I expected, I got upon my feet and endeavour'd to make on towards the land as fast as I could, before another wave should return and take me up again. But I soon found it was impossible to avoid it, for I saw a wave come after me as high as a great hill and as furious as an enemy, which I had no means or strength to contend with. My business was to hold my breath and raise myself upon the water, if I could, and so by swimming to preserve my breathing and pilot myself towards the shore if possible. My greatest concern now being that the wave, as it would carry me a great way towards the shore when it came on, might not carry me back again with it when it gave back towards the sea.

The wave came upon me again and bury'd me at once twenty or thirty foot deep in its own body, and I could feel myself carry'd with a mighty force and swiftness towards the shore a very great way. But I held my breath and as-sisted myself to swim still forward with all my might. I was ready to burst with holding my breath when, as I felt myself rizing up, so to my immediate relief, I found my head and hands shoot out above the surface of the water, and tho' it was not two seconds of time that I could keep myself so, yet it reliev'd me greatly and gave me breath and new courage. I was cover'd again with water a good while, but not so long but I held it out; and finding the water had spent itself, and began to return, I strook forward against the return of the waves and felt ground again with my feet. I stood still a few moments to recover breath and till the water went from me, and then took to my heels and ran with what strength I had farther towards the shore. But neither would this deliver me from the fury of the sea, which came pouring in after me again, and twice more I was lifted up by the waves and carry'd forwards as before, the shore being very flat.

The last time of these two had well near been fatal to me; for the sea having hurry'd me along as before, landed me, or rather dash'd me against a piece of a rock, and that with such force as it left me senseless, and indeed helpless, as to my own deliverance; for the blow taking my side and breast, beat the breath as it were quite out of my body; but had it return'd again immediately, I must have been strangl'd in the water. But I recover'd a little before the return of the waves and, seeing I should be cover'd again with the water, I resolv'd to hold fast by a piece of the rock and so to hold my breath, if possible, till the wave went back. Now as the waves were not so high as at first, being nearer land, I held my hold till the wave abated and then fetch'd another run, which brought me so near the shore that the next wave, tho' it went over me, yet did not so swallow me up as to carry me away; and the next run I took, I got to the main-land, where, to my great comfort, I clamber'd up the cliffs of the shore and sat me down upon the grass, free from danger and quite out of the reach of the water.

I was now landed and safe on shore, and I began to look up and thank God that my life was sav'd in a case wherein there was some minutes before scarce any room to hope. I believe it is impossible to express to the life what the extasies and transports of the soul are, when it is so sav'd, as I may say, out of the very grave. And I do not wonder now at that custom, viz., that when a malefactor who has the halter about his neck is ty'd up, and just going to be turn'd off, and has a reprieve brought to him,

I say, I do not wonder that they bring a surgeon with it, to let him blood that very moment they tell him of it, that the surprize may not drive the animal spirits from the heart, and overwhelm him:

For sudden joys, like griefs, confound at first.

I walk'd about on the shore, lifting up my hands, and my whole being, as I may say, wrapt up in the contemplation of my deliverance, making a thousand gestures and motions which I cannot describe, reflecting upon all my comrades that were drown'd and that there should not be one soul sav'd but myself; for, as for them, I never saw them afterwards, or any sign of them, except three of their hats, one cap, and two shoes that were not fellows.

I cast my eyes to the stranded vessel, when the breach and froth of the sea being so big, I could hardly see it, it lay so far off, and consider'd, Lord! how was it possible I could get on shore?

After I had solac'd my mind with the comfortable part of my condition, I began to look round me to see what kind of place I was in and what was next to be done, and I soon found my comforts abate, and that in a word I had a dreadful deliverance: For I was wet, had no cloaths to shift me, nor any thing either to eat or drink to comfort me, neither did I see any prospect before me, but that of perishing with hunger, or being devour'd by wild beasts; and that which was particularly afflicting to me was that I had no weapon either to hunt and kill any creature for my sustenance or to defend myself against any other creature that might desire to kill me for their's. In a word, I had nothing about me but a knife, a tobacco-pipe, and a little tobacco in a box, this was all my provision; and this threw me into terrible agonies of mind, that for a while I ran about like a mad-man. Night coming upon me, I began with a heavy heart to consider what would be my lot if there were any ravenous beasts in that country, seeing at night they always come abroad for their prey.

All the remedy that offer'd to my thoughts at that time was to get up into a thick bushy tree, like a firr but thorny, which grew near me, and where I resolv'd to sit all night and consider the next day what death I should die, for as yet I saw no prospect of life. I walk'd about a furlong from the shore to see if I could find any fresh water to drink, which I did, to my great joy; and having drank and put a little tobacco in my mouth to prevent hunger, I went to the tree and, getting up into it, endeavour'd to place myself so that if I should sleep I might not fall; and having cut me a short stick, like a truncheon, for my defense, I took up my lodging, and being excessively fatigu'd, I fell fast a-sleep and slept as comfortably as, I believe, few could have done in my condition, and found myself the most refresh'd with it that I think I ever was on such an occasion.

When I wak'd it was broad day, the weather clear, and the storm abated, so that the sea did not rage and swell as before. But that which surpriz'd me most was that the ship was lifted off in the night from the sand where she lay, by the swelling of the tide, and was driven up almost as far as the rock which I first mention'd, where I had been so bruis'd by the dashing of me against it. This being within about a mile from the shore where I was, and the ship seeming to stand upright still, I wish'd myself on board that, at least, I might save some necessary things for my use.

When I came down from my appartment in the tree,
I look'd about me again, and the first thing I found was
the boat, which lay as the wind and the sea had toss'd her
up upon the land, about two miles on my right hand. I
walk'd as far as I could upon the shore to have got to her,
but found a neck or inlet of water between me and the
boat, which was about half a mile broad, so I came back
for the present, being more intent upon getting at the ship,
where I hop'd to find something for my present subsistence.

A little after noon I found the sea very calm and the
tide ebb'd so far out that I could come within a quarter of
a mile of the ship; and here I found a fresh renewing of
my grief, for I saw evidently, that if we had kept on board,
we had been all safe, that is to say, we had all got safe on
shore, and I had not been so miserable as to be left entirely destitute of all comfort and company, as I now was.
This forc'd tears from my eyes again, but as there was
little relief in that, I resolv'd, if possible, to get to the ship.
So I pull'd off my cloaths, for the weather was hot to extremity, and took to the water; but when I came to the
ship my difficulty was still greater to know how to get on
board, for, as she lay a-ground and high out of the water,
there was nothing within my reach to lay hold of. I swam
round her twice, and the second time I spy'd a small piece
of a rope, which I wonder'd I did not see at first, hang
down by the fore-chains, so low that with great difficulty
I got hold of it and, by the help of that rope, got up into
the forecastle of the ship. Here I found that the ship was
bulg'd and had a great deal of water in her hold, but that
she lay so on the side of a bank of hard sand, or rather
earth, that her stern lay lifted up upon the bank and her
head low almost to the water. By this means all her quarter

was free, and all that was in that part was dry, for you may be sure my first work was to search and to see what was spoil'd and what was free; and first I found that all the ship's provisions were dry and untouch'd by the water and, being very well dispos'd to eat, I went to the bread-room and fill'd my pockets with bisket, and ate it as I went about other things, for I had no time to lose. I also found some rum in the great cabbin, of which I took a large dram, and which I had indeed need enough of to spirit me for what was before me. Now I wanted nothing but a boat to furnish myself with many things which I foresaw would be very necessary to me.

It was in vain to sit still and wish for what was not to be had, and this extremity rouz'd my application. We had several spare yards, and two or three large sparrs of wood, and a spare topmast or two in the ship; I resolv'd to fall to work with these, and I flung as many of them overboard as I could manage for their weight, tying every one with a rope that they might not drive away. When this was done I went down the ship's-side, and pull'd them to me. I ty'd four of them fast together at both ends as well as I could in the form of a raft, and, laying two or three short pieces of plank upon them crossways, I found I could walk upon it very well, but that it was not able to bear any great weight, the pieces being too light. So I went to work, and with the carpenter's saw I cut a spare topmast into three lengths and added them to my raft with a great deal of labour and pains; but hope of furnishing myself with necessaries encourag'd me to go beyond what I should have been able to have done upon another occasion.

My raft was now strong enough to bear any reasonable weight; my next care was what to load it with and how to preserve what I lay'd upon it from the surf of the sea. But I was not long considering this; I first lay'd all the plank or boards upon it that I could get and, having consider'd well what I most wanted, I first got three of the seamen's chests, which I had broken open and empty'd, and lower'd them down upon my raft; the first of these I fill'd with provision, viz., bread, rice, three Dutch cheeses, five pieces of dry'd goat's flesh, which we liv'd much upon, and a little remainder of European corn which had been lay'd by for some fowls which we brought to sea with us, but the fowls were kill'd. There had been some barley and wheat together, but, to my great disappointment, I found afterwards that the rats had eaten or spoil'd it all. As for liquor, I found several cases of bottles belonging to our skipper, in which were some cordial waters, and in all about five or six gallons of rack; these I stow'd by themselves, there being no need to put them into the chest, nor no room for them. While I was doing this, I found the tide began to flow, tho' very calm, and I had the mortification to see my coat, shirt, and waistcoat, which I had left on shore upon the sand, swim away; as for my breeches, which were only linnen and open-knee'd, I swam on board in them and my stockings. However, this put me upon rummaging for cloaths, of which I found enough, but took no more than I wanted for present use, for I had other things which my eye was more upon. First, tools to work with on shore, and it was after long searching that I found out the carpenter's chest, which was indeed a very useful prize to me, and much more valuable than a ship-loading of gold would have been at that time. I got it down to my raft, even whole as it was, without losing time to look into it, for I knew in general what it contain'd.

My next care was for some ammunition and arms. There were two very good fowling-pieces in the great cabbin and two pistols. These I secur'd first, with some powder-horns, and a small bag of shot, and two old rusty swords. I knew there were three barrels of powder in the ship, but knew not where our gunner had stow'd them, but with much search I found them, two of them dry and good; the third had taken water. Those two I got to my raft, with the arms, and now I thought myself pretty well freighted and began to think how I should get to shore with them, having neither sail, oar, or rudder, and the least capful of wind would have overset all my navigation.

I had three encouragements, 1. A smooth calm sea, 2. The tide rizing and setting in to the shore, 3. What little wind there was blew me towards the land. And thus, having found two or three broken oars belonging to the boat, and besides the tools which were in the chest, I found two saws, an axe, and a hammer, and with this cargo I put to sea. For a mile, or thereabouts, my raft went very well, only that I found it drive a little distant from the place where I had landed before, by which I perceiv'd that there was some in-draft of the water, and consequently I hop'd to find some creek or river there, which I might make use of as a port to get to land with my cargo.

As I imagin'd, so it was, there appear'd before me a little opening of the land, and I found a strong current of the tide set into it, so I guided my raft as well as I could to keep in the middle of the stream. But here I had like to have suffer'd a second shipwreck, which, if I had, I think verily would have broke my heart, for knowing nothing of the coast, my raft ran a-ground at one end of it upon a shoal, and not being a-ground at the other end, it wanted

but a little that all my cargo had flipp'd off towards that
end that was a-float, and so fall'n into the water. I did my
utmost by setting my back against the chests to keep them
in their places, but could not thrust off the raft with all my
strength, neither durst I stir from the posture I was in;
but holding up the chests with all my might, stood in that
manner near half an hour, in which time the rizing of the
water brought me a little more upon a level, and a little
after, the water still rizing, my raft floated again, and I
thrust her off with the oar I had, into the channel, and
then driving up higher, I at length found myself in the
mouth of a little river, with land on both sides and a
strong current or tide running up. I look'd on both sides
for a proper place to get to shore, for I was not willing
to be driven too high up the river, hoping in time to see
some ship at sea, and therefore resolv'd to place myself
as near the coast as I could.

At length I spy'd a little cove on the right shore of the
creek, to which with great pain and difficulty I guided my
raft, and at last got so near that, reaching ground with
my oar, I could thrust her directly in. But here I had like
to have dipp'd all my cargo in the sea again, for that shore
lying pretty steep, that is to say sloping, there was no place
to land, but where one end of my raft, if it ran on shore,
would lie so high, and the other sink lower as before, that it
would endanger my cargo again. All that I could do was to
wait till the tide was at highest, keeping the raft with my
oar like an anchor to hold the side of it fast to the shore,
near a flat piece of ground, which I expected the water
would flow over; and so it did. As soon as I found water
enough (for my raft drew about a foot of water) I thrust
her on upon that flat piece of ground, and there fasten'd

Having found two or three broken oars belonging to the boat,
and besides the tools which were in the chest, I found two
saws, an axe, and a hammer, and with this cargo I put to sea.

(page 57)

or moor'd her by sticking my two broken oars into the ground; one on one side near one end, and one on the other side near the other end. Thus I lay till the water ebb'd away and left my raft and all my cargo safe on shore.

My next work was to view the country and seek a proper place for my habitation, and where to stow my goods to secure them from whatever might happen. Where I was I yet knew not, whether on the continent or on an island, whether inhabited or not inhabited, whether in danger of wild beasts or not. There was a hill not above a mile from me, which riz'd up very steep and high, and which seem'd to overtop some other hills, which lay as in a ridge from it northward. I took out one of the fowling-pieces, and one of the pistols, and an horn of powder, and thus arm'd I travell'd for discovery up to the top of that hill; where, after I had with great labour and difficulty got to the top, I saw my fate to my great affliction, viz., that I was on an island environ'd every way with the sea, no land to be seen, except some rocks which lay a great way off, and two small islands less than this, which lay about three leagues to the west.

I found also that the island I was on was barren, and, as I saw good reason to believe, uninhabited, except by wild beasts, of whom however I saw none; yet I saw an abundance of fowls, but knew not their kinds, neither when I kill'd them could I tell what was fit for food and what not. At my coming back, I shot at a great bird which I saw sitting upon a tree on the side of a great wood; I believe it was the first gun that had been fir'd there since the creation of the world. I had no sooner fir'd, but from all the parts of the wood there a-riz'd an innumerable number of fowls of many sorts, making a confus'd screaming, and crying every one according to his usual note; but not one of them of any kind that I knew. As for the creature I kill'd, I took it to be a kind of hawk, its colour and beak resembling it, but it had no talons or claws more than common; its flesh was carrion and fit for nothing.

Contented with this discovery, I came back to my raft and fell to work to bring my cargo on shore, which took me up the rest of that day, and what to do with myself at night I knew not, nor indeed where to rest. I was afraid to lie down on the ground, not knowing but some wild beast might devour me, tho' as I afterwards found, there was really no need for those fears.

However, as well as I could, I barricado'd myself round with the chests and boards that I had brought on shore and made a kind of a hut for that night's lodging. As for food, I yet saw not which way to supply myself, except that I had seen two or three creatures like hares run out of the wood where I shot the fowl.

I now began to consider that I might yet get a great many things out of the ship, which would be useful to me, and particularly some of the rigging, and sails, and such other things as might come to land, and I resolv'd to make another voyage on board the vessel, if possible, as I knew that the first storm that blew must necessarily break her all in pieces. I resolv'd to set all other things apart till I got every thing out of the ship that I could get. Then I call'd a council, that is to say, in my thoughts, whether I should take back the raft, but this appear'd impracticable; so I resolv'd to go as before, when the tide was down, and I did so, only that I stripp'd before I went from my hut, having nothing on but a chequer'd shirt, and a pair of linnen drawers, and a pair of pumps on my feet.

I got on board the ship, as before, and prepar'd a second raft, and having had experience of the first, I neither made this so unwieldy, nor loaded it so hard. Yet I brought away several things very useful to me; as first, in the carpenter's stores I found two or three bagsful of nails and spikes, a great skrew-jack, a dozen or two of hatchets, and above all, that most useful thing call'd a grindstone. All these I secur'd together, with several things belonging to the gunner, particularly two or three iron crows, and two barrels of musquet bullets, seven musquets, and another fowling-piece, with some small quantity of powder more; a large bagful of small-shot, and a great roll of sheet lead, but this last was so heavy I could not hoist it up to get it over the ship's-side.

Besides these things, I took all the men's cloaths that I could find, and a spare fore-topsail, a hammock, and some bedding. With this I loaded my second raft, and brought them all safe on shore to my very great comfort.

I was under some apprehensions during my absence from the land that at least my provisions might be devour'd on shore; but when I came back, I found no sign of any visitor, only there sat a creature like a wild cat upon one of the chests, which, when I came towards it, ran away a little distance and then stood still; she sat very compos'd, and unconcern'd, and look'd full in my face, as if she had a mind to be acquainted with me. I presented my gun at her, but as she did not understand it, she was perfectly unconcern'd at it, nor did she offer to stir away; upon which I toss'd her a bit of bisket, tho' by the way I was not very free of it, for my store was not great. However, I spar'd her a bit, I say, and she went to it, smell'd of it, and ate it, and look'd (as pleas'd) for more, but I thank'd her, and could spare no more; so she march'd off.

Having got my second cargo on shore, tho' I was fain to open the barrels of powder and bring them by parcels, for they were too heavy, being large casks, I went to work to make me a little tent with the sail and some poles which I cut for that purpose. Into this tent I brought every thing that I knew would spoil, either with rain or sun, and I pil'd all the empty chests and casks up in a circle round the tent, to fortify it from any sudden attempt, either from man or beast.

When I had done this I block'd up the door of the tent with some boards within, and an empty chest set up on end without, and spreading one of the beds upon the ground, laying my two pistols just at my head, and my gun at length by me, I went to bed for the first time. I slept very quietly all night, for I was very weary and heavy, for the night before I had slept little and had labour'd very hard all day, as well to fetch all those things from the ship, as to get them on shore.

I had the biggest magazine of all kinds now that ever were lay'd up, I believe, for one man, but I was not satisfy'd still; for while the ship sat upright in that posture, I thought I ought to get every thing out of her that I could. So every day at low water I went on board and brought away some thing or other. The third time I went, I brought away as much of the rigging as I could, as also all the small ropes and rope-twine I could get, with a piece of spare canvass, which was to mend the sails upon occasion, and the barrel of wet gun-powder. In a word, I brought away all the sails first and last, only that I was fain to cut them in pieces, and bring as much at a time as I could; for they were no more useful to be sails, but as meer canvass only.

But that which comforted me more still was, that at last of all, after I had made five or six such voyages as these, and thought I had nothing more to expect from the ship that was worth my meddling with, I say, after all this, I found a great hogshead of bread and three large runlets of rum or spirits, and a box of sugar, and a barrel of fine flour; this was surprizing to me, because I had given over expecting any more provisions, except what was spoil'd by the water. I soon empty'd the hogshead of that bread and wrapp'd it up parcel by parcel in pieces of the sails, which I cut out. In a word, I got all this safe on shore also.

The next day I made another voyage; and now having plunder'd the ship of what was portable and fit to hand out, I began with the cables. Cutting the great cable into pieces, such as I could move, I got two cables and a hawser on shore, with all the iron-work I could get; and having cut down the spritsail-yard and the missen-yard, and every thing I could to make a large raft, I loaded it with all those heavy goods, and came away. But my good luck began now to leave me, for this raft was so unwieldy, and so overloaden, that after I enter'd the little cove where I had landed the rest of my goods, not being able to guide it so handily as I did the others, it overset, and threw me and all my cargo into the water. As for myself it was no great harm, for I was near the shore, but as to my cargo, it was great part of it lost, especially the iron, which I expected would have been of great use to me. However, when the tide was out, I got most of the pieces of cable ashore, and some of the iron, tho' with infinite labour, for I was fain to dip for it into the water, a work which fatigu'd me very much. After this I went every day on board, and brought away what I could get.

I had been now thirteen days on shore, and had been

eleven times on board the ship, in which time I had brought away all that one pair of hands could well be suppos'd capable to bring, tho' I believe verily, had the calm weather held, I should have brought away the whole ship piece by piece. But preparing the twelfth time to go on board, I found the wind begin to rize; however, at low water I went on board, and tho' I thought I had rummag'd the cabbin so effectually as that nothing more could be found, yet I discover'd a locker with drawers in it, in one of which I found two or three razors, and one pair of large scissars, with some ten or a dozen of good knives and forks; in another I found about 36 pounds value in money, some European coin, some Brasil, some pieces of eight, some gold, some silver.

I smil'd to myself at the sight of this money, "O Drug!" said I aloud, "what art thou good for? Thou art not worth to me, no not the taking off of the ground; one of those knives is worth all this heap. I have no manner of use for thee, e'en remain where thou art, and go to the bottom as a creature whose life is not worth saving." However, upon second thoughts, I took it away, and wrapping all this in a piece of canvass, I began to think of making another raft. But while I was preparing this, I found the sky overcast, and the wind began to rize, and in a quarter of an hour it blew a fresh gale from the shore. It presently occurr'd to me that it was in vain to pretend to make a raft with the wind off shore, and that it was my business to be gone before the tide of flood began, otherwise I might not be able to reach the shore at all. Accordingly, I let myself down into the water, and swam cross the channel, which lay between the ship and the sands, and even that with difficulty enough, partly with the weight of the things

I had about me, and partly the roughness of the water, for the wind riz'd very hastily, and before it was quite high water, it blew a storm.

But I was gotten home to my little tent, where I lay with all my wealth about me very secure. It blew very hard all that night, and in the morning when I look'd out, behold no more ship was to be seen. I was a little surpriz'd, but recover'd myself with this satisfactory reflection, viz., that I had lost no time, nor abated no diligence to get every thing out of her that could be useful to me, and that indeed there was little left in her that I was able to bring away if I had had more time.

I now gave over any more thoughts of the ship, or of any thing out of her, except what might drive on shore from her wreck, as indeed diverse pieces of her afterwards did; but those things were of small use to me.

My thoughts were now wholly employ'd about securing myself against either savages, if any should appear, or wild beasts, if any were on the island. I had many thoughts of the method how to do this and what kind of dwelling to make, whether I should make me a cave in the earth or a tent upon the earth. In short, I resolv'd upon both, the manner and description of which it may not be improper to give an account of.

I soon found the place I was in was not for my settlement, particularly because it was upon a low moorish ground near the sea, and I believ'd would not be wholesome and, more particularly, because there was no fresh water near it. So I resolv'd to find a more healthy and more convenient spot of ground.

I consulted several things in my situation which I found would be proper for me: *1stly.* Health, and fresh water I just now mention'd; 2dly. Shelter from the heat of the sun; 3dly. Security from ravenous creatures, whether men or beasts; 4thly. A view to the sea, that if God sent any ship in sight, I might not lose any advantage for my deliverance, of which I was not willing to banish all my expectation yet.

In search of a place proper for this, I found a little plain on the side of a rising hill, whose front towards this little plain was steep as a house-side, so that nothing could come down upon me from the top; on the side of this rock there was a hollow place worn a little way in like the entrance or door of a cave, but there was not really any cave or way into the rock at all.

On the flat of the green, just before this hollow place, I resolv'd to pitch my tent. This plain was not above an hundred yards broad, and about twice as long, and lay like a green before my door, and at the end of it descended irregularly every way down into the low-grounds by the sea-side. It was on the NNW side of the hill, so that I was shelter'd from the heat every day, till it came to a W by S sun, or thereabouts, which in those countries is near the setting.

Before I set up my tent, I drew a half circle before the hollow place, which took in about ten yards in its semi-diameter from the rock, and twenty yards in its diameter, from its beginning and ending.

In this half circle I pitch'd two rows of strong stakes, driving them into the ground till they stood very firm like piles, the biggest end being out of the ground about five foot and a half, and sharpen'd on the top. The two rows did not stand above six inches from one another.

Then I took the pieces of cable which I had cut in the ship, and I lay'd them in rows one upon another, within the circle, between these two rows of stakes, up to the top, placing other stakes in the in-side, leaning against them, about two foot and a half high, like a spurr to a post. And this fence was so strong that neither man or beast could get into it or over it. This cost me a great deal of time and labour, especially to cut the piles in the woods, bring them to the place, and drive them into the earth.

The entrance into this place I made to be not by a door, but by a short ladder to go over the top, which ladder, when I was in, I lifted over after me, and so I was compleatly fenc'd in, and fortify'd, as I thought, from all the world, and consequently slept secure in the night, which otherwise I could not have done, tho', as it appear'd afterwards, there was no need of all this caution from the enemies that I apprehended danger from.

Into this fence or fortress, with infinite labour, I carry'd all my riches, all my provisions, ammunition, and stores, of which you have the account above, and I made me a large tent, which, to preserve me from the rains that in one part of the year are very violent there, I made double, viz., one smaller tent within, and one larger tent above it, and cover'd the uppermost with a large tarpaulin which I had sav'd among the sails.

And now I lay no more for a while in the bed which I had brought on shore, but in a hammock, which was indeed a very good one, and belong'd to the mate of the ship.

Into this tent I brought all my provisions, and every thing that would spoil by the wet, and having thus enclos'd all my goods, I made up the entrance, which till now I had left open, and so pass'd and re-pass'd, as I said, by a short ladder.

When I had done this, I began to work my way into the

rock, and bringing all the earth and stones that I dug down out thro' my tent, I lay'd them up within my fence in the nature of a terrass, that so it rais'd the ground within about a foot and a half; and thus I made me a cave just behind my tent, which serv'd me like a cellar to my house.

It cost me much labour, and many days, before all these things were brought to perfection, and therefore I must go back to some other things which took up some of my thoughts. At the same time it happen'd, after I had lay'd my scheme for the setting up my tent and making the cave, that a storm of rain falling from a thick dark cloud, a sudden flash of lightning happen'd, and after that a great clap of thunder, as is naturally the effect of it. I was not so much surpriz'd with the lightning as I was with a thought which darted into my mind as swift as the lightning itself: O my powder! My very heart sunk within me when I thought that at one blast all my powder might be destroy'd on which, not my defence only, but the providing me food, as I thought, entirely depended; I was nothing near so anxious about my own danger, tho' had the powder took fire, I had never known what had hurt me.

Such impression did this make upon me that after the storm was over, I lay'd aside all my works, my building, and fortifying, and apply'd myself to make bags and boxes to separate the powder, and keep it a little and a little in a parcel, in hopes that whatever might come, it might not all take fire at once, and to keep it so apart that it should not be possible to make one part fire another. I finish'd this work in about a fortnight, and I think my powder, which in all was about 240 pounds weight, was divided in not less than an hundred parcels. As to the barrel that had been wet, I did not apprehend any danger from that, so I plac'd it in my new cave, which in my fancy I call'd my kitchen, and the rest I hid up and down in holes among the rocks, so that no wet might come to it, marking very carefully where I lay'd it.

In the interval of time while this was doing I went out once at least every day with my gun, as well to divert myself as to see if I could kill any thing fit for food, and as near as I could to acquaint myself with what the island produc'd. The first time I went out I presently discover'd that there were goats on the island, which was a great satisfaction to me; but then it was attended with this misfortune to me, viz., that they were so shy, so subtile, and so swift of foot, that it was the difficultest thing in the world to come at them. But I was not discourag'd at this, not doubting that I might now and then shoot one, as it soon happen'd, for after I had found their haunts a little, I lay'd wait in this manner for them: I observ'd if they saw me in the valleys, tho' they were upon the rocks, they would run away as in a terrible fright; but if they were feeding in the valleys, and I was upon the rocks, they took no notice of me, whence I concluded, that by the position of their opticks, their sight was so directed downward, that they did not readily see objects that were above them. So afterwards I took this method: I always clim'd the rocks first to get above them, and then had frequently a fair mark. The first shot I made among these creatures, I kill'd a she-goat which had a little kid by her which she gave suck to, which griev'd me heartily; but when the old one fell, the kid stood stock still by her till I came and took her up, and not only so, but when I carry'd the old one with me upon my shoulders, the kid follow'd me quite to my enclosure, upon which I lay'd down the dam, and took the kid in my arms, and carry'd it over my pale, in hopes to have bred it up tame. But it would not eat, so I was forc'd to kill it and eat it myself; these two supply'd me with flesh a great while, for I ate sparingly and sav'd my provisions (my bread especially) as much as possibly I could.

Having now fix'd my habitation, I found it absolutely necessary to provide a place to make a fire in, and fuel to burn; and what I did for that, as also how I enlarg'd my cave, and what conveniencies I made, I shall give a full account of in its place. But I must first give some little account of myself, and of my thoughts about living, which it may well be suppos'd were not a few.

I had a dismal prospect of my condition, for as I was not cast away upon that island without being driven, as is said, by a violent storm quite out of the course of our intended voyage, and a great way, viz., some hundreds of leagues out of the ordinary course of the trade of mankind, I had great reason to consider it as a determination of heaven, that in this desolate place, and in this desolate manner I should end my life. The tears would run plentifully down my face when I made these reflections, and sometimes I would expostulate with myself why Providence should thus compleatly ruine its creatures and render them so absolutely miserable, so without help abandon'd, so entirely depress'd that it could hardly be rational to be thankful for such a life.

But something always return'd swift upon me to check these thoughts and to reprove me; and one day walking with my gun in my hand by the sea-side, I was very pensive upon the subject of my present condition, when reason as it were expostulated with me t'other way, thus: Well, you are in a desolate condition 'tis true, but pray remember, where are the rest of you? Did not you come eleven of you into the boat; where are the ten? Why were not they sav'd and you lost? Why were you singl'd out? Is it better to be here or there? And then I pointed to the sea. All evils are to be consider'd with the good that is in them and with what worse attends them.

Then it occurr'd to me again how well I was furnish'd for my subsistence, and what would have been my case if it had not happen'd, which was a hundred thousand to one, that the ship floated from the place where she first struck and was driven so near to the shore that I had time to get all these things out of her. What would have been my case, if I had to have liv'd in the condition in which I at first came on shore, without the necessaries of life or the necessaries to supply and procure them? "Particularly," said I aloud (tho' to myself), "what should I have done without a gun, without ammunition, without any tools to make anything, or to work with, without cloaths, bedding, a tent, or any manner of covering." Now I had all these to a sufficient quantity and was in a fair way to provide myself in such a manner as to live without my gun when my ammunition was spent; so that I had a tolerable view of subsisting without any want as long as I liv'd; for I consider'd from the beginning how I would provide for the accidents that might happen and for the time that was to come, not only after my ammunition should be spent, but even after my health or strength should decay.

I confess I had not entertain'd any notion of my ammunition being destroy'd at one blast, I mean my powder being blown up by lightning, and this made the thoughts of it so surprizing to me when it lighten'd and thunder'd, as I observed just now.

And now being to enter into a melancholy relation of a scene of silent life, such perhaps as was never heard of in the world before, I shall take it from its beginning, and continue it in its order. It was, by my account, the 30th of September when, in the manner as above said, I first set foot upon this horrid island, when the sun being, to us, in its autumnal equinox, was almost just over my head, for I reckon'd myself, by observation, to be in the latitude of 9 degrees 22 minutes north of the Line.

After I had been there about ten or twelve days, it came into my thoughts that I should lose my reckoning of time for want of books and pen and ink, and should even forget the Sabbath days from the working days; but to prevent this I cut it with my knife upon a large post, in capital letters, and making it into a great cross I set it up on the shore where I first landed, viz., I came on shore here on the 30th of September, 1659. Upon the sides of this square post I cut every day a notch with my knife, and every seventh notch was as long again as the rest, and every first day of the month as long again as that long one, and thus I kept my kalender, or weekly, monthly, and yearly reckoning of time.

In the next place we are to observe that, among the many things which I brought out of the ship in the several voyages, which, as above mention'd, I made to it, I got several things of less value, but not all less useful to me, which I omitted setting down before. In particular, pens, ink, and paper, several parcels in the captain's, mate's, gunner's, and carpenter's keeping, three or four compasses, some mathematical instruments, dials, perspectives, charts, and books of navigation, all which I huddel'd together, whether I might want them or no. Also, I found three very good Bibles which came to me in my cargo from England, and which I had pack'd up among my things; some Portugueze books also, and among them two or three Popish prayer books, and several other books, all which I carefully secur'd. And I must not forget, that we had in the ship a dog and two cats, of whose eminent history I may have occasion to say something in its place; for I carry'd both the cats with me, and as for the dog, he jump'd out of the ship of himself and swam on shore to me, the day after I went on shore with my first cargo, and was a trusty servant to me many years. I wanted nothing that he could not fetch me, nor any company that he could not make up to me; I only wanted to have him talk to me, but that would not do. As I observ'd before, I found pen, ink, and paper, and I husbanded them to the utmost, and I shall shew that, while my ink lasted, I kept things very exact, but after that was gone I could not, for I could not make any ink by any means that I could devize.

And this put me in mind that I wanted many things, notwithstanding all that I had amass'd together, and of these, this of ink was one, as also spade, pick-axe, and shovel to dig or remove the earth; needles, pins, and thread; as for linnen, I soon learn'd to want that without much difficulty.

This want of tools made every work I did go on heavily, and it was near a whole year before I had entirely finish'd my little pale or surrounded habitation. The piles or stakes, which were as heavy as I could well lift, were a long time in cutting and preparing in the woods, and more by far in bringing home. So I spent sometimes two days in cutting and bringing home one of those posts, and a third day in driving it into the ground; for which purpose I got a heavy piece of wood at first, but at last bethought myself of one of the iron crows, which however tho' I found it, yet it made driving those posts or piles very laborious and tedious work.

But what need I have been concern'd at the tediousness of any thing I had to do, seeing I had time enough to do it in, nor had I any other employment if that had been over, at least, that I could foresee, except the ranging of the island to seek for food, which I did more or less every day.

I now began to consider seriously my condition, and the circumstance I was reduc'd to, and I drew up the state of my affairs in writing, not so much to leave them to any that were to come after me, for I was like to have but few heirs, as to deliver my thoughts from daily poring upon them, and afflicting my mind. And as my reason began now to master my despondency, I began to comfort myself as well as I could and to set the good against the evil, that I might have something to distinguish my case from worse, and I stated it very impartially, like debtor and creditor, the comforts I enjoy'd, against the miseries I suffer'd, thus:

Evil	*Good*
I am cast upon a horrible desolate island, void of all hope of recovery.	But I am alive and not drown'd as all my ship's company was.

I am singl'd out and separated, as it were, from all the world to be miserable.	But I am singl'd out too from all the ship's crew to be spar'd from death; and He that miraculously sav'd me from death can deliver me from this condition.
I am divided from mankind, a solitaire, one banish'd from human society.	But I am not starv'd and perishing on a barren place affording no sustenance.
I have not cloaths to cover me.	But I am in a hot climate, where if I had cloaths I could hardly wear them.
I am without any defence or means to resist any violence of man or beast.	But I am cast on an island where I see no wild beasts to hurt me, as I saw on the coast of Africa. And what if I had been shipwreck'd there?
I have no soul to speak to or relieve me.	But God wonderfully sent the ship in near enough to the shore, that I have gotten out so many necessary things as will either supply my wants or enable me to supply myself even as long as I live.

Upon the whole, here was an undoubted testimony that there was scarce any condition in the world so miserable, but there was something negative or something positive to be thankful for in it. And let this stand as a direction from the experience of the most miserable of all conditions in this world, that we may always find in it something to comfort ourselves from and to set in the description of good and evil on the credit side of the account.

Having now brought my mind a little to relish my condition, and given over looking out to sea to see if I could spy a ship, I say, giving over these things, I began to apply myself to accommodate my way of living, and to make things as easy to me as I could.

I have already describ'd my habitation, which was a tent under the side of a rock, surrounded with a strong pale of posts and cables, but I might now rather call it a wall, for I rais'd a kind of wall up against it of turfs, about two-foot thick on the out-side, and after some time, I think it was a year and a half, I rais'd rafters from it leaning to the rock, and thatch'd or cover'd it with bows of trees, and such things as I could get to keep out the rain, which I found at some times of the year very violent.

I have already observ'd how I brought all my goods into this pale and into the cave which I had made behind me. But I must observe too, that at first this was a confus'd heap of goods, which as they lay in no order, so they took up all my place. I had no room to turn myself, so I set myself to enlarge my cave and works farther into the earth. It was a loose sandy rock, which yielded easily to the labour I bestow'd on it, so when I found I was pretty safe as to beasts of prey, I work'd sideways to the right hand into the rock, and then turning to the right again, work'd quite out and made me a door to come out, on the out-side of my pale or fortification.

This gave me not only egress and regress, as it were a back way to my tent and to my storehouse, but gave me room to stow my goods.

And now I began to apply myself to make such necessary things as I found I most wanted, as particularly a chair and a table, for without these I was not able to enjoy the few comforts I had in the world; I could not write, or eat, or do several things with so much pleasure without a table.

So I went to work; and here I must needs observe, that as reason is the substance and original of the Mathematicks, so by stating and squaring every thing by reason, and by making the most rational judgment of things, every man may be in time master of every mechanick art. I had never handl'd a tool in my life, and yet in time by labour, application, and contrivance, I found at last that I wanted nothing but I could have made it, especially if I had had tools. However, I made an abundance of things, even without tools, and some with no more tools than an adze and a hatchet, which perhaps were never made that way before, and that with infinite labour. For example, if I wanted a board, I had no other way but to cut down a tree, set it on an edge before me, and hew it flat on either side with my axe, till I had brought it to be thin as a plank, and then dubb it smooth with my adze. It is true, by this method I could make but one board out of a whole tree, but this I had no remedy for but patience, any more than I had for the prodigious deal of time and labour which it took me up to make a plank or board. But my time or labour was little worth, and so it was as well employ'd one way as another.

However, I made me a table and a chair, as I observ'd

above, in the first place, and this I did out of the short pieces of boards that I brought on my raft from the ship. When I had wrought out some boards, as above, I made large shelves of the breadth of a foot and half one over another, all along one side of my cave, to lay all my tools, nails, and iron-work, and in a word, to separate every thing at large in their places, that I must come easily to them. I knock'd pieces into the wall of the rock to hang my guns and all things that would hang up.

So that had my cave been to be seen, it look'd like a general magazine of all necessary things, and I had every thing so ready at my hand, that it was a great pleasure to me to see all my goods in such order, and especially to find my stock of all necessaries so great.

And now it was when I began to keep a Journal of every day's employment. Indeed, at first I was in too much hurry, and not only hurry as to labour, but in too much discomposure of mind, and my Journal would ha' been full of many dull things. For example, I must have said thus: *Sept. the 30th.* After I got to shore and had escap'd drowning, instead of being thankful to God for my deliverance, having first vomited with the great quantity of salt water which was gotten into my stomach, and recovering myself a little, I ran about the shore, wringing my hands and beating my head and face, exclaiming at my misery, and crying out I was undone, undone, till tyr'd and faint I was forc'd to lie down on the ground to repose, but durst not sleep for fear of being devour'd.

Some days after this, and after I had been on board the ship and got all that I could out of her, yet I could not forbear getting up to the top of a little mountain and looking out to sea in hopes of seeing a ship, then fancy at a vast distance I spy'd a sail, pleas'd myself with the hopes of it, and then after looking steadily till I was almost blind, lose it quite, and sit down and weep like a child, and thus encrease my misery by my folly.

But having gotten over these things in some measure, and having settl'd my household stuff and habitation, made me a table and a chair, and all as handsome about me as I could, I began to keep my Journal, of which I shall here give you the copy (tho' in it will be told all these particulars over again) as long as it lasted, for having no more ink I was forc'd to leave it off.

The Journal

September 30, 1659. I, poor miserable Robinson Crusoe, being shipwreck'd, during a dreadful storm, in the offing, came on shore on this dismal unfortunate island, which I call'd the Island of Despair, all the rest of the ship's company being drown'd, and myself almost dead.

All the rest of that day I spent in afflicting myself at the dismal circumstances I was brought to, *viz.*, I had neither food, house, cloaths, weapon, or place to fly to, and in despair of any relief, saw nothing but death before me, either that I should be devour'd by wild beasts, murther'd by savages, or starv'd to death for want of food. At the approach of night, I slept in a tree for fear of wild creatures, but slept soundly tho' it rain'd all night.

October 1. In the morning I saw to my great surprize the ship had floated with the high tide and was driven on shore again much nearer the island, which as it was some comfort on one hand, for seeing her sit upright and not broken to pieces, I hop'd, if the wind abated, I might get on board

and get some food and necessaries out of her for my relief;
so on the other hand, it renew'd my grief at the loss of my
comrades, who I imagin'd if we had all stay'd on board
might have sav'd the ship, or at least that they would not
have been all drown'd as they were; and that had the men
been sav'd, we might perhaps have built us a boat out of
the ruins of the ship to have carry'd us to some other part
of the world. I spent great part of this day in perplexing
myself on these things; but at length seeing the ship almost
dry, I went upon the sand as near as I could and then swam
on board; this day also it continu'd raining, tho' with no
wind at all.

From the 1st of October to the 24th. All these days entirely spent in many several voyages to get all I could out
of the ship, which I brought on shore, every tide of flood,
upon rafts. Much rain also in these days, tho' with some
intervals of fair weather. But it seems this was the rainy
season.

Oct. 20. I overset my raft and all the goods I had got
upon it, but being in shoal water, and the things being
chiefly heavy, I recover'd many of them when the tide was
out.

Oct. 25. It rain'd all night and all day, with some gusts
of wind, during which time the ship broke in pieces, the
wind blowing a little harder than before, and was no more
to be seen, except the wreck of her, and that only at low
water. I spent this day in covering and securing the goods
which I had sav'd, that the rain might not spoil them.

Oct. 26. I walk'd about the shore almost all day to
find out a place to fix my habitation, greatly concern'd to
secure myself from an attack in the night, either from wild

beasts or men. Towards night I fix'd upon a proper place under a rock and mark'd out a semicircle for my encampment, which I resolv'd to strengthen with a work, wall, or fortification made of double piles, lin'd within with cables and without with turf.

From the 26th to the 30th. I work'd very hard in carrying all my goods to my new habitation, tho' some part of the time it rain'd exceeding hard.

The 31st. In the morning I went out into the island with my gun to see for some food and discover the country, when I kill'd a she-goat, and her kid follow'd me home, which I afterwards kill'd also because it would not feed.

November 1. I set up my tent under a rock and lay there for the first night, making it as large as I could with stakes driven in to swing my hammock upon.

Nov. 2. I set up all my chests and boards, and the pieces of timber which made my rafts, and with them form'd a fence round me, a little within the place I had mark'd out for my fortification.

Nov. 3. I went out with my gun and kill'd two fowls like ducks, which were very good food. In the afternoon went to work to make me a table.

Nov. 4. This morning I began to order my times of work, of going out with my gun, time of sleep, and time of diversion, viz., every morning I walk'd out with my gun for two or three hours if it did not rain, then employ'd myself to work till about eleven a-clock, then ate what I had to live on, and from twelve to two I lay down to sleep, the weather being excessive hot, and then in the evening to work again. The working part of this day and of the next were wholly employ'd in making my table, for I was yet but a very sorry workman, tho' time and necessity made me a compleat natural mechanick soon after, as I believe it would do any one else.

Nov. 5. This day went abroad with my gun and my dog, and kill'd a wild cat, her skin pretty soft, but her flesh good for nothing. Every creature I kill'd I took off the skins and preserv'd them. Coming back by the seashore, I saw many sorts of sea fowls which I did not understand, but was surpriz'd and almost frighted with two or three seals, which, while I was gazing at, not well knowing what they were, got into the sea and escap'd me for that time.

Nov. 6. After my morning walk I went to work with my table again and finish'd it, tho' not to my liking; nor was it long before I learn'd to mend it.

Nov. 7. Now it began to be settl'd fair weather. The 7th, 8th, 9th, 10th, and part of the 12th (for the 11th was Sunday), I took wholly up to make me a chair and with much ado brought it to a tolerable shape, but never to please me, and even in the making I pull'd it to pieces several times. *Note,* I soon neglected my keeping Sundays, for omitting my mark for them on my post, I forgot which was which.

Nov. 13. This day it rain'd, which refresh'd me exceedingly and cool'd the earth; but it was accompany'd with terrible thunder and lightning, which frighted me dreadfully for fear of my powder. As soon as it was over, I resolv'd to separate my stock of powder into as many little parcels as possible, that it might not be in danger.

Nov. 14, 15, 16. These three days I spent in making little square chests or boxes, which might hold about a pound or two pounds, at most, of powder, and so putting the powder in, I stow'd it in places as secure and remote from one another as possible. On one of these three days

I kill'd a large bird that was good to eat, but I know not what to call it.

Nov. 17. This day I began to dig behind my tent into the rock to make room for my further conveniency. *Note,* two things I wanted exceedingly for this work, *viz.,* a pick-axe, a shovel, and a wheel-barrow or basket, so I desisted from my work, and began to consider how to supply that want and make me some tools. As for a pick-axe, I made use of the iron crows, which were proper enough, tho' heavy; but the next thing was a shovel or spade. This was so absolutely necessary that indeed I could do nothing effectually without it, but what kind of one to make I knew not.

Nov. 18. The next day in searching the woods I found a tree of that wood, or like it, which, in the Brasils they call the Iron Tree, for its exceeding hardness. Of this, with great labour and almost spoiling my axe, I cut a piece, and brought it home too, with difficulty enough, for it was exceeding heavy.

The excessive hardness of the wood, and having no other way, made me a long while upon this machine, for I work'd it effectually by little and little into the form of a shovel or spade, the handle exactly shap'd like ours in England, only that the broad part having no iron shod upon it at bottom, it would not last me so long. However, it serv'd well enough for the uses which I had occasion to put it to; but never was a shovel, I believe, made after that fashion, or so long a-making.

I was still deficient, for I wanted a basket or a wheel-barrow. A basket I could not make by any means, having no such things as twigs that would bend to make wicker-ware, at least none yet found out; and as to a wheel-barrow,

I fancy'd I could make all but the wheel, but that I had no notion of, neither did I know how to go about it. Besides, I had no possible way to make the iron gudgeons for the spindle or axis of the wheel to run in, so I gave it over, and, for carrying away the earth which I dug out of the cave, I made me a thing like a hodd, which the labourers carry mortar in when they serve the bricklayers.

This was not so difficult to me as the making of the shovel; and yet this, and the shovel, and the attempt which I made in vain to make a wheel-barrow, took me up no less than four days, I mean all the day, excepting my morning walk with my gun, which I seldom fail'd, and very seldom fail'd also bringing home something fit to eat.

Nov. 23. My other work now stood still, because of my making these tools. When they were finish'd, I went on, and working every day, as my strength and time allow'd, I spent eighteen days entirely in widening and deepening my cave, that it might hold my goods commodiously. *Note*, during all this time, I work'd to make this room or cave spacious enough to accommodate me as a warehouse or magazine, a kitchen, a dining room, and a cellar. As for my lodging, I kept to the tent, except that sometimes in the wet season of the year, it rain'd so hard that I could not keep myself dry, which caused me afterwards to cover all my place within my pale with long poles in the form of rafters leaning against the rock, and load them with flaggs and large leaves of trees like a thatch.

December 10. I began now to think my cave or vault finish'd, when on a sudden (it seems I had made it too large) a great quantity of earth fell down from the top and one side, so much that, in short, it frighted me, and not without reason too, for if I had been under it I had never wanted a grave-digger. Upon this disaster I had a great deal of work to do over again, for I had the loose earth to carry out, and which was of more importance, I had the ceiling to prop up, so that I might be sure no more would come down.

Dec. 11. This day I went to work with it accordingly and got two shores or posts pitch'd upright to the top, with two pieces of boards across over each post. This I finish'd the next day, and setting more posts up with boards, in about a week more I had the roof secur'd; and the posts standing in rows serv'd me for partitions to part of my house.

Dec. 17. From this day to the 20th I plac'd shelves, and knock'd up nails on the posts to hang every thing up that could be hung up, and now I began to be in some order within doors.

Dec. 20. Now I carry'd every thing into the cave, and began to furnish my house and set up some pieces of boards, like a dresser, to order my victuals upon, but boards began to be very scarce with me; also I made me another table.

Dec. 24. Much rain all night and all day, no stirring out.

Dec. 25. Rain all day.

Dec. 26. No rain, and the earth much cooler than before, and pleasanter.

Dec. 27. Kill'd a young goat and lam'd another so as that I catch'd it, and led it home on a string. When I had it home, I bound and splinter'd up its leg, which was broke. *Note*, I took such care of it that it liv'd, and the leg grew well and as strong as ever; but by my nursing it so long it grew tame, and fed upon the little green at my door, and would not go away. This was the first time that I entertain'd a thought of breeding up some tame creatures, that I might have food when my powder and shot was all spent.

Dec. 28, 29, 30. Great heats and no breeze, so that there was no stirring abroad except in the evening for food; this time I spent in putting all my things in order within doors.

January 1. Very hot still, but I went abroad early and late with my gun and lay still in the middle of the day; this evening going farther into the valleys which lay towards the center of the island, I found there was plenty of goats, tho' exceeding shy and hard to come at. However, I resolv'd to try if I could not bring my dog to hunt them down.

Jan. 2. Accordingly, the next day I went out with my dog, and set him upon the goats; but I was mistaken, for they all fac'd about upon the dog, and he knew his danger too well, for he would not come near them.

Jan. 3. I began my fence or wall; which being still jealous of my being attack'd by some body, I resolv'd to make very thick and strong. Note, this wall being describ'd before, I purposely omit what was said in the Journal; it is sufficient to observe that I was no less time than from the 3rd of January to the 14th of April, working, finishing, and perfecting this wall, tho' it was no more than about twenty-four yards in length, being a half circle from one place in the rock to another place about eight yards from it; the door of the cave being in the center behind it.

All this time I work'd very hard, the rains hind'ring me many days, nay, sometimes weeks together; but I thought I should never be perfectly secure till this wall was finish'd; and it is scarce credible what inexpressible labour every thing was done with, especially the bringing piles out of the woods and driving them into the ground, for I made them much bigger than I need to have done.

When this wall was finish'd, and the out-side double fenc'd with a turfwall rais'd up close to it, I persuaded myself that if any people were to come on shore there, they would not perceive any thing like a habitation. It was very well I did so, as may be observ'd hereafter upon a very remarkable occasion.

During this time, I made my rounds in the woods for game every day when the rain admitted me and made frequent discoveries in these walks of something or other to my advantage. Particularly, I found a kind of wild pidgeons, who built not as wood pidgeons in a tree, but rather as house pidgeons, in the holes of the rocks; and taking some young ones, I endeavour'd to breed them up tame, and did so. But when they grew older they flew all away, which perhaps was at first for want of feeding them, for I had nothing to give them; however, I frequently found their nests, and got their young ones, which were very good meat.

And now, in the managing of my household affairs, I found myself wanting in many things, which I thought at first it was impossible for me to make, as indeed as to some of them it was. For instance, I could never make a cask to be hoop'd; I had a small runlet or two, as I observ'd before, but I could never arrive to the capacity of making one by them, tho' I spent many weeks about it; I could neither put in the heads or joint the staves so true to one another as to make them hold water, so I gave that also over.

In the next place, I was at a great loss for candle, so that as soon as ever it was dark, which was generally by seven a-

clock, I was oblig'd to go to bed. I remember'd the lump
of beeswax with which I made candles on my African adventure, but I had none of that now; the only remedy I
had was that when I had kill'd a goat, I sav'd the tallow,
and with a little dish made of clay, which I bak'd in the
sun, to which I added a wick of some oakum, I made me a
lamp, and this gave me light, tho' not a clear steady light
like a candle. In the middle of all my labours it happen'd
that, rummaging my things, I found a little bag, which, as
I hinted before, had been fill'd with corn for the feeding
of poultry, not for this voyage, but before, as I suppose,
when the ship came from Lisbon. What little remainder
of corn had been in the bag was all devour'd by the rats,
and I saw nothing in the bag but husks and dust. But
being willing to have the bag for some other use, I think
it was to put powder in, when I divided it for fear of the
lightning, or some such use, I shook the husks of corn out
of it on one side of my fortification under the rock.

It was a little before the great rains, just now mention'd,
that I threw this stuff away, taking no notice of any thing
and not so much as rememb'ring that I had thrown any
thing there; when about a month after, or thereabout, I
saw some few stalks of something green shooting out of the
ground, which I fancy'd might be some plant I had not
seen, but I was surpriz'd and perfectly astonish'd when,
after a little longer time, I saw about ten or twelve ears
come out, which were perfect green barley of the same kind
as our European, nay, as our English barley.

It is impossible to express the astonishment and confusion of my thoughts on this occasion; I had hitherto acted
upon no religious foundation at all, indeed I had very few
notions of religion in my head, or had entertain'd any sense

For an oven, I made some earthen vessels very broad, but
deep, that is to say, about two foot diameter and not above
nine inches deep. (page 141)

of any thing that had befallen me, otherwise than as a chance, or, as we lightly say, what pleases God; without so much as enquiring into the end of Providence in these things, or His order in governing events in the world. But after I saw barley grow there, in a climate which I know was not proper for corn, and especially that I knew not how it came there, it startl'd me strangely, and I began to suggest that God had miraculously caus'd this grain to grow without any help of seed sown and that it was so directed purely for my sustenance on that wild miserable place.

This touch'd my heart a little and brought tears out of my eyes, and I began to bless myself that such a prodigy of nature should happen upon my account; and this was the more strange to me because I saw near it, still all along by the side of the rock, some other straggling stalks, which prov'd to be stalks of rice, and which I knew because I had seen it grow in Africa when I was ashore there.

I not only thought these the pure productions of Providence for my support, but not doubting that there was more in the place, I went all over that part of the island, where I had been before, peering in every corner, and under every rock, to see for more of it, but I could not find any. At last it occurr'd to my thoughts that I had shook a bag of chicken's meat out in that place, and then the wonder began to cease; and I must confess, my religious thankfulness to God's providence began to abate too upon the discov'ring that all this was nothing but what was common; tho' I ought to have been as thankful for so strange and unforeseen providence, as if it had been miraculous; for it was really the work of Providence as to me, that should order or appoint, that ten or twelve grains of corn should remain unspoil'd (when the rats had destroy'd all the rest), as if it had been dropp'd from Heaven. Also, that I should throw it out in that particular place, where it being in the shade of a high rock, it sprang up immediately; whereas, if I had thrown it anywhere else, at that time, it had been burnt up and destroy'd.

I carefully sav'd the ears of this corn you may be sure in their season, which was about the end of June; and laying up every ear, I resolv'd to sow them all again, hoping in time to have some quantity sufficient to supply me with bread. But it was not till the fourth year that I could allow myself the least grain of this corn to eat, and even then but sparingly, as I shall say afterwards in its order, for I lost all that I sow'd the first season by not observing the proper time; for I sow'd it just before the dry season, so that it never came up at all, at least, not as it would have done. Of which account in its place.

Besides this barley there was, as above, twenty or thirty stalks of rice, which I preserv'd with the same care and whose use was of the same kind or to the same purpose, viz., to make me bread, or rather food; for I found ways to cook it up without baking, tho' I did that also after some time. But to return to my Journal.

I work'd excessive hard these three or four months to get my wall done; and the 14th of April I clos'd it up, contriving to go into it, not by a door, but over the wall by a ladder, that there might be no sign on the out-side of my habitation.

April 16. I finish'd the ladder, so I went up with the ladder to the top, and then pull'd it up after me, and let it down in the in-side. This was a compleat enclosure to me; for within I had room enough, and nothing could come at me from without, unless it could first mount my wall.

The very next day after this wall was finish'd, I almost had all my labour overthrown at once and myself kill'd. The case was thus: As I was busy in the in-side of it, behind my tent, just in the entrance to my cave, I was terribly frighted with a most dreadful surprizing thing indeed; for all on a sudden I found the earth come crumbling down from the roof of my cave, and from the edge of the hill over my head, and two of the posts I had set up in the cave crack'd in a frightful manner. I was heartily scar'd, but thought nothing of what was really the cause, only thinking that the top of my cave was falling in, as some of it had done before; and for fear I should be bury'd in it, I ran forward to my ladder, and not thinking myself safe there neither, I got over my wall for fear of the pieces of the hill which I expected might roll down upon me. I was no sooner stepp'd down upon the firm ground, but I plainly saw it was a terrible earthquake, for the ground I stood on shook three times at about eight minutes' distance, with three such shocks as would have overturn'd the strongest building that could be suppos'd to have stood on the earth. And a great piece of the top of a rock, which stood about half a mile from me next the sea, fell down with such a terrible noise as I never heard in all my life. I perceiv'd also the very sea was put into violent motion by it, and I believe the shocks were stronger under the water than on the island.

I was so amaz'd with the thing itself, having never felt the like, or discours'd with any one who had, that I was like one dead or stupify'd; and the motion of the earth made my stomach sick like one that was toss'd at sea. The noise of the falling of the rock awak'd me, as it were, and rouzing me from the stupify'd condition I was in, fill'd me with horror, and I thought of nothing then but the hill falling upon my tent and all my household goods and burying all at once; and this sunk my very soul within me a second time.

After the third shock was over, and I felt no more for some time, I began to take courage, and yet I had not heart enough to go over my wall again, for fear of being bury'd alive, but sat still upon the ground, greatly cast down and disconsolate, not knowing what to do. All this while I had not the least serious religious thought, nothing but the common, *Lord have mercy upon me*; and when it was over, that went away too.

While I sat thus, I found the air overcast, and grow cloudy, as if it would rain; soon after that the wind riz'd by little and little, so that, in less than half an hour, it blew a most dreadful hurricane. The sea was all on a sudden cover'd over with foam and froth; the shore was cover'd with the breach of the water; the trees were torn up by the roots; and a terrible storm it was. This held about three hours, and then began to abate, and in two hours more it was stark calm and began to rain very hard.

All this while I sat upon the ground very much terrify'd and dejected, when on a sudden it came into my thoughts that these winds and rain being the consequences of the earthquake, the earthquake itself was spent and over, and I might venture into my cave again. With this thought my spirits began to revive, and the rain also helping to persuade me, I went in and sat down in my tent; but the rain was so violent that my tent was ready to be beaten down with it, and I was forc'd to go into my cave, tho' very much afraid and uneasy for fear it should fall on my head.

This violent rain forc'd me to a new work, viz., to cut a

hole thro' my new fortification like a sink to let the water go out, which would else have drown'd my cave. After I had been in my cave some time, and found still no more shocks of the earthquake follow, I began to be more compos'd; and now to support my spirits, which indeed wanted it very much, I went to my little store and took a small sup of rum, which however I did then and always very sparingly, knowing I could have no more when that was gone.

It continu'd raining all that night and great part of the next day, so that I could not stir abroad. But my mind being more compos'd, I began to think of what I had best do, concluding that if the island was subject to these earthquakes, there would be no living for me in a cave; but I must consider of building me some little hut in an open place which I might surround with a wall as I had done here and so make myself secure from wild beasts or men; but concluded if I stay'd where I was, I should certainly, one time or other, be bury'd alive.

With these thoughts I resolv'd to remove my tent from the place where it stood, which was just under the hanging precipice of the hill, and which, if it should be shaken again, would certainly fall upon my tent. I spent the two next days, being the 19th and 20th of April, in contriving where and how to remove my habitation.

The fear of being swallow'd up alive, made me that I never slept in quiet, and yet the apprehensions of lying abroad without any fence was almost equal to it; but still when I look'd about and saw how every thing was put in order, how pleasantly conceal'd I was, and how safe from danger, it made me very loath to remove.

In the meantime it occurr'd to me that it would require

a fast deal of time for me to do this, and that I must be contented to run the venture where I was till I had form'd a camp for myself and had secur'd it so as to remove to it. So with this resolution I compos'd myself for a time and resolv'd that I would go to work with all speed to build me a wall with piles and cables, &c. in a circle as before, and set my tent up in it when it was finish'd, but that I would venture to stay where I was till it was finish'd and fit to remove to. This was the 21st.

April 22. The next morning I began to consider of means to put this resolve in execution, but I was at a great loss about my tools. I had three large axes and an abundance of hatchets (for we carried the hatchets for traffick with the Indians), but with much chopping and cutting knotty hard wood, they were all full of notches and dull, and tho' I had a grindstone, I could not turn it and grind my tools too. This cost me as much thought as a statesman would have bestow'd upon a grand point of politicks, or a judge upon the life and death of a man. At length I contriv'd a wheel with a string to turn it with my foot, that I might have both my hands at liberty. Note, I had never seen any such thing in England, or at least not to take notice how it was done, tho' since I have observ'd it is very common there. Besides that, my grindstone was very large and heavy; this machine cost me a full week's work to bring it to perfection.

April 28, 29. These two whole days I took up in grinding my tools, my machine for turning my grindstone performing very well.

April 30. Having perceiv'd my bread had been low a great while, now I took a survey of it and reduc'd myself to one bisket-cake a day, which made my heart very heavy.

May 1. In the morning looking towards the seaside, the tide being low, I saw something lie on the shore bigger than ordinary, and it look'd like a cask. When I came to it, I found a small barrel and two or three pieces of the wreck of the ship, which were driven on shore by the late hurricane; and looking towards the wreck itself, I thought it seem'd to lie higher out of the water than it used to do. I examin'd the barrel which was driven on shore, and soon found it was a barrel of gunpowder, but it had taken water, and the powder was cak'd as hard as a stone. However, I roll'd it farther on shore for the present and went on upon the sands as near as I could to the wreck of the ship to look for more.

When I came down to the ship I found it strangely remov'd; the forecastle, which lay before bury'd in sand, was heav'd up at least six foot; and the stern, which was broke to pieces and parted from the rest by the force of the sea soon after I had left rummaging her, was toss'd, as it were, up, and cast on one side; and the sand was thrown so high on that side next her stern that, whereas there was a great place of water before, so that I could not come within a quarter of a mile of the wreck without swimming, I could now walk quite up to her when the tide was out. I was surpriz'd with this at first, but soon concluded it must be done by the earthquake, and as by this violence the ship was more broken open than formerly, so many things came daily on shore, which the sea had loosen'd, and which the winds and water roll'd by degrees to the land.

This wholly diverted my thoughts from the design of removing my habitation; and I busy'd myself mightily that day especially, in searching whether I could make any way into the ship, but I found nothing was to be expected of that kind, for that all the in-side of the ship was choack'd up with sand. However, as I had learn'd not to despair of any thing, I resolv'd to pull every thing to pieces that I could of the ship, concluding that every thing I could get from her would be of some use or other to me.

May 3. I began with my saw and cut a piece of a beam thro', which I thought held some of the upper part or quarter-deck together, and when I had cut it thro' I clear'd away the sand as well as I could from the side which lay highest; but the tide coming in, I was oblig'd to give over for that time.

May 4. I went a-fishing, but caught not one fish that I durst eat of, till I was weary of my sport, when just going to leave off, I caught a young dolphin. I had made me a long line of some rope yarn, but I had no hooks, yet I frequently caught fish enough, as much as I car'd to eat; all which I dry'd in the sun and ate them dry.

May 5. Work'd on the wreck, cut another beam a-sunder, and brought three great firr planks off from the decks, which I ty'd together, and made swim on shore when the tide of flood came on.

May 6. Work'd on the wreck, got several iron bolts out of her and other pieces of iron-work; work'd very hard, and came home very much tyr'd, and had thoughts of giving it over.

May 7. Went to the wreck again, but with an intent not to work, but found the weight of the wreck had broken it-self down. The beams being cut, several pieces of the ship seem'd to lie loose, and the in-side of the hold lay so open that I could see into it, but almost full of water and sand.

May 8. Went to the wreck and carry'd an iron crow to wrench up the deck, which lay now quite clear of the water or sand. I wrench'd open two planks and brought them on shore also with the tide; I left the iron crow in the wreck for next day.

May 9. Went to the wreck, and with the crow made way into the body of the wreck, and felt several casks, and loosen'd them with the crow, but could not break them up; I felt also the roll of English lead, and could stir it, but it was too heavy to remove.

May 10, 11, 12, 13, 14. Went every day to the wreck and got a great deal of pieces of timber, and boards, or plank and 200 or 300 weight of iron.

May 15. I carry'd two hatchets to try if I could not cut a piece off of the roll of lead by placing the edge of one hatchet and driving it with the other; but, as it lay about a foot and a half in the water, I could not make any blow to drive the hatchet.

May 16. It had blow'd hard in the night, and the wreck appear'd more broken by the force of the water; but I stay'd so long in the woods to get pidgeons for food that the tide prevented me going to the wreck that day.

May 17. I saw some pieces of the wreck blown on shore, at a great distance, near two miles off me, but resolv'd to see what they were, and found it was a piece of the head, but too heavy for me to bring away.

May 24. Every day to this day I work'd on the wreck, and with hard labour I loosen'd some things so much with the crow that with the first blowing tide several casks floated out, and two of the seamen's chests; but the wind blowing from the shore, nothing came to land that day, but pieces of timber and a hogshead, which had some Brasil pork in it, but the salt water and the sand had spoil'd it.

I continu'd this work every day to the 15th of June, except the time necessary to get food, which I always appointed, during this part of my employment, to be when the tide was up, that I might be ready when it was ebb'd out. And by this time I had gotten timber, and plank, and iron-work enough to have builded a good boat, if I had known how; and also, I got at several times, and in several pieces, near 100 weight of the sheet lead.

June 16. Going down to the seaside, I found a large tortoise or turtle. This was the first I had seen, which it seems was only my misfortune, not any defect of the place, or scarcity, for had I happen'd to be on the other side of the island, I might have had hundreds of them every day, as I found afterwards; but perhaps had paid dear enough for them.

June 17. I spent in cooking the turtle; I found in her threescore eggs; and her flesh was to me at that time the most savoury and pleasant that ever I tasted in my life, having had no flesh, but of goats and fowls, since I landed in this horrid place.

June 18. Rain'd all day, and I stay'd within. I thought at this time the rain felt cold, and I was somewhat chilly, which I knew was not usual in that latitude.

June 19. Very ill, and shivering, as if the weather had been cold.

June 20. No rest all night, violent pains in my head, and feverish.

June 21. Very ill, frighted almost to death with the apprehensions of my sad condition, to be sick and no help. Pray'd to God for the first time since the storm off of Hull, but scarce knew what I said, or why, my thoughts being all confused.

June 22. A little better, but under dreadful apprehensions of sickness.

June 23. Very bad again, cold and shivering, and then a violent head-ache.

June 24. Much better.

June 25. An ague very violent; the fit held me seven hours, cold fit and hot, with faint sweats after it.

June 26. Better; and having no victuals to eat, took my gun, but found myself very weak. However, I kill'd a she-goat, and with much difficulty got it home, and broil'd some of it, and ate; I would fain have stew'd it and made some broth, but had no pot.

June 27. The ague again so violent that I lay a-bed all day and neither ate or drank. I was ready to perish for thirst, but so weak I had not strength to stand up or to get myself any water to drink. Pray'd to God again, but was light-headed, and when I was not, I was so ignorant that I knew not what to say; only I lay and cry'd, "Lord look upon me, Lord pity me, Lord have mercy upon me." I suppose I did nothing else for two or three hours till, the fit wearing off, I fell asleep and did not wake till far in the night. When I wak'd, I found myself much refresh'd, but weak and exceeding thirsty. However, as I had no water in my whole habitation, I was forc'd to lie till morning and went to sleep again; in this second sleep, I had this terrible dream.

I thought that I was sitting on the ground on the outside of my wall, where I sat when the storm blew after the earthquake, and that I saw a man descend from a great black cloud, in a bright flame of fire and light upon the ground. He was all over as bright as a flame, so that I could but just bear to look towards him; his countenance was most inexpressibly dreadful, impossible for words to describe. When he stepp'd upon the ground with his feet, I thought the earth trembl'd, just as it had done before in the earthquake, and all the air look'd, to my apprehension, as if it had been fill'd with flashes of fire.

He was no sooner landed upon the earth, but he moved forward towards me with a long spear or weapon in his hand to kill me; and when he came to a rizing ground at some distance, he spoke to me, or I heard a voice so terrible that it is impossible to express the terror of it. All that I can say I understood was this, "Seeing all these things have not brought thee to repentance, now thou shalt die." At which words, I thought he lifted up the spear that was in his hand to kill me.

No one, that shall ever read this account, will expect that I should be able to describe the horrors of my soul at this terrible vision, I mean, that even while it was a dream, I even dream'd of those horrors; nor is it any more possible to describe the impression that remain'd upon my mind when I awak'd and found it was but a dream.

I had, alas, no divine knowledge! What I had receiv'd by the good instruction of my father was then worn out by an uninterrupted series, for eight years of seafaring wickedness and a constant conversation with no thing but such as were like myself, wicked and prophane to the last degree. I do not remember that I had in all that time one thought that so much as tended either to looking upwards toward God or inwards toward a reflection upon my own ways. But a certain stupidity of soul, without desire of good, or conscience of evil, had entirely overwhelm'd me, and I was all that the most harden'd, unthinking, wicked creature among our common sailors, can be suppos'd to be, not having the least sense, either of the fear of God in danger or of thankfulness to God in deliverances.

In the relating what is already past of my story, this will be the more easily believ'd, when I shall add, that thro' all the variety of miseries that had to this day befallen me, I never had so much as one thought of it being the hand of God or that it was a just punishment for my sin; my rebellious behaviour against my father, or my present sins which were great; or so much as a punishment for the general course of my wicked life. When I was on the desperate expedition on the desert shores of Africa, I never had so much as one thought of what would become of me or one wish to God to direct me whether I should go, or to keep me from the danger which apparently surrounded me, as well from voracious creatures as cruel savages. But I was meerly thoughtless of a God, or a Providence; acted like a meer brute from the principles of nature and by the dictates of common sense only, and indeed hardly that.

When I was deliver'd and taken up at sea by the Portugueze captain, well used, and dealt justly and honourably with, as well as charitably, I had not the least thankfulness in my thoughts. When again I was shipwreck'd, ruin'd, and in danger of drowning on this island, I was as far from remorse, or looking on it as a judgment; I only said to myself often that I was an unfortunate dog, and born to be always miserable.

It is true, when I got on shore first here, and found all my ship's crew drown'd and myself spar'd, I was surpriz'd with a kind of extasie and some transports of soul, which, had the grace of God assisted, might have come up to true thankfulness; but it ended where it began, in a meer common flight of joy, or as I may say, being glad I was alive, without the least reflection upon the distinguishing goodness of the hand which had preserv'd me and had singl'd me out to be preserv'd when all the rest were destroy'd; or an enquiry why Providence had been thus merciful to me; even just the same common sort of joy which seamen generally have after they are got safe ashore from a shipwreck, which they drown all in the next bowl of punch, and forget almost as soon as it is over, and all the rest of my life was like it.

Even when I was afterwards, on due consideration, made sensible of my condition, how I was cast on this dreadful place, out of the reach of human kind, out of all hope of relief, or prospect of redemption, as soon as I saw but a prospect of living, and that I should not starve and perish for hunger, all the sense of my affliction wore off. I began to be very easy, apply'd myself to the works proper for my preservation and supply, and was far enough from being afflicted at my condition as a judgment from Heaven or as the hand of God against me; these were thoughts which very seldom enter'd into my head.

The growing up of the corn, as is hinted in my Journal, had at first some little influence upon me and began to affect me with seriousness as long as I thought it had something miraculous in it; but as soon as ever that part of the thought was remov'd, all the impression which was rais'd from it wore off also, as I have noted already.

Even the earthquake, tho' nothing could be more terrible in its nature, or more immediately directing to the Invisible Power which alone directs such things, yet no sooner was the first fright over, but the impression it had made went off also. I had no more sense of God or His judgments, much less of the present affliction of my circumstances being from His hand, than if I had been in the most prosperous condition of life.

But now when I began to be sick, and a leisurely view of the miseries of death came to place itself before me; when my spirits began to sink under the burthen of a strong distemper, and nature was exhausted with the violence of the fever; conscience that had slept so long began to awake, and I began to reproach myself with my past life, in which I had so evidently, by uncommon wickedness, provok'd the justice of God to lay me under uncommon strokes and to deal with me in so vindictive a manner.

These reflections oppress'd me for the second or third day of my distemper, and in the violence, as well of the fever as of the dreadful reproaches of my conscience, extorted some words from me, like praying to God, tho' I cannot say they were either a prayer attended with desires or with hopes. It was rather the voice of meer fright and distress; my thoughts were confus'd, the convictions great upon my mind, and the horror of dying in such a miserable condition rais'd vapours into my head with the meer apprehensions. In these hurries of my soul, I know not what my tongue might express, but it was rather exclamation, such as, "Lord! what a miserable creature am I! If I should be sick, I shall certainly die for want of help, and what will become of me!" Then the tears burst out of my eyes, and I could say no more for a good while.

In this interval, the good advice of my father came to my mind, and presently his prediction which I mention'd at the beginning of this story, viz.: That if I did take this foolish step, God would not bless me, and I would have leisure hereafter to reflect upon having neglected his counsel, when there might be none to assist in my recovery. "Now," said I aloud, "my dear father's words come to pass: God's justice has overtaken me, and I have none to help or hear me. I rejected the voice of Providence, which had mercifully put me in a posture or station of life, wherein I might have been happy and easy; but I would neither see it myself or learn to know the blessing of it from my parents; I left them to mourn over my folly, and now I am left to mourn under the consequences of it. I refus'd their help and assistance who would have lifted me into the world and would have made every thing easy to me, and now I have difficulties to struggle with too great for even nature itself to support, and no assistance, no help, no comfort, no advice." Then I cry'd out, "Lord be my Help, for I am in great Distress!"

This was the first prayer, if I may call it so, that I had made for many years. But I return to my Journal.

June 28. Having been somewhat refresh'd with the sleep I had had, and the fit being entirely off, I got up; and tho' the fright and terror of my dream was very great, yet I consider'd, that the fit of the ague would return again the next day and now was my time to get some thing to refresh and support myself when I should be ill. The first thing I did, I fill'd a large square case bottle with water and set it upon my table in reach of my bed; and to take off the chill or aguish disposition of the water, I put about a quarter of a pint of rum into it, and mix'd them together. Then I got me a piece of the goat's flesh and broil'd it on the coals, but could eat very little. I walk'd about, but was very weak, and withal very sad and heavy-hearted in the sense of my miserable condition, dreading the return of my distemper the next day. At night, I made my supper of three of the turtle's eggs, which I roasted in the ashes, and ate, as we call it, in the shell. This was the first bit of meat I had ever ask'd God's blessing to, even as I could remember, in my whole life.

After I had eaten, I try'd to walk, but found myself so weak that I could hardly carry the gun, for I never went out without it. So I went but a little way, and sat down upon the ground, looking out upon the sea, which was just before me and very calm and smooth. As I sat here, some such thoughts as these occurr'd to me.

What is this earth and sea of which I have seen so much? Whence is it produc'd, and what am I, and all the other creatures, wild and tame, humane and brutal, whence are we?

Sure we are all made by some secret Power, who form'd the earth and sea, the air and sky; and who is that?

Then it follow'd most naturally, It is God that has made it all. Well, but then it came on strangely, if God has made all these things, He guides and governs them all, and all things that concern them; for the Power that could make all things must certainly have power to guide and direct them.

If so, nothing can happen in the great circuit of His works either without His knowledge or appointment.

And if nothing happens without His knowledge, He knows that I am here and am in this dreadful condition; and if nothing happens without His appointment, He has appointed all this to befall me.

Nothing occurr'd to my thought to contradict any of these conclusions; and therefore it rested upon me with the greater force that it must needs be that God had appointed all this to befall me; that I was brought to this miserable circumstance by His direction, He having the sole power, not of me only, but of every thing that happen'd in the world. Immediately it follow'd:

Why has God done this to me? What have I done to be thus used?

My conscience presently check'd me in that enquiry, as if I had blasphem'd, and methought it spoke to me like a voice: "WRETCH! dost thou ask what thou hast done! Look back upon a dreadful mis-spent life and ask thyself what thou hast not done; ask why is it that thou wert not long ago destroy'd? Why wert thou not drown'd in Yarmouth Roads? Kill'd in the fight when the ship was taken by the Sallee man of war? Devour'd by the wild beasts on the coast of Africa? Or, drown'd *here*, when all the crew perish'd but thyself? Durst thou ask, What have I done?"

I was struck dumb with these reflections, as one astonish'd, and had not a word to say, no not to answer to myself, but rize up pensive and sad, walk'd back to my retreat, and went up over my wall, as if I had been going to bed. But my thoughts were sadly disturb'd, and I had no inclination to sleep; so I sat down in my chair and lighted my lamp, for it began to be dark. Now as the apprehension of the return of my distemper terrify'd me very much, it occurr'd to my thought that the Brasilians take no physick but their tobacco for almost all distempers; and I had a piece of a roll of tobacco in one of the chests, which was quite cur'd, and some also that was green and not quite cur'd.

I went, directed by Heaven no doubt, for in this chest I found a cure, both for soul and body; I open'd the chest and found what I look'd for, *viz.*, the tobacco; and as the few books I had sav'd lay there too, I took out one of the

Bibles, which I mention'd before and which to this time I had not found leisure or so much as inclination to look into; I say, I took it out, and brought both that and the tobacco with me to the table.

What use to make of the tobacco I knew not, as to my distemper, or whether it was good for it or no; but I try'd several experiments with it, as if I was resolv'd it should hit one way or other. I first took a piece of a leaf, and chew'd it in my mouth, which indeed at first almost stupify'd my brain, the tobacco being green and strong, and that I had not been much used to it; then I took some and steeped it an hour or two in some rum, and resolv'd to take a dose of it when I lay down; and lastly, I burnt some upon a pan of coals and held my nose close over the smoke of it as long as I could bear it, as well for the heat as almost for suffocation.

In the interval of this operation, I took up the Bible and began to read, but my head was too much disturb'd with the tobacco to bear reading, at least that time; only having open'd the Book casually, the first words that occurr'd to me were these: *Call on Me in the day of trouble, and I will deliver, and thou shalt glorify Me.*

The words were very apt to my case and made some impression upon my thoughts at the time of reading them, tho' not so much as they did afterwards; for as for being deliver'd, the word had no sound, as I may say, to me; the thing was so remote, so impossible in my apprehension of things, that I began to say as the Children of Israel did when they were promis'd flesh to eat, *Can God spread a table in the wilderness?* So I began to say, "Can God Himself deliver me from this place?" and as it was not for many years that any hope appear'd, this prevail'd very often upon my thoughts; however the words made a great impression upon me, and I mus'd upon them very often. It grew now late, and the tobacco had, as I said, doz'd my head so much that I inclin'd to sleep; so I left my lamp burning in the cave, lest I should want any thing in the night, and went to bed. But before I lay down, I did what I never had done in all my life, I kneel'd down and pray'd to God to fulfill the promise to me, that if I call'd upon Him in the day of trouble, He would deliver me. After my broken and imperfect prayer was over, I drank the rum in which I had steep'd the tobacco, which was so strong and rank of the tobacco that indeed I could scarce get it down; immediately upon this I went to bed. I found presently it flew up in my head violently, but I fell into a sound sleep and wak'd no more till by the sun it must necessarily be near three a-clock in the afternoon the next day; nay, to this hour, I'm partly of the opinion that I slept all the next day and night, and till almost three that day after, for otherwise I knew not how I should lose a day out of my reckoning in the days of the week, as it appear'd some years after I had done. If I had lost it by crossing and re-crossing the Line, I should have lost more than one day; but certainly I lost a day in my account and never knew which way.

Be that however one way or t'other, when I awak'd I found myself exceedingly refresh'd and my spirits lively and cheerful. When I got up, I was stronger than I was the day before, and my stomach better, for I was hungry; and in short, I had no fit the next day, but continu'd much alter'd for the better. This was the 29th.

The 30th was my well day of course, and I went abroad with my gun, but did not care to travel too far. I kill'd a sea fowl or two, something like a brand goose, and brought them home, but was not very forward to eat them; so I ate some more of the turtle's eggs, which were very good. This evening I renew'd the medicine which I had suppos'd did me good the day before, viz., the tobacco steep'd in rum, only I did not take so much as before, nor did I chew any of the leaf, or hold my head over the smoke. However, I was not so well the next day, which was the 1st of July, as I hop'd I should have been, for I had a little spice of the cold fit, but it was not much.

July 2. I renew'd the medicine all the three ways, and doz'd myself with it as at first, and doubled the quantity which I drank.

July 3. I miss'd the fit for good and all, tho' I did not recover my full strength for some weeks after; while I was thus gathering strength, my thoughts ran exceedingly upon this scripture, *I will deliver thee*, and the impossibility of my deliverance lay much upon my mind in barr of my ever expecting it. But as I was discouraging myself with such thoughts, it occurr'd to my mind that I por'd so much upon my deliverance from the main affliction that I disregarded the deliverance I had receiv'd; and I was, as it were, made to ask myself such questions as these, viz.: Have I not been deliver'd, and wonderfully too, from sickness? from the most distress'd condition that could be and that was so frightful to me? and what notice I had taken of it? Had I done my part, God had deliver'd me, but I had not glorify'd Him; that is to say, I had not own'd and been thankful for that as a deliverance, and how could I expect greater deliverance?

This touch'd my heart very much, and immediately I kneel'd down and gave God thanks aloud for my recovery from my sickness.

July 4. In the morning I took the Bible and, beginning at

the New Testament, I began seriously to read it, and impos'd upon myself to read awhile every morning and every night, not tying myself to the number of chapters, but as long as my thoughts should engage me. It was not long after I set seriously to this work, but I found my heart more deeply and sincerely affected with the wickedness of my past life. The impression of my dream reviv'd, and the words, *All these things have not brought thee to repentance,* ran seriously in my thought. I was earnestly begging of God to give me repentance when it happen'd providentially the very day that, reading the Scripture, I came to these words: *He is exalted a Prince and a Saviour, to give repentance and to give remission.* I threw down the Book, and with my heart as well as my hands lifted up to Heaven, in a kind of extasie of joy, I cry'd out aloud, "Jesus, thou son of David, Jesus, thou exalted Prince and Saviour, give me repentance!"

This was the first time that I could say, in the true sense of the words, that I pray'd in all my life, for now I pray'd with a sense of my condition and with a true Scripture view of hope, founded on the encouragement of the Word of God. From this time, I may say, I began to have hope that God would hear me.

Now I began to construe the words mention'd above, *Call on Me and I will deliver you,* in a different sense from what I had ever done before; for then I had no notion of any thing being call'd deliverance but my being deliver'd from the captivity I was in; for tho' I was indeed at large in the place, yet the island was certainly a prison to me, and that in the worst sense in the world. But now I learn'd to take it in another sense: Now I look'd back upon my past life with such horror, and my sins appear'd so dreadful, that my soul sought nothing of God but deliverance from the load of guilt that bore down all my comfort. As for my solitary life, it was nothing; I did not so much as pray to be deliver'd from it or think of it; it was all of no consideration in comparison to this. And I add this part here, to hint to whoever shall read it, that whenever they come to a true sense of things they will find deliverance from sin a much greater blessing, than deliverance from affliction.

But leaving this part, I return to my Journal.

My condition began now to be, tho' not less miserable as to my way of living, yet much easier to my mind; and my thoughts being directed, by a constant reading of the Scripture and praying to God, to things of a higher nature, I had a great deal of comfort within, which till now I knew nothing of; also, as my health and strength return'd, I bestirr'd myself to furnish myself with every thing that I wanted, and make my way of living as regular as I could.

From the 4th of July to the 14th, I was chiefly employ'd in walking about with my gun in my hand, a little and a little at a time, as a man that was gath'ring up his strength after a fit of sickness. For it is hardly to be imagin'd how low I was and to what weakness I was reduc'd. The application which I made use of was perfectly new, and perhaps what had never cur'd an ague before, neither can I recommend it to any one to practise, by this experiment, for tho' it did carry off the fit, yet it rather contributed to weakening me, for I had frequent convulsions in my nerves and limbs for some time.

I learn'd from it also this in particular, that being abroad in the rainy season was the most pernicious thing to my health that could be, especially in those rains which came attended with storms and hurricanes of wind; for as the rain which came in the dry season was always most accompany'd with such storms, so I found that rain was much more dangerous than the rain which fell in September and October.

I had been now in this unhappy island about ten months; all possibility of deliverance from this condition seem'd to be entirely taken from me; and I firmly believ'd that no human shape had ever set foot upon that place. Having now secur'd my habitation, as I thought, fully to my mind, I had a great desire to make a more perfect discovery of the island and to see what other productions I might find, which I yet knew nothing of.

It was the 15th of July that I began to take a more particular survey of the island itself. I went up the creek first, where, as I hinted, I brought my rafts on shore; I found, after I came about two miles up, that the tide did not flow any higher and that it was no more than a little brook of running water and very fresh and good; but this being the dry season, there was hardly any water in some parts of it, at least, not enough to run in any stream, so as it could be perceiv'd.

On the bank of this brook I found many pleasant savannas, or meadows, plain, smooth, and cover'd with grass; and on the rizing parts of them next to the higher grounds, where the water, as it might be suppos'd, never overflow'd, I found a great deal of tobacco, green, and growing to a great and very strong stalk; there were divers other plants which I had no notion of, or understanding about, and might perhaps have virtues of their own, which I could not find out.

I searched for the cassava root, which the Indians in all that climate make their bread of, but I could find none.

I saw large plants of alloes, but did not then understand them. I saw several sugar canes, but wild and, for want of cultivation, imperfect. I contented myself with these discoveries for this time and came back musing with myself what course I might take to know the virtue and goodness of any of the fruits or plants which I should discover; but I could bring it to no conclusion for, in short, I had made so little observation while I was in the Brasils, that I knew little of the plants in the field, at least very little that might serve me to any purpose now in my distress.

The next day, the 16th, I went up the same way again, and after going something farther than I had gone the day before, I found the brook, and the savannas began to cease, and the country became more woody than before; in this part I found different fruits, and particularly I found melons upon the ground in great abundance, and grapes upon the trees; the vines had spread indeed over the trees, and the clusters of grapes were just now in their prime, very ripe and rich. This was a surprizing discovery, and I was exceeding glad of them; but I was warn'd by my experience to eat sparingly of them, rememb'ring that when I was ashore in Barbary, the eating of grapes kill'd several of our Englishmen who were slaves there, by throwing them into fluxes and fevers. But I found an excellent use for these grapes, and that was to cure or dry them in the sun, and keep them as dry'd grapes or raisins are kept, which I thought would be, as indeed they were, as wholesome as agreeable to eat when no grapes might be to be had.

I spent all that evening there and went not back to my habitation, which by the way was the first night, as I might say, I had lain from home. In the night I took my first contrivance and got up into a tree, where I slept well, and the next morning proceeded upon my discovery, travelling near four miles, as I might judge by the length of the valley, keeping still due north, with a ridge of hills on the south and north sides of me.

At the end of this march I came to an opening, where the country seem'd to descend to the west, and a little spring of fresh water which issued out of the side of the hill by me, ran the other way, that is due east; and the country appear'd so fresh, so green, so flourishing, every thing being in a constant verdure, or flourish of spring, that it looked like a planted garden.

I descended a little on the side of that delicious vale, surveying it with a secret kind of pleasure (tho' mix'd with my other afflicting thoughts) to think that this was all my own, that I was king and lord of all this country indefeasibly and had a right of possession; and if I could convey it, I might have it in inheritance, as compleatly as any lord of a manor in England. I saw here an abundance of cocoa trees, orange and lemon and citron trees; but all wild, and very few bearing any fruit, at least not then. However, the green limes that I gather'd were not only pleasant to eat, but very wholesome; and I mix'd their juice afterwards with water, which made it very wholesome, and very cool and refreshing.

I found now I had business enough to gather and carry home; and I resolv'd to lay up a store, as well of grapes as of limes and lemons, to furnish myself for the wet season, which I knew was approaching.

In order to this, I gather'd a great heap of grapes in one place, and a lesser heap in another place, and a great parcel of limes and lemons in another place; and taking a few of each with me, I travell'd homewards, and resolv'd to come again, and bring a bag or sack, or what I could make to carry the rest home.

Accordingly, having spent three days on this journey, I came home, so I must now call my tent and my cave. But before I got thither, the grapes were spoil'd; the richness of the fruits, and the weight of the juice having broken them and bruis'd them, they were good for little or nothing. As to the limes, they were good, but I could bring but a few.

The next day, being the 19th, I went back, having made me two small bags to bring home my harvest. But I was surpriz'd, when coming to my heap of grapes, which were so rich and fine when I gather'd them, I found them all spread about, trod to pieces, and dragg'd about, some here, some there, and an abundance eaten and devour'd. By this, I concluded there were some wild creatures thereabouts which had done this; but what they were, I knew not.

However, I found there was no laying them up on heaps, and no carrying them away in a sack, but that one way they would be destroy'd and the other way they would be crush'd with their own weight. I took another course, and gather'd a large quantity of the grapes and hung them up upon the outer branches of the trees that they might cure and dry in the sun; and as for the limes and lemons, I carry'd as many back as I could well stand under.

When I came home from this journey, I contemplated with great pleasure the fruitfulness of that valley and the pleasantness of the situation, the security from storms on that side the water, and the woods, and concluded that I had until now pitch'd upon a place to fix my abode which was by far the worst part of the country. Upon the whole I began to consider of removing my habitation, and to look out for a place equally safe as where I now was situate, if possible, in that pleasant fruitful part of the island.

This thought ran long in my head, and I was exceeding fond of it for some time, the pleasantness of the place tempting me; but then I came to a nearer view of it, and consider'd that I was now by the seaside, where it was at least possible that something might happen to my advantage, and by the same ill fate that brought me hither, might bring some other unhappy wretches to the same place, tho' it was scarce probable that any such thing should ever happen. Yet to enclose myself among the hills and woods, in the center of the island, was to anticipate my bondage and to rend such an affair not only improbable, but impossible; therefore I ought not by any means to remove.

However, I was so enamour'd of this place that I spent much of my time there, for the whole remaining part of the month of July; and tho' upon second thoughts I resolv'd as above, not to remove, yet I built me a little kind of bower and surrounded it at a distance with a strong fence, being a double hedge, as high as I could reach, well stak'd, and fill'd between with brushwood. Here I lay very secure, sometimes two or three nights together, always going over it with a ladder, as before, so that I fancy'd now I had my country house and my seacoast house. This work took me up to the beginning of August.

I had but newly finish'd my fence and begun to enjoy my labour, but the rains came on and made me stick close to my first habitation; for tho' I had made me a tent like the other, with a piece of sail, and spread it very well, yet I had not the shelter of a hill to keep me from storms nor a cave behind me to retreat into when the rains were extraordinary.

About the beginning of August, as I said, I had finish'd my bower, and began to enjoy myself. The 3rd of August, I found the grapes I had hung up were perfectly dry'd and, indeed, were excellent good raisins of the sun. So I began to take them down from the trees, and it was very happy that I did so, for the rains which follow'd would have spoil'd them, and I had lost the best part of my winter food, for I had above two hundred large bunches of them. No sooner had I taken them all down and carry'd most of them home to my cave, but it began to rain, and from hence, which was the 14th of August, it rain'd more or less every day till the middle of October; and sometimes so violently that I could not stir out of my cave for several days.

In this season I was much surpriz'd with the encrease of my family; I had been concern'd for the loss of one of my cats, who ran away from me, or as I thought had been dead, and I heard no more tale or tidings of her till, to my astonishment, she came home about the end of August with three kittens; this was the more strange to me, because tho' I had kill'd a wild cat, as I call'd it, with my gun, yet I thought it was a quite diff'ring kind from our European cats; yet these young cats were the same kind of house-breed like the old one; and both my cats being females, I thought it very strange. But from these three kittens, I afterwards came to be so pester'd with cats that I was forc'd to kill them like vermin, or wild beasts, and to drive them from my house as much as possible.

From the 14th of August to the 26th. Incessant rain, so

that I could not stir, and was now very careful not to be much wet. In this confinement I began to be strain'd for food, but venturing out twice, I one day kill'd a goat, and the last day, which was the 26th, found a very large tortoise, which was a treat to me, and my food was regulated thus: I ate a bunch of raisins for my breakfast; a piece of the goat's flesh, or of the turtle for my dinner broil'd (for to my great misfortune, I had no vessel to boil or stew any thing) ; and two or three of the turtle's eggs for my supper.

During this confinement to my cover by the rain, I work'd daily two or three hours at enlarging my cave, and by degrees work'd it on towards one side, till I came to the out-side of the hill and made a door or way out, which came beyond my fence or wall, and so I came in and out this way. But I was not perfectly easy at lying so open, for as I had manag'd myself before, I was in a perfect enclosure, whereas now I thought I lay expos'd and open for any thing to come in upon me. Yet I could not perceive that there was any living thing to fear, the biggest creature that I had yet seen upon the island being a goat.

September 30. I was now come to the unhappy anniversary of my landing. I cast up the notches on my post, and found I had been on shore three hundred and sixty-five days. I kept this day as a solemn fast, setting it apart to religious exercize, prostrating myself on the ground with the most serious humiliation, confessing my sins to God, acknowledging His righteous judgments upon me, and praying to Him to have mercy on me through Jesus Christ; and having not tasted the least refreshment for twelve hours, even till the going-down of the sun, I then ate a bisket-cake and a bunch of grapes and went to bed, finishing the day as I began it.

*I made an umbrella that cast off the rains like a penthouse,
and kept off the sun so effectually that I could walk out in the
hottest of the weather.* (pages 155–6)

I had all this time observ'd no Sabbath-day, for as at first I had no sense of religion upon my mind, I had after some time omitted to distinguish the weeks by making a longer notch than ordinary for the Sabbath-day, and so did not really know what any of the days were. Now, having cast up the days, as above, I found I had been there a year, so I divided it into weeks, and set apart every seventh day for a Sabbath, though I found at the end of my account I had lost a day or two in my reckoning.

A little after this my ink began to fail me, and so I contented myself to use it more sparingly and to write down only the most remarkable events of my life, without continuing a daily memorandum of other things.

The rainy season and the dry season began now to appear regular to me, and I learn'd to divide them so as to provide for them accordingly. But I bought all my experience before I had it, and this, I am going to relate, was one of the most discouraging experiments that I made at all. I have mention'd that I had sav'd the few ears of barley and rice, which I had so surprizingly found spring up, as I thought, of themselves, and believe there were about thirty stalks of rice and about twenty of barley, and now I thought it a proper time to sow it after the rains, the sun being in its southern position going from me.

Accordingly, I dug up a piece of ground as well as I could with my wooden spade and, dividing it into two parts, I sow'd my grain. As I was sowing it, it casually occurr'd to my thoughts that I would not sow it all at first, because I did not know when was the proper time for it; so I sow'd about two-thirds of the seed, leaving about a handful of each.

It was a great comfort to me afterwards that I did so, for

not one grain of that I sow'd this time came to any thing; for the dry months following, the earth having no rain after the seed was sown, it had no moisture to assist its growth, and never came up at all till the wet season had come again, and then it grew as if it had been but newly sown.

Finding my first seed did not grow, which I easily imagin'd was by the drought, I sought for a moister piece of ground to make another trial in. I dug up a piece of ground near my new bower, and sow'd the rest of my seed in February, a little before the vernal equinox; and thus having the rainy months of March and April to water it, it sprung up very pleasantly and yielded a very good crop. But having part of the seed left only, and not daring to sow all that I had, I had but a small quantity at last, my whole crop not amounting to above half a peck of each kind.

But by this experiment I was made master of my business, and knew exactly when the proper season was to sow, and that I might expect two seed times and two harvests every year.

While this corn was growing, I made a little discovery which was of use to me afterwards. As soon as the rains were over and the weather began to settle, which was about the month of November, I made a visit up the country to my bower, where though I had not been some months, yet I found all things just as I left them. The circle, or double hedge, that I had made was not only firm and entire, but the stakes which I had cut out of some trees that grew thereabouts were all shot out and grown with long branches, as much as a willow-tree usually shoots the first year after lopping its head. I could not tell what tree to call it that these stakes were cut from. I was surpriz'd, and yet very well pleas'd, to see the young trees grow. I prun'd them, and led them up to grow as much alike as I could, and it is scarce credible how beautiful a figure they grew into in three years; so that though the hedge made a circle of about twenty-five yards in diameter, yet the trees, for such I might now call them, soon cover'd it; and it was a compleat shade, sufficient to lodge under all the dry season.

This made me resolve to cut some more stakes and make me a hedge like this in a semicircle round my wall; I mean that of my first dwelling, which I did; and placing the trees or stakes in a double row, at about eight yards distance from my first fence, they grew presently and were at first a fine cover to my habitation, and afterwards serv'd for a defence also, as I shall observe in its order.

I found now that the seasons of the year might generally be divided, not into summer and winter as in Europe, but into the rainy seasons and the dry seasons, which were generally thus:

Half February, March, Half April,	Rainy, the sun being then on or near the equinox.
Half April, May, June, July, Half August,	Dry, the sun being then to the north of the Line.
Half August, September, Half October,	Rainy, the sun being then come back.

Half October,
November,
December, } Dry, the sun being then to the south
January, of the Line.
Half February,

The rainy season sometimes held longer or shorter, as the winds happen'd to blow, but this was the general observation I made. After I had found by experience the ill consequence of being abroad in the rain, I took care to furnish myself with provisions beforehand, that I might not be oblig'd to go out; and I sat within doors as much as possible during the wet months.

This time I found much employment (and very suitable also to the time), for I found great occasion of many things which I had no way to furnish myself with but by hard labour and constant application; particularly, I try'd many ways to make myself a basket. But all the twigs I could get for the purpose prov'd so brittle that they would do nothing. It prov'd of excellent advantage to me now that when I was a boy I used to take great delight in standing at a basket-maker's, in the town where my father liv'd, to see them make their wicker-ware; and being as boys usually are, very officious to help and a great observer of the manner how they work'd those things, and sometimes lending a hand, I had by this means full knowledge of the methods of it. I wanted now nothing but the materials; and when it came into my mind that the twigs of that tree whence I cut my stakes might possibly be as tough as the sallows, willows, and osiers in England, I resolv'd to try.

Accordingly, the next day I went to my country-house, as I call'd it, and cutting some of the smaller twigs, I found them to my purpose as much as I could desire; whereupon I came the next time prepar'd with a hatchet to cut down a quantity, which I soon found, for there was great plenty of them. These I set up to dry within my circle or hedge, and when they were fit for use I carry'd them to my cave, and here during the next season, I employ'd myself in making, as well as I could, a great many baskets, both to carry earth, or to carry or lay up any thing as I had occasion. Tho' I did not finish them very handsomely, yet I made them sufficiently serviceable for my purpose; and thus afterwards I took care never to be without them. And as my wicker-ware decay'd, I made more; especially, I made strong deep baskets to place my corn in, instead of sacks, when I should come to have any quantity of it.

Having master'd this difficulty and employ'd a world of time about it, I bestirr'd myself to see if possible how to supply two wants. I had no vessels to hold any thing that was liquid, except two runlets, which were almost full of rum, and some glass bottles, some of the common size, and others which were case-bottles square, for the holding of waters, spirits, &c. I had not so much as a pot to boil any thing, except a great kettle, which I sav'd out of the ship, and which was too big for such use as I desir'd it, viz., to make broth and stew a bit of meat by itself. The second thing I would fain ha' had was a tobacco-pipe, but it was impossible to me to make one; however, I found a contrivance for that too at last.

I employ'd myself in planting my second rows of stakes or piles and in this wicker-working all the summer, or dry season, when another business took me up more time than it could be imagin'd I could spare.

I mention'd before that I had a great mind to see the

whole island, and that I had travell'd up the brook and so on to where I built my bower and where I had an opening quite to the sea on the other side of the island; I now re-solv'd to travel quite cross to the seashore on that side. So, taking my gun, a hatchet, and my dog, and a larger quan-tity of powder and shot than usual, with two bisket-cakes, and a great bunch of raisins in my pouch for my store, I began my journey. When I had pass'd the vale where my bower stood, as above, I came within view of the sea to the west, and, it being a very clear day, I fairly descry'd land, whether an island or a continent, I could not tell; but it lay very high, extending from the west, to the WSW at a very great distance; by my guess it could not be less than fifteen or twenty leagues off.

I could not tell what part of the world this might be, otherwise than that I know it must be part of America and, as I concluded by all my observations, must be near the Spanish dominions, and perhaps was all inhabited by sav-ages, where if I should have landed, I had been in a worse condition than I was now. Therefore I acquiesced in the dispositions of Providence which, I began now to own and to believe, order'd every thing for the best; I say, I quieted my mind with this and left afflicting myself with fruitless wishes of being there.

Besides, after some pause upon this affair, I consider'd that if this land was the Spanish coast, I should certainly, one time or other, see some vessel pass or re-pass one way or other; but if not, then it was the savage coast between the Spanish country and the Brasils, which are indeed the worst of savages; for they are canibals, or men-eaters, and fail not to murther and devour all the human bodies that fall into their hands.

With these considerations I walk'd very leisurely forward. I found that side of the island where I now was much pleasanter than mine, the open or savanna fields sweet, adorn'd with flowers and grass, and full of very fine woods. I saw an abundance of parrots, and fain I would have caught one, if possible, to have kept it to be tame and taught it to speak to me. I did, after some pains-taking, catch a young parrot, for I knock'd it down with a stick and, having recover'd it, I brought it home; but it was some years before I could make him speak. However, at last I taught him to call me by my name very familiarly. But the accident that follow'd, tho' it be a trifle, will be very diverting in its place.

I was exceedingly diverted with this journey. I found in the low grounds hares, as I thought them to be, and foxes, but they differ'd greatly from all the other kinds I had met with; nor could I satisfy myself to eat them, tho' I kill'd several. But I had no need to be venturous, for I had no want of food, and of that which was very good too; especially these three sorts, viz., goats, pidgeons, and turtle or tortoise, which, added to my grapes, Leaden Hall Market could not have furnish'd a table better than I, in proportion to the company. Tho' my case was deplorable enough, yet I had great cause for thankfulness that I was not driven to any extremities for food, but rather plenty, even to dainties.

I never travell'd in this journey above two miles outright in a day or thereabouts; but I took so many turns and returns, to see what discoveries I could make, that I came weary enough to the place where I resolv'd to sit down for all night. Then I either repos'd myself in a tree or surrounded myself with a row of stakes set upright on the ground, either from one tree to another, or so as no wild creature could come at me without waking me.

As soon as I came to the seashore, I was surpriz'd to see that I had taken up my lot on the worst side of the island; for here indeed the shore was cover'd with innumerable turtles, whereas on the other side I had found but three in a year and a half. Here was also an infinite number of fowls of many kinds, some which I had seen and some which I had not seen before, and many of them very good meat; but such as I knew not the names of except those call'd penguins.

I could have shot as many as I pleas'd, but was very sparing of my powder and shot; and therefore had more mind to kill a she-goat, if I could, which I could better feed on; and though there were many goats here more than on my side the island, yet it was with much more difficulty that I could come near them, the country being flat and even, and they saw me much sooner than when I was on the hill.

I confess this side of the country was much pleasanter than mine, but yet I had not the least inclination to remove; for as I was fix'd in my habitation, it became natural to me, and I seem'd all the while I was here, to be as it were upon a journey, and from home. However, I travell'd along the shore of the sea, towards the east, I suppose about twelve miles; and then setting up a great pole upon the shore for a mark, I concluded I would go home again and that the next journey I took should be on the other side of the island, east from my dwelling, and so round till I came to my post again. Of which in its place.

I took another way to come back than that I went, thinking I could easily keep all the island so much in my view that I could not miss finding my first dwelling by viewing the country. But I found myself mistaken; for being come about two or three miles, I found myself descended into a very large valley, but so surrounded with hills, and those hills cover'd with wood, that I could not see which was my way by any direction but that of the sun, nor even then, unless I knew very well the position of the sun at that time of the day.

It happen'd, to my further misfortune, that the weather prov'd hazey for three or four days while I was in this valley; and, not being able to see the sun, I wander'd about very uncomfortably and at last was oblig'd to find out the seaside, look for my post, and come back the same way I went. Then by easy journies I turn'd homeward, the weather being exceeding hot, and my gun, ammunition, hatchet, and other things very heavy.

In this journey my dog surpriz'd a young kid and seiz'd upon it; and I, running in to take hold of it, caught it, and sav'd it alive from the dog. I had a great mind to bring it home if I could, for I had often been musing whether it might not be possible to get a kid or two and so raise a breed of tame goats, which might supply me when my powder and shot should be all spent.

I made a collar to this little creature, and with a string which I made of some rope-yarn, which I always carry'd about me, I led him along, tho' with some difficulty, till I came to my bower, and there I enclos'd him and left him. I was very impatient to be at home, whence I had been absent above a month.

I cannot express what a satisfaction it was to me to come into my old hutch and lie down in my hammock-bed. This little wand'ring journey, without settled place of abode, had been so unpleasant to me that my own house, as I call'd it to myself, was a perfect settlement to me compar'd to that; it render'd every thing about me so comfortable, that I resolv'd I would never go a great way from it again, while it should be my lot to stay on the island.

I repos'd myself here a week, to rest and regale myself after my long journey, during which, most of the time was taken up in the weighty affair of making a cage for my Poll, who began now to be a meer domestick and to be mighty well acquainted with me. Then I began to think of the poor kid, which I had penn'd in within my little circle, and resolv'd to go and fetch it home or give it some food. Accordingly I went, and found it where I left it, for indeed it could not get out, but almost starv'd for want of food. I went and cut bows of trees, and branches of such shrubs as I could find and threw them over, and, having fed it, I ty'd it as I did before to lead it away. But it was so tame with being hungry that I had no need to have ty'd it, for it follow'd me like a dog, and, as I continually fed it, the creature became so loving, so gentle, and so fond, that it became from that time one of my domesticks also and would never leave me afterwards.

The rainy season of the autumnal equinox was now come, and I kept the 30th of September in the same solemn manner as before, being the anniversary of my landing on the island, having now been there two years and no more prospect of being deliver'd than the first day I came there. I spent the whole day in humble and thankful acknowledgments of the many wonderful mercies which my solitary condition was attended with and without which it might have been infinitely more miserable. I gave humble and hearty thanks that God had been pleas'd to discover to me even that it was possible I might be more happy in this solitary condition than I should have been in a liberty of society and in all the pleasures of the world. That He could fully make up to me the deficiencies of my solitary state and the want of human society by His presence and the communications of His grace to my soul, supporting, comforting, and encouraging me to depend upon His providence here and hope for His eternal presence hereafter.

It was now that I began sensibly to feel how much more happy this life I now led was, with all its miserable circumstances, than the wicked, cursed, abominable life I had led all the past part of my days. Now I chang'd both my sorrows and my joys; my very desires alter'd, my affections changed their gusts, and my delights were perfectly new from what they were at my first coming or indeed for the two years past.

Before, as I walk'd about, either on my hunting or for viewing the country, the anguish of my soul at my condition would break out upon me on a sudden and my very heart would die within me to think of the woods, the mountains, the deserts I was in; how I was a prisoner, lock'd up with the eternal bars and bolts of the ocean in an uninhabited wilderness, without redemption. In the midst of the greatest composures of my mind, this would break out upon me like a storm, and make me wring my hands and weep like a child; sometimes it would take me in the middle of my work, and I would immediately sit down and sigh, and look upon the ground for an hour or two together; and this was still worse to me, for, if I could burst out into tears or vent myself by words, it would go off, and the grief having exhausted itself would abate.

But now I began to exercize myself with new thoughts,

and I daily read the Word of God and apply'd all the comforts of it to my present state. One morning being very sad,
I open'd the Bible upon these words, *I will never, never
leave thee, nor forsake thee*; immediately it occurr'd that
these words were to me; why else should they be directed in
such a manner, just at the moment when I was mourning
over my condition as one forsaken of God and man? Well
then, thought I, if God does not forsake me, of what ill
consequence can it be, or what matters it, though the
world should all forsake me, seeing on the other hand, if I
had all the world and should lose the favour and blessing
of God, there would be no comparison in the loss.

From this moment, I began to conclude in my mind that
it was possible for me to be more happy in this forsaken
solitary condition than it was probable I should ever have
been in any other particular state in the world; and with
this thought I was going to give thanks to God for bringing
me to this place.

I know not what it was, but something shock'd my mind
at that thought, and I durst not speak the words. "How
canst thou be such a hypocrite," said I (even audibly), "to
pretend to be thankful for a condition which, however thou
may'st endeavour to be contented with, thou would'st
rather pray heartily to be deliver'd from?" so I stopp'd
there. But though I could not say I thank'd God for being
there, yet I sincerely gave thanks to God for opening my
eyes, by whatever afflicting providences, to see the former
condition of my life and to mourn for my wickedness and
repent. I never open'd the Bible, or shut it, but my very
soul within me bless'd God for directing my friend in England, without any order of mine, to pack it up among my
goods; and for assisting me afterwards to save it out of the
wreck of the ship.

Thus, and in this disposition of mind, I began my third year; and tho' I have not given the reader the trouble of so particular account of my works this year as the first, yet, in general, it may be observ'd that I was very seldom idle; but having regularly divided my time, according to the several daily employments that were before me, such as, *1*, My duty to God and the reading the Scriptures, which I constantly set apart some time for thrice every day. 2, The going abroad with my gun for food, which generally took me up three hours in every morning when it did not rain. 3, The ordering, curing, preserving, and cooking what I had kill'd or catch'd for my supply. These took up great part of the day. Also, it is to be consider'd that the middle of the day, when the sun was in the zenith, the violence of the heat was too great to stir out, so that about four hours in the evening was all the time I could be suppos'd to work in; with this exception, that sometimes I chang'd my hours of hunting and working and went to work in the morning and abroad with my gun in the afternoon.

To this short time allow'd for labour, I desire may be added the exceeding laboriousness of my work; the many hours which, for want of tools, want of help, and want of skill, every thing I did took up out of my time. For example, I was full two-and-forty days making me a board for a long shelf, which I wanted in my cave; whereas two sawyers with their tools, and a saw-pit, would have cut six of them out of the same tree in half a day.

My case was this: It was to be a large tree, which was to be cut down, because my board was to be a broad one. This tree I was three days a-cutting down, and two more cutting off the bows, and reducing it to a log or piece of timber. With inexpressible hacking and hewing I reduc'd both the sides of it into chips, till it began to be light enough to move. Then I turn'd it and made one side of it smooth and flat as a board from end to end; then turning that side downward, cut the other side, till I brought the plank to be about three inches thick and smooth on both sides. Any one may judge the labour of my hands in such a piece of work, but labour and patience carry'd me through that and many other things. I only observe this in particular, to shew the reason why so much of my time went away with so little work, viz., that what might be a little to be done with help and tools was a vast labour and requir'd a prodigious time to do alone and by hand.

But notwithstanding this, with patience and labour I went through many things; and indeed every thing that my circumstances made necessary to me to do, as will appear by what follows.

I was now, in the months of November and December, expecting my crop of barley and rice. The ground I had manur'd or dug up for them was not great; for as I observ'd, my seed of each was not above the quantity of half a peck, for I had lost one whole crop by sowing in the dry season. Now my crop promis'd very well, when on a sudden I found I was in danger of losing it all again by enemies of several sorts, which it was scarce possible to keep from it: first, the goats, and wild creatures which I call'd hares, who tasting the sweetness of the blade, lay in it night and day, as soon as it came up, and ate it so close that it could get no time to shoot up into stalk.

This I saw no remedy for, but by making an enclosure about it with a hedge, which I did with a great deal of toil and the more, because it requir'd speed. However, as my arable land was but small, suited to my crop, I got it totally well fenc'd in about three weeks' time. Shooting some of the creatures in the day-time, I set my dog to guard it in the night, tying him up to a stake at the gate, where he would stand and bark all night long; so in a little time the enemies forsook the place, and the corn grew very strong and well, and began to ripen a-pace.

But as the beasts ruin'd me before, while my corn was in the blade, so the birds were as likely to ruine me now when it was in the ear, for going along by the place to see how it throve, I saw my little crop surrounded with fowls of I know not how many sorts, who stood as it were watching till I should be gone. I immediately let fly among them (for I always had my gun with me), and I had no sooner shot but there riz'd up a little cloud of fowls, which I had not seen at all, from among the corn itself.

This touch'd me sensibly, for I foresaw that in a few days they would devour all my hopes, that I should be starv'd, and never be able to raise a crop at all, and what to do I could not tell. However, I resolv'd not to lose my corn, if possible, tho' I should watch it night and day. In the first place, I went among it to see what damage was already done and found they had spoil'd a good deal of it, but that as it was yet too green for them, the loss was not so great but that the remainder was like to be a good crop if it could be sav'd.

I stay'd by it to load my gun, and then coming away I could easily see the thieves sitting upon all the trees about me, as if they only waited till I was gone away, and the event prov'd it to be so. For as I walk'd off as if I was gone, I was no sooner out of their sight, but they dropp'd down one by one into the corn again. I was so provok'd that I could not have patience to stay till more came on, knowing that every grain that they ate now was, as it might be said,

a peck-loaf to me in the consequence. But coming up to
the hedge, I fir'd again and kill'd three of them. This was
what I wish'd for; so I took them up and serv'd them, as we
serve notorious thieves in England, viz., hang'd them in
chains for a terror to others. It is impossible to imagine
almost that this should have such an effect as it had, for
the fowls would not only not come at the corn, but in short
they forsook all that part of the island, and I could never
see a bird near the place as long as my scare-crows hung
there.

This I was very glad of, you may be sure, and about the
latter end of December, which was my second harvest of
the year, I reap'd my crop.

I was sadly put to it for a scythe or a sickle to cut it
down, and all I could do was to make one as well as I could
out of one of the broad swords or cutlasses, which I sav'd
among the arms out of the ship. However, as my first crop
was but small I had no great difficulty to cut it down; in
short, I reap'd it my way, for I cut nothing off but the ears
and carry'd it away in a great basket which I had made, and
so rubb'd it out with my hands. At the end of all my har-
vesting, I found that out of my half peck of seed, I had near
two bushels of rice and above two bushels and a half of
barley, that is to say, by my guess, for I had no measure at
that time.

However, this was a great encouragement to me, and I
foresaw that in time, it would please God to supply me
with bread. And yet here I was perplex'd again, for I neither
knew how to grind or make meal of my corn, or indeed how
to clean it and part it; nor if made into meal, how to make
bread of it, and if how to make it, yet I knew not how to
bake it. These things being added to my desire of having

a good quantity for store and to secure a constant supply, I resolv'd not to taste any of this crop but to preserve it all for seed against the next season, and in the meantime to employ all my study and hours of working to accomplish this great work of providing myself with corn and bread.

It might be truly said that now I work'd for my bread; 'tis a little wonderful, and what I believe few people have thought much upon, viz., the strange multitude of little things necessary in the providing, producing, curing, dressing, making, and finishing this one article of bread.

I, that was reduc'd to a meer state of nature, found this to my daily discouragement and was made more and more sensible of it every hour, even after I had got the first handful of seed-corn, which, as I have said, came up unexpectedly and indeed to a surprize.

First, I had no plow to turn up the earth, no spade or shovel to dig it. Well, this I conquer'd, by making a wooden spade, as I observ'd before; but this did my work in but a wooden manner, and tho' it cost me a great many days to make it, yet for want of iron it not only wore out the sooner, but made my work the harder and made it be perform'd much worse.

However, this I bore with and was content to work it out with patience and bear with the badness of the performance. When the corn was sow'd, I had no harrow, but was forc'd to go over it myself and drag a great heavy bough of a tree over it, to scratch it, as it may be call'd, rather than rake or harrow it.

When it was growing and grown, I have observ'd already, how many things I wanted; to fence it, secure it, mow or reap it, cure and carry it home, thrash it, part it from the chaff, and save it. Then I wanted a mill to grind it, sieves to dress it, yeast and salt to make it into bread, and an oven to bake it, and yet all these things I did without, as shall be observ'd; and yet the corn was an inestimable comfort and advantage to me too. All this, as I said, made every thing laborious and tedious to me, but that there was no help for; neither was my time so much lost to me, because as I had divided it, a certain part of it was every day appointed to these works; and as I resolv'd to use none of the corn for bread till I had a greater quantity by me, I had the next six months to apply myself wholly by labour and invention to furnish myself with utensils proper for the performing all the operations necessary for the making the corn (when I had it) fit for my use.

But first, I was to prepare more land, for I had now seed enough to sow above an acre of ground. Before I did this, I had a week's work at least to make me a spade, which when it was done was but a sorry one indeed, and very heavy, and requir'd double labour to work with it. However, I went thro' that and sow'd my seed in two large flat pieces of ground, as near my house as I could find them to my mind, and fenc'd them in with a good hedge, the stakes of which were all cut of that wood which I had set before. I knew it would grow, so that in one year's time I knew I should have a quick or living-hedge that would want but little repair. This work was not so little as to take me up less than three months, because great part of that time was of the wet season, when I could not go abroad.

Within doors, that is, when it rain'd, and I could not go out, I found employment on the following occasions. Always observing that all the while I was at work I diverted myself with talking to my parrot and teaching him to speak, I quickly teach'd him to know his own name and at last to

136

speak it out pretty loud, "Poll," which was the first word I ever heard spoken in the island by any mouth but my own. This therefore was not my work, but an assistant to my work, for now, as I said, I had a great employment upon my hands, as follows, viz., I had long study'd by some means or other, to make myself some earthen vessels, which indeed I wanted sorely, but knew not where to come at them. However, considering the heat of the climate, I did not doubt but if I could find out any such clay, I might botch up some such pot, as might, being dry'd in the sun, be hard enough and strong enough to bear handling, and to hold any thing that was dry and requir'd to be kept so. As this was necessary in the preparing corn, meal, &c. which was the thing I was upon, I resolv'd to make some as large as I could and fit only to stand like jarrs to hold what should be put into them.

It would make the reader pity me, or rather laugh at me, to tell how many awkward ways I took to raise this paste, what odd mis-shapen ugly things I made, how many of them fell in, and how many fell out, the clay not being stiff enough to bear its own weight; how many crack'd by the over-violent heat of the sun being set out too hastily; and how many fell in pieces with only removing, as well before as after they were dry'd; and in a word, how after having labour'd hard to find the clay, to dig it, to temper it, to bring it home and work it, I could not make above two large earthen ugly things, I cannot call them jarrs, in about two months' labour.

However, as the sun bak'd these two very dry and hard, I lifted them very gently up and set them down again in two great wicker-baskets, which I had made on purpose for them that they might not break; and as between the pot and the basket there was a little room to spare, I stuff'd it full of the rice and barley straw; and these two pots being to stand always dry, I thought would hold my dry corn and perhaps the meal, when the corn was bruis'd.

Tho' I miscarry'd so much in my design for large pots, yet I made several smaller things with better success, such as little round pots, flat dishes, pitchers and pipkins, and any things my hand turn'd to, and the heat of the sun bak'd them strangely hard.

But all this would not answer my end, which was to get an earthen pot to hold what was liquid and bear the fire, which none of these could do. It happen'd after some time, making a pretty large fire for cooking my meat, when I went to put it out after I had done with it, I found a broken piece of one of my earthen-ware vessels in the fire, burnt as hard as a stone and red as a tile. I was agreeably surpriz'd to see it and said to myself that certainly they might be made to burn whole if they would burn broken.

This set me to studying how to order my fire, so as to make it burn me some pots. I had no notion of a kiln, such as the potters burn in, or of glazing them with lead, tho' I had some lead to do it with; but I plac'd three large pipkins and two or three pots in a pile one upon another and plac'd my fire-wood all round it with a great heap of embers under them. I ply'd the fire with fresh fuel round the out-side and upon the top, till I saw the pots in the in-side red hot quite thro', and observ'd that they did not crack at all. When I saw them clear red, I let them stand in that heat about five or six hours, till I found one of them, tho' it did not crack, did melt or run, for the sand which was mix'd with the clay melted by the violence of the heat, and would have run into glass if I had gone on. So I slack'd my fire gradually till the pots began to abate of the red colour, and watching them all night, that I might not let the fire abate too fast, in the morning I had three very good (I will not say handsome) pipkins; and two other earthen pots, as hard burnt as could be desir'd; and one of them perfectly glaz'd with the running of the sand.

After this experiment, I need not say that I wanted no sort of earthen-ware for my use. But I must needs say, as to the shapes of them, they were very indifferent, as any one may suppose, when I had no way of making them but as the children make dirt-pies or as a woman would make pies that never learn'd to raise paste.

No joy at a thing of so mean a nature was ever equal to mine when I found I had made an earthen pot that would bear the fire; and I had hardly patience to stay till they were cold before I set one upon the fire again, with some water in it, to boil me some meat, which it did admirably well; and with a piece of a kid, I made some very good broth, though I wanted oatmeal, and several other ingredients, requisite to make it so good as I would have had it been.

My next concern was to get me a stone mortar to stamp or beat some corn in; for as to the mill, there was no thought of arriving to that perfection of art with one pair of hands. To supply this want I was at a great loss; for of all trades in the world I was as perfectly unqualify'd for a stone-cutter as for any whatever; neither had I any tools to go about it with. I spent many a day to find out a great stone big enough to cut hollow, and make fit for a mortar, and could find none at all, except what was in the solid rock and which I had no way to dig or cut out. Nor indeed were the rocks on the island of hardness sufficient, but were all of a sandy crumbling stone, which neither would bear the weight of a heavy pestle, or would break the corn without filling it with sand. So after a great deal of time lost in searching for a stone, I gave it over and resolv'd to look out for a great block of hard wood, which I found indeed much easier. Getting one as big as I had strength to stir, I rounded it, and form'd it on the out-side with my axe and hatchet, and then with the help of fire and infinite labour made a hollow place in it, as the Indians in the Brasils make their canoes. After this, I made a great heavy pestle or beater of the wood call'd the iron wood, and this I prepar'd and lay'd by against I had my next crop of corn, when I propos'd to myself to grind, or rather pound, my corn into meal to make my bread.

My next difficulty was to make a sieve, or search, to dress my meal, and to part it from the bran and the husk, without which I did not see it possible I could have any bread. This was a most difficult thing, so much as but to think on, for to be sure I had nothing like the necessary thing to make it; I mean fine thin canvass, or stuff, to search the meal through. And here I was at a full stop for many months, nor did I really know what to do. Linnen I had none left, but what was meer rags; I had goat's hair, but neither knew I how to weave it or spin it; and had I known how, there were no tools to work it with; all the remedy that I found for this was that at last I did remember I had among the seamen's cloaths, which were sav'd out of the ship, some neck-cloaths of calicoe, or muslin, and with some pieces of these, I made three small sieves, but proper enough for the work. Thus I made shift for some years; how I did afterwards, I shall show in its place.

The baking part was the next thing to be consider'd, and how I should make bread when I came to have corn. First,

I had no yeast; as to that part, as there was no supplying the want, I did not concern myself much about it. But for an oven I was indeed in great pain; at length I found out an experiment for that also, which was this: I made some earthen vessels very broad, but deep, that is to say, about two foot diameter and not above nine inches deep; these I burnt in the fire, as I had done the other, and lay'd them by; and when I wanted to bake, I made a great fire upon my hearth, which I had pav'd with some square tiles of my own making, and burning also, but I should not call them square.

When the fire-wood was burnt pretty much into embers, or live coals, I drew them forward upon this hearth, so as to cover it all over, and there I let them lie, till the hearth was very hot. Then sweeping away all the embers, I set down my loaf, or loaves, and whelming down the earthen pot upon them, drew the embers all round the out-side of the pot, to keep in, and add to the heat; and thus, as well as in the best oven in the world, I bak'd my barley loaves, and became in little time a meer pastry-cook into the bar-gain. For I made myself several cakes of the rice, and puddings; indeed I made no pies, neither had I any thing to put into them, supposing I had, except the flesh either of fowls or goats.

It need not be wonder'd at if all these things took me up most part of the third year of my abode here; for it is to be observ'd that in the intervals of these things, I had my new harvest and husbandry to manage; for I reap'd my corn in its season, and carry'd it home as well as I could, and lay'd it up in the ear, in my large baskets, till I had time to rub it out; for I had no floor to thrash it on or instrument to thrash it with.

And now indeed my stock of corn encreasing, I really wanted to build my barns bigger. I wanted a place to lay it up in, for the encrease of the corn now yielded me so much that I had of the barley about twenty bushels, and of the rice as much or more; insomuch, that now I resolv'd to begin to use it freely, for my bread had been quite gone a great while. Also I resolv'd to see what quantity would be sufficient for me a whole year, and to sow but once a year.

Upon the whole, I found that the forty bushels of barley and rice was much more than I could consume in a year, so I resolv'd to sow just the same quantity every year that I sow'd in the last, in hopes that such a quantity would fully provide me with bread, &c.

All the while these things were doing, you may be sure my thoughts ran many times upon the prospect of land which I had seen from the other side of the island, and I was not without secret wishes that I were on shore there, fancying the seeing the main-land, and in an inhabited country, I might find some way or other to convey myself farther, and perhaps at last find some means of escape.

But all this while I made no allowance for the dangers of such a condition, and how I might fall into the hands of savages, and perhaps such as I might have reason to think far worse than the lyons and tygers of Africa. That if I once came into their power, I should run a hazard more than a thousand to one of being kill'd, and perhaps of being eaten; for I had heard that the people of the Carribeen coast were canibals, or man-eaters; and I knew by the latitude that I could not be far off from that shore. That suppose they were not canibals, yet that they might kill me, as many Europeans who had fallen into their hands had

been serv'd, even when they had been ten or twenty together; much more I that was but one, and could make
little or no defence. All these things, I say, which I ought
to have consider'd well of, and did cast up in my thoughts
afterwards, yet took up none of my apprehensions at first;
but my head ran mightily upon the thought of getting over
to the shore.

Now I wish'd for my boy, Xury, and the longboat, with
the shoulder-of-mutton sail, with which I sail'd above a
thousand miles on the coast of Africa; but this was in vain.
Then I thought I would go and look at our ship's boat,
which, as I have said, was blown up upon the shore a great
way in the storm, when we were first cast away. She lay
almost where she did at first, but not quite; and was turn'd
by the force of the waves and the winds almost bottom upward, against a high ridge of beachy rough sand, but no
water about her as before.

If I had had hands to have refitted her, and to have
launch'd her into the water, the boat would have done well
enough, and I might have gone back into the Brasils with
her easily enough. But I might have foreseen that I could
no more turn her and set her upright upon her bottom than
I could remove the island. However, I went to the woods
and cut levers and rollers and brought them to the boat,
resolv'd to try what I could do, suggesting to myself that if
I could but turn her down, I might easily repair the damage
she had receiv'd, and she would be a very good boat, and I
might go to sea in her very easily.

I spar'd no pains indeed in this piece of fruitless toil, and
spent, I think, three or four weeks about it. At last, finding
it impossible to heave it up with my little strength, I fell to

digging away the sand, to undermine it, and so to make it fall down, setting pieces of wood to thrust and guide it right in the fall.

But when I had done this, I was unable to stir it up again, or to get under it, much less to move it forward towards the water, so I was forc'd to give it over; and yet, though I gave over the hopes of the boat, my desire to venture over for the main encreas'd, rather than decreas'd, as the means for it seem'd impossible.

This at length put me upon thinking whether it was not possible to make myself a canoe, or periagua, such as the natives of those climates make, even without tools, or, as I might say, without hands, viz., of the trunk of a great tree. This I not only thought possible, but easy, and pleased myself extremely with the thoughts of making it, and with my having much more convenience for it than any of the Negroes or Indians; but not at all considering the particular inconveniences which I lay under, more than the Indians did, viz., want of hands to move it, when it was made, into the water; a difficulty much harder for me to surmount than all the consequences of want of tools could be to them; for what was it to me that, when I had chosen a vast tree in the woods, I might with much trouble cut it down, if after I might be able with my tools to hew and dubb the out-side into the proper shape of a boat, and burn or cut out the in-side to make it hollow, so to make a boat of it, if, after all this, I must leave it just where I found it and was not able to launch it into the water?

One would have thought I could not have had the least reflection upon my mind of my circumstance while I was making this boat, but I should have immediately thought how I should get it into the sea. But my thoughts were so intent upon my voyage over the sea in it, that I never once consider'd how I should get it off of the land; it was really in its own nature more easy for me to guide it over forty-five miles of sea, than about forty-five fathoms of land, where it lay, to set it a-float in the water.

I went to work upon this boat the most like a fool that ever man did who had any of his senses awake. I pleas'd myself with the design, without determining whether I was ever able to undertake it, not but that the difficulty of launching my boat came often into my head; but I put a stop to my own enquiries into it by this foolish answer which I gave myself: "Let's first make it; I'll warrant I'll find some way or other to get it along, when 'tis done."

This was a most preposterous method, but the eagerness of my fancy prevail'd, and to work I went. I fell'd a cedar tree; I question much whether Solomon ever had such a one for the building of the temple of Jerusalem. It was five foot ten inches diameter at the lower part next the stump, and four foot eleven inches diameter at the end of twenty-two foot, after which it lessen'd for a while, and then parted into branches. It was not without infinite labour that I fell'd this tree. I was twenty days hacking and hewing at it at the bottom. I was fourteen more getting the branches and limbs and the vast spreading head of it cut off, which I hack'd and hew'd through the axe and hatchet and inexpressible labour. After this, it cost me a month to shape it, and dubb it to a proportion, and to something like the bottom of a boat, that it might swim upright as it ought to do. It cost me near three months more to clear the in-side, and work it out so as to make an exact boat of it. This I did indeed without fire, by meer malett and chissel, and by the dint of hard labour, till I had brought it to be a very handsome periagua, and big enough to have carry'd six-and-twenty men, and consequently big enough to have carry'd me and all my cargo.

When I had gone through this work, I was extremely delighted with it. The boat was really much bigger than I ever saw a canoe or periagua that was made of one tree in my life. Many a weary stroke it had cost, you may be sure. There remain'd nothing but to get it into the water, and had I gotten it into the water I make no question but I should have begun the maddest voyage, and the most unlikely to be perform'd, that ever was undertaken.

But all my devices to get it into the water fail'd me, tho' they cost me infinite labour too. It lay about one hundred yards from the water, and not more. But the first inconvenience was it was up hill towards the creek; well, to take away this discouragement, I resolv'd to dig into the surface of the earth, and so make a declivity. This I began, and it cost me a prodigious deal of pains; but who grudges pains that has his deliverance in view? But when this was work'd through and this difficulty manag'd, it was still much at one; for I could no more stir the canoe than I could the other boat.

Then I measur'd the distance of ground and resolv'd to cut a dock, or canal, to bring the water up to the canoe, seeing I could not bring the canoe down to the water. Well, I began this work, and when I began to enter into it and calculate how deep it was to be dug, how broad, and how much the stuff to be thrown out, I found that by the number of hands I had, being none but my own, it must have been ten or twelve years before I should have gone through with it; for the shore lay high, so that at the upper end it must have been at least twenty foot deep; so at length, tho' with great reluctancy, I gave this attempt over also.

This griev'd me heartily, and now I saw, tho' too late, the folly of beginning a work before we count the cost, and before we judge rightly of our own strength to go through with it.

In the middle of this work, I finish'd my fourth year in this place, and kept my anniversary with the same devotion, and with as much comfort as ever before; for by a constant study, and serious application of the Word of God, and by the assistance of His grace, I gain'd a different knowledge from what I had before. I entertain'd different notions of things. I look'd now upon the world as a thing remote, which I had nothing to do with, no expectation from, and indeed no desires about. In a word, I had nothing indeed to do with it, nor was ever like to have; so I thought it look'd as we may perhaps look upon it hereafter, viz., as a place I had liv'd in, but was come out of it; and well might I say, as Father Abraham to Dives, *Between me and thee is a great gulph fix'd.*

In the first place, I was remov'd from all the wickedness of the world here. I had neither the lust of the flesh, the lust of the eye, or the pride of life. I had nothing to covet, for I had all that I was now capable of enjoying. I was lord of the whole manor, or if I pleas'd, I might call myself king, or emperor over the whole country which I had possession of. There were no rivals. I had no competitor, none to dispute sovereignty or command with me. I might have rais'd ship-loadings of corn; but I had no use for it, so I let as little grow as I thought enough for my occasion. I had tortoise or turtles enough; but now and then one was as much as I could put to any use. I had timber enough to have built a fleet of ships. I had grapes enough to have made wine, or to have cur'd into raisins, to have loaded that fleet when it had been built.

But all I could make use of was all that was valuable. I had enough to eat, and to supply my wants, and what was all the rest to me? If I kill'd more flesh than I could eat, the dog must eat it, or the vermin. If I sow'd more corn than I could eat, it must be spoil'd. The trees that I cut down were lying to rot on the ground. I could make no more use of them than for fuel, and that I had no occasion for but to dress my food.

In a word, the nature and experience of things dictated to me upon just reflection, that all the good things of this world are no further good to us than they are for our use; and that whatever we may heap up indeed to give others, we enjoy just as much as we can use, and no more. The most covetous, griping miser in the world would have been cur'd of the vice of covetousness if he had been in my case, for I possess'd infinitely more than I knew what to do with. I had no room for desire, except it was of things which I had not, and they were but trifles, though indeed of great use to me. I had, as I hinted before, a parcel of money, as well gold as silver, about thirty-six pounds sterling. Alas, there the nasty sorry useless stuff lay! I had no manner of business for it; and I often thought with myself that I would have given a handful of it for a gross of tobacco-pipes, or for a hand-mill to grind my corn; nay, I would have given it all for sixpenny-worth of turnip and carrot seed out of England, or a handful of pease and beans, and a bottle of ink. As it was, I had not the least advantage by it, or benefit from it; but there it lay in a drawer

My dog, sat always at my right hand; and two cats, one on one side of the table, and one on the other, expecting now and then a bit from my hand, as a mark of special favour.
(page 170)

and grew mouldy with the damp of the cave in the wet season; and if I had had the drawer full of diamonds, it had been the same case, and they had been of no manner of value to me because of no use.

I had now brought my state of life to be much easier in itself than it was at first, and much easier to my mind, as well as to my body. I frequently sat down to my meat with thankfulness, and admir'd the hand of God's providence, which had thus spread my table in the wilderness. I learn'd to look more upon the bright side of my condition, and less upon the dark side; and to consider what I enjoy'd rather than what I wanted. This gave me sometimes such secret comforts, that I cannot express them; and which I take notice of here to put those discontented people in mind of it, who cannot enjoy comfortably what God has given them; because they see and covet something that He has not given them. All our discontents about what we want appear'd to me to spring from the want of thankfulness for what we have.

Another reflection was of great use to me, and doubtless would be so to any one that should fall into such distress as mine was; and this was to compare my present condition with what I at first expected it should be; nay, with what it would certainly have been, if the good providence of God had not wonderfully order'd the ship to be cast up nearer to the shore, where I not only could come at her, but could bring what I got out of her to the shore, for my relief and comfort, without which I had wanted for tools to work, weapons for defence, or gun-powder and shot for getting my food.

I spent whole hours, I may say whole days, in representing to myself in the most lively colours how I must have acted if I had got nothing out of the ship. How I could not have so much as got any food, except fish and turtles, and that as it was long before I found any of them, I must have perish'd first. That I should have liv'd, if I had not perish'd, like a meer savage; that if I had kill'd a goat, or a fowl, by any contrivance, I had no way to flea or open them, or part the flesh from the skin and the bowels, or to cut it up, but must gnaw it with my teeth, and pull it with my claws like a beast.

These reflections made me very sensible of the goodness of Providence to me and very thankful for my present condition, with all its hardships and misfortunes. And this part also I cannot but recommend to the reflection of those who are apt in their misery to say, "Is any affliction like mine!" Let them consider how much worse the cases of some people are, and their case might have been, if Providence had thought fit.

I had another reflection which assisted me also to comfort my mind with hopes, and this was comparing my present condition with what I had deserv'd, and had therefore reason to expect from the hand of Providence. I had liv'd a dreadful life, perfectly destitute of the knowledge and fear of God. I had been well instructed by father and mother; neither had they been wanting to me, in their early endeavours, to infuse a religious awe of God into my mind, a sense of my duty, and of what the nature and end of my being requir'd of me. But alas! Falling early into the seafaring life, which of all the lives is the most destitute of the fear of God, though His terrors are always before them; I say, falling early into the seafaring life, and into seafaring company, all that little sense of religion which I had entertain'd, was laugh'd out of me by my messmates, by a harden'd despizing of dangers; and the views of death, which grew habitual to me, by my long absence from all manner of opportunities to converse with any thing but what was like myself, or to hear any thing that was good, or tended towards it.

So void was I of every thing that was good, or of the least sense of what I was, or was to be, that in the greatest deliverances I enjoy'd, such as my escape from Sallee, my being taken up by the Portugueze master of the ship, my being planted so well in the Brasils, my receiving the cargo from England, and the like, I never had once the words "Thank God" so much as on my mind or in my mouth. Nor in the greatest distress, had I so much as a thought to pray to Him, or so much as to say, "Lord have mercy upon me"; no nor to mention the name of God, unless it was to swear by and blaspheme it.

I had terrible reflections upon my mind for many months, as I have already observ'd, on the account of my wicked and harden'd life past. And when I look'd about me and considered what particular providences had attended me since my coming into this place, and how God had dealt bountifully with me; had not only punish'd me less than my iniquity had deserv'd, but had so plentifully provided for me, this gave me great hopes that my repentance was accepted and that God hath yet mercy in store for me.

With these reflections I work'd my mind up, not only to resignation to the will of God in the present disposition of my circumstances, but even to a sincere thankfulness for my condition; and that I, who was yet a living man, ought not to complain, seeing I had not the due punishment of my sins; that I enjoy'd so many mercies which I had no reason to have expected in that place; that I ought never more to repine at my condition, but to rejoyce and to give daily thanks for that daily bread, which nothing but a croud of wonders could have brought; that I ought to consider I had been fed even by a miracle, even as great as that of feeding Elijah by the ravens; nay, by a long series of miracles, and that I could hardly have nam'd a place in the unhabitable part of the world where I could have been cast more to my advantage; a place, where as I had no society, which was my affliction on one hand, so I found no ravenous beast, no furious wolves or tygers to threaten my life, no venomous creatures or poisonous, which I might feed on to my hurt, no savages to murther and devour me.

In a word, as my life was a life of sorrow one way, so it was a life of mercy another. I wanted nothing to make it a life of comfort, but to be able to make my sense of God's goodness to me, and care over me in this condition, be my daily consolation, and after I did make a just improvement of these things, I went away and was no more sad.

I had now been here so long that many things which I brought on shore for my help were either quite gone, or very much wasted and near spent.

My ink, as I observ'd, had been gone sometime, all but a very little, which I eek'd out with water a little and a little, till it was so pale it scarce left any appearance of black upon the paper. As long as it lasted, I made use of it to minute down the days of the month on which any remarkable thing happen'd to me, and first by casting up times past. I remember that there was a strange concurrence of days, in the various providences which befell me, and which, if I had been superstitiously inclin'd to observe days as fatal or fortunate, I might have had reason to have look'd upon with a great deal of curiosity.

First, I had observ'd that the same day that I broke away from my father and my friends, and ran away to Hull in order to go to sea, the same day afterwards I was taken by the Sallee man of war and made a slave.

The same day of the year that I escap'd out of the wreck of that ship in Yarmouth roads, that same day-year afterwards I made my escape from Sallee in the boat.

The same day of the year I was born on, viz., the 30th of September, that same day, I had my life so miraculously sav'd twenty-six years after, when I was cast on shore in this island, so that my wicked life and my solitary life began both on a day.

The next thing to my ink's being wasted was that of my bread, I mean the bisket which I brought out of the ship. This I had husbanded to the last degree, allowing myself but one cake of bread a day for above a year, and yet I was quite without bread for near a year before I got any corn of my own, and great reason I had to be thankful that I had any at all, the getting it being, as has been already observ'd, next to miraculous.

My cloaths began to decay too mightily. As to linnen, I had had none a good while, except some chequer'd shirts which I found in the chests of the other seamen and which I carefully preserv'd, because many times I could bear no other cloaths on but a shirt; and it was a very great help to me that I had among all the men's cloaths of the ship almost three dozen of shirts. There were also several thick watch-coats of the seamen, which were left indeed, but they were too hot to wear; and tho' it is true that the weather was so violent hot that there was no need of cloaths, yet I could not go quite naked; no, tho' I had been enclin'd to it, which I was not, nor could not abide the thoughts of it, tho' I was all alone.

The reason why I could not go quite naked was, I could not bear the heat of the sun so well when quite naked as with some cloaths on; nay, the very heat frequently blister'd my skin, whereas with a shirt on, the air itself made some motion and whistling under that shirt was twofold cooler than without it. No more could I ever bring myself to go out in the heat of sun without a cap or a hat; the heat of the sun beating with such violence as it does in that place would give me the head-ache presently, by darting so directly on my head, without a cap or hat on, so that I could not bear it, whereas, if I put on my hat, it would presently go away.

Upon those views I began to consider about putting the few rags I had, which I call'd cloaths, into some order. I had worn out all the waistcoats I had, and my business was now to try if I could not make jackets out of the great watch-coats which I had by me, and with such other materials as I had, so I set to work a-tayloring, or rather indeed a-botching, for I made most piteous work of it. However, I made shift to make two or three new waistcoats, which I hoped would serve me a great while; as for breeches or drawers, I made but a very sorry shift indeed, till afterwards.

I have mention'd that I sav'd the skins of all the creatures that I kill'd, I mean four-footed ones, and I had hung them up stretch'd out with sticks in the sun, by which means some of them were so dry and hard that they were fit for little, but others it seems were very useful. The first

thing I made of these was a great cap for my head, with
the hair on the out-side to shoor off the rain; and this I
perform'd so well, that after this I made me a suit of
cloaths wholly of these skins, that is to say, a waistcoat, and
breeches open at knees, and both loose, for they were
rather wanting to keep me cool than to keep me warm. I
must not omit to acknowledge that they were wretchedly
made; for if I was a bad carpenter, I was a worse taylor.
However, they were such as I made very good shift with;
and when I was abroad, if it happen'd to rain, the hair
of my waistcoat and cap being outermost, I was kept very
dry.

After this I spent a great deal of time and pains to make
me an umbrella; I was indeed in great want of one and
had a great mind to make one. I had seen them made in
the Brasils, where they are very useful in the great heats
which are there, and I felt the heats every jot as great
here, and greater too, being nearer the equinox. Besides,
as I was oblig'd to be much abroad, it was a most useful
thing to me, as well for the rains as the heats. I took a
world of pains at it, and it was a great while before I could
make any thing likely to hold; nay, after I thought I had
hit the way, I spoil'd two or three before I made one to
my mind, but at last I made one that answer'd indifferently
well. The main difficulty I found was to make it to let
down. I could make it to spread, but if it did not let down
too, and draw in, it was not portable for me any way but
just over my head, which would not do. However, at last,
as I said, I made one to answer, and cover'd it with skins,
the hair upwards, so that it cast off the rains like a penthouse, and kept off the sun so effectually that I could walk

out in the hottest of the weather with greater advantage than I could before in the coolest, and when I had no need of it, could close it and carry it under my arm.

Thus I liv'd mighty comfortably, my mind being entirely compos'd by resigning to the will of God and throwing myself wholly upon the disposal of His providence. This made my life better than sociable, for when I began to regret the want of conversation, I would ask myself whether thus conversing mutually with my own thoughts, and, as I hope I may say, with even God Himself by ejaculations, was not better than the utmost enjoyment of human society in the world.

I cannot say that after this, for five years, any extraordinary things happen'd to me, but I liv'd on in the same course, in the same posture and place, just as before. The chief things I was employ'd in, besides my yearly labour of planting my barley and rice, and curing my raisins, of both which I always kept up just enough to have sufficient stock of one year's provisions beforehand; I say, besides this yearly labour, and my daily labour of going out with my gun, I had one labour to make me a canoe, which at last I finish'd. So that by digging a canal to it of six-foot wide, and four-foot deep, I brought it into the creek, almost half a mile. As for the first, which was so vastly big, as I made it without considering beforehand, as I ought to do, how I should be able to launch it; so never being able to bring it to the water, or bring the water to it, I was oblig'd to let it lie where it was, as a memorandum to teach me to be wiser next time. Indeed, the next time, tho' I could not get a tree proper for it, and in a place where I could not get the water to it, at any less distance than as I have said, near half a mile; yet as I saw it was practicable at last, I never gave it over, and tho' I was near two years about it, yet I never grudged my labour, in hopes of having a boat to go off to sea at last.

However, though my little periagua was finish'd, the size of it was not at all answerable to the design which I had in view when I made the first attempt, I mean, of venturing over to the *terra firma*, where it was above forty miles broad. Accordingly, the smallness of my boat assisted to put an end to that design, and now I thought no more of it. But as I had a boat, my next design was to make a tour round the island; for as I had been on the other side, in one place crossing as I have already describ'd it, over the land, so the discoveries I made in that little journey made me very eager to see other parts of the coast; and now I had a boat, I thought of nothing but sailing round the island.

For this purpose, that I might do every thing with discretion and consideration, I fitted up a little mast to my boat and made a sail to it out of some of the pieces of the ship's sail, which lay in store, and of which I had a great stock by me.

Having fitted my mast and sail and try'd the boat, I found she would sail very well. Then I made little lockers, or boxes, at either end of my boat, to put provisions, necessaries, and ammunition, &c. into, to be kept dry, either from rain or the sprye of the sea; and a little long hollow place I cut in the in-side of the boat, where I could lay my gun, making a flap to hang down over it to keep it dry.

I fix'd my umbrella also in a step at the stern, like a mast, to stand over my head and keep the heat of the sun off of me like an auning. Thus I every now and then took a little voyage upon the sea, but never went far out nor far from the little creek. But, at last, being eager to view the circumference of my little kingdom, I resolv'd upon my tour, and accordingly I victuall'd my ship for the voyage, putting in two dozen of my loaves (cakes I should rather call them) of barley bread, an earthen pot full of parch'd rice (a food I ate a great deal of), a little bottle of rum, half a goat, and powder and shot for killing more, and two large watch-coats, of those which, as I mention'd before, I had sav'd out of the seamen's chests; these I took, one to lie upon, and the other to cover me in the night.

It was the 6th of November, in the sixth year of my reign, or my captivity, which you please, that I set out on this voyage, and I found it much longer than I expected; for though the island itself was not very large, yet when I came to the east side of it, I found a great ledge of rocks lay out above two leagues into the sea, some above water, some under it, and beyond that, a shoal of sand, lying dry half a league more, so that I was oblig'd to go a great way out to sea to double the point.

When first I discover'd them, I was going to give over my enterprize and come back again, not knowing how far it might oblige me to go out to sea; and above all, doubting how I should get back again; so I came to anchor, for I had made me a kind of an anchor with a piece of a broken graplin, which I got out of the ship.

Having secur'd my boat, I took my gun and went on shore, climbing up upon a hill, which seem'd to overlook that point, where I saw the full extent of it and resolv'd to venture.

In my viewing the sea from that hill where I stood, I perceiv'd a strong, and indeed, a most furious current, which ran to the east, and even came close to the point. I took the more notice of it because I saw there might be some danger; that when I came into it, I might be carry'd out to sea by the strength of it and not be able to make the island again; and indeed, had I not gotten first up upon this hill, I believe it would have been so, for there was the same current on the other side the island, only that it set off at a farther distance. And I saw there was a strong eddy under the shore, so I had nothing to do but to get in out of the first current, and I should presently be in an eddy.

I lay here, however, two days, because the wind blowing pretty fresh at ESE, and that being just contrary to the said current, made a great breach of the sea upon the point, so that it was not safe for me to keep too close to the shore for the breach, nor to go too far off because of the stream.

The third day in the morning, the wind having abated over night, the sea was calm, and I ventur'd; but I am a-warning piece again to all rash and ignorant pilots, for no sooner was I come to the point, when even I was not my boat's length from the shore, but I found myself in a great depth of water and a current like the sluice of a mill. It carry'd my boat along with it with such violence that all I could do could not keep her so much as on the edge of it; but I found it hurry'd me farther and farther out from the eddy, which was on my left hand. There was no wind stirring to help me, and all I could do with my paddlers signify'd nothing, and now I began to give myself over for lost; for as the current was on both sides the island, I knew in a few leagues distance they must join again, and then I was irrecoverably gone. Nor did I see any possibility of avoiding it, so that I had no prospect before me but of perishing; not by the sea, for that was calm enough, but of starving for hunger. I had indeed found a tortoise on the shore, as big almost as I could lift, and had toss'd it into the boat; and I had a great jarr of fresh water, that is to say, one of my earthen pots, but what was all this to being driven into the vast ocean, where to be sure, there was no shore, no main-land, or island, for a thousand leagues at least.

And now I saw how easy it was for the providence of God to make the most miserable condition mankind could be in worse. Now I look'd back upon my desolate solitary island as the most pleasant place in the world, and all the happiness my heart could wish for was to be but there again. I stretch'd out my hands to it with eager wishes. O happy desert, thought I, I shall never see thee more! O miserable creature, thought I, whither am I going? Then I reproach'd myself with my unthankful temper, and how I had repin'd at my solitary condition; and now what would I give to be on shore there again. Thus we never see the true state of our condition till it is illustrated to us by its contraries; nor know how to value what we enjoy but by the want of it. It is scarce possible to imagine the consternation I was now in, being driven from my belov'd island (for so it appear'd to me now to be) into the wide ocean, almost two leagues, and in the utmost despair of ever recov'ring it again. However, I work'd hard, till indeed my strength was almost exhausted, and kept my boat as much to the nor'ward, that is, towards the side of the current which the eddy lay on, as possibly I could; when about noon, as the sun pass'd the meridian, I thought I felt a little breeze of wind in my face, springing up from the SSE. This cheer'd my heart a little, and especially when in about half an hour more it blew a pretty small, gentle gale. By this time I was gotten at a frightful distance from the island, and had the least cloud or hazey weather interven'd, I had been undone another way too; for I had no compass on board, and should never have known how to have steer'd towards the island if I had but once lost sight of it. But the weather continuing clear, I apply'd myself to get up my mast again, spread my sail, standing away to the north as much as possible, to get out of the current.

Just as I had set my mast and sail, and the boat began to stretch away, I saw by the clearness of the water some alteration of the current was near; for where the current was so strong, the water was foul; but perceiving the water clear, I found the current abate, and presently I found to the east, at about half a mile, a breach of the sea upon some rocks. These rocks I found caus'd the current to part again, and as the main stress of it ran away more southerly, leaving the rocks to the north-east, so the other return'd by the repulse of the rocks and made a strong eddy, which ran back again to the north-west with a very sharp stream.

They who know what it is to have a reprieve brought to them upon the ladder, or to be rescu'd from thieves just a-going to murther them, or, who have been in such like extremities, may guess what my present surprize of joy was and how gladly I put my boat into the stream of this eddy; and the wind also fresh'ning, how gladly I spread my sail to it, running cheerfully before the wind and with a strong tide or eddy under foot.

This eddy carry'd me about a league on my way back again directly towards the island, but about two leagues more to the nor'ward than the current which carry'd me away at first; so that when I came near the island, I found myself open to the northern shore of it, that is to say, the other end of the island opposite to that which I went out from.

When I had made something more than a league of way by the help of this current or eddy, I found it was spent and serv'd me no further. However, I found that being between the two great currents, viz., that on the south side which had hurry'd me away, and that on the north, which lay about a league on the other side, I say between these two, in the wake of the island, I found the water at last still and running no way, and having still a breeze of wind fair for me, I kept on steering directly for the island, tho' not making such fresh way as I did before.

About four a-clock in the evening, being then within about a league of the island, I found the point of the rocks which occasion'd this disaster, stretching out as is describ'd before to the southward, and casting off the current more southwardly, had of course made another eddy to the north, and this I found very strong, but not directly setting the way my course lay which was due west, but almost full north. However, having a fresh gale I stretch'd across this eddy slanting north-west, and in about an hour came within about a mile of the shore, where it being smooth water, I soon got to land.

When I was on shore I fell on my knees and gave God thanks for my deliverance, resolving to lay a-side all thoughts of my deliverance by my boat. Refreshing myself with such things as I had, I brought my boat close to the shore in a little cove that I had spy'd under some trees and lay'd me down to sleep, being quite spent with the labour and fatigue of the voyage.

I was now at a great loss which way to get home with my

boat. I had run so much hazard, and knew too much the case, to think of attempting it by the way I went out, and what might be at the other side (I mean the west side) I knew not, nor had I any mind to run any more ventures; so I only resolv'd in the morning to make my way westward along the shore and to see if there was no creek where I might lay up my frigate in safety, so as to have her again if I wanted her. In about three miles or thereabout, coasting the shore, I came to a very good inlet or bay about a mile over, which narrow'd till it came to a very little rivulet or brook, where I found a very convenient harbour for my boat, and where she lay as if she had been in a little dock made on purpose for her. Here I put in and, having stow'd my boat very safe, I went on shore to look about me and see where I was.

I soon found I had but a little pass'd by the place where I had been before, when I travell'd on foot to the shore. So taking nothing out of my boat but my gun and my umbrella, for it was exceeding hot, I began my march. The way was comfortable enough after such a voyage as I had been upon, and I reach'd my old bower in the evening, where I found every thing standing as I left it; for I always kept it in good order, being, as I said before, my country-house.

I got over the fence, and lay'd me down in the shade to rest my limbs; for I was very weary, and fell a-sleep. But judge you, if you can, that read my story, what a surprize I must be in, when I was wak'd out of my sleep by a voice calling me by my name several times, "Robin, Robin, Robin Crusoe, poor Robin Crusoe, where are you Robin Crusoe? Where are you? Where have you been?"

I was so dead a-sleep at first, being fatigu'd with rowing,

or paddling, as it is call'd, the first part of the day, and with walking the latter part, that I did not wake thoroughly, but dozing between sleeping and waking, thought I dream'd that some body spoke to me. But as the voice continu'd to repeat, "Robin Crusoe, Robin Crusoe," at last I began to wake more perfectly, and was at first dreadfully frighted, and started up in the utmost consternation. But no sooner were my eyes open, but I saw my Poll sitting on the top of the hedge, and immediately knew that it was he that spoke to me. Just in such bemoaning language I had used to talk to him and teach him; and he had learn'd it so perfectly that he would sit upon my finger and lay his bill close to my face and cry, "Poor Robin Crusoe. Where are you? Where have you been? How come you here?" And such things as I had taught him.

However, even tho' I knew it was the parrot, and that indeed it could be no body else, it was a good while before I could compose myself. First, I was amaz'd how the creature got thither, and then, how he should just keep about the place and no where else. But as I was well satisfy'd it could be no body but honest Poll, I got it over. Holding out my hand, I call'd him by his name, Poll, and the sociable creature came to me and sat upon my thumb, as he used to do, and continu'd talking to me, "Poor Robin Crusoe," and how did I come here? and where had I been? just as if he had been overjoy'd to see me again; and so I carry'd him home along with me.

I had now had enough of rambling to sea for some time, and had enough to do for many days to sit still and reflect upon the danger I had been in. I would have been very glad to have had my boat again on my side of the island, but I knew not how it was practicable to get it about as to the east side of the island, which I had gone round. I knew well enough there was no venturing that way; my very heart would shrink and my very blood run chill but to think of it. And as to the other side of the island, I did not know how it might be there; for supposing the current ran with the same force against the shore at the east as it pass'd by it on the other, I might run the same risk of being driven down the stream and carry'd by the island, as I had been before of being carry'd away from it; so with these thoughts I contented myself to be without any boat, though it had been the product of so many months' labour to make it, and of so many more to get it unto the sea.

In this government of my temper I remain'd near a year, and liv'd a very sedate retir'd life, as you may well suppose. My thoughts being very much compos'd as to my condition, and fully comforted in resigning myself to the dispositions of Providence, I thought I liv'd really very happily in all things, except that of society.

I improv'd myself in this time in all the mechanick exercises which my necessities put me upon applying myself to, and I believe could, upon occasion, make a very good carpenter, especially considering how few tools I had.

Besides this, I arriv'd at an unexpected perfection in my earthen-ware, and contriv'd well enough to make them with a wheel, which I found infinitely easier and better, because I made things round and shapable which before were filthy things indeed to look on. But I think I was never more vain of my own performance, or more joyful for any thing I found out, than for my being able to make a tobacco-pipe. And tho' it was a very ugly clumsy thing when it was done, and only burnt red like other earthen-ware, yet as it was hard and firm and would draw the smoke, I was exceedingly comforted with it, for I had been always used to smoke. There were pipes in the ship, but I forgot them at first, not knowing that there was tobacco on the island; and afterwards, when I search'd the ship again, I could not come at any pipes at all.

In my wicker-ware also I improv'd much and made abundance of necessary baskets, as well as my invention shew'd me, tho' not very handsome, yet they were such as were very handy and convenient for my laying things up in or fetching things home in. For example, if I kill'd a goat abroad, I could hang it up in a tree, flea it, and dress it, and cut it in pieces, and bring it home in a basket; and the like by a turtle, I could cut it up, take out the eggs, and a piece or two of the flesh, which was enough for me, and bring them home in a basket, and leave the rest behind me. Also large deep baskets were my receivers for my corn, which I always rubb'd out as soon as it was dry, and cur'd, and kept it in great baskets.

I began now to perceive my powder abated considerably, and this was a want which it was impossible for me to supply. I began seriously to consider what I must do when I should have no more powder; that is to say, how I should do to kill any goat. I had, as is observ'd in the third year of my being here, kept a young kid and bred her up tame; and I was in hope of getting a he-goat, but I could not by any means bring it to pass, till my kid grew an old goat, and I could never find in my heart to kill her, till she dy'd at last of meer age.

But being now in the eleventh year of my residence, and, as I have said, my ammunition growing low, I set myself to study some art to trap and snare the goats, to see whether I could not catch some of them alive, and particularly I wanted a she-goat great with young.

To this purpose I made snares to hamper them, and I do believe they were more than once taken in them. But my tackle was not good, for I had no wire, and always found them broken, and my bait devour'd.

At length I resolv'd to try a pit-fall, so I dug several large pits in the earth, in places where I had observ'd the goats used to feed, and over these pits I plac'd hurdles of my own making too, with a great weight upon them. Several times I put ears of barley, and dry rice, without setting the trap, and I could easily perceive that the goats had gone in and eaten up the corn, for I could see the mark of their feet. At length I set three traps in one night, and going the next morning I found them all standing, and yet the bait eaten and gone. This was very discouraging. However, I alter'd my trap and, not to trouble you with particulars, going one morning to see my trap, I found in one of them a large old he-goat, and in one of the others, three kids, a male and two females.

As to the old one, I knew not what to do with him, he was so fierce I durst not go into the pit to him; that is to say, to go about to bring him away alive, which was what I wanted. I could have kill'd him, but that was not my business, nor would it answer my end. So I e'en let him out, and he ran away as if he had been frighted out of his wits. But I had forgot then what I learn'd afterwards, that hunger will tame a lyon. If I had let him stay there three or four days without food, and then have carry'd him some water to drink, and then a little corn, he would have been as tame as one of the kids, for they are mighty sagacious tractable creatures where they are well used.

However, for the present I let him go, knowing no better at that time. Then I went to the three kids, and taking them one by one, I ty'd them with strings together, and with some difficulty brought them all home.

It was a good while before they would feed, but throwing them some sweet corn, it tempted them and they began to be tame. Now I found that if I expected to supply myself with goat-flesh when I had no powder or shot left, breeding some up tame was my only way, when perhaps I might have them about my house like a flock of sheep.

But then it presently occurr'd to me that I must keep the tame from the wild, or else they would always run wild when they grew up, and the only way for this was to have some enclos'd piece of ground, well fenc'd either with hedge or pale, to keep them in so effectually that those within might not break out, or those without break in.

This was a great undertaking for one pair of hands, yet as I saw there was an absolute necessity of doing it, my first piece of work was to find out a proper piece of ground, viz., where there was likely to be herbage for them to eat, water for them to drink, and cover to keep them from the sun.

Those who understand such enclosures will think I had very little contrivance, when I pitch'd upon a place very proper for all these, being a plain open piece of meadow-land, or savanna (as our people call it in the western colonies), which had two or three little drills of fresh water in it, and at one end was very woody. I say they will smile at my forecast, when I shall tell them I began my enclosing of this piece of ground in such a manner that my hedge or pale must have been at least two mile about. Nor was the madness of it so great as to the compass, for if it was ten mile about I was like to have time enough to do it in. But I did not consider that my goats would be as wild in so much compass as if they had had the whole island, and I should have so much room to chase them in, that I should never catch them.

My hedge was begun and carry'd on, I believe, about fifty yards, when this thought occurr'd to me, so I presently stopp'd short, and for the first beginning I resolv'd to enclose a piece of about 150 yards in length, and 100 yard in breadth, which as it would maintain as many as I should have in any reasonable time, so as my flock encreas'd, I could add more ground to my enclosure.

This was acting with some prudence, and I went to work with courage. I was about three months hedging in the first piece, and till I had done it I tether'd the three kids in the best part of it, and used them to feed as near me as possible to make them familiar. Very often I would go and carry them some ears of barley, or a handful of rice, and feed them out of my hand; so that after my enclosure was finish'd, and I let them loose, they would follow me up and down, bleating after me for a handful of corn.

This answer'd my end, and in about a year and a half I had a flock of about twelve goats, kids and all; and in two years more I had three-and-forty, besides several that I took and kill'd for my food. And after that I enclos'd several pieces of ground to feed them in, with little pens to drive them into, to take them as I wanted, and gates out of one piece of ground into another.

But this was not all, for now I not only had goat's-flesh to feed on when I pleas'd, but milk too, a thing which indeed in my beginning I did not so much as think of, and which, when it came into my thoughts, was really an agreeable surprize. For now I set up my dairy and had sometimes a gallon or two of milk in a day; and as nature, who gives supplies of food to every creature, dictates even naturally how to make use of it, so I that had never milk'd a cow, much less a goat, or seen butter or cheese made, very readily and handily, tho' after a great many essays and miscarriages, made me both butter and cheese at last, and never wanted for it afterwards.

How mercifully can our great Creator treat His creatures, even in those conditions in which they seem'd to be overwhelm'd in destruction! How can He sweeten the bitterest provinces and give us cause to praise Him for dungeons and prisons! What a table was here spre'd for me in a wilderness, where I saw nothing at first but to perish for hunger!

It would have made a stoick smile to have seen me and my little family sit down to dinner; there was my majesty the prince and lord of the whole island; I had the lives of all my subjects at my absolute command. I could hang, draw, give liberty, and take it away, and no rebels among all my subjects.

Then to see how like a king I din'd too all alone, attended by my servants; Poll, as if he had been my favourite, was the only person permitted to talk to me. My dog, who was now grown very old and crazy, and had found no species to multiply his kind upon, sat always at my right hand; and two cats, one on one side of the table, and one on the other, expecting now and then a bit from my hand, as a mark of special favour.

But these were not the two cats which I brought on shore at first, for they were both of them dead, and had been interr'd near my habitation by my own hand; but one of them having multiply'd by I know not what kind of creature, these were two which I had preserv'd tame, whereas the rest ran wild in the woods and became indeed troublesome to me at last; for they would often come into my house and plunder me too, till at last I was oblig'd to shoot them, and did kill a great many. At length they left me with this attendance, and in this plentiful manner I lived; neither could I be said to want any thing but society, and of that in some time after this, I was like to have too much.

I was something impatient, as I have observ'd, to have the use of my boat; though very loath to run any more hazards; and therefore sometimes I sat contriving ways to get her about the island, and at other times I sat myself down contented enough without her. But I had a strange uneasiness in my mind to go down to the point of the island where, as I have said, in my last ramble I went up the hill to see how the shore lay and how the current set, that I might see what I had to do. This inclination en-creas'd upon me every day, and at length I resolv'd to travel thither by land, following the edge of the shore. I did so, but had any one in England been to meet such a man as I was, it must either have frighted them or rais'd a great deal of laughter. And as I frequently stood still to look at myself, I could not but smile at the notion of my travelling through Yorkshire with such an equipage and in such a dress. Be pleas'd to take a sketch of my figure as follows.

I had a great, high, shapeless cap, made of a goat's skin, with a flap hanging down behind, as well to keep the sun from me as to shoot the rain off from running into my neck; nothing being so hurtful in these climates as the rain upon the flesh under the cloaths.

I had a short jacket of goat-skin, the skirts coming down

to about the middle of my thighs, and a pair of open-knee'd
breeches of the same; the breeches were made of the skin
of an old he-goat, whose hair hung down such a length
on either side, that like pantaloons it reach'd to the middle
of my legs. Stockings and shoes I had none, but had made
me a pair of some things, I scarce know what to call them,
like buskins to flap over my legs and lace on either side like
spatter-dashes, but of a most barbarous shape, as indeed
were all the rest of my cloaths.

I had on a broad belt of goat-skin dry'd, which I drew
together with two thongs of the same, instead of buckles,
and in a kind of a frog on either side of this. Instead of
a sword and a dagger, hung a little saw and a hatchet, one
on one side, one on the other. I had another belt not so
broad, and fasten'd in the same manner, which hung over
my shoulder; and at the end of it, under my left arm, hung
two pouches, both made of goat-skin too; in one of which
hung my powder, in the other my shot. At my back I
carry'd my basket, on my shoulder my gun, and over my
head a great, clumsy, ugly goat-skin umbrella, but which,
after all, was the most necessary thing I had about me,
next to my gun. As for my face, the colour of it was really
not so moletta–like as one might expect from a man not
at all careful of it and living within 19 degrees of the equinox. My beard I had once suffer'd to grow till it was about
a quarter of a yard long; but as I had both scissars and
razors sufficient, I had cut it pretty short, except what
grew on my upper lip, which I had trimm'd into a large
pair of Mahometan whiskers, such as I had seen worn by
some Turks, who I saw at Sallee; for the Moors did not
wear such, tho' the Turks did. Of these muschatoes or
whiskers, I will not say they were long enough to hang my

hat upon them; but they were of a length and shape monstrous enough, and such as in England would have pass'd for frightful.

But all this is by the by; for as to my figure, I had so few to observe me that it was of no manner of consequence, so I say no more to that part. In this kind of figure I went my new journey, and was out five or six days. I travell'd first along the seashore, directly to the place where I first brought my boat to anchor, to get up upon the rocks. Having no boat now to take care of, I went over the land a nearer way to the same height that I was upon before, when looking forward to the point of the rocks which lay out, and which I was oblig'd to double with my boat, as is said above, I was surpriz'd to see the sea all smooth and quiet, no rippling, no motion, no current, any more there than in other places.

I was at a strange loss to understand this, and resolv'd to spend some time in the observing it, to see if nothing from the sets of the tide had occasion'd it; but I was presently convinc'd how it was, viz., that the tide of ebb setting from the west, and joining with the current of waters from some great river on the shore, must be the occasion of this current; and that according as the wind blew more forcibly from the west, or from the north, this current came nearer, or went farther from the shore. Waiting thereabouts till evening, I went up to the rock again, and then the tide of ebb being made, I plainly saw the current again as before, only that it ran farther off, being near half a league from the shore; whereas in my case, it set close upon the shore, and hurry'd me and my canoe along with it, which at another time it would not have done.

This observation convinc'd me that I had nothing to do

but to observe the ebbing and the flowing of the tide, and I might very easily bring my boat about the island again. But when I began to think of putting it in practise, I had such a terror upon my spirits at the remembrance of the danger I had been in that I could not think of it again with any patience; but on the contrary, I took up another resolution which was more safe, though more laborious; and this was that I would build, or rather make me another periagua or canoe; and so have one for one side of the island, and one for the other.

You are to understand that now I had, as I may call it, two plantations on the island; one my little fortification or tent, with the wall about it under the rock, with the cave behind me, which by this time I had enlarg'd into several appartments, or caves, one within another. One of these, which was the dryest, and largest, had a door out beyond my wall or fortification; that is to say, beyond where my wall join'd to the rock, was all fill'd up with the large earthen pots, of which I have given an account, and with fourteen or fifteen great baskets, which would hold five or six bushels each, where I lay'd up my stores of provision, especially my corn, some in the ear cut off short from the straw, and the other rubb'd out with my hand.

As for my wall, made as before with long stakes or piles, those piles grew all like trees, and were by this time grown so big, and spread so very much, that there was not the least appearance to any one's view of any habitation behind them.

Near this dwelling of mine, but a little farther within the land, and upon lower ground, lay my two pieces of corn-ground, which I kept duly cultivated and sow'd, and which duly yielded me their harvest in its season; and whenever I had occasion for more corn, I had more land adjoining as fit as that.

Besides this, I had my country-seat, and I had now a tolerable plantation there also. First, I had my little bower, as I call'd it, which I kept in repair; that is to say, I kept the hedge which circl'd it in, constantly fitted up to its usual height, the ladder standing always in the in-side. I kept the trees which at first were no more than my stakes, but were now grown very firm and tall; I kept them always so cut that they might spread and grow thick and wild and make the more agreeable shade, which they did effectually to my mind. In the middle of this I had my tent always standing, being a piece of a sail spread over poles set up for that purpose, and which never wanted any repair or renewing; and under this I had made me a squab or couch, with the skins of the creatures I had kill'd, and with other soft things, and a blanket lay'd on them, such as belong'd to our sea-bedding, which I had sav'd, and a great watch-coat to cover me. And here, whenever I had occasion to be absent from my chief seat, I took up my country habitation.

Adjoining to this I had my enclosures for my cattle, that is to say, my goats. And as I had taken an inconceivable deal of pains to fence and enclose this ground, so I was so uneasy to see it kept entire, lest the goats should break thro', that I never left off till with infinite labour I had stuck the out-side of the hedge so full of small stakes, and so near to one another, that it was rather a pale than a hedge, and there was scarce room to put a hand thro' between them, which afterwards when those stakes grew, as they all did in the next rainy season, made the enclosure strong like a wall, indeed stronger than any wall.

This will testify for me that I was not idle and that I spared no pains to bring to pass whatever appear'd necessary for my comfortable support. I consider'd the keeping up a breed of tame creatures thus at my hand would be a living magazine of flesh, milk, butter, and cheese for me as long as I liv'd in the place, if it were to be forty years; and that keeping them in my reach depended entirely upon my perfecting my enclosures to such a degree that I might be sure of keeping them together; which by this method indeed I so effectually secur'd that when these little stakes began to grow, I had planted them so very thick I was forc'd to pull some of them up again.

In this place also I had my grapes growing, which I principally depended on for my winter store of raisins; and which I never fail'd to preserve very carefully, as the best and most agreeable dainty of my whole diet. Indeed they were not agreeable only, but physical, wholesome, nourishing, and refreshing to the last degree.

As this was also about half way between my other habitation, and the place where I had lay'd up my boat, I generally stay'd and lay here in my way thither, for I used frequently to visit my boat, and I kept all things about or belonging to her in very good order. Sometimes I went out in her to divert myself, but no more hazardous voyages would I go, nor scarce ever above a stone's cast or two from the shore, I was so apprehensive of being hurry'd out of my knowledge again by the currents, or winds, or any other accident. But now I come to a new scene of my life.

It happen'd one day about noon going towards my boat, I was exceedingly surpriz'd with the print of a man's naked foot on the shore, which was very plain to be seen in the sand. I stood like one thunder-struck, or as if I had seen an apparition; I listen'd, I look'd round me, I could hear nothing, nor see any thing. I went up to a rizing ground to look farther; I went up the shore and down the shore, but it was all one, I could see no other impression but that one; I went to it again to see if there were any more and to observe if it might not be my fancy; but there was no room for that, for there was exactly the very print of a foot, toes, heel, and every part of a foot; how it came thither, I knew not, nor could in the least imagine. But after innumerable fluttering thoughts, like a man perfectly confus'd and out of myself, I came home to my fortification, not feeling, as we say, the ground I went on, but terrify'd to the last degree, looking behind me at every two or three steps, mistaking every bush and tree, and fancying every stump at a distance to be a man. Nor is it possible to describe how many various shapes affrighted imagination represented things to me in how many wild ideas were found every moment in my fancy, and what strange unaccountable whimsies came into my thoughts by the way.

When I came to my castle, for so I think I call'd it ever after this, I fled into it like one pursu'd; whether I went over by the ladder as first contriv'd, or went in at the hole in the rock, which I call'd a door, I cannot remember; no, nor could I remember the next morning, for never frighted hare fled to cover, or fox to earth, with more terror of mind than I to this retreat.

I slept none that night; the farther I was from the occasion of my fright, the greater my apprehensions were, which is something contrary to the nature of such things, and especially to the usual practise of all creatures in fear.

But I was so embarrass'd with my own frightful ideas of the thing, that I form'd nothing but dismal imaginations to myself, even tho' I was now a great way off of it. Sometimes I fancy'd it must be the Devil; and reason join'd in with me upon this supposition. For how should any other thing in human shape come into the place? Where was the vessel that brought them? What marks was there of any other footsteps? And how was it possible a man should come there? But then to think that Satan should take human shape upon him in such a place where there could be no manner of occasion for it, but to leave the print of his foot behind him, and that even for no purpose too, for he could not be sure I should see it; this was an amusement the other way. I consider'd that the Devil might have found out an abundance of other ways to have terrify'd me than this of the single print of a foot. That as I liv'd quite on the other side of the island, he would never have been so simple to leave a mark in a place where 'twas ten thousand to one whether I should ever see it or not, and in the sand too, which the first surge of the sea upon a high wind would have defac'd entirely. All this seem'd inconsistent with the thing itself and with all the notions we usually entertain of the subtilty of the Devil.

Abundance of such things as these assisted to argue me out of all apprehensions of its being the Devil, and I presently concluded then that it must be some more dangerous creature, viz., that it must be some of the savages of the main-land over-against me, who had wander'd out to sea in their canoes; and either driven by the currents or by contrary winds had made the island; and had been on shore, but were gone away again to sea, being as loath,

*It happen'd one day about noon going towards my boat, I was
exceedingly surpriz'd with the print of a man's naked foot on
the shore.* (page 176)

perhaps, to have stay'd in this desolate island, as I would have been to have had them.

While these reflections were rowling upon my mind, I was very thankful in my thoughts, that I was so happy as not to be thereabouts at that time, or that they did not see my boat, by which they would have concluded that some inhabitants had been in the place, and perhaps have search'd farther for me. Then terrible thoughts rack'd my imagination about their having found my boat, and that there were people here; and that if so, I should certainly have them come again in greater numbers and devour me; that if it should happen so that they should not find me, yet they would find my enclosure, destroy all my corn, carry away all my flock of tame goats, and I should perish at last for meer want.

Thus my fear banish'd all my religious hope; all that former confidence in God which was founded upon such wonderful experience as I had had of His goodness, now vanish'd, as if He that had fed me by miracle hitherto, could not preserve by His power the provision which He had made for me by His goodness. I reproach'd myself with my easiness, that would not sow any more corn one year than would just serve me till the next season, as if no acci-dent could intervene to prevent my enjoying the crop that was upon the ground; and this I thought so just a reproof, that I resolv'd for the future to have two or three years corn beforehand, so that whatever might come, I might not perish for want of bread.

How strange a chequer-work of Providence is the life of man! and by what secret differing springs are the affections hurry'd about as differing circumstance present! Today we love what tomorrow we hate; today we seek what tomorrow we shun; today we desire what tomorrow we fear, nay, even tremble at the apprehensions of. This was exemplify'd in me at this time in the most lively manner imaginable; for I, whose only affliction was that I seem'd banish'd from human society, that I was alone, circum-scrib'd by the boundless ocean, cut off from mankind, and condemn'd to what I call'd silent life; that I was as one who Heaven thought not worthy to be number'd among the living, or to appear among the rest of His creatures; that to have seen one of my own species, would have seem'd to me a rizing me from death to life, and the greatest blessing that Heaven itself, next to the supreme blessing of salvation, could bestow; I say, that I should now tremble at the very apprehensions of seeing a man, and was ready to sink into the ground as but the shadow or silent appearance of a man's having set his foot in the island.

Such is the uneven state of human life. And it afforded me a great many curious speculations afterwards, when I had a little recover'd my first surprize. I consider'd that this was the station of life the infinitely wise and good providence of God had determin'd for me; that as I could not foresee what the ends of divine wisdom might be in all this, so I was not to dispute His sovereignty, who, as I was His creature, had an undoubted right by creation to govern and dispose of me absolutely as He thought fit; and who, as I was a creature who had offended Him, had like-wise a judicial right to condemn me to what punishment He thought fit; and that it was my part to submit to bear His indignation because I had sinn'd against Him.

I then reflected that God, who was not only righteous

but omnipotent, as He had thought fit thus to punish and afflict me, so He was able to deliver me; that if He did not think fit to do it, 'twas my unquestion'd duty to resign myself absolutely and entirely to His will; and on the other hand, it was my duty also to hope in Him, pray to Him, and quietly to attend the dictates and directions of His daily providence.

These thoughts took me up many hours, days, nay, I may say weeks and months; and one particular effect of my cogitations on this occasion, I cannot omit, viz.: one morning early, lying in my bed, and fill'd with thoughts about my danger from the appearance of savages, I found it discompos'd me very much, upon which those words of the Scripture came into my thoughts, *Call upon Me in the day of trouble, and I will deliver, and thou shalt glorify Me.*

Upon this, rizing cheerfully out of my bed, my heart was not only comforted, but I was guided and encourag'd to pray earnestly to God for deliverance. When I had done praying, I took up my Bible, and opening it to read, the first words that presented to me were *Wait on the Lord, and be of good cheer, and He shall strengthen thy heart; wait, I say, on the Lord.* It is impossible to express the comfort this gave me. In answer, I thankfully lay'd down the Book, and was no more sad, at least, not on that occasion.

In the middle of these cogitations, apprehensions, and reflections, it came into my thought one day, that all this might be a meer chimera of my own, and that this foot might be the print of my own foot, when I came on shore from my boat. This cheer'd me up a little too, and I began to persuade myself it was all a delusion; that it was nothing else but my own foot, and why might not I come that way from the boat, as well as I was going that way to the boat; again, I consider'd also that I could by no means tell for certain where I had trod, and where I had not; and that if at last this was only the print of my own foot, I had play'd the part of those fools who strive to make stories of spectres, and apparitions, and then are frighted at them more than any body.

Now I began to take courage and to peep abroad again; for I had not stirr'd out of my castle for three days and nights. So I began to starve for provision, for I had little or nothing within doors but some barley-cakes and water. Then I knew that my goats wanted to be milk'd too, which usually was my evening diversion, and the poor creatures were in great pain and inconvenience for want of it; and indeed, it almost spoil'd some of them, and almost dry'd up their milk.

Heartening myself therefore with the belief that this was nothing but the print of one of my own feet, and so I might be truly said to start at my own shadow, I began to go abroad again, and went to my country-house, to milk my flock; but to see with what fear I went forward, how often I look'd behind me, how I was ready every now and then to lay down my basket and run for my life, it would have made any one have thought I was haunted with an evil conscience or that I had been lately most terribly frighted, and so indeed I had.

However, as I went down thus two or three days, and having seen nothing, I began to be a little bolder and to think there was really nothing in it but my own imagination. But I could not persuade myself fully of this, till I should go down to the shore again, and see this print of a foot, and measure it by my own, and see if there was any similitude or fitness, that I might be assur'd it was my own foot. When I came to the place, first, it appear'd evidently to me, that when I lay'd up my boat, I could not possibly be on shore anywhere there about. Secondly, when I came to measure the mark with my own foot, I found my foot not so large by a great deal. Both these things fill'd my head with new imaginations, and gave me the vapours again, to the highest degree, so that I shook with cold, like one in an ague. And I went home again, fill'd with the belief that some man or men had been on shore there; or in short, that the island was inhabited, and I might be surpriz'd before I was aware; and what course to take for my security I knew not.

O what ridiculous resolutions men take, when possess'd with fear! It deprives them of the use of those means which reason offers for their relief. The first thing I propos'd to myself was to throw down my enclosures, and turn all my tame cattle wild into the woods, that the enemy might not find them; and then frequent the island in prospect of the fame or the like booty. Then to the simple thing of digging up my two corn fields, that they might not find such a grain there, and still be prompted to frequent the island; then to demolish my bower, and tent, that they might not see any vestiges of habitation, and be prompted to look farther, in order to find out the persons inhabiting.

These were the subject of the first night's cogitation, after I was come home again, while the apprehensions which had so overrun my mind were fresh upon me, and my head was full of vapours, as above. Thus fear of danger is ten thousand times more terrifying than danger itself, when apparent to the eyes; and we find the burthen of anxiety greater by much, than the evil which we are anxious about; and which was worse than all this, I had not that relief in this trouble from the resignation I used to practise, that I hop'd to have. I look'd, I thought, like Saul, who complain'd not only that the Philistines were upon him, but that God had forsaken him; for I did not now take due ways to compose my mind, by crying to God in my distress, and resting upon His providence, as I had done before, for my defence and deliverance; which if I had done, I had, at least, been more cheerfully supported under this new surprize, and perhaps carry'd through it with more resolution.

This confusion of my thoughts kept me waking all night; but in the morning I fell a-sleep, and having by the amusement of my mind, been, as it were, tyr'd, and my spirits exhausted, I slept very soundly, and wak'd much better compos'd than I had ever been before. Now I began to think sedately, and upon the utmost debate with myself, I concluded that this island, which was so exceeding pleasant, fruitful, and no farther from the main-land than as I had seen, was not so entirely abandon'd as I might imagine; that altho' there were no stated inhabitants who liv'd on the spot, yet that there might sometimes come boats off from the shore, who either with design, or perhaps never, but when they were driven by cross winds, might come to this place.

That I had liv'd here fifteen years now and had not met with the least shadow or figure of any people yet; and that if at any time they should be driven here, it was probably they went away again as soon as ever they could, seeing they had never thought fit to fix there upon any occasion to this time.

That the most I could suggest any danger from was, from any such casual accidental landing of straggling people from the main, who, as it was likely if they were driven hither, were here against their wills; so they made no stay here, but went off again with all possible speed, seldom staying one night on shore, lest they should not have the help of the tides and daylight back again; and that therefore I had nothing to do but to consider of some safe retreat, in case I should see any savages land upon the spot.

Now I began sorely to repent that I had dug my cave so large as to bring a door through again, which door, as I said, came out beyond where my fortification join'd to the rock; upon maturely considering this therefore, I resolv'd to draw me a second fortification, in the same manner of a semicircle, at a distance from my wall just where I had planted a double row of trees, about twelve years before, of which I made mention. These trees having been planted so thick before, they wanted but a few piles to be driven between them that they should be thicker, and stronger, and my wall would be soon finish'd.

So that I had now a double wall, and my outer wall was thicken'd with pieces of timber, old cables, and every thing I could think of, to make it strong; having in it seven little holes, about as big as I might put my arm out at. In the in-side of this, I thicken'd my wall to above ten foot thick, with continual bringing earth out of my cave, and laying it at the foot of the wall, and walking upon it; and through the seven holes I contriv'd to plant the musquets, of which I took notice, that I got seven on shore out of the ship; these, I say, I planted like my cannon, and fitted them into frames that held them like a carriage, that so I could fire all the seven guns in two minutes' time. This wall I was many a weary month a-finishing, and yet never thought myself safe till it was done.

When this was done, I stuck all the ground without my wall, for a great way every way, as full with stakes or sticks of the osier like wood, which I found so apt to grow, as they could well stand; insomuch, that I believe I might set in near twenty thousand of them, leaving a pretty large space between them and my wall, that I might have room to see an enemy, and they might have no shelter from the young trees if they attempted to approach my outer wall.

Thus in two years' time I had a thick grove and in five or six years' time I had a wood before my dwelling, growing so monstrous thick and strong that it was indeed perfectly impassable; and no men of what kind soever would ever imagine that there was any thing beyond it, much less a habitation. As for the way which I propos'd to myself to go in and out, for I left no avenue, it was by setting two ladders, one to a part of the rock which was low, and then broke in, and left room to place another ladder upon that; so when the two ladders were taken down, no man living could come down to me without mischieving himself; and if they had come down, they were still on the out-side of my outer wall.

Thus I took all the measures human prudence could suggest for my own preservation, and it will be seen at length that they were not altogether without just reason, though I foresaw nothing at that time, more than my meer fear suggested to me.

While this was doing, I was not altogether careless of my other affairs; for I had a great concern upon me for my little herd of goats. They were not only a pleasant supply to me upon every occasion and began to be sufficient to me without the expense of powder and shot, but also without the fatigue of hunting after the wild ones; and I was loath to lose the advantage of them and to have them all to nurse up over again.

To this purpose, after long consideration, I could think of but two ways to preserve them; one was to find another convenient place to dig a cave under-ground and to drive them into it every night; and the other was to enclose two or three little bits of land, remote from one another and as much conceal'd as I could, where I might keep about half a dozen young goats in each place. Then if any disaster happen'd to the flock in general, I might be able to raise them again with little trouble and time, and this, tho' it would require a great deal of time and labour, I thought was the most rational design.

Accordingly I spent some time to find out the most retir'd parts of the island, and I pitch'd upon one which was as private indeed as my heart could wish for. It was a little damp piece of ground in the middle of the hollow and thick woods, where, as is observ'd, I almost lost myself once before, endeavouring to come back that way from the eastern part of the island. Here I found a clear piece of land near three acres, so surrounded with woods that it was almost an enclosure by nature; at least it did not want near so much labour to make it so as the other pieces of ground I had work'd so hard at.

I immediately went to work with this piece of ground, and in less than a month's time I had so fenc'd it round that my flock or herd, call it which you please, who were not so wild now as at first they might be suppos'd to be, were well enough secur'd in it. So, without any further delay, I remov'd ten young she-goats and two he-goats to this piece; and when they were there, I continu'd to perfect the fence till I had made it as secure as the other, which, however, I did at more leisure, and it took me up more time by a great deal.

All this labour I was at the expense of purely from my apprehensions on the account of the print of a man's foot which I had seen. As yet I never saw any human creature come near the island, and I had now liv'd two years under these uneasinesses, which indeed made my life much less comfortable than it was before; as may well be imagin'd by any who know what it is to live in the constant snare of the fear of man. This I must observe with grief too, that the discomposure of my mind had too great impressions also upon the religious part of my thoughts, for the dread and terror of falling into the hands of savages and canibals lay so upon my spirits that I seldom found myself in a due temper for application to my Maker, at least not with the sedate calmness and resignation of soul which I was wont to do. I rather pray'd to God as under great affliction and pressure of mind, surrounded with danger and in expectation every night of being murther'd and devour'd before morning. But I must testify from my experience that a temper of peace, thankfulness, love, and affection is much more the proper frame for prayer than that of terror and discomposure; and that under the dread of mischief impending, a man is no more fit for a comforting performance of the duty of praying to God than he is for repentance on a sick bed. These discomposures affect the mind as the others do the body; and the discomposure of the mind must necessarily be as great a disability as that of the body, and much greater, praying to God being properly an act of the mind, not of the body.

But to go on. After I had thus secur'd one part of my little living stock, I went about the whole island, searching for another private place to make such another deposit; when wand'ring more to the west point of the island than I had ever gone yet, and looking out to sea, I thought I saw a boat upon the sea at a great distance. I had found a perspective-glass or two in one of the seamen's chests which I sav'd out of our ship; but I had it not about me, and this thing was so remote that I could not tell what to make of it, though I look'd at it till my eyes were not able to hold to look any longer. Whether it was a boat or not I do not know; but as I descended from the hill, I could see no more of it, so I gave it over; only I resolv'd to go no more out without a perspective-glass in my pocket.

When I was come down the hill to the end of the island, where indeed I had never been before, I was presently convinc'd that the seeing the print of a man's foot was not such a strange thing in the island as I imagin'd, and but that it was a special providence that I was cast upon the side of the island where the savages never came. I should easily have known that nothing was more frequent than the canoes from the main, when they happen'd to be a little too far out at sea, to shoot over to that side of the island for harbour; likewise as they often met and fought in their canoes, the victors having taken any prisoners would bring them over to this shore where, according to their dreadful customs, being all canibals, they would kill and eat them; of which hereafter.

When I was come down the hill to the shore, as I said above, being the SW point of the island, I was perfectly confounded and amaz'd, nor is it possible for me to express the horror of my mind, at seeing the shore spread with skulls, hands, feet, and other bones of human bodies; and particularly I observ'd a place where there had been a fire made, and a circle dug in the earth, like a cockpit, where it is suppos'd the savage wretches had sat down to their inhuman feastings upon the bodies of their fellow-creatures.

I was so astonish'd with the sight of these things that I entertain'd no notions of any danger to myself from it for a long while. All my apprehensions were bury'd in the thoughts of such a pitch of inhuman, hellish brutality, and the horror of the degeneracy of human nature, which tho' I had heard of often, yet I never had so near a view of before. In short, I turn'd away my face from the horrid spectacle; my stomach grew sick, and I was just at the point of fainting, when nature discharg'd the disorder from my stomach. Having vomited with an uncommon violence, I was a little reliev'd, but could not bear to stay in the place a moment; so I got me up the hill again, with all the speed I could, and walk'd on towards my own habitation.

When I came a little out of that part of the island, I stood still a while as amaz'd; and then recovering myself, I looked up with the utmost affection of my soul and, with a flood of tears in my eyes, gave God thanks that had cast my first lot in a part of the world where I was distinguish'd from such dreadful creatures as these; and that tho' I had esteem'd my present condition very miserable, had yet given me so many comforts in it that I had still more to give thanks for than to complain of; and this above all, that I had even in this miserable condition been comforted with the knowledge of Himself and the hope of His blessing, which was a felicity more than sufficiently equivalent to all the misery which I had suffer'd or could suffer.

In this frame of thankfulness, I went home to my castle, and began to be much easier now as to the safety of my circumstances than ever I was before; for I observ'd that these wretches never came to this island in search of what they could get, perhaps not seeking, not wanting, or not expecting any thing here; and having often, no doubt, been up in the cover'd woody part of it without finding any thing to their purpose. I knew I had been here now almost eighteen years and never saw the least foot-steps of human creature there before; and I might be here eighteen more, as entirely conceal'd as I was now, if I did not discover myself to them, which I had no manner of occasion to do, it being my only business to keep myself entirely conceal'd where I was, unless I found a better sort of creature than canibals to make myself known to.

Yet I entertain'd such an abhorrence of the savage wretches that I have been speaking of, and of the wretched inhuman custom of their devouring and eating one another up, that I continu'd pensive, and sad, and kept close within my own circle for almost two years after this. When I say my own circle, I mean by it, my three plantations, viz., my castle, my country-seat, which I call'd my bower, and my enclosure in the woods. I look'd not after this for any other use than as an enclosure for my goats, for the aversion which nature gave me to these hellish wretches was such that I was fearful of seeing them as of seeing the Devil himself; nor did I so much as go to look after my boat in all this time, but began rather to think of making me another; for I could not think of ever making any more attempts to bring the other boat round the island to me, lest I should meet with some of these creatures at sea, in which, if I had happen'd to have fallen into their hands, I knew what would have been my lot.

Time, however, and the satisfaction I had that I was in

no danger of being discover'd by these people, began to wear off my uneasiness about them, and I began to live just in the same compos'd manner as before, only with this difference: that I used more caution and kept my eyes more about me than I did before, lest I should happen to be seen by any of them; and particularly, I was more cautious of firing my gun, lest any of them being on the island, should happen to hear of it. And it was therefore a very good providence to me that I had furnish'd myself with a tame breed of goats, that I needed not hunt any more about the woods or shoot at them; and if I did catch any of them after this, it was by traps and snares, as I had done before. So that for two years after this, I believe I never fir'd my gun once off, though I never went out without it; and which was more, as I had sav'd three pistols out of the ship, I always carry'd them out with me, or at least two of them, sticking them in my goat-skin belt. Also, I furbish'd up one of the great cutlashes, that I had out of the ship, and made me a belt to put it on also, so that I was now a most formidable fellow to look at when I went abroad, if you add to the former description of myself, the particular of two pistols, and a great broad sword hanging at my side in a belt, but without a scabbard.

Things going on thus, as I have said, for some time, I seem'd, excepting these cautions, to be reduc'd to my former calm, sedate way of living; all these things tended to shew me more and more how far my condition was from being miserable, compar'd to some others; nay, to many other particulars of life, which it might have pleased God to have made my lot. It put me upon reflecting how little repining there would be among mankind, at any condition of life, if people would rather compare their condition with those that are worse, in order to be thankful, than be always comparing them with those which are better, to assist their murmurings and complainings.

As in my present condition there were not really many things which I wanted, so indeed I thought that the frights I had been in about these savage wretches, and the concern I had been in for my own preservation, had taken off the edge of my invention for my own conveniences. I had dropp'd a good design, which I had once bent my thoughts too much upon, and that was to try if I could not make some of my barley into malt, and then try to brew myself some beer. This was really a whimsical thought, and I reprov'd myself often for the simplicity of it, for I presently saw there would be the want of several things necessary to the making my beer that it would be impossible for me to supply; as, first, casks to preserve it in, which was a thing, that as I have observ'd already, I could never compass; no, though I spent not many days, but weeks, nay, months in attempting it, but to no purpose. In the next place, I had no hops to make it keep, no yeast to make it work, no copper or kettle to make it boil; and yet all these things, notwithstanding, I verily believe, had not these things interven'd, I mean the frights and terrors I was in about the savages, I had undertaken it, and perhaps brought it to pass too, for I seldom gave any thing over without accomplishing it when I once had it in my head enough to begin it.

But my invention now ran quite another way; for night and day, I could think of nothing but how I might destroy some of these monsters in their cruel bloody entertainment and, if possible, save the victim they should bring hither to destroy. It would take up a larger volume than this whole work is intended to be to set down all the contrivances I hatch'd, or rather brooded upon in my thought, for the destroying these creatures, or at least frighting them, so as to prevent their coming hither anymore. But all was abortive, nothing could be possible to take effect, unless I was to be there to do it myself; and what could one man do among them, when perhaps there might be twenty or thirty of them together, with their darts, or their bows and arrows, with which they could shoot as true to a mark as I could with my gun?

Sometimes I contriv'd to dig a hole under the place where they made their fire and put in five or six pound of gun-powder, which when they kindl'd their fire, would consequently take fire, and blow up all that was near it. But, as in the first place I should be very loath to waste so much powder upon them, my store being now within the quantity of one barrel, so neither could I be sure of its going off, at any certain time, when it might surprize them, and at best, that it would do little more than just blow the fire about their ears and fright them, but not sufficient to make them forsake the place; so I lay'd it aside and then propos'd that I would place myself in ambush, in some convenient place, with my three guns all double loaded, and in the middle of their bloody ceremony, let fly at them, when I should be sure to kill or wound perhaps two or three at every shot; and then falling in upon them with my three pistols, and my sword, I made no doubt but that if there were twenty I should kill them all. This fancy pleas'd my thoughts for some weeks, and I was so full of it that I often dream'd of it; and sometimes that I was just going to let fly at them in my sleep.

I went so far with it, in my imagination, that I employ'd

myself several days to find out proper places to put myself in ambuscade, as I said, to watch for them; and I went frequently to the place itself, which was now grown more familiar to me; and especially while my mind was thus fill'd with thoughts of revenge, and of a bloody putting twenty or thirty of them to the sword, as I may call it; the horror I had at the place, and at the signals of the barbarous wretches devouring one another, abated my malice.

Well, at length I found a place in the side of the hill where I was satisfy'd I might securely wait till I saw any of their boats coming, and might then, even before they would be ready to come on shore, convey myself unseen into thickets of trees, in one of which there was a hollow large enough to conceal me entirely. Here I might sit, and observe all their bloody doings, and take my full aim at their heads, when they were so close together as that it would be next to impossible that I should miss my shot or that I could fail wounding three or four of them at the first shot.

In this place then I resolv'd to fix my design, and accordingly I prepar'd two musquets and my ordinary fowling-piece. The two musquets I loaded with a brace of slugs each, and four or five smaller bullets, about the size of pistol bullets; and the fowling-piece I loaded with near a handful of swan-shot, of the largest size. I also loaded my pistols with about four bullets each, and in this posture, well provided with ammunition for a second and third charge, I prepar'd myself for my expedition.

After I had thus lay'd the scheme of my design and in my imagination put it in practise, I continually made my tour every morning up to the top of the hill, which was from my castle, as I call'd it, about three miles, or more, to see if I could observe any boats upon the sea, coming near the island or standing over towards it; but I began to tire of this hard duty after I had for two or three months constantly kept my watch, but came always back without any discovery, there having not in all that time been the least appearance, not only on, or near the shore; but not on the whole ocean, so far as my eyes or glasses could reach every way.

As long as I kept up my daily tour to the hill to look out, so long also I kept up the vigour of my design, and my spirits seem'd to be all the while in a suitable form, for so outrageous an execution as the killing twenty or thirty naked savages, for an offence which I had not at all enter'd into a discussion of in my thoughts, any further than my passions were at first fir'd by the horror I conceiv'd at the unnatural custom of that people of the country, who it seems had been suffer'd by Providence in His wise disposition of the world, to have no other guide than that of their own abominable and vitiated passions; and consequently were left, and perhaps had been so for some ages, to act such horrid things, and receive such dreadful customs, as nothing but nature entirely abandon'd of Heaven, and acted by some hellish degeneracy, could have run them into. But now, when as I have said, I began to be weary of the fruitless excursion which I had made so long, and so far, every morning in vain, so my opinion of the action itself began to alter, and I began with cooler and calmer thoughts to consider what it was I was going to engage in. What authority or call had I to pretend to be judge and executioner upon these men as criminals, whom Heaven had thought fit for so many ages to suffer unpunish'd, to go on, and to be as it were, the executioners of His judgments one upon another? How far were these people offenders against me, and what right had I to engage in the quarrel of that blood, which they shed promiscuously one upon another? I debated this very often with myself thus: How do I know what God Himself judges in this particular case; it is certain these people either do not commit this as a crime; it is not against their own consciences reproving, or their light reproaching them. They do not know it be an offence, and then commit it in defiance of divine justice, as we do in almost all the sins we commit. They think it no more a crime to kill a captive taken in war than we do to kill an ox; nor to eat human flesh than we do to eat mutton.

When I had consider'd this a little, it follow'd necessarily that I was certainly in the wrong in it; that these people were not murtherers in the sense that I had before condemn'd them in my thoughts, any more than those Christians were murtherers, who often put to death the prisoners taken in battle; or more frequently, upon many occasions, put whole troops of men to the sword, without giving quarter, tho' they threw down their arms and submitted.

In the next place it occurr'd to me, that albeit the usage they thus gave one another was thus brutish and inhuman, yet it was really nothing to me. These people had done me no injury. That if they attempted me, or I saw it necessary for my immediate preservation to fall upon them, something might be said for it; but that as I was yet out of their power, and they had really no knowledge of me, and consequently no design upon me; and therefore it could not be just for me to fall upon them. That this would justify the conduct of the Spaniards in all their barbarities practis'd in America, and where they destroy'd millions of these people, who however they were idolaters and barbarians, and had several bloody and barbarous rites in their customs, such as sacrificing human bodies to their idols, were yet, as to the Spaniards, very innocent people; and that the rooting them out of the country is spoken of with the utmost abhorrence and detestation by even the Spaniards themselves at this time; and by all other Christian nations of Europe, as a meer butchery, a bloody and unnatural piece of cruelty, unjustifiable either to God or man; and such, as for which the very name of a Spaniard is reckon'd to be frightful and terrible to all people of humanity, or of Christian compassion; as if the kingdom of Spain were particularly eminent for the product of a race of men who were without principles of tenderness or the common bowels of pity to the miserable, which is reckon'd to be a mark of generous temper in the mind.

These considerations really put me to a pause and to a kind of a full-stop; and I began by little and little to be off of my design and to conclude I had taken wrong measures in my resolutions to attack the savages; that it was not my business to meddle with them unless they first attack'd me, and this it was my business if possible to prevent; but that if I were discover'd, and attack'd, then I knew my duty.

On the other hand, I argu'd with myself that this really was the way not to deliver myself, but entirely to ruine and destroy myself; for unless I was sure to kill every one that not only should be on shore at that time, but that should ever come on shore afterwards, if but one of them escap'd to tell their country people what had happen'd, they would come over again by thousands to revenge the death of their fellows, and I should only bring upon myself a certain destruction, which at present I had no manner of occasion for.

Upon the whole I concluded that neither in principle or in policy, I ought one way or other to concern myself in this affair; that my business was by all possible means to conceal myself from them and not to leave the least signal to them to guess by that there were any living creatures upon the island, I mean of human shape.

Religion join'd in with this prudential, and I was convinc'd now many ways that I was perfectly out of my duty when I was laying all my bloody schemes for the destruction of innocent creatures, I mean innocent as to me. As to the crimes they were guilty of towards one another, I had nothing to do with them; they were national, and I ought to leave them to the justice of God, who is the Governour of nations and knows how by national punishments to make a just retribution for national offences, and to bring publick judgments upon those who offend in a publick manner, by such ways as best pleases Him.

This appear'd so clear to me now that nothing was a greater satisfaction to me than that I had not been suffer'd to do a thing which I now saw so much reason to believe would have been no less a sin, than that of willful murther, if I had committed it. And I gave most humble thanks on my knees to God that had thus deliver'd me from bloodguiltiness, beseeching Him to grant me the protection of His providence, that I might not fall into the hands of the barbarians; or that I might not lay my hands upon them, unless I had a more clear call from Heaven to do it in defence of my own life.

In this disposition I continu'd for near a year after this;

and so far was I from desiring an occasion for falling upon these wretches that in all that time I never once went up the hill to see whether there were any of them in sight or to know whether any of them had been on shore there, or not, that I might not be tempted to renew any of my contrivances against them or be provok'd by any advantage which might present itself to fall upon them. Only this I did: I went and remov'd my boat, which I had on the other side of island, and carry'd it down to the east end of the whole island, where I ran it into a little cove which I found under some high rocks, and where I knew, by reason of the currents, the savages durst not, at least would not come with their boats upon any account whatsoever.

With my boat I carry'd away every thing that I had left there belonging to her, though not necessary for the bare going thither, viz., a mast and a sail which I had made for her and a thing like an anchor, but indeed which could not be call'd either anchor or grapling; however, it was the best I could make of its kind. All these I remov'd that there might not be the least shadow of any discovery, or any appearance of any boat, or of any human habitation upon the island.

Besides this, I kept myself, as I said, more retir'd than ever, and seldom went from my cell, other than upon my constant employment, viz., to milk my she-goats and manage my little flock in the wood, which, as it was quite on the other part of the island, was quite out of danger; for certain it is, that these savage people who sometimes haunted this island never came with any thoughts of finding any thing here; and consequently never wander'd off from the coast; and I doubt not, but they might have been several times on shore, after my apprehensions of them had made me cautious as well as before; and indeed, I look'd back with some horror upon the thoughts of what my condition would have been, if I had chop'd upon them, and been discover'd before that, when naked and unarm'd, except with one gun, and that loaden often only with small-shot, I walk'd everywhere, peeping and peeping about the island to see what I could get; what a surprize should I have been in, if when I discover'd the print of a man's foot, I had instead of that, seen fifteen or twenty savages, and found them pursuing me, and by the swiftness of their running, no possibility of my escaping them.

The thoughts of this sometimes sunk my very soul within me and distress'd my mind so much that I could not soon recover it to think what I should have done, and how I not only should not have been able to resist them, but even should not have had presence of mind enough to do what I might have done; much less, what now after so much consideration and preparation I might be able to do. Indeed, after serious thinking of these things, I should be very melancholy, and sometimes it would last a great while. But I resolv'd it at last all into thankfulness to that Providence which had deliver'd me from so many unseen dangers and had kept me from those mischiefs which I could no way have been the agent in delivering myself from, because I had not the least notion of any such thing depending, or the least supposition of it being possible.

This renew'd a contemplation, which often had come to my thoughts in former time when first I began to see the merciful disposition of Heaven in the dangers we run through in this life. How wonderfully we are deliver'd, when we know nothing of it. How when we are in a quandary, as we call it, a doubt or hesitation whether to go this way or that way, a secret hint shall direct us this way when we intended to go that way; nay, when sense, our own inclination, and perhaps business has call'd us to go the other way, yet a strange impression upon the mind, from we know not what springs, and by we know not what power, shall overrule us to go this way; and it shall afterwards appear that, had we gone that way which we should have gone, and even to our imagination ought to have gone, we should have been ruin'd and lost. Upon these and many like reflections, I afterwards made it a certain rule with me that whenever I found those secret hints or pressings of my mind to doing or not doing any thing that presented, or to going this way or that way, I never fail'd to obey the secret dictate; though I knew no other reason for it, than that such a pressure or such a hint hung upon my mind. I could give many examples of the success of this conduct in the course of my life; but more especially in the latter part of my inhabiting this unhappy island; besides many occasions which it is very likely I might have taken notice of, if I had seen with the same eyes then that I saw with now. But 'tis never too late to be wise, and I cannot but advise all considering men, whose lives are attended with such extraordinary incidents as mine, or even though not so extraordinary, not to slight such secret intimations of Providence; let them come from what invisible intelligence they will, that I shall not discuss, and perhaps cannot account for; but certainly they are a proof of the converse of spirits and of the secret communication between those embody'd and those unembody'd; and such a proof can never be withstood, of which I shall have occasion to give some very remarkable instances in the remainder of my solitary residence in this dismal place.

I believe the reader of this will not think it strange if I confess that these anxieties, these constant dangers I liv'd in, and the concern that was now upon me, put an end to all invention and to all the contrivances that I had lay'd for my future accommodations and conveniencies. I had the care of my safety more now upon my hands than that of my food. I car'd not to drive a nail, or chop a stick of wood now, for fear the noise I should make should be heard; much less would I fire a gun, for the same reason; and above all, I was intolerably uneasy at making any fire, lest the smoke which is visible at a great distance in the day should betray me. For this reason I remov'd that part of my business which requir'd fire, such as burning of pots and pipes, &c. into my new appartment in the woods where, after I had been some time, I found to my unspeakable consolation a meer natural cave in the earth, which went in a vast way, and where, I dare say, no savage, had he been at the mouth of it, would be so hardy as to venture in, nor indeed, would any man else; but one who like me wanted nothing so much as safe retreat.

The mouth of this hollow was at the bottom of a great rock, where by meer accident (I would say, if I did not see abundant reason to ascribe all such things now to Providence) I was cutting down some thick branches of trees to make charcoal. But before I go on, I must observe the reason of my making this charcoal, which was thus.

I was afraid of making a smoke about my habitation, as I said before; and yet I could not live there without baking my bread, cooking my meat, &c. So I contriv'd to burn some wood here, as I had seen done in England, under turf, till it became chark, or dry coal; and then putting the fire out, I preserv'd the coal to carry home, and perform the other services which fire was wanting for at home without danger of smoke.

But this is by the by. While I was cutting down some wood here, I perceiv'd that behind a very thick branch of low brushwood, or under wood, there was a kind of hollow place. I was curious to look into it and, getting with difficulty into the mouth of it, I found it was pretty large, that is to say, sufficient for me to stand upright in it, and perhaps another with me. But I must confess to you, I made more haste out than I did in when, looking farther into the place, and which was perfectly dark, I saw two broad shining eyes of some creature, whether Devil or man I knew not, which twinkl'd like two stars, the dim light from the cave's mouth shining directly in and making the reflection.

However, after some pause, I recover'd myself, and began to call myself a thousand fools and tell myself that he that was afraid to see the Devil was not fit to live twenty years in an island all alone; and that I durst to believe there was nothing in this cave that was more frightful than myself. Upon this, plucking up my courage, I took up a great firebrand and in I rush'd again, with the stick flaming in my hand. I had not gone three steps in, but I was almost as much frighted as I was before, for I heard a very loud sigh, like that of a man in some pain, and it was follow'd by a broken noise, as if of words half express'd, and then a deep sigh again. I stepp'd back, and was indeed struck with such a surprize that it put me into a cold sweat; and if I had had a hat on my head, I will not answer for it, that my hair might not have lifted it off. But still plucking up my spirits as well as I could, and encouraging myself a little with considering that the power and presence of God was everywhere, and was able to protect me; upon this

I stepp'd forward again, and by the light of the firebrand, holding it up a little over my head, I saw lying on the ground a most monstrous frightful old he-goat, just making his will, as we say, and gasping for life, and dying indeed of meer old age.

I stirr'd him a little to see if I could get him out, and he essay'd to get up, but was not able to rize himself; and I thought with myself, he might even lie there; for if he had frighted me so, he would certainly fright any of the savages, if any of them should be so hardy as to come in there while he had any life in him.

I was now recover'd from my surprize and began to look round me, when I found the cave was but very small, that is to say, it might be about twelve foot over, but in no manner of shape either round or square, no hands having ever been employ'd in making it, but those of meer nature. I observ'd also that there was a place at the farther side of it that went in farther, but was so low that it requir'd me to creep upon my hands and knees to go into it, and whither I went I knew not. So having no candle, I gave it over for some time, but resolv'd to come again the next day, provided with candles, and a tinder-box, which I had made of the lock of one of the musquets, with some wild-fire in the pan.

Accordingly the next day, I came provided with six large candles of my own making, for I made very good candles now of goat's-tallow. Going into this low place, I was oblig'd to creep upon all fours, as I have said, almost ten yards; which by the way, I thought was a venture bold enough, considering that I knew not how far it might go nor what was beyond it. When I was got through the strait, I found the roof riz'd higher up, I believe near twenty foot, but never was such a glorious sight seen on the island, I dare say, as it was to look round the sides and roof of this vault or cave. The walls reflected a hundred thousand lights to me from my two candles; what it was in rock, whether diamonds, or any other precious stones, or gold, which I rather suppos'd it to be, I knew not.

The place I was in was a most delightful cavity, or grotto, of its kind, as could be expected, though perfectly dark; the floor was dry and level, and had a sort of small loose gravel upon it, so that there was no nauseous or venemous creature to be seen, neither was there any damp, or wet, on the sides or roof. The only difficulty in it was the entrance, which however, as it was a place of security and such a retreat as I wanted, I thought that was a convenience; so that I was really rejoyc'd at the discovery and resolv'd without any delay to bring some of those things which I was most anxious about to this place; particularly, I resolv'd to bring hither my magazine of powder and all my spare arms, viz., two fowling-pieces, for I had three in all; and three musquets, for of them I had eight in all; so I kept at my castle only five, which stood ready mounted like pieces of cannon on my out-most fence, and were ready also to take out upon any expedition.

Upon this occasion of removing my ammunition, I took occasion to open the barrel of powder which I took up out of the sea and which had been wet; and I found that the water had penetrated about three or four inches into the powder on every side, which, caking and growing hard, had preserv'd the in-side like a kernel in a shell; so that I had near sixty pound of very good powder in the center of the cask, and this was an agreeable discovery to me at that time. So I carry'd all away thither, never keeping above two or three pound of powder with me in my castle, for fear of a surprize of any kind. I also carry'd thither all the lead I had left for bullets.

I fancy'd myself now like one of the ancient giants, which are said to live in caves, and holes, in the rocks, where none could come at them; for I persuaded myself while I was here, if five hundred savages were to hunt me, they would never find me out; or if they did, they would not venture to attack me here.

The old goat who I found expiring, dy'd in the mouth of the cave the next day after I made this discovery; and I found it much easier to dig a great hole there, and throw him in, and cover him with earth, than to drag him out; so I interr'd him there, to prevent the offence to my nose.

I was now in my twenty-third year of residence on this island and was so naturaliz'd to the place, and to the manner of living, that could I have but enjoy'd the certainty that no savages would come to the place to disturb me, I could have been content to have capitulated for spending the rest of my time there, even to the last moment, till I had lay'd me down and dy'd, like the old goat in the cave. I had also arriv'd to some little diversions and amusements, which made the time pass more pleasantly with me a great deal than it did before. First, I had taught my Poll, as I noted before, to speak; and he did it so familiarly, and talk'd so articulately and plain, that it was very pleasant to me; and he liv'd with me no less than six-and-twenty years. How long he might have liv'd afterwards, I know not; though I know they have a notion in the Brasils that they live a hundred years; perhaps poor Poll may be alive there still, calling after Poor Robin Crusoe to this day. I wish no Englishman the ill luck to come there and hear him; but if he did, he would certainly believe it was the Devil. My dog was a very pleasant and loving companion to me, for no less than sixteen years of my time, and then dy'd of meer old age; as for my cats, they multiply'd, as I have observ'd, to that degree that I was oblig'd to shoot several of them at first, to keep them from devouring me and all I had; but at length, when the two old ones I had brought with me were gone, and after some time continually driving them from me and letting them have no provision with me, they all ran wild into the woods, except two or three favourites, which I kept tame; and whose young when they had any, I always drown'd; and these were part of my family. Besides these, I always kept two or three household kids about me, who I taught to feed out of my hand; and I had two more parrots which talk'd pretty well and would all call Robin Crusoe; but none like my first; nor indeed did I take the pains with any of them that I had done with him. I had also several tame sea-fowls, whose names I know not, who I caught upon the shore, and cut their wings; and the little stakes which I had planted before my castle wall being now grown up to a good thick grove, these fowls all liv'd among these low trees and bred there, which was very agreeable to me. So that as I said above, I began to be very well contented with the life I led, if it might but have been secur'd from the dread of the savages.

But it was otherwise directed; and it may not be amiss for all people who shall meet with my story to make this just observation from it, viz., how frequently in the course of our lives the evil which in itself we seek most to shun and which, when we are fallen into it, is the most dreadful to us, is oftentimes the very means or door of our deliverance, by which alone we can be riz'd again from the afflic-

*Here I observ'd, by the help of my perspective-glass, that they
were all dancing in I know not how many barbarous gestures
and figures, their own way, round the fire.* (page 232)

tion we are fallen into. I could give many examples of this in the course of my unaccountable life, but in nothing was it more particularly remarkable than in the circumstances of my last years of solitary residence in this island.

It was now the month of December, as I said above, in my twenty-third year. This being the southern solstice, for winter I cannot call it, it was the particular time of my harvest and requir'd my being pretty much abroad in the fields; but going out pretty early one morning, even before it was thorow daylight, I was surpriz'd with seeing a light of some fire upon the shore, at a distance from me of about two mile towards the end of the island where I had observ'd some savages had been as before, but not on the other side; but to my great affliction, it was on my side of the island.

I was indeed terribly surpriz'd at the sight and stepp'd short within my grove, not daring to go out, lest I might be surpriz'd. Yet I had no more peace within, from the apprehensions I had that if these savages, in rambling over the island, should find my corn standing, or cut, or any of my works and improvements, they would immediately conclude that there were people in the place, and would then never give over till they had found me out. In this extremity I went back directly to my castle, pull'd up the ladder after me, and made all things without look as wild and natural as I could.

Then I prepar'd myself within, putting myself in a posture of defence. I loaded all my cannon, as I call'd them, that is to say, my musquets, which were mounted upon my new fortification, and all my pistols, and resolv'd to defend myself to the last gasp, not forgetting seriously to commend myself to the divine protection, and earnestly to pray to

God to deliver me out of the hands of the barbarians. In this posture I continu'd about two hours, but began to be mighty impatient for intelligence abroad, for I had no spys to send out.

After sitting awhile longer and musing what I should do in this case, I was not able to bear sitting in ignorance any longer; so setting up my ladder to the side of the hill, where there was a flat place, as I observ'd before, and then pulling the ladder up after me, I set it up again and mounted to the top of the hill. Pulling out my perspective-glass, which I had taken on purpose, I lay'd me down flat on my belly, on the ground, and began to look for the place; I presently found there was no less than nine naked savages sitting round a small fire they had made, not to warm them, for they had no need of that, the weather being extreme hot, but as I suppos'd, to dress some of their barbarous diet of human flesh, which they had brought with them, whether alive or dead I could not know.

They had two canoes with them, which they had hal'd up upon the shore; and as it was then tide of ebb, they seem'd to me to wait for the return of the flood, to go away again. It is not easy to imagine what confusion this sight put me into, especially seeing them come on my side the island, and so near me too. But when I observ'd their coming must be always with the current of the ebb, I began afterwards to be more sedate in my mind, being satisfy'd that I might go abroad with safety all the time of the tide of flood, if they were not on shore before. Having made this observation, I went abroad about my harvest work with the more composure.

As I expected, so it proved; for as soon as the tide made to the westward, I saw them all take boat and row (or paddle as we call it) all away. I should have observ'd that for an hour and more before they went off, they went to dancing, and I could easily discern their postures and gestures by my glasses. I could not perceive by my nicest observation, but that they were stark-naked and had not the least covering upon them; but whether they were men or women, that I could not distinguish.

As soon as I saw them shipp'd and gone, I took two guns upon my shoulders, and two pistols at my girdle, and my great sword by my side, without a scabbard, and with all the speed I was able to make, I went away to the hill, where I had discover'd the first appearance of all. I got thither not less than two hours later, for I could not go a-pace, being so loaden with arms as I was. I perceiv'd there had been three canoes more of savages on that place; and looking out farther, I saw they were all at sea together, making over for the main.

This was a dreadful sight to me, especially when going down to the shore, I could see the marks of horror, which the dismal work they had been about had left behind it, viz., the blood, the bones, and part of the flesh of human bodies, eaten and devour'd by those wretches, with merriment and sport. I was so fill'd with indignation at the sight that I began now to premeditate the destruction of the next that I saw there, let them be who or how many soever.

It seem'd evident to me that the visits which they thus made to this island were not very frequent, for it was above fifteen months before any more of them came on shore there again; that is to say, I neither saw them, or any footsteps, or signals of them, in all that time; for as to the rainy seasons, then they were sure not to come abroad, at least not so far. Yet all this while I liv'd uncomfortably by reason of the constant apprehensions I was in of their coming upon me by surprize; whence I observ'd, that the expectation of evil is more bitter than the suffering, especially if there is no room to shake off that expectation or those apprehensions.

During all this time I was in the murthering humour and took up most of my hours, which should have been better employ'd, in contriving how to circumvent and fall upon them the very next time I should see them; especially if they should be divided, as they were the last time, into two parties. Nor did I consider at all that if I kill'd one party, suppose ten, or a dozen, I was still the next day, or week, or month, to kill another, and so another, even *ad infinitum*, till I should be at length no less a murtherer than they were in being man-eaters, and perhaps much more so.

I spent my days now in great perplexity and anxiety of mind, expecting that I should one day or other fall into the hands of these merciless creatures; and if I did at any time venture abroad, it was not without looking round me with the greatest care and caution imaginable. Now I found to my great comfort, how happy it was that I provided for a tame flock or herd of goats; for I durst not upon any account fire my gun, especially near that side of the island where they usually came, lest I should alarm the savages; and if they had fled from me now, I was sure to have them come back again, with perhaps two or three hundred canoes with them, in a few days, and then I knew what to expect.

However, I wore out a year and three months more before I ever saw any more of the savages, and then I found them again, as I shall soon observe. It is true, they might have been there once or twice, but either they made no stay, or at least I did not hear them. But in the month of May, as near as I could calculate, and in my four-and-twentieth year, I had a very strange encounter with them, of which in its place.

The perturbation of my mind, during this fifteen or sixteen months' interval, was very great; I slept unquiet, dream'd always frightful dreams, and often started out of my sleep in the night. In the day great troubles overwhelm'd my mind, and in the night I dream'd often of killing the savages and of the reasons why I might justify the doing of it. But to wave all this for a while. It was in the middle of May, on the 16th day I think, as well as my poor wooden kalender would reckon, for I mark'd all upon the post still; I say, it was the 16th of May, that it blew a very great storm of wind, all day, with a great deal of lightning and thunder, and a very foul night it was after it; I know not what was the particular occasion of it, but as I was reading in the Bible and taken up with very serious thoughts about my present condition, I was surpriz'd with a noise of a gun as I thought fir'd at sea.

This was to be sure a surprize of a quite different nature from any I had met with before, for the notions this put into my thoughts were quite of another kind. I started up in the greatest haste imaginable and in a trice clapp'd my ladder to the middle place of the rock, and pull'd it after me and, mounting it the second time, got to the top of the hill the very moment that a flash of fire bid me listen for a second gun, which accordingly, in about half a minute I heard; and by the sound, knew that it was from that part of the sea where I was driven down the current in my boat.

I immediately consider'd that this must be some ship

in distress and that they had some comrade or some other ship in company, and fir'd these guns for signals of distress and to obtain help. I had this presence of mind at that minute, as to think, that tho' I could not help them, it may be they might help me; so I brought together all the dry wood I could get at hand and, making a good handsome pile, I set it on fire upon the hill. The wood was dry and blaz'd freely, and tho' the wind blew very hard, yet it burnt fairly out; that I was certain, if there was any such thing as a ship, they must needs see it, and no doubt they did, for as soon as ever my fire blaz'd up, I heard another gun, and after that several others, all from the same quarter. I ply'd my fire all night long, till day broke; and when it was broad day, and the air clear'd up, I saw something at a great distance at sea, full east of the island, whether a sail or a hull I could not distinguish; no, not with my glasses, the distance was so great, and the weather still something hazey also, at least it was so out at sea.

I look'd frequently at it all that day and soon perceiv'd that it did not move; so I presently concluded that it was a ship at anchor, and being eager, you may be sure, to be satisfy'd, I took my gun in my hand and ran towards the south side of the island to the rocks where I had formerly been carry'd away with the current, and getting up there, the weather by this time being perfectly clear, I could plainly see to my great sorrow the wreck of a ship, cast away in the night upon those conceal'd rocks which I found when I was out in my boat; and which rocks, as they check'd the violence of the stream and made a kind of counter-stream or eddy, were the occasion of my recovering from the most desperate hopeless condition that ever I had been in in all my life.

Thus what is one man's safety is another man's destruction; for it seems these men, whoever they were, being out of their knowledge, and the rocks being wholly under water, had been driven upon them in the night, the wind blowing hard at E and ENE. Had they seen the island, as I must necessarily suppose they had not, they must, as I thought, have endeavour'd to have sav'd themselves on shore by the help of their boat; but their firing of guns for help, especially when they saw, as I imagin'd, my fire, fill'd me with many thoughts. First, I imagin'd that upon seeing my light, they might have put themselves into their boat and have endeavour'd to make the shore, but that the sea going very high, they might have been cast away; other times I imagin'd that they might have lost their boat before, as might be the case many ways; as particularly by the breaking of the sea upon their ship, which many times obliges men to stave or take in pieces their boat, and sometimes to throw it overboard with their own hands. Other times I imagin'd they had some other ship, or ships in company, who upon the signals of distress they had made, had taken them up and carry'd them off. Other whiles I fancy'd they were all gone off to sea in their boat and, being hurry'd away by the current that I had been formerly in, were carry'd out into the great ocean, where there was nothing but misery and perishing; and that perhaps they might by this time think of starving and of being in a condition to eat one another.

As all these were but conjectures at best, so in the condition I was in I could do no more than look on upon the misery of the poor men and pity them, which had still this good effect on my side that it gave me more and more cause to give thanks to God, who had so happily and comfortably provided for me in my desolate condition; and that of two ships' companies who were now cast away upon this part of the world, not one life should be spar'd but mine. I learn'd here again to observe that it is very rare that the providence of God casts us into any condition of life so low, or any misery so great, but we may see some thing or other to be thankful for; and may see others in worse circumstances than our own.

Such certainly was the case of these men, of whom I could not so much as see room to suppose any of them were sav'd; nothing could make it rational, so much as to wish or expect that they did not all perish there; except the possibility only of their being taken up by another ship in company, and this was but meer possibility indeed, for I saw not the least signal or appearance of any such thing.

I cannot explain by any possible energy of words what a strange longing or hankering of desires I felt in my soul upon this sight, breaking out sometimes thus, "O, that there had been but one or two; nay, or but one soul sav'd out of this ship, to have escap'd to me, that I might but have had one companion, one fellow-creature to have spoken to me, and to have convers'd with!" In all the time of my solitary life, I never felt so earnest, so strong a desire after the society of my fellow-creatures, or so deep a regret at the want of it.

There are some secret moving springs in the affections which, when they are set a-going by some object in view, or be it some object, though not in view, yet render'd present to the mind by the power of imagination, that motion carrys out the soul by its impetuosity to such violent eager embracings of the object, that the absence of it is insupportable.

Such were these earnest wishings that but one man had been sav'd! "O that it had been but one!" I believe I repeated the words, "O that it had been but one!" a thousand times; and the desires were so mov'd by it that, when I spoke the words, my hands would clinch together and my fingers press the palms of my hands, that if I had had any soft thing in my hand, it would have crush'd it involuntarily; and my teeth in my head would strike together and set against one another so strong that for some time I could not part with them again.

Let the naturalists explain these things and the reason and manner of them; all I can say to them is to describe the fact, which was even surprizing to me when I found it, though I knew not from what it should proceed. It was doubtless the effect of ardent wishes and of strong ideas form'd in my mind, realizing the comfort which the conversation of one of my fellow-Christians would have been to me.

But it was not to be; either their fate or mine, or both, forbid it; for till the last year of my being on this island, I never knew whether any were sav'd out of that ship or no; and had only the affliction some days after, to see the corpse of a drown'd boy come on shore at the end of the island which was next the shipwreck. He had on no cloaths but a seaman's waistcoat, a pair of open-knee'd linnen drawers, and a blue linnen shirt; but nothing to direct me so much as to guess what nation he was of. He had nothing in his pocket but two pieces of eight and a tobacco-pipe; the last was to me of ten times more value than the first.

It was now calm, and I had a great mind to venture out in my boat to this wreck, not doubting but I might find some thing on board that might be useful to me. But that did not altogether press me so much as the possibility that there might be yet some living creature on board, whose life I might not only save, but might by saving that life comfort my own to the last degree. This thought clung so to my heart that I could not be quiet, night or day, but I must venture out in my boat on board this wreck; and committing the rest to God's providence, I thought the impression was so strong upon my mind, that it could not be resisted, that it must come from some invisible direction, and that I should be wanting to myself if I did not go.

Under the power of this impression, I hasten'd back to my castle, prepar'd every thing for my voyage, took a quantity of bread, a great pot for fresh water, a compass to steer by, a bottle of rum (for I had still a great deal of that left), and a basketful of raisins. Thus loading myself with every thing necessary, I went down to my boat, got the water out of her, and got her a-float; loaded all my cargo in her, and then went home again for more. My second cargo was a great bagful of rice; the umbrella to set up over my head for shade; another large potful of fresh water; and about two dozen of my small loaves or barley cakes, more than before; with a bottle of goat's-milk, and a cheese. All which, with great labour and sweat, I brought to my boat; and praying to God to direct my voyage, I put out. Rowing or paddling the canoe along the shore, I came at last to the utmost point of the island on that side, viz., NE. And now I was to launch out into the ocean, and either to venture or not to venture. I look'd on the rapid currents which ran constantly on both sides of the island, at a distance, and which were very terrible to me, from the remembrance of the hazard I had been in before, and my heart began to fail me; for I foresaw that if I was driven into either of those currents, I should be carry'd a vast way out to sea and perhaps out of my reach or sight of the island again; and that then, as my boat was but small, if any little gale of wind should rize, I should be inevitably lost.

These thoughts so oppress'd my mind, that I began to give over my enterprize and, having hal'd my boat into a little creek on the shore, I stepp'd out and sat me down upon a little rizing bit of ground, very pensive and anxious, between fear and desire about my voyage. While as I was musing, I could perceive that the tide was turn'd, and the flood come on, upon which my going was for so many hours impracticable. Upon this presently it occurr'd to me that I should go up to the highest piece of ground I could find, and observe, if I could, how the sets of the tide, or currents lay, when the flood came in, that I might judge whether if I was driven one way out, I might not expect to be driven another way home, with the same rapidness of the currents. This thought was no sooner in my head, but I cast my eye upon a little hill, which sufficiently overlook'd the sea both ways, and from whence I had a clear view of the currents, or sets of the tide, and which way I was to guide myself on my return. Here I found that as the current of the ebb set out close by the south point of the island, so the current of the flood set in close by the shore of the north side, and that I had nothing to do but to keep to the north of the island on my return, and I should do well enough.

Encourag'd with this observation, I resolv'd the next morning to set out with the first of the tide; and reposing myself for the night in the canoe, under the great watch-coat I mention'd, I launched out. I made first a little out to sea full north, till I began to feel the benefit of the current, which set eastward and which carry'd me at a great rate, and yet did not so hurry me as the southern side current had done before, and so as to take from me all government of the boat; but having a strong steerage with my paddle, I went at a great rate directly for the wreck, and in less than two hours I came up to it.

It was a dismal sight to look at. The ship, which by its building was Spanish, stuck fast, jaum'd in between two rocks. All the stern and quarter of her was beaten to pieces with the sea; and as her forecastle, which stuck in the rocks, had run on with great violence, her mainmast and foremast were brought by the board; that is to say, broken short off; but her boltsprit was sound, and the head and bow appear'd firm. When I came close to her, a dog appear'd upon her who, seeing me coming yelp'd and cry'd, and as soon as I call'd him, jump'd into the sea to come to me, and I took him into the boat, but found him almost dead for hunger and thirst. I gave him a cake of my bread, and he ate it like a ravenous wolf that had been starving a fortnight in the snow. I then gave the poor creature some fresh water, with which, if I would have let him, he would have burst himself.

After this I went on board; but the first sight I met with was two men drown'd in the cook-room, or forecastle of the ship, with their arms fast about one another. I concluded, as is indeed probable, that when the ship struck, it being in a storm, the sea broke so high and so continually over her that the men were not able to bear it and were strangl'd with the constant rushing in of the water, as much as if they had been under water. Besides the dog, there was nothing left in the ship that had life; nor any goods that I could see, but what were spoil'd by the water. There were some casks of liquor, whether wine or brandy, I knew not, which lay lower in the hold and which, the water being ebb'd out, I could see; but they were too big to meddle with. I saw several chests, which I believ'd belong'd to some of the seamen; and I got two of them into the boat, without examining what was in them.

Had the stern of the ship been fix'd and the forepart broken off, I am persuaded I might have made a good voyage; for by what I found in these two chests, I had room to suppose the ship had a great deal of wealth on board; and if I may guess by the course she steer'd, she must have been bound from the Buenos Ayres, or the Rio de la Plata, in the south part of America, beyond the Brasils, to the Havana in the Gulph of Mexico, and so perhaps to Spain. She had no doubt a great treasure in her, but of no use at that time to any body; and what became of the rest of her people, I then knew not.

I found besides these chests a little cask full of liquor of about twenty gallons, which I got into my boat with much difficulty; there were several musquets in a cabbin, and a great powder-horn, with about four pounds of powder in it; as for the musquets, I had no occasion for them; so I left them, but took the powder-horn. I took a fire-shovel and tongs, which I wanted extremely; as also two little brass kettles, a copper pot to make chocolate, and a gridiron. With this cargo, and the dog, I came away, the tide beginning to make home again; and the same evening, about an hour within night, I reach'd the island again, weary and fatigu'd to the last degree.

I repos'd that night in the boat, and in the morning I

resolv'd to harbour what I had gotten in my new cave, not to carry it home to my castle. After refreshing myself, I got all my cargo on shore and began to examine the particulars. The cask of liquor I found to be a kind of rum, but not such as we had in the Brasils and, in a word, not at all good. But when I came to open the chests, I found several things of great use to me. For example, I found in one a fine case of bottles of an extraordinary kind and fill'd with cordial waters, fine, and very good. The bottles held about three pints each and were tipp'd with silver. I found two pots of very good succades, or sweet-meats, so fasten'd also on top that the salt water had not hurt them; and two more of the same, which the water had spoil'd. I found some very good shirts, which were very welcome to me; and about a dozen and a half of linnen white handkerchiefs and colour'd neckcloths; the former were also very welcome, being exceeding refreshing to wipe my face on a hot day. Besides this, when I came to the till in the chest, I found there three great bags of pieces of eight, which held about eleven hundred pieces in all; and in one of them, wrapp'd up in a paper, six doubloons of gold, and some small bars or wedges of gold; I suppose they might all weigh near a pound.

The other chest I found had some cloaths in it, but of little value. By the circumstances it must have belong'd to the gunner's mate, though there was no powder in it; but about two pound of fine glaz'd powder in three small flasks, kept, I suppose for charging their fowling-pieces on occasion. Upon the whole, I got very little by this voyage that was of any use to me; for as to the money, I had no manner of occasion for it. 'Twas to me as the dirt under my feet, and I would have given it all for three or four pair of English shoes and stockings, which were things I greatly wanted, but had not had on my feet now for many years. I had indeed gotten two pair of shoes now, which I took off of the feet of the two drown'd men who I saw in the wreck; and I found two pair more in one of the chests, which were very welcome to me, but they were not like our English shoes, either for ease or service, being rather what we call pumps, than shoes. I found in this seaman's chest about fifty pieces of eight in riyals, but no gold; I suppose this belong'd to a poorer man than the other, which seem'd to belong to some officer.

Well, however, I lugg'd this money home to my cave and lay'd it up, as I had done that before which I brought from our own ship. But it was great pity, as I said, that the other part of this ship had not come to my shore; for I am satisfy'd I might have loaded my canoe several times over with money, which if I had ever escap'd to England, would have lain here safe enough, till I might have come again and fetch'd it.

Having now brought all my things on shore and secur'd them, I went back to my boat and row'd or paddl'd her along the shore to her old harbour, where I lay'd her up and made the best of my way to my old habitation, where I found every thing safe and quiet. So I began to repose myself, live after my old fashion, and take care of my family affairs; and for a while, I liv'd easy enough, only that I was more vigilant than I used to be, look'd out oftner, and did not go abroad so much; and if at any time I did stir with any freedom, it was always to the east part of the island, where I was pretty well satisfy'd the savages never came and where I could go without so many precautions and such a load of arms and ammunition as I always carry'd with me if I went the other way.

I liv'd in this condition near two years more, but my unlucky head, that was always to let me know it was born to make my body miserable, was all this two years fill'd with projects and designs; how, if it were possible, I might get away from this island; for sometimes I was for making another voyage to the wreck, though my reason told me that there was nothing left there worth the hazard of my voyage. Sometimes for a ramble one way, sometimes another; and I believe verily, if I had had the boat that I went from Sallee in, I should have ventur'd to sea, bound anywhere, I knew not whither.

I have been in all my circumstances a memento to those who are touch'd with the general plague of mankind, whence, for ought I know, one half of their miseries flow; I mean, that of not being satisfy'd with the station wherein God and nature has plac'd them; for not to look back upon my primitive condition and the excellent advice of my father, the opposition to which was, as I may call it, my *original sin*. My subsequent mistakes of the same kind had been the means of my coming into this miserable condition; for had that Providence, which so happily had seated me at the Brasils, as a planter, bless'd me with confin'd desires, I could have been contented to have gone on gradually. I might have been by this time (I mean, in the time of my being on this island), one of the most considerable planters in the Brasils, nay, I am persuaded, that by the improvements I had made in that little time I liv'd there, and the encrease I should probably have made if I had stay'd, I might have been worth a hundred thousand moidores; and what business had I to leave a settl'd fortune, a well-stock'd plantation, improving and encreasing, to turn supra-cargo to Guiney to fetch Negroes, which patience and time would have so encreas'd our stock at home that we could have bought them at our own door from those whose business it was to fetch them; and though it had cost us something more, yet the difference of that price was by no means worth saving at so great a hazard.

But as this is ordinarily the fate of young heads, so reflection upon the folly of it is as ordinarily the exercise of more years, or of the dear-bought experience of time; and so it was with me now. Yet so deep had the mistake taken root in my temper, that I could not satisfy myself in my station, but was continually poring upon the means and possibility of my escape from this place. That I may with the greater pleasure to the reader bring on the remaining part of my story, it may not be improper to give some account of my first conceptions on the subject of this foolish scheme for my escape, and how and upon what foundation I acted.

I am now to be suppos'd retir'd into my castle, after my last voyage to the wreck, my frigate lay'd up and secur'd under water, as usual, and my condition restor'd to what it was before. I had more wealth indeed than I had before, but was not at all the richer; for I had no more use for it than the Indians of Peru had before the Spaniards came there.

It was one of the nights in the rainy season in March, the four-and-twentieth year of my first setting foot on this island of solitariness; I was lying in my bed, or hammock, awake, very well in health, had no pain, no distemper, no uneasiness of body; no, nor any uneasiness of mind, more than ordinary; but could by no means close my eyes, that is, so as to sleep; no, not a wink all night long, otherwise than as follows.

It is impossible as needless to set down the innumerable crowd of thoughts that whirl'd through that great thorowfare of the brain, the memory, in this night's time. I ran over the whole history of my life in miniature, or by abridgment, as I may call it, to my coming to this island, and also of the part of my life since I came to this island. In my reflections upon the state of my case, since I came on shore on this island, I was comparing the happy posture of my affairs, in the first years of my habitation here, compar'd to the life of anxiety, fear, and care, which I had liv'd ever since I had seen the print of a foot in the sand; not that I did not believe the savages had frequented the island even all the while, and might have been several hundreds of them at time on shore there; but I had never known it and was incapable of any apprehensions about it; my satisfaction was perfect, though my danger was the same; and I was as happy in not knowing my danger as if I had never really been expos'd to it. This furnish'd my thoughts with many very profitable reflections, and particularly this one: How infinitely good that Providence is, which has provided in its government of mankind such narrow bounds to his sight and knowledge of things; and though he walks in the midst of so many thousand dangers, the sight of which, if discover'd to him, would distract his mind and sink his spirits, he is kept serene and calm by having the events of things hid from his eyes and knowing nothing of the dangers which surround him.

After these thoughts had for some time entertain'd me, I came to reflect seriously upon the real danger I had been in for so many years on this very island; and how I had walk'd about in the greatest security and with all possible tranquility, even when perhaps nothing but a brow of a hill, a great tree, or the casual approach of night, had been between me and the worst kind of destruction, viz., that of falling into the hands of canibals and savages, who would have seiz'd on me with the same view as I did of a goat or a turtle; and have thought it no more a crime to kill and devour me, than I did of a pidgeon or a curlieu. I would unjustly slander myself if I should say I was not sincerely thankful to my great Preserver, to whose singular protection I acknowledg'd, with great humility, that all these unknown deliverances were due and without which, I must inevitably have fallen into their merciless hands.

When these thoughts were over, my head was for some time taken up in considering the nature of these wretched creatures; I mean, the savages, and how it came to pass in the world that the wise Governour of all things should give up any of His creatures to such inhumanity; nay, to some thing so much below, even brutality itself, as to devour its own kind. But as this ended in some (at that time fruitless) speculations, it occurr'd to me to enquire what part of the world these wretches liv'd in; how far off the coast was whence they came; what they ventur'd over so far from home for; what kind of boats they had; and why I might not order myself and my business so that I might be as able to go over thither as they were to come to me.

I never so much as troubl'd myself to consider what I should do with myself when I came thither; what would become of me if I fell into the hands of the savages; or how I should escape from them if they attempted me; no, nor so much as how it was possible for me to reach the coast and not to be attempted by some or other of them, without any possibility of delivering myself; and if I should not fall into their hands, what I should do for provision, or whither I should bend my course. None of these thoughts, I say, so much as came in my way; my mind was wholly bent upon the notion of my passing over in my boat to the main-land. I look'd back upon my present condition as the most miserable that could possibly be; that I was not able to throw myself into any thing but death that could be call'd worse; that if I reach'd the shore of the main, I might perhaps meet with relief, or I might coast along, as I did on the shore of Africa, till I came to some inhabited country where I might find some relief; and after all, perhaps I might fall in with some Christian ship that might take me in. And if the worse came to the worst, I could but die, which would put an end to all these miseries at once. Pray note, all this was the fruit of a disturb'd mind, an impatient temper, made as it were desperate by the long continuance of my troubles and the disappointments I had met in the wreck I had been on board of; and where I had been so near the obtaining what I so earnestly long'd for, viz., some body to speak to, and to learn some knowledge from of the place where I was, and of the probable means of my deliverance; I say, I was agitated wholly by these thoughts. All my calm of mind in my resignation to Providence, and waiting the issue of the dispositions of Heaven, seem'd to be suspended; and I had, as it were, no power to turn my thoughts to any thing but to the project of a voyage to the main, which came upon me with such force, and such an impetuosity of desire, that it was not to be resisted.

When this had agitated my thoughts for two hours, or

more, with such violence that it set my very blood into a ferment, and my pulse beat as high as if I had been in a fever, meerly with the extraordinary fervour of my mind about it; nature, as if I had been fatigu'd and exhausted with the very thought of it, threw me into a sound sleep. One would have thought I should have dream'd of it, but I did not, nor of any thing relating to it; but I dream'd that as I was going out in the morning as usual from my castle, I saw upon the shore two canoes and eleven savages coming to land, and that they brought with them another savage, who they were going to kill in order to eat him; when on a sudden, the savage that they were going to kill jump'd away and ran for his life; and I thought in my sleep that he came running into my little thick grove, before my fortification, to hide himself; and that I seeing him alone, and not perceiving that the others sought him that way, shew'd myself to him and, smiling upon him, encourag'd him; that he kneel'd down to me, seeming to pray me to assist him; upon which I shew'd my ladder, made him go up, and carry'd him into my cave, and he became my servant; and that as soon as I had gotten this man, I said to myself, now I may certainly venture to the main-land, for this fellow will serve me as a pilot and will tell me what to do and whether to go for provisions; and whether not to go for fear of being devour'd, what places to venture into, and what to escape. I wak'd with this thought and was under such inexpressible impressions of joy at the prospect of my escape in my dream, that the disappointments which I felt upon coming to myself, and finding it was no more than a dream, were equally extravagant the other way and threw me into a very great dejection of spirit.

Upon this however, I made this conclusion: that my

only way to go about an attempt for an escape was, if possible, to get a savage into my possession; and if possible, it should be one of their prisoners, who they had condemn'd to be eaten, and should bring thither to kill. But these thoughts still were attended with this difficulty: that it was impossible to effect this without attacking a whole caravan of them and killing them all; and this was not only a very desperate attempt and might miscarry, but on the other hand, I had greatly scrupl'd the lawfulness of it to me; and my heart trembl'd at the thoughts of shedding so much blood, tho' it was for my deliverance. I need not repeat the arguments which occurr'd to me against this, they being the same mention'd before; but tho' I had other reasons to offer now, viz., that those men were enemies to my life and would devour me if they could; that it was self-preservation in the highest degree to deliver myself from this death of a life and was acting in my own defence, as much as if they were actually assaulting me, and the like. I say, tho' these things argu'd for it, yet the thoughts of shedding human blood for my deliverance were very terrible to me and such as I could by no means reconcile myself to a great while.

However, at last, after many secret disputes with myself, and after great perplexities about it, for all these arguments one way and another struggl'd in my head a long time, the eager prevailing desire of deliverance at length master'd all the rest, and I resolv'd, if possible, to get one of those savages into my hands, cost what it would. My next thing then was to contrive how to do it, and this indeed was very difficult to resolve on. But as I could pitch upon no probable means for it, so I resolv'd to put myself upon the watch to see them when they came on shore, and leave the rest to the event, taking such measures as the opportunity should present, let be what would be.

With these resolutions in my thoughts, I set myself upon the scout, as often as possible, and indeed so often till I was heartily tir'd of it, for it was above a year and a half that I waited, and for great part of that time went out to the west end and to the south-west corner of the island, almost every day, to see for canoes, but none appear'd. This was very discouraging and began to trouble me much, tho' I cannot say that it did in this case as it had done sometime before that, viz., wear off the edge of my desire to the thing. But the longer it seem'd to be delay'd, the more eager I was for it; in a word, I was not at first so careful to shun the sight of these savages and avoid being seen by them, as I was now eager to be upon them.

Besides, I fancy'd myself able to manage one, nay, two or three savages, if I had them so as to make them entirely slaves to me, to do whatever I should direct them, and to prevent their being able at any time to do me any hurt. It was a great while that I pleas'd myself with this affair, but nothing still presented; all my fancies and schemes came to nothing, for no savage came near me for a great while.

About a year and a half after I had entertain'd these notions, and by long musing, had as it were resolv'd them all into nothing for want of an occasion to put them in execution, I was surpriz'd one morning early with seeing no less than five canoes all on shore together on my side the island; and the people who belong'd to them all landed and out of my sight. The number of them broke all my measures for, seeing so many and knowing that they always came four or six or sometimes more in a boat, I could not tell what to think of it or how to take my measures to attack twenty or thirty men single-handed; so I lay still in my castle, perplex'd and discomforted. However, I put myself into all the same postures for an attack that I had formerly provided and was ready for action if any thing had presented. Having waited a good while, listening to hear if they made any noise, at length, being very impatient, I set my guns at the foot of my ladder and clamber'd up to the top of the hill by my two stages as usual; standing so, however, that my head did not appear above the hill, so that they could not perceive me by any means. Here I observ'd, by the help of my perspective-glass, that they were no less than thirty in number, that they had a fire kindl'd, that they had meat dress'd. How they had cook'd it, that I knew not, or what it was; but they were all dancing in I know not how many barbarous gestures and figures, their own way, round the fire.

While I was thus looking on them, I perceiv'd by my perspective, two miserable wretches dragg'd from the boats, where it seems they were lay'd by, and were now brought out for the slaughter. I perceiv'd one of them immediately fell, being knock'd down, I suppose with a club or wooden sword, for that was their way; and two or three others were at work immediately cutting him open for their cookery, while the other victim was left standing by himself, till they should be ready for him. In that very moment this poor wretch, seeing himself a little at liberty, nature inspir'd him with hopes of life, and he started away from them and ran with incredible swiftness along the sands directly towards me, I mean towards that part of the coast where my habitation was.

I was dreadfully frighted (that I must acknowledge)

when I perceiv'd him to run my way; and especially, when as I thought I saw him pursu'd by the whole body; and now I expected that part of my dream was coming to pass, and that he would certainly take shelter in my grove. But I could not depend by any means upon my dream for the rest of it, viz., that the other savages would not pursue him thither and find him there. However, I kept my station, and my spirits began to recover when I found that there was not above three men that follow'd him; and still more was I encourag'd when I found that he outstripp'd them exceedingly in running and gain'd ground of them, so that if he could but hold it for half an hour, I saw easily he would fairly get away from them all.

There was between them and my castle the creek which I mention'd often at the first part of my story, when I landed my cargoes out of the ship; and this I saw plainly, he must necessarily swim over, or the poor wretch would be taken there. But when the savage escaping came thither, he made nothing of it, tho' the tide was then up, but plunging in, swam thro' in about thirty strokes or thereabouts, landed and ran on with exceeding strength and swiftness. When the three persons came to the creek, I found that two of them could swim, but the third could not, and that standing on the other side, he look'd at the other, but went no farther; and soon after went softly back again, which, as it happen'd, was very well for him in the main.

I observ'd that the two who swam were yet more than twice as long swimming over the creek as the fellow was that fled from them. It came now very warmly upon my thoughts, and indeed irresistibly, that now was my time to get me a servant, and perhaps a companion or assistant; and that I was call'd plainly by Providence to save this poor creature's life. I immediately ran down the ladders with all possible expedition, fetch'd my two guns, for they were both but at the foot of the ladders, as I observ'd above; and getting up again, with the same haste, to the top of the hill, I cross'd towards the sea; and having a very short cut, and all down hill, clapp'd myself in the way between the pursuers and the pursu'd. Hollowing aloud to him that fled, who looking back was at first perhaps as much frighted at me as at them, I beckon'd with my hand to him to come back. In the meantime, I slowly advanc'd towards the two that follow'd, then rushing at once upon the foremost, I knock'd him down with the stock of my piece. I was loath to fire, because I would not have the rest hear, though at that distance, it would not have been easily heard; and being out of sight of the smoke too, they would not have easily known what to make of it. Having knock'd this fellow down, the other who pursu'd with him stopp'd, as if he had been frighted, and I advanc'd a-pace towards him; but as I came nearer, I perceiv'd presently he had a bow and arrow and was fitting it to shoot at me; so I was then necessitated to shoot at him first, which I did, and kill'd him at the first shot. The poor savage who fled had stopp'd, though he saw both his enemies fallen, and kill'd, as he thought; yet he was so frighted with the fire and noise of my piece, that he stood stock still, and neither came forward or went backward, tho' he seem'd rather enclin'd to fly still, than to come on. I hollow'd again to him and made signs to come forward, which he easily understood, and came a little way, then stopp'd again, and then a little farther, and stopp'd again, and I could then perceive that he stood trembling, as if he had been taken prisoner and had just been to be kill'd, as his two enemies were. I beckon'd him again to come to me and gave him all the signs of encouragement that I could think of, and he came nearer and nearer, kneeling down every ten or twelve steps in token of acknowledgment for my saving his life. I smil'd at him, and look'd pleasantly, and beckon'd to him to come still nearer; at length he came close to me, and then he kneel'd down again, kiss'd the ground, and lay'd his head upon the ground, and taking me by the foot, set my foot upon his head; this it seems was in token of swearing to be my slave forever. I took him up, and made much of him, and encourag'd him all I could. But there was more work to do yet, for I perceiv'd the savage who I knock'd down was not kill'd, but stunn'd with the blow and began to come to himself; so I pointed to him, and showing him the savage, that he was not dead; upon this he spoke some words to me, and tho' I could not understand them, yet I thought they were pleasant to hear, for they were the first sound of a man's voice that I had heard, my own excepted, for above twenty-five years. But there was no time for such reflections now; the savage who was knock'd down recover'd himself so far as to sit up upon the ground, and I perceiv'd that my savage began to be afraid; but when I saw that, I presented my other piece at the man, as if I would shoot him, upon this my savage, for so I call'd him now, made a motion to me to lend him my sword, which hung naked in a belt by my side. So I did; he no sooner had it, but he ran to his enemy, and at one blow cut off his head as cleverly, no executioner in Germany could have done it sooner or better; which I thought very strange, for one who I had reason to believe never saw a sword in his life before, except their own wooden swords. However, it seems, as I learn'd afterwards, they make their wooden swords so sharp, so heavy, and the wood is so hard, that they will cut off heads even with them, aye, and arms, and that at one blow too. When he had done this, he came laughing to me in sign of triumph and brought me the sword again and, with an abundance of gestures which I did not understand, lay'd it down with the head of the savage that he had kill'd just before me.

But that which astonish'd him most was to know how I had kill'd the other Indian so far off, and pointing to him, he made signs to me to let him go to him, so I bade him go, as well as I could. When he came to him, he stood like one amaz'd, looking at him, turn'd him first on one side, then on t'other, look'd at the wound the bullet had made, which it seems was just in his breast, where it had made a hole, and no great quantity of blood had follow'd, but he had bled inwardly, for he was quite dead. My savage then took up his bow, and arrows, and came back, so I turn'd to go away, and beckon'd to him to follow me, making signs to him, that more might come after them.

Upon this he sign'd to me that he should bury them with sand, that they might not be seen by the rest if they follow'd; and so I made signs again to him to do so. He fell to work, and in an instant he had scrap'd a hole in the sands with his hands, big enough to bury the first in, and then dragg'd him into it, and cover'd him, and did so also by the other; I believe he had bury'd them both in a quarter of an hour. Then, calling him away, I carry'd him not to my castle, but quite away to my cave, on the farther part of the island; so I did not let my dream come to pass in that part, viz., that he came into my grove for shelter.

Here I gave him bread, and a bunch of raisins to eat, and a draught of water, which I found he was indeed in great distress for by his running; and having refresh'd him, I made signs for him to go lie down and sleep; pointing to a place where I had lay'd a great parcel of rice-straw, and a blanket upon it, which I used to sleep upon myself sometimes. So the poor creature lay'd down and went to sleep.

He was a comely handsome fellow, perfectly well made, with straight strong limbs, not too large; tall and well shap'd, and as I reckon, about twenty-six years of age. He had a very good countenance, not a fierce and surly aspect; but seem'd to have something very manly in his face, and yet he had all the sweetness and softness of a European in his countenance too, especially when he smil'd. His hair was long and black, not curl'd like wool; his forehead very high and large, and a great vivacity and sparkling sharpness in his eyes. The colour of his skin was not quite black, but very tawny; and yet not of an ugly yellow, nauseous tawny as the Brasilians, and Virginians, and other natives of America are, but of a bright kind of a dun-olive colour that had in it something very agreeable, tho' not very easy to describe. His face was round and plump; his nose small, not flat like the Negroes'; a very good mouth, thin lips, and his fine teeth well set, and white as ivory. After he had slumber'd, rather than slept, about half an hour, he wak'd again and came out of the cave to me; for I had been milking my goats, which I had in the enclosure just by. When he espy'd me, he came running to me, laying himself down again upon the ground, with all the possible signs of an humble thankful disposition, making a many antick gestures to show it. At last he lay'd his head flat upon the ground, close to my foot, and set my other foot upon his head, as he had done before; and after this, made all the signs to me of subjection, servitude, and submission imaginable, to let me know how he would serve me as long as he liv'd. I understood him in many things, and let him know I was very well pleas'd with him. In a little time I began to speak to him and teach him to speak to me. First, I made him know his name should be Friday, which was the day I sav'd his life, and I call'd him so for the memory of the time. I likewise taught him to say *Master*, and then let him know that was to be my name. I likewise taught him to say Yes and No, and to know the meaning of them; I gave him some milk, in an earthen pot, and let him see me drink it before him and sop my bread in it; and I gave him a cake of bread to do the like, which he quickly comply'd with and made signs that it was very good for him.

I kept there with him all that night; but as soon as it was day, I beckon'd to him to come with me and let him know I would give him some cloaths, at which he seem'd very glad, for he was stark-naked. As we went by the place where he had bury'd the two men, he pointed exactly to the place and shew'd me the marks that he had made to find them again, making signs to me that we should dig them up again and eat them. At this I appear'd very angry, express'd my abhorrence of it, made as if I would vomit at the thought of it, and beckon'd with my hand to him to come away, which he did immediately, with great submission. I then led him up to the top of the hill to see if his enemies were gone; and pulling out my glass, I look'd and saw plainly the place where they had been, but no appearance of them or of their canoes; so that it was plain

He was a comely handsome fellow, perfectly well made, with straight strong limbs, not too large; tall and well shap'd, and as I reckon, about twenty-six years of age. (page 237)

they were gone and had left their two comrades behind them, without any search after them.

But I was not content with this discovery. Having now more courage and consequently more curiosity, I took my man Friday with me, giving him the sword in his hand, with the bows and arrows at his back, which I found he could use very dextrously, making him carry one gun for me, and I two for myself, and away we march'd to the place where these creatures had been, for I had a mind now to get some fuller intelligence of them. When I came to the place, my very blood ran chill in my veins and my heart sunk within me at the horror of the spectacle. Indeed, it was a dreadful sight, at least it was so to me, tho' Friday made nothing of it. The place was cover'd with human bones, the ground dy'd with their blood, great pieces of flesh left here and there, half eaten, mangl'd and scorch'd; in short, all the tokens of the triumphant feast they had been making there, after a victory over their enemies. I saw three skulls, five hands, and the bones of three or four legs and feet, and an abundance of other parts of the bodies. Friday, by his signs, made me understand that they brought over four prisoners to feast upon; that three of them were eaten up, and that he, pointing to himself, was the fourth; that there had been a great battle between them and their next king, whose subjects it seems he had been one of; and that they had taken a great number of prisoners, all which were carry'd to several places by those that had taken them in the fight, in order to feast upon them, as was done here by these wretches upon those they brought hither.

I caus'd Friday to gather all the skulls, bones, flesh, and whatever remain'd, and lay them together on a heap, and make a great fire upon it, and burn them all to ashes. I found Friday had still a hankering stomach after some of the flesh and was still a canibal in his nature; but I shew'd so much abhorrence at the very thoughts of it, and at the least appearance of it, that he durst not discover it; for I had by some means let him know that I would kill him if he offer'd it.

When we had done this, we came back to our castle, and there I fell to work for my man Friday. First of all, I gave him a pair of linnen drawers, which I had out of the poor gunner's chest I mentioned, and which I found in the wreck, and which with a little alteration fitted him very well; then I made him a jerkin of goat-skin, as well as my skill would allow; and I was now grown a tolerable good taylor; and I gave him a cap, which I had made of a hare-skin, very convenient, and fashionable enough. Thus he was cloath'd for the present, tolerably well, and was mighty well pleas'd to see himself almost as well cloath'd as his master. It is true, he went awkwardly in these things at first; wearing the drawers was very awkward to him, and the sleeves of the waistcoat gall'd his shoulders, and the in-side of his arms; but a little easing them where he complain'd they hurt him, and using himself to them, at length he took to them very well.

The next day after I came home to my hutch with him, I began to consider where I should lodge him, and that I might do well for him and yet be perfectly easy myself. I made a little tent for him in the vacant place between my two fortifications, in the in-side of the last, and in the out-side of the first; and as there was a door or entrance there into my cave, I made a formal fram'd door-case, and a door to it of boards, and set it up in the passage, a little within the entrance. And causing the door to open on the in-side, I barr'd it up in the night, taking in my ladders too; so that Friday could no way come at me in the in-side of my innermost wall without making so much noise in getting over that it must needs waken me. My first wall had now a compleat roof over it of long poles, covering all my tent, and leaning up to the side of the hill, which was again lay'd cross with smaller sticks instead of laths, and then thatch'd over a great thickness, with the rice-straw, which was strong like reeds; and at the hole or place which was left to go in or out by the ladder, I had plac'd a kind of trap-door, which if it had been attempted on the out-side, would not have open'd at all, but would have fallen down, and made a great noise. As to weapons, I took them all in to my side every night.

But I needed none of all these precautions, for never man had a more faithful, loving, sincere servant than Friday was to me; without passions, sullenness or designs, perfectly oblig'd and engag'd; his very affections were ty'd to me, like those of a child to a father; and I dare say, he would have sacrific'd his life for the saving of mine upon any occasion whatsoever. The many testimoniels he gave me of this put it out of doubt and soon convinc'd me that I needed to use no precautions as to my safety on his account.

This frequently gave me occasion to observe, and that with wonder, that however it had pleas'd God, in His providence and in the government of the works of His hands, to take from so great a part of the world of his creatures, the best uses to which their faculties and the powers of their souls are adapted; yet that He has bestow'd upon them the same powers, the same reason, the same affections, the same sentiments of kindness and obligation, the same passions and resentments of wrongs; the same sense of gratitude, sincerity, fidelity, and all the capacities of doing good, and receiving good, that he has given to us; and that when He pleases to offer to them occasions of exerting these, they are as ready, nay, more ready to apply them to the right uses for which they were bestow'd than we are. This made me very melancholy sometimes, in reflecting as the several occasions presented, how mean a use we make of all these, even though we have these powers enlighten'd by the great lamp of instruction, the spirit of God, and by the knowledge of His Word, added to our understanding; and why it has pleas'd God to hide the like saving knowledge from so many millions of souls who, if I might judge by this poor savage, would make a much better use of it than we did.

Hence, I sometimes was led too far to invade the sovereignty of Providence and, as it were, arraign the justice of so arbitrary a disposition of things that should hide that light from some and reveal it to others, and yet expect a like duty from both. But I shut it up and check'd my thoughts with this conclusion, first, that we did not know by what light and law these should be condemn'd; but that as God was necessarily and, by the nature of His being, infinitely holy and just, so it could not be; but that if these creatures were all sentenc'd to absence from Himself, it was on account of sinning against that light which, as the Scripture says, was a law to themselves, and by such rules as their consciences would acknowledge to be just, tho' the foundation was not discover'd to us. And secondly, that still as we are all the clay in the hand of the Potter, no vessel could say to Him, Why hast Thou form'd me thus?

But to return to my new companion. I was greatly delighted with him and made it my business to teach him every thing that was proper to make him useful, handy, and helpful; but especially to make him speak and understand me when I spake, and he was the aptest scholar that ever was, and particularly was so merry, so constantly diligent, and so pleas'd when he could but understand me, or make me understand him, that it was very pleasant to me to talk to him. Now my life began to be so easy that I began to say to myself that could I but have been safe from more savages, I car'd not if I was never to remove from the place while I liv'd.

After I had been two or three days return'd to my castle, I thought that, in order to bring Friday off from his horrid way of feeding and from the relish of a canibal's stomach, I ought to let him taste other flesh. So I took him out with me one morning to the woods. I went indeed intending to kill a kid out of my own flock and bring him home and dress it. But as I was going, I saw a she-goat lying down in the shade and two young kids sitting by her. I catch'd hold of Friday. "Hold," said I, "stand still," and made signs to him not to stir. Immediately, I presented my piece, shot and kill'd one of the kids. The poor creature who had at a distance indeed seen me kill the savage his enemy, but did not know, or could imagine how it was done, was sensibly surpriz'd; he trembled, and shook, and look'd so amaz'd that I thought he would have sunk down. He did not see the kid I shot at, or perceive I had kill'd it, but ripp'd up his waistcoat to feel if he was not wounded, and as I found presently, thought I was resolv'd to kill him; for he came and kneel'd down to me and, embracing my knees, said a great many things I did not understand, but I could easily see that the meaning was to pray me not to kill him.

I soon found a way to convince him that I would do him no harm, and taking him up by the hand, laugh'd at him, and pointing to the kid which I had kill'd, beckon'd to him to run and fetch it, which he did. And while he was wond'ring and looking to see how the creature was kill'd, I loaded my gun again, and by and by I saw a great fowl like a hawk sit upon a tree within shot. So to let Friday understand a little what I would do, I call'd him to me again, pointed at the fowl which was indeed a parrot, tho' I thought it had been a hawk, I say, pointing to the parrot, and to my gun, and to the ground under the parrot, to let him see I would make it fall, I made him understand that I would shoot and kill that bird. Accordingly, I fir'd and bade him look, and immediately he saw the parrot fall, he stood like one frighted again, notwithstanding all I had said to him; and I found he was the more amaz'd because he did not see me put any thing into the gun, but thought that there must be some wonderful fund of death and destruction in that thing, able to kill man, beast, bird, or any thing near, or far off. The astonishment this created in him was such as could not wear off for a long time, and I believe, if I would have let him, he would have worship'd me and my gun. As for the gun itself, he would not so much as touch it for several days after; but would speak to it and talk to it, as if it had answer'd him, when he was by himself; which, as I afterwards learn'd of him, was to desire it not to kill him.

Well, after this astonishment was a little over, I pointed

to him to run and fetch the bird I had shot, which he did, but stay'd some time; for the parrot not being quite dead, was flutter'd away a good way off from the place where she fell. However, Friday found her, took her up, and brought her to me; and as I had perceiv'd his ignorance about the gun before, I took this advantage to charge the gun again, and not let him see me do it, that I might be ready for any other mark that might present, but nothing more offer'd at that time. So I brought home the kid, and the same evening I took the skin off and cut it out as well as I could; and having a pot for that purpose, I boil'd or stew'd some of the flesh and made some very good broth. After I had begun to eat some, I gave some to my man, who seem'd very glad of it, and lik'd it very well. But that which was strangest to him was to see me eat salt with it; he made a sign to me that the salt was not good to eat, and putting a little into his own mouth, he seem'd to nauseate it and would spit and sputter at it, washing his mouth with fresh water after it; on the other hand, I took some meat in my mouth without salt, and I pretended to spit and sputter for want of salt, as fast as he had done at the salt; but it would not do, he would never care for salt with his meat or in his broth; at least not for a great while, and then but a very little.

Having thus fed him with boil'd meat and broth, I was resolv'd to feast him the next day with roasting a piece of the kid; this I did by hanging it before the fire on a string, as I had seen many people do in England: setting two poles up, one on each side the fire, and one cross on the top, and tying the string to the cross-stick, letting the meat turn continually. This Friday admir'd very much, but when he came to taste the flesh, he took so many ways to tell me how well he lik'd it that I could not but understand him; and at last he told me he would never eat man's flesh anymore, which I was very glad to hear.

The next day I set him to work to beating some corn out and sifting it in the manner I used to do, as I observ'd before, and he soon understood how to do it as well as I, especially after he had seen what the meaning of it was and that it was to make bread of. After that I let him see me make my bread, and bake it too, and in a little time Friday was able to do all the work for me, as well as I could do it myself.

I began now to consider that having two mouths to feed, instead of one, I must provide more ground for my harvest and plant a larger quantity of corn than I used to do. So I mark'd out a larger piece of land and began the fence in the same manner as before, in which Friday not only work'd very willingly and very hard, but did it very cheerfully. I told him what it was for, that it was for corn to make more bread, because he was now with me, and that I might have enough for him and myself too. He appear'd very sensible of that part, and let me know that he thought I had much more labour upon me on his account than I had had for myself, and that he would work the harder for me if I would tell him what to do.

This was the pleasantest year of all the life I led in this place. Friday began to talk pretty well, and understand the names of almost every thing I had occasion to call for and of every place I had to send him to, and talk'd a great deal to me. So I began now to have some use for my tongue again, which indeed I had had very little occasion for before, that is to say, about speech. Besides the pleasure of talking to him, I had a singular satisfaction in the fellow himself; his simple, unfeign'd honesty appear'd to me more and more every day, and I began really to love the creature; and on his side, I believe he lov'd me more than it was possible for him ever to love any thing before.

I had a mind once to try if he had any hankering inclination to his own country again, and having learn'd him English so well that he could answer me almost any questions, I ask'd him whether the nation that he belong'd to never conquer'd in battle, at which he smil'd, and said, "Yes, yes, we always fight the better"; that is, he meant always get the better in fight; and so we began the following discourse: "You always fight the better," said I, "how came you to be taken prisoner then, Friday?"

Friday. My nation beat much, for all that.

Master. How beat? If your nation beat them, how came you to be taken?

Friday. They more many than my nation in the place where me was; they take one, two, three, and me; my nation over-beat them in the yonder place, where me no was. There my nation take one, two, great thousand.

Master. But why did not your side recover you from the hands of your enemies then?

Friday. They run one, two, three, and me, and make go in the canoe; my nation have no canoe that time.

Master. Well, Friday, and what does your nation do with the men they take? Do they carry them away, and eat them, as these did?

Friday. Yes, my nation eat mans too, eat all up.

Master. Where do they carry them?

Friday. Go to other place where they think.

Master. Do they come hither?

Friday. Yes, yes, they come hither; come other else place.

Master. Have you been here with them?

Friday. Yes, I been here. *[Points to the NW side of the island which it seems was their side.]*

By this I understood that my man Friday had formerly been among the savages who used to come on shore on the farther part of the island, on the same man-eating occasions that he was now brought for; and sometime after, when I took the courage to carry him to that side, being the same I formerly mention'd, he presently knew the place and told me he was there once when they ate up twenty men, two women, and one child; he could not tell twenty in English, but he number'd them by laying so many stones in a row and pointing to me to tell them over.

I have told this passage because it introduces what follows; that after I had had this discourse with him, I ask'd him how far it was from our island to the shore and whether the canoes were not often lost; he told me there was no danger, no canoes ever lost; but that after a little ways out to the sea, there was a current, and wind, always one way in the morning, the other in the afternoon.

This I understood to be no more than the sets of the tide, as going out or coming in; but I afterwards understood it was occasion'd by the great draft and reflux of the mighty river Oronoque; in the mouth, or the gulph of which river, as I found afterwards, our island lay; and this land which I perceiv'd to the W and NW was the great island Trinidad, on the north point of the mouth of the river. I ask'd Friday a thousand questions about the country, the inhabitants, the sea, the coast, and what nation were near; he told me all he knew with the greatest openness imaginable. I ask'd him the names of the several nations of this sort of people; but could get no other name than Caribs; whence I easily understood, that these were the Caribbees, which our maps place on the part of America which reaches from the mouth of the river Oronoque to Guiana, and onwards to St. Martha. He told me that up a great way beyond the moon, that was, beyond the setting of the moon, which must be west from their country, there dwelt white, bearded men, like me; and pointed to my great whiskers, which I mention'd before; and that they had kill'd much mans, that was his word. By all which I understood, he meant the Spaniards, whose cruelties in America had been spread over the whole countries and was remember'd by all the nations from father to son.

I enquir'd if he could tell me how I might come from this island and get among those white men; he told me, yes, yes, I might go in "two canoe"; I could not understand what he meant, or make him describe to me what he meant by two canoe, till at last, with great difficulty, I found he meant it must be a large great boat, as big as two canoes.

This part of Friday's discourse began to relish with me very well, and from this time I entertain'd some hopes that one time or other I might find an opportunity to make my escape from this place and that this poor savage might be a means to help me to do it.

During the long time that Friday had now been with me, and that he began to speak to me and understand me, I was now wanting to lay a foundation of religious knowledge in his mind; particularly I ask'd him one time who made him? The poor creature did not understand me at all, but thought I had ask'd him who was his father. But I took it by another handle and ask'd him who made the sea, the ground we walk'd on, and the hills, and woods; he told me it was one old Benamuckee, that liv'd beyond all. He could describe nothing of this great person, but that he was very old; much older he said than the sea or the land, than the moon or the stars. I ask'd him then, if this old person had made all things, why did not all things worship him? He look'd very grave and with a perfect look of innocence, said, "All things do say 'O' to him." I ask'd him if the people who die in his country went away anywhere, and he said yes, they all went to Benamuckee. Then I ask'd him whether those they ate up went thither too, and he said yes.

From these things, I began to instruct him in the knowledge of the true God. I told him that the great maker of all things liv'd up there, pointing up towards Heaven; that He governs the world by the same power and providence by which He had made it; that He was omnipotent, could do every thing for us, give every thing to us, and take every thing from us; thus by degrees I open'd his eyes. He listen'd with great attention and receiv'd with pleasure the notion of Jesus Christ being sent to redeem us, and of the manner of making our prayers to God, and His being able to hear us, even into Heaven. He told me one day that if our God could hear us up beyond the sun, He must needs be a greater god than their Benamuckee, who liv'd but a little way off, and yet could not hear till they went up to the great mountains where he dwelt to speak to him; I ask'd him if ever he went thither to speak to him; he said no, they never went that were young men; none went thither but the old men, who he call'd their Oowocakee, that is, as I made him explain it to me, their religious, or clergy, and that they went to say "O" (so he call'd saying prayers), and then came back and told

250

them what Benamuckee said. By this I observ'd that there is priestcraft even amongst the most blinded ignorant pagans in the world; and the policy of making a secret religion, in order to preserve the veneration of the people to the clergy, is not only to be found in the Roman, but perhaps among all religions in the world, even among the most brutish and barbarous savages.

I endeavour'd to clear up this fraud to my man Friday and told him that the pretence of their old men going up to the mountains to say "O" to their god Benamuckee was a cheat, and their bringing word thence what he said was much more so; that if they met with any answers, or spake with any one there, it must be with an evil spirit. Then I enter'd into a long discourse with him about the Devil, the original of him, his rebellion against God, his enmity to man, the reason of it, his setting himself up in the dark parts of the world to be worship'd instead of God and as God; and the many stratagems he made use of to delude mankind to his ruine; how he had a secret access to our passions, and to our affections, to adapt his snares so to our inclinations as to cause us even to be our own tempters and to run upon our destruction by our own choice.

I found it was not so easy to imprint right notions in his mind about the Devil, as it was about the being of God. Nature assisted all my arguments to evidence to him, even the necessity of a great first cause and overruling governing power; a secret directing Providence, and of the equity and justice of paying homage to Him that made us, and the like. But there appear'd nothing of all this in the notion of an evil spirit; of his original, his being, his nature, and above all of his inclinations to do evil and to draw us in to do so too; and the poor creature puzzl'd me once in such a manner, by a question meerly natural and innocent, that I scarce knew what to say to him. I had been talking a great deal to him of the power of God, His omnipotence, His dreadful nature to sin, His being a consuming fire to the workers of iniquity; how, as He had made us all, He could destroy us and all the world in a moment; and he listen'd with great seriousness to me all the while.

After this, I had been telling him how the Devil was God's enemy in the hearts of men, and used all his malice and skill to defeat the good designs of Providence, and to ruine the kingdom of Christ in the world, and the like. "Well," said Friday, "but you say God is so strong, so great, is He not much strong, much might as the Devil?" "Yes, yes," said I, "Friday, God is stronger than the Devil, God is above the Devil, and therefore we pray to God to tread him down under our feet and enable us to resist his temptations and quench his fiery darts." "But," said he again, "if God much strong, much might as the Devil, why God no kill the Devil, so make him no more do wicked?"

I was strangely surpriz'd at his question, and after all, tho' I was now an old man, yet I was but a young doctor, and ill-enough qualify'd for a casuist or a solver of difficulties. And at first I could not tell what to say, so I pretended not to hear him and ask'd him what he said. But he was too earnest for an answer to forget his question, so that he repeated it in the very same broken words as above. By this time I had recover'd myself a little, and I said, "God will at last punish him severely; he is reserv'd for the judgment and is to be cast into the bottomless-pit to dwell with everlasting fire." This did not satisfy Friday, but he return'd upon me, repeating my words, "Reserve, at last, me no understand; but why not kill Devil now, not kill great ago?" "You may as well ask me," said I, "why God does not kill you and me, when we do wicked things here that offend him. We are preserv'd to repent and be pardon'd." He mus'd awhile at this; "Well, well," said he, mighty affectionately, "that well; so you, I, Devil, all wicked, all preserve, repent, God pardon all." Here I was run down again by him to the last degree, and it was a testimony to me how the meer notions of nature, though they will guide reasonable creatures to the knowledge of God, and of a worship or homage due to the Supreme Being, of God as the consequence of our nature, yet nothing but divine revelation can from the knowledge of Jesus Christ, and of a redemption purchas'd for us, of a mediator of the new covenant, and of an intercessor at the foot-stool of God's throne; I say, nothing but a revelation from Heaven can form these in the soul, and that therefore the Gospel of our Lord and Saviour Jesus Christ; I mean, the Word of God, and the spirit of God promis'd for the guide and sanctifier of His people, are the absolutely necessary instructors of the souls of men in the saving knowledge of God and the means of salvation.

I therefore diverted the present discourse between me and my man, rizing up hastily, as upon some sudden occasion of going out; then sending him for some thing a good way off, I seriously pray'd to God that he would enable me to instruct savingly this poor savage, assisting by His spirit the heart of the poor ignorant creature, to receive the light of the knowledge of God in Christ, reconciling him to himself, and would guide me to speak so to him from the Word of God, as his conscience might be convinc'd, his eyes open'd, and his soul sav'd. When he came again to me, I enter'd into a long discourse with him upon the subject of the redemption of man by the Saviour of the world and of the doctrine of the Gospel preach'd from Heaven, *viz.*, of repentance towards God and faith in our Blessed Lord Jesus. I then explain'd to him, as well as I could, why our Blessed Redeemer took not on Him the nature of angels, but the seed of Abraham, and how for that reason the fallen angels had no share in the redemption; that He came only to the lost sheep of the house of Israel, and the like.

I had, God knows, more sincerity than knowledge in all the methods I took for this poor creature's instruction, and must acknowledge what I believe all that act upon the same principle will find; that in laying things open to him, I really inform'd and instructed myself in many things that either I did not know or had not fully consider'd before; but which occurr'd naturally to my mind, upon my searching into them for the information of this poor savage. And I had more affection in my enquiry after things upon this occasion than ever I felt before; so that whether this poor wild wretch was the better for me, or no, I had great reason to be thankful that ever he came to me. My grief set lighter upon me, my habitation grew comfortable to me beyond measure; and, when I reflected that in this solitary life which I had been confin'd to, I had not only been moved myself to look up to Heaven and to seek to the hand that had brought me there, but was now to be made an instrument under Providence to save the life and, for ought I know, the soul of a poor savage, and bring him to the true knowledge of religion, and of the Christian doctrine, that he might know Christ Jesus, to know whom is life eternal. I say, when I reflected upon all these things, a secret joy ran through every part of my soul, and I frequently rejoyc'd that ever I was brought to this place, which I had so often thought the most dreadful of all afflictions that could possibly have befallen me.

In this thankful frame I continu'd all the remainder of my time, and the conversation which employ'd the hours between Friday and me was such as made the three years which we liv'd there together perfectly and compleatly happy; if any such thing as compleat happiness can be form'd in a sublunary state. The savage was now a good Christian, a much better than I; though I have reason to hope, and bless God for it, that we were equally penitent, and comforted, restor'd penitents; we had here the Word of God to read, and no farther off from His spirit to instruct than if we had been in England.

I always apply'd myself in reading the Scripture, to let him know, as well as I could, the meaning of what I read; and he again, by his serious enquiries and questionings, made me, as I said before, a much better scholar in the Scripture knowledge, than I should ever have been by my own private meer reading. Another thing I cannot refrain from observing here also from experience, in this retir'd part of my life, viz., how infinite and inexpressible a blessing it is that the knowledge of God and of the doctrine of salvation by Christ Jesus is so plainly lay'd down in the Word of God, so easy to be receiv'd and understood. That as the bare reading the Scripture made me capable of understanding enough of my duty to carry me directly on to the great work of sincere repentance for my sins; and laying hold of a Saviour for life and salvation, to a stated reformation in practise and obedience to all God's commands, and this without any teacher or instructer; I mean, human; so the same plain instruction sufficiently serv'd to the enlight-

'ning this savage creature and bringing him to be such a Christian as I have known few equal to him in my life.

As to all the disputes, wranglings, strife and contention which has happen'd in the world about religion, whether niceties in doctrines, or schemes of church government, they were all perfectly useless to us; as for ought I can yet see, they have been to all the rest of the world. We had the sure guide to Heaven, viz., the Word of God; and we had, blessed be God, comfortable views of the spirit of God teaching and instructing us by His Word, leading us into all truth, and making us both willing and obedient to the instruction of His Word; and I cannot see the least use that the greatest knowledge of the disputed points in religion, which have made such confusions in the world would have been to us, if we could have obtain'd it. But I must go on with the historical part of things, and take every part in its order.

After Friday and I became more intimately acquainted, and after he could understand almost all I said to him and speak fluently, though in broken English to me, I acquainted him with my own story, or at least so much of it as related to my coming into this place, how I had liv'd here, and how long. I let him into the mystery, for such it was to him, of gun-powder, and bullet, and taught him how to shoot. I gave him a knife, which he was wonderfully delighted with, and I made him a belt, with a frog hanging to it, such as in England we wear hangers on. In the frog, instead of a hanger, I gave him a hatchet, which was not only as good a weapon in some cases, but much more useful upon other occasions.

I describ'd to him the country of Europe, and particularly England, which I came from; how we liv'd; how we worship'd God; how we behav'd to one another; and how we traded in ships to all parts of the world. I gave him an account of the wreck which I had been on board of, and shew'd him, as near as I could, the place where she lay; but she was all beaten in pieces before and gone.

I shew'd him the ruines of our boat, which we lost when we escap'd, and which I could not stir with my whole strength then; but was now fallen almost all to pieces. Upon seeing this boat, Friday stood musing a great while and said nothing. I ask'd him what it was he study'd upon, and at last said he, "Me see such boat like come to place at my nation."

I did not understand him a good while; but at last, when I had examin'd further into it, I understood by him that a boat, such as that had been, came on shore upon the country where he liv'd. That is, as he explain'd it, it was driven thither by stress of weather. I presently imagin'd that some European ship must have been cast away upon their coast, and the boat must get loose and drive a-shore; but was so dull, that I never once thought of men making escape from a wreck thither, much less whence they might come. So I only enquir'd after a description of the boat.

Friday describ'd the boat to me well enough; but brought me better to understand him, when he added with some warmth, "We save the white mans from drown." Then, I presently ask'd him if there was any white mans, as he call'd them, in the boat. "Yes," he said, "the boat full white mans." I ask'd him how many; he told upon his fingers seventeen. I ask'd him then what became of them; he told me, "They live, they dwell at my nation."

This put new thoughts into my head, for I presently imagin'd that these might be the men belonging to the ship that was cast away in sight of my island, as I now call it; and who after the ship was struck on the rock, and they saw her inevitably lost, had sav'd themselves in their boat, and were landed upon that wild shore among the savages.

Upon this, I enquir'd of him more critically what was become of them? He assur'd me they liv'd still there; that they had been there about four years; that the savages let them alone and gave them victuals to live. I ask'd him how it came to pass they did not kill them and eat them? He said, "No, they make brother with them"; that is, as I understood him, a truce. And then he added, "They no eat man but when makes the war fight"; that is to say, they never eat any men but such as come to fight with them and are taken in battle.

It was after this some considerable time, being upon the top of the hill at the east side of the island, whence as I have said, I had on a clear day discover'd the main, or continent of America, that Friday, the weather being very serene, look'd very earnestly towards the main-land and in a kind of surprize, fell to a-jumping and a-dancing and call'd out to me, for I was at some distance from him. I ask'd him what was the matter? "O joy!" said he, "O glad! There see my country, there my nation!"

I observ'd an extraordinary sense of pleasure appear'd in his face, and his eyes sparkl'd and his countenance discover'd a strange eagerness, as if he had a mind to be in his own country again. This observation of mine put a great many thoughts into me, which made me at first not so easy about my man Friday as I was before; and I made no doubt but that if Friday could get back to his own nation again, he would not only forget all his religion, but all his obligation to me; and would be forward enough to give his countryman an account of me, and come back perhaps with an hundred or two of them, and make a feast upon me, at which he might be as merry as he used to be with those of his enemies when they were taken in war.

But I wrong'd the poor honest creature very much, for which I was very sorry afterwards. However, as my jealousy encreas'd, and held me some weeks, I was a little more circumspect and not so familiar and kind to him as before; in which I was certainly in the wrong too, the honest grateful creature having no thought about it but what consisted with the best principles, both as a religious Christian, and as a grateful friend, as appear'd afterwards to my full satisfaction.

While my jealousy of him lasted, you may be sure I was every day pumping him to see if he would discover any of the new thoughts, which I suspected were in him; but I found everything he said was so honest, and so innocent, that I could find nothing to nourish my suspicion; and in spite of all my uneasiness he made me at last entirely his own again, nor did he in the least perceive that I was uneasy, and therefore I could not suspect him of deceit.

One day walking up the same hill, but the weather being hazey at sea, so that we could not see the continent, I call'd to him, and said, "Friday, do not you wish yourself in your own country, your own nation?" "Yes," he said, "he be much O glad to be at his own nation." "What would you do there?" said I. "Would you turn wild again, eat men's flesh again, and be a savage as you were before?" He look'd full of concern, and shaking his head said, "No, no, Friday tell them to live good, tell them to pray God, tell them to eat corn-bread, cattle-flesh, milk, no eat man again." "Why then," said I to him, "they will kill you." He look'd grave at that, and then said, "No, they no kill me, they willing love learn." He meant by this they would be willing to learn. He added then that they learn'd much of the bearded mans that came in the boat. Then I ask'd him if he would go back to them? He smil'd at that and told me he could not swim so far. I told him I would make a canoe for him. He told me he would go, if I would go with him. "I go!" said I. "Why they will eat me as I come there!" "No, no," said he, "me make they no eat you; me make they much love you." He meant he would tell them how I had kill'd his enemies and sav'd his life, and so he would make them love me; then he told me, as well as he could, how kind they were to seventeen white mans, or bearded mans, as he call'd them, who came on shore there in distress.

From this time I confess I had a mind to venture over, and see if I could possibly join with these bearded men, who I made no doubt were Spaniards or Portugueze; not doubting but if I could we might find some method to escape thence, being upon the continent, and a good company together; better than I could from an island forty miles off the shore, and alone without help. So after some days I took Friday to work again, by way of discourse, and told him I would give him a boat to go back to his own nation. Accordingly, I carry'd him to my frigate, which lay on the other side of the island, and having clear'd it of water, for I always kept it sunk in the water, I brought it out, shew'd it him, and we both went into it.

I found he was a most dextrous fellow at managing it; would make it go almost as swift and fast again as I could. So when he was in, I said to him, "Well now, Friday, shall we go to your nation?" He look'd very dull at my saying so, which it seems was because he thought the boat too small to go so far. I told him then I had a bigger; so the next day we went to the place where the first boat lay which I had made, but which I could not get into the water. He said that it was big enough. But as I had taken no care of it, and it had lay'd two- or three-and-twenty years there, the sun had split and dry'd it, it was in a manner rotten. Friday told me such a boat would do very well, and would carry "much enough vittle, drink, bread"; that was his way of talking.

Upon the whole, I was by this time so fix'd upon my design of going over with him to the continent that I told him we would go and make a boat as big as that, and he should go home in it. He answer'd not one word, but look'd very grave and sad. I ask'd him what was the matter with him? He ask'd me again thus, "Why, you angry mad with Friday, what me done?" I ask'd him what he meant; I told him I was not angry with him at all. "No angry! No angry!" said he, repeating the words several times. "Why send Friday home away to my nation?" "Why," said I, "Friday, did you not say you wish'd you were there?" "Yes, yes," said he, "wish be both there, no wish Friday there, no Master there." In a word, he would not think of going there without me. "I go there! Friday, what shall I do there?" He turn'd very quick upon me at this: "You do great deal much good," said he, "you teach wild mans be good, sober, tame mans; you tell them know God, pray God, and live new life!" "Alas Friday, thou knowest not what thou sayest! I am but an ignorant man myself." "Yes, yes," said he, "you teachee me good you teachee them good!" "No, no, Friday, you shall go without me, leave me here to live by myself, as I did before." He look'd confus'd again at that word, and running to one of the hatchets which he used to wear, he took it up hastily, came and gave it me. "What must I do with this?" said I. "You take, kill Friday," said he. "What must I kill you for?" said I again. He return'd very quick, "What you send Friday away for? Take, kill Friday, no send Friday away." This he spoke so earnestly that I saw tears stand in his eyes. In a word, I so plainly discover'd the utmost affection in him to me, and a firm resolution in him, that I told him then, and often after, that I would never send him away from me if he was willing to stay with me.

Upon the whole, as I found by all his discourse a settled affection to me, and that nothing should part him from me, so I found all the foundation of his desire to go to his own country was lay'd in his ardent affection to his people, and his hopes of my doing them good; a thing which as I had no notion of myself, so I had not the least thought or intention, or desire of undertaking it. But still I found a strong inclination to my attempting an escape as above, founded on the supposition gather'd from the discourse, viz., that there were seventeen bearded men there; and therefore, without any more delay, I went to work with Friday to find out a great tree proper to fell, and make a large periagua or canoe to undertake the voyage. There were trees enough in the island to have built a little fleet, not of periaguas and canoes, but even of good large vessels. But the main thing I look'd at was to get one so near the water that we might launch it when it was made, to avoid the mistake I committed at first.

At last, Friday pitch'd upon a tree, for I found he knew much better than I what kind of wood was fittest for it, nor can I tell to this day what wood to call the tree we cut down, except that it was very like the tree we call *fustic*, or between that and the Nicaragua wood, for it was much of the same colour and smell. Friday was for burning the hollow or cavity of this tree out to make it for a boat. But I shew'd him how rather to cut it out with tools, which, after I had shew'd him how to use, he did very handily. In about a month's hard labour, we finish'd it and made it very handsome, especially when with our axes, which I shew'd him how to handle, we cut and hew'd the out-side into the true shape of a boat; after this, however, it cost us near a fortnight's time to get her along as it were inch by inch upon great rowlers into the water. But when she was in, she would have carry'd twenty men with great ease.

When she was in the water, and tho' she was so big it amaz'd me to see with what dexterity and how swift my man Friday could manage her, turn her, and paddle her along; so I ask'd him if he would, and if we might venture over in her. "Yes," he said, "we venture over in her very well, tho' great blow wind." However, I had a further design that he knew nothing of, and that was to make a mast and sail and to fit her with an anchor and cable. As to a mast, that was easy enough to get; so I pitch'd upon a strait young cedar-tree, which I found near the place, and which there was great plenty of on the island, and I set Friday to work to cut it down, and gave him directions how to shape and order it. But as to the sail, that was my particular care. I knew I had old sails, or rather pieces of old sails enough, but as I had had them now six-and-twenty years by me, and had not been very careful to preserve them, not imagining that I should ever have this kind of use for them, I did not doubt but they were all rotten; indeed most of them were so. However, I found two pieces which appear'd pretty good, and with these I went to work, and with a great deal of pains, and awkward tedious stitching (you may be sure) for want of needles, I at length made a three-corner'd ugly thing, like what we call in England a shoulder-of-mutton sail, to go with a boom at bottom, and a little short sprit at the top, such as usually our ship's longboats sail with, and such as I best knew how to manage; because it was such a one as I had to the boat in which I made my escape from Barbary, as related in the first part of my story.

I was near two months performing this last work, viz., rigging and fitting my mast and sails; for I finish'd them very compleat, making a small stay, and a sail, or foresail to it, to assist, if we should turn to windward. But which was more than all, I fix'd a rudder to the stern of her to steer with; and though I was but a bungling shipwright, yet as I knew the usefulness and even necessity of such a thing, I apply'd myself with so much pains to do it that at last I brought it to pass. But considering the many dull contrivances I had for it that sail'd, I think it cost me almost as much labour as making the boat.

After all this was done too, I had my man Friday to teach as to what belong'd to the navigation of my boat; for tho' he knew very well how to paddle a canoe, he knew nothing what belong'd to a sail and a rudder, and was the most amaz'd when he saw me work the two, and again in the sea by the rudder, and how the sail gyb'd, and fill'd this way, or that way, as the course we sail'd chang'd. I say, when he saw this, he stood like one astonish'd and amaz'd. However, with a little use, I made all these things familiar to him, and he became an expert sailor, except as to the compass; I could make him understand very little of that. On the other hand, as there was very little cloudy weather, and seldom or never any fogs in those parts, there was the less occasion for a compass, seeing the stars were always to be seen by night, and the shore by day, except in the rainy season, and then no body car'd to stir abroad, either by land or sea.

I was now enter'd on the seven-and-twentieth year of my captivity in this place, though the three last years that I had this creature with me ought rather to be left out of the account; my habitation being quite of another kind than in all the rest of the time. I kept the anniversary of my landing here with the same thankfulness to God for His mercys, as at first; and if I had such cause of acknowledgment at first, I had much more so now, having such additional testimonies of the care of Providence over me, and the great hopes I had of being effectually and speedily deliver'd; for I had an invincible impression upon my thoughts that my deliverance was at hand, and that I should not be another year in this place. However, I went on with my husbandry, digging, planting, fencing as usual; I gather'd and cur'd my grapes, and did every necessary thing as before.

The rainy season was in the meantime upon me, when I kept more within doors than at other times. So I had stow'd our new vessel as secure as we could, bringing her up into the creek, where as I said in the beginning, I landed my rafts from the ship, and haling her up to the shore, at high-water-mark, I made my man Friday dig a little dock, just big enough to hold her, and just deep enough to give her water enough to float in. Then when the tide was out, we made a strong dam cross the end of it to keep the water out. So she lay dry as to the tide from the sea; and to keep the rain off, we lay'd a great many boughs of trees, so thick that she was as well thatch'd as a house, and thus we waited

for the months of November and December, in which I design'd to make my adventure.

When the settl'd season began to come in, and as the
thought of my design return'd with the fair weather, I was
preparing daily for the voyage; and the first thing I did was
to lay by a certain quantity of provisions, being the stores
for our voyage, and I intended in a week or a fortnight's
time, to open the dock and launch out our boat. I was busy
one morning upon some thing of this kind, when I call'd
to Friday, and bade him go to the seashore and see if he
could find a turtle, or tortoise, a thing which we generally
got once a week, for the sake of the eggs as well as the
flesh. Friday had not been long gone, when he came
running back, and flew over my outer wall, or fence, like
one that felt not the ground, or the steps he set his feet
on! Before I had time to speak to him, he cry'd out to me,
"O Master! O Master! O sorrow! O bad!" "What's the
matter, Friday?" said I. "O yonder, there," said he, "one,
two, three canoe! one, two, three!" By his way of speaking,
I concluded there were six; but on enquiry, I found it was
but three. "Well, Friday," said I, "do not be frighted"; so
I hearten'd him up as well as I could. However, I saw the
poor fellow was most terribly scar'd, for nothing ran in his
head but that they were come to look for him, and would
cut him in pieces and eat him; and the poor fellow trembl'd
so that I scarce knew what to do with him. I comforted
him as well as I could, and told him I was in as much
danger as he, and that they would eat me as well as him.
"But," said I, "Friday, we must resolve to fight them. Can
you fight, Friday?" "Me shoot," said he, "but there come
many great number." "No matter for that," said I again,
"our guns will fright them so that we do not kill." I ask'd

him whether if I resolv'd to defend him, he would defend me, and stand by me, and do just as I bid him? He said, "Me die when you bid die, Master"; so I went and fetch'd a good dram of rum and gave him, for I had been so good a husband of my rum that I had a great deal left. When he had drank it, I made him take the two fowling-pieces, which we always carry'd, and load them with large swan-shot, as big as small pistol bullets. Then I took four musquets and loaded them with two slugs and five small bullets each; and my two pistols I loaded with a brace of bullets each. Then I hung my great sword as usual, naked by my side, and gave Friday his hatchet.

When I had thus prepar'd myself, I took my perspective-glass and went up to the side of the hill to see what I could discover. I found quickly, by my glass, that there were one-and-twenty savages, three prisoners, and three canoes, and that their whole business seem'd to be the triumphant banquet upon these three human bodies (a barbarous feast indeed), but nothing else more than as I had observ'd was usual with them.

I observ'd also that they were landed not where they had done when Friday made his escape, but nearer to my creek, where the shore was low and where a thick wood came close almost down to the sea. This, with the abhorrence of the inhumane errand these wretches came about, fill'd me with such indignation that I came down again to Friday and told him I was resolv'd to go down to them and kill them all, and ask'd him if he would stand by me. He was now gotten over his fright, and his spirits being a little riz'd with the dram I had given him, he was very cheerful and told me, as before, he would die when I bid die.

In this fit of fury, I took first and divided the arms which

I had charg'd, as before, between us. I gave Friday one pistol to stick in his girdle and three guns upon his shoulder; and I took one pistol and the other three myself, and in this posture we march'd out. I took a small bottle of rum in my pocket and gave Friday a large bag with more powder and bullet; and as to orders, I charg'd him to keep close behind me, and not to stir, or shoot, or anything, till I bid him; and in the meantime, not to speak a word. In this posture I fetch'd a compass to my right hand, of near a mile, as well to get over the creek as to get into the wood, so that I might come within shot of them before I should be discover'd, which I had seen by my glass it was easy to do.

While I was making this march, my former thoughts returning, I began to abate my resolution. I do not mean that I entertain'd any fear of their number, for as they were naked, unarm'd wretches 'tis certain I was superior to them, nay, tho' I had been alone; but it occurr'd to my thoughts, What call? What occasion? Much less, what necessity was I in to go and dip my hands in blood, to attack people who had neither done or intended me any wrong? Who as to me were innocent, and whose barbarous customs were their own disaster, being in them a token indeed of God's having left them, with the other nations of that part of the world, to such stupidity, and to such inhumane courses, but did not call me to take upon myself to be a judge of their actions, much less an executioner of His justice; that whenever He thought fit, He would take the cause into His own hands, and by national vengeance punish them as a people, for national crimes; but that in the meantime, it was none of my business; that it was true, Friday might justify it, because he was a declar'd enemy,

*When the boat was in the water, it amaz'd me to see with
what dexterity and how swift my man Friday could manage
her, turn her, and paddle her along. (page 263)*

and in a state of war with those very particular people, and it was lawful for him to attack them, but I could not say the same with respect to me. These things were so warmly press'd upon my thoughts, all the way as I went, that I resolv'd I would only go and place myself near them, that I might observe their barbarous feast, and that I would act then as God should direct but that unless something offer'd that was more a call to me than yet I knew of, I would not meddle with them.

With this resolution I enter'd the wood, and with all possible waryness and silence, Friday following close at my heels, I march'd till I came to the skirt of the wood, on the side which was next to them; only that one corner of the wood lay between me and them. Here I call'd softly to Friday, and shewing him a great tree, which was just at the corner of the wood, I bade him go to the tree and bring me word if he could see there plainly what they were doing. He did so, and came immediately back to me, and told me they might be plainly view'd there; that they were all about their fire, eating the flesh of one of their prisoners; and that another lay bound upon the sand, a little from them, which he said they would kill next, and which fir'd all the very soul within me. He told me it was not one of their nation, but one of the bearded men, who he had told me of, that came to their country in the boat. I was fill'd with horror at the very naming the white bearded men and, going to the tree, I saw plainly by my glass a white man who lay upon the beach of the sea, with his hands and his feet ty'd with flags, or things like rushes, and that he was a European and had cloaths on.

There was another tree, and a little thicket beyond it, about fifty yards nearer to them than the place where I was, which by going a little way about, I saw I might come at undiscover'd, and that then I should be within half-shot of them. So I withheld my passion, though I was indeed enrag'd to the highest degree. Going back about twenty paces, I got behind some bushes, which held all the way till I came to the other tree, and then I came to a little riz-ing ground, which gave me a full view of them, at the dis-tance of about eighty yards.

I had now not a moment to lose, for nineteen of the dreadful wretches sat upon the ground, all close huddl'd together, and had just sent the other two to butcher the poor Christian and bring him perhaps limb by limb to their fire, and they were stoop'd down to untie the bands at his feet. I turn'd to Friday, "Now Friday," said I, "do as I bid thee"; Friday said he would. "Then Friday," said I, "do exactly as you see me do; fail in nothing." So I set down one of the musquets and the fowling-piece upon the ground, and Friday did the like by his; and with the other musquet, I took my aim at the savages, bidding him do the like, then asking him if he was ready? He said, "Yes." "Then fire at them," said I, and the same moment I fir'd also.

Friday took his aim so much better than I that on the side that he shot he kill'd two of them and wounded three more; and on my side I kill'd one and wounded two. They were, you may be sure, in a dreadful consternation; and all of them who were not hurt jump'd up upon their feet, but did not immediately know which way to run or which way to look, for they knew not whence their destruction came. Friday kept his eyes close upon me that, as I had bade him, he might observe what I did. So as soon as the first shot was made, I threw down the piece and took up the fowling-piece, and Friday did the like; he saw me cock and present; he did the same again. "Are you ready, Friday?" said I. "Yes," said he. "Let fly then," said I, "in the name of God." With that I fir'd again among the amaz'd wretches, and so did Friday; and as our pieces were now loaden with what I call'd swan-shot, or small pistol bullets, we found only two drop; but so many were wounded that they ran about yelling and screaming like mad creatures, all bloody and miserably wounded, most of them; whereof three more fell quickly after, though not quite dead.

"Now Friday," said I, laying down the discharg'd pieces and taking up the musquet, which was yet loaden, "follow me," which he did, with a great deal of courage; upon which I rush'd out of the wood and shew'd myself, with Friday close at my foot. As soon as I perceiv'd they saw me, I shouted as loud as I could and bade Friday do so too; and running as fast as I could, which by the way, was not very fast, being loaden with arms as I was, I made directly towards the poor victim, who was, as I said, lay'd upon the beach, or shore, between the place where they sat and the sea. The two butchers who were just going to work with him had left him, at the surprize of our first fire, and fled in a terrible fright to the seaside, and had jump'd into a canoe, and three more of the rest made the same way. I turn'd to Friday and bade him step forwards and fire at them. He understood me immediately, and running about forty yards, to be near them, he shot at them, and I thought he had kill'd them all, for I saw them all fall of a heap into the boat, tho' I saw two of them up again quickly. However, he had kill'd two of them and wounded the third, so that he lay down in the bottom of the boat, as if he had been dead.

While my man Friday fir'd at them, I pull'd out my knife and cut the flags that bound the poor victim, and loosing his hands and feet, I lifted him up and ask'd him in the Portugueze tongue what he was? He answer'd in Latin, *Christianus*. But he was so weak and faint that he could scarce stand or speak. I took my bottle out of my pocket and gave it him, making signs that he should drink, which he did; and I gave him a piece of bread, which he ate. Then I ask'd him what countryman he was? And he said *Espagniole*, and being a little recover'd, let me know by all the signs he could possibly make how much he was in my debt for his deliverance: "Seignoir," said I, with as much Spanish as I could make up, "we will talk afterwards; but we must fight now. If you have any strength left, take this pistol and sword and lay about you." He took them very thankfully, and no sooner had he the arms in his hands, but as if they had put new vigour into him, he flew upon his murtherers like a fury and had cut two of them in pieces in an instant. The truth is, as the whole was a surprize to them, so the poor creatures were so much frighted with the noise of our pieces that they fell down for meer amazement and fear and had no more power to attempt their own escape than their flesh had to resist our shot. That was the case of those five that Friday shot at in the boat; for as three of them fell with the hurt they receiv'd, so the other two fell with the fright.

I kept my piece in my hand still, without firing, being willing to keep my charge ready, because I had given the Spaniard my pistol and sword. So I call'd to Friday and bade him run up to the tree, whence we first fir'd, and fetch the arms which lay there that had been discharg'd, which he did with great swiftness. Then giving him my musquet, I sat down myself to load all the rest again and bade them come to me when they wanted. While I was loading these pieces, there happen'd a fierce engagement between the Spaniard and one of the savages, who made at him with one of their great wooden swords, the same weapon that was to have kill'd him before if I had not prevented it. The Spaniard, who was as bold and as brave as could be imagin'd, though weak, had fought this Indian a good while and had cut him two great wounds on his head; but the savage being a stout lusty fellow, closing in with him, had thrown him down (being faint) and was wringing my sword out of his hand, when the Spaniard, tho' undermost, wisely quitting the sword, drew the pistol from his girdle, shot the savage thro' the body, and kill'd him upon the spot, before I, who was running to help him, could come near him.

Friday, being now left to his liberty, pursu'd the flying wretches with no weapon in his hand but his hatchet, and with that he dispatch'd those three, who, as I said before, were wounded at first and fallen, and all the rest he could come up with, and the Spaniard coming to me for a gun, I gave him one of the fowling-pieces, with which he pursu'd two of the savages and wounded them both. But as he was not able to run, they both got from him into the wood, where Friday pursu'd them and kill'd one of them. But the other was too nimble for him, and though he was wounded, yet had plunged himself into the sea and swam with all his might off to those two who were left in the canoe, which three in the canoe, with one wounded, who we know not whether he dy'd or no, were all that escap'd our hands of one-and-twenty. The account of the rest is as follows:

3 kill'd at our first shot from the tree
2 kill'd at the next shot
2 kill'd by Friday in the boat
3 kill'd by ditto, of those at first wounded
1 killed by ditto, in the wood
3 kill'd by the Spaniard
4 kill'd, being found dropp'd here and there of their wounds, or kill'd by Friday in his chase of them.
4 escap'd in the boat, whereof one wounded if not dead.

———

21 in all

———

Those that were in the canoe work'd hard to get out of gun-shot, and tho' Friday made two or three shots at them, I did not find that he hit any of them. Friday would fain have had me take one of their canoes and pursue them; and indeed I was very anxious about their escape, lest carrying the news home to their people, they should come back perhaps with two or three hundred of their canoes and devour us by mere multitude. So I contented to pursue them by sea and, running to one of their canoes, I jump'd in and bade Friday follow me. But when I was in the canoe, I was surpriz'd to find another poor creature lay there alive, bound hand and foot as the Spaniard was for the slaughter, and almost dead with fear, not knowing what the matter was, for he had not been able to look up over the side of the boat, he was ty'd so hard, neck and heels, and had been ty'd so long that he had really but little life in him. I immediately cut the twisted flags, or rushes, which they had bound him with, and would have help'd him up; but he could not stand, or speak, but groan'd most piteously, believing it seems still that he was only unbound in order to be kill'd.

When Friday came to him, I bade him speak to him and tell him of his deliverance, and, pulling out my bottle, made him give the poor wretch a dram, which, with the news of his being deliver'd, reviv'd him, and he sat up in the boat. But when Friday came to hear him speak and look in his face, it would have mov'd any one to tears to have seen how Friday kiss'd him, embrac'd him, hugg'd him, cry'd, laugh'd, hollow'd, jump'd about, danc'd, sung, then cry'd again, wrung his hands, beat his own face and head, and then sung and jump'd about again like a distracted creature. It was a good while before I could make him speak to me or tell me what was the matter; but when he came a little to himself, he told me that it was his father.

It is not easy for me to express how it mov'd me to see what extasie and filial affection had work'd in this poor savage at the sight of his father and of his being deliver'd from death; nor indeed can I describe half the extravagancies of his affection after this; for he went into the boat and out of the boat a great many times. When he went in to his father, he would sit down by him, open his breast, and hold his father's head close to his bosom, half an hour together, to nourish it. Then he took his arms and ankles, which were numb'd and stiff with the binding, and chaf'd and rubb'd them with his hands. Perceiving what the case was, I gave him some rum out of my bottle to rub them with, which did them a great deal of good.

This action put an end to our pursuit of the canoe with

the other savages, who were now gotten almost out of sight; and it was happy for us that we did not, for it blew so hard within two hours after, and before they could be gotten a quarter of their way, and continu'd blowing so hard all night, and that from the north-west, which was against them, that I could not suppose their boat could live or that they ever reach'd to their own coast.

But to return to Friday. He was so busy about his father that I could not find in my heart to take him off for some time. But after I thought he could leave him a little, I call'd him to me, and he came jumping and laughing and pleas'd to the highest extreme. Then I ask'd him if he had given his father any bread? He shook his head, and said, "None. Ugly dog eat all up self." So I gave him a cake of bread out of a little pouch I carry'd on purpose; I also gave him a dram for himself, but he would not taste it, but carry'd it to his father. I had in my pocket also two or three bunches of my raisins, so I gave him a handful of them for his father. He had no sooner given his father these raisins, but I saw him come out of the boat, and run away, as if he had been bewitch'd. He ran at such a rate, for he was the swiftest fellow of his foot that ever I saw; I say, he ran at such a rate that he was out of sight, as it were, in an instant; and though I call'd, and hollow'd too, after him, it was all one, away he went, and in a quarter of an hour, I saw him come back again, though not so fast as he went; and as he came nearer, I found his pace was slacker, because he had some thing in his hand.

When he came up to me, I found he had been quite home for an earthen jugg or pot to bring his father some fresh water, and that he had got two more cakes, or loaves of bread. The bread he gave me, but the water he carry'd to his father. However, as I was very thirsty too, I took a little sup of it. This water reviv'd his father more than all the rum or spirits I had given him, for he was just fainting with thirst.

When his father had drank, I call'd to him to know if there was any water left; he said yes; and I bade him give it to the poor Spaniard, who was in as much want of it as his father. Then I sent one of the cakes that Friday brought to the Spaniard too, who was indeed very weak and was reposing himself upon a green place under the shade of a tree, and whose limbs were also very stiff and very much swell'd with the rude bandage he had been ty'd with. When I saw that upon Friday's coming to him with the water, he sat up and drank, and took the bread, and began to eat, I went to him and gave him a handful of raisins. He look'd up in my face, and with all the tokens of gratitude and thankfulness that could appear in any countenance. But he was so weak, notwithstanding he had so exerted himself in the fight, that he could not stand up upon his feet. He try'd to do it two or three times, but was really not able, his ankles were so swell'd and so painful to him; so I bade him sit still, and caused Friday to rub his ankles and bathe them with rum, as he had done his father's.

I observ'd the poor affectionate creature every two minutes, or perhaps less, all the while he was there, turn'd his head about to see if his father was in the same place, and posture, as he left him sitting; and at last he found he was not to be seen, at which he started up and, without speaking a word, flew with that swiftness to him that one could scarce perceive his feet to touch the ground as he went. But when he return'd, he only found he had lay'd himself down to ease his limbs. So Friday came back to me presently, and I then spoke to the Spaniard to let Friday help him up if he could and lead him to the boat, and then he should carry him to our dwelling, where I would take care of him. But Friday, a lusty strong fellow, took the Spaniard quite up upon his back, and carry'd him away to the boat, and set him down softly upon the side or gunnel of the canoe, with his feet in the inside of it, and then lifted him quite in and set him close to his father, and presently stepping out again, launch'd the boat off and paddl'd it along the shore faster than I could walk, tho' the wind blew pretty hard too. So he brought them both safe into our creek and, leaving them in the boat, ran away to fetch the other canoe. As he pass'd me, I spoke to him and ask'd him whither he went. He told me, "Go fetch more boat." So away he went like the wind, for sure never man or horse ran like him, and he had the other canoe in the creek almost as soon as I got to it by land. So he wafted me over and then went to help our new guests out of the boat, which he did; but they were neither of them able to walk, so that poor Friday knew not what to do.

To remedy this, I went to work in my thoughts and, calling to Friday to bid them sit down on the bank while he came to me, I soon made a kind of hand-barrow to lay them on, and Friday and I carry'd them up both together upon it between us. But when we got them to the out-side of our wall or fortification, we were at a worse loss than before, for it was impossible to get them over. I was resolv'd not to break it down, so I set to work again; and Friday and I, in about two hours' time, made a very handsome tent, cover'd with old sails, and above that with boughs of trees, being in the space without our out-side fence, and between that and the grove of young wood which I had planted. And here we made them two beds of such things as I had, viz., of good rice-straw, with blankets lay'd upon them to lie on, and another to cover them on each bed.

My island was now peopl'd, and I thought myself very rich in subjects; and it was a merry reflection which I frequently made, how like a king I look'd. First of all, the whole country was my own meer property, so that I had an undoubted right of dominion. Secondly, my people were perfectly subjected; I was absolute lord and lawgiver; they all ow'd their lives to me and were ready to lay down their lives, if there had been occasion of it, for me. It was remarkable too, I had but three subjects, and they were of three different religions: my man Friday was a Protestant, his father was a pagan and a canibal, and the Spaniard was a Papist; however, I allow'd liberty of conscience throughout my dominions. But this is by the way.

As soon as I had secur'd my two weak rescu'd prisoners and given them shelter and a place to rest them upon, I began to think of making some provision for them. And the first thing I did, I order'd Friday to take a yearling goat, betwixt a kid and a goat, out of my particular flock, to be kill'd. Then I cut off the hinder quarter and, chopping it into small pieces, I set Friday to work to boiling and stewing, and made them a very good dish, I assure you, of flesh and broth, having put some barley and rice also into the broth. As I cook'd it without doors, for I made no fire within my inner wall, so I carry'd it all into the new tent; and having set a table there for them, I sat down and ate my own dinner also with them, and, as well as I could, cheer'd them and encourag'd them, Friday being my interpreter, especially to his father, and indeed to the Spaniard too; for the Spaniard spoke the language of the savages pretty well.

After we had din'd, or rather supp'd, I order'd Friday to take one of the canoes and go and fetch our musquets and other fire-arms, which for want of time we had left upon the place of battle. The next day I order'd him to go and bury the dead bodies of the savages, which lay open to the sun and would presently be offensive; I also order'd him to bury the horrid remains of their barbarous feast, which I knew were pretty much, and which I could not think of doing myself; nay, I could not bear to see them, if I went that way. All which he punctually perform'd, and defac'd the very appearance of the savages being there, so that when I went again I could scarce know where it was, otherwise than by the corner of the wood pointing to the place.

I then began to enter into a little conversation with my two new subjects. First I set Friday to enquire of his father what he thought of the escape of the savages in that canoe and whether we might expect a return of them with a power too great for us to resist. His first opinion was that the savages in the boat never could live out the storm which blew that night they went off, but must of necessity be drown'd or driven south to those other shores where they were as sure to be devour'd as they were to be drown'd if they were cast away; but as to what they would do if they came safe on shore, he said he knew not; but it was his opinion that they were so dreadfully frighted with the manner of their being attack'd, the noise and the fire, that he believ'd they would tell their people they were all kill'd by thunder and lightning, not by the hand of man, and that the two which appear'd, viz., Friday and me, were two heavenly spirits or furies, come down to destroy them, and not men with weapons. This he said he knew, because he heard them all cry out so in their language to one another, for it was impossible to them to conceive that a man could dart fire, and speak thunder, and kill at a distance without lifting up the hand, as was done now. And this old savage was in the right, for, as I understood since by other hands, the savages never attempted to go over to the island afterwards. They were so terrify'd with the accounts given by those four men (for it seems they did escape the sea) that they believ'd whoever went to that enchanted island would be destroy'd with fire from the gods.

This however I knew not and therefore was under continual apprehensions for a good while and kept always upon my guard, me and all my army; for as we were now four of us, I would have ventur'd upon a hundred of those savages fairly in the open field at any time.

In a little time, however, no more canoes appearing, the fear of their coming wore off, and I began to take my former thoughts of a voyage to the main into consideration, being likewise assur'd by Friday's father that I might depend upon good usage from their nation on his account if I would go.

But my thoughts were a little suspended when I had a serious discourse with the Spaniard, and when I understood that there were sixteen more of his countrymen and Portugueze, which is near that number who, having been cast away and made their escape to that side, liv'd there at peace indeed with the savages, but were very sore put to it for necessaries, and indeed for life. I ask'd him all the particulars of their voyage, and found they had been a Spanish ship bound from the Rio de la Plata to the Havana, being directed to leave their loading there, which was chiefly hides and silver, and to bring back what European goods they could meet with there; that they had five Portugueze seamen on board, who they took out of another wreck; that five of their own men were drown'd when the first ship was lost and that these escap'd thro' infinite dangers and hazards and arriv'd almost starv'd on the canibal coast, where they expected to have been devour'd every moment.

He told me they had some arms with them, but they were perfectly useless, for that they had neither powder or ball, the washing of the sea having spoil'd all their powder but a little, which they used at their first landing to provide themselves some food.

I ask'd him what he thought would become of them there and if they had form'd no design of making any escape. He said they had had many consultations about it, but that having neither vessel nor tools to build one, or provisions of any kind, their councils always ended in tears and despair.

I ask'd him how he thought they would receive a proposal from me, which might tend towards an escape. And whether, if they were all here, it might not be done. I told him with freedom, I fear'd mostly their treachery and ill usage of me, if I put my life in their hands, for that gratitude was no inherent virtue in the nature of man, nor did men always square their dealings by the obligations they had receiv'd, so much as they did by the advantages they expected. I told him it would be very hard that I should be the instrument of their deliverance and that they should afterwards make me their prisoner in New Spain, where an Englishman was certain to be made a sacrifice, no matter what necessity, or what accident, brought him thither. And that I had rather be deliver'd up to the savages and be devour'd alive than fall into the merciless claws of the priests and be carry'd into the Inquisition. I added that otherwise I was persuaded, if they were all here, we might, with so many hands, build a bark large enough to carry us all away, either to the Brasils southward or to the islands or Spanish coast nor'ward. But that if in requital they should, when I had put weapons into their hands, carry me by force among their own people, I might be ill used for my kindness to them and make my case worse than it was before.

He answer'd, with a great deal of candour and ingenuity, that their condition was so miserable, and they were so sensible of it, that he believ'd they would abhor the thought of using any man unkindly that should contribute to their deliverance; and that, if I pleas'd, he would go to them with the old man and discourse with them about it, and return again and bring me their answer. That he would make conditions with them upon their solemn oath that they should be absolutely under my leading, as their commander and captain; and that they should swear upon the holy sacraments and the Gospel to be true to me and to go to such Christian country as that I should agree to, and no other; and to be directed wholly and absolutely to my orders, till they were landed safely in such country as I intended; and that he would bring a contract from them under their hands for this purpose.

Then he told me he would first swear to me himself that he would never stir from me as long as he liv'd, till I gave him orders; and that he would take my side to the last drop of his blood if there should happen the least breach of faith among his countrymen.

He told me they were all of them very civil honest men, and they were under the greatest distress imaginable, having neither weapons or cloaths, nor any food, but at the mercy and discretion of the savages; out of all hopes of ever returning to their own country; and that he was sure, if I would undertake their relief, they would live and die by me.

Upon these assurances, I resolv'd to venture to relieve them, if possible, and to send the old savage and the Spaniard over to them to treat. But when we had gotten all things in a readiness to go, the Spaniard himself started an objection, which had so much prudence in it on one hand, and so much sincerity on the other hand, that I could not but be very well satisfy'd in it; by his advice, I put off the deliverance of his comrades for at least half a year. The case was thus.

He had been with us now about a month, during which time I had let him see in what manner I had provided, with the assistance of Providence, for my support. He saw evidently what stock of corn and rice I had lay'd up, which as it was more than sufficient for myself, so it was not sufficient, at least without good husbandry, for my family; now it was encreas'd to number four. But much less would it be sufficient, if his countrymen, who were, as he said, fourteen still alive, should come over. And least of all should it be sufficient to victual our vessel, if we should build one, for a voyage to any of the Christian colonies of America. So he told me he thought it would be more advisable to let him and the two other dig and cultivate some more land, as much as I could spare seed to sow; and that we should wait another harvest, that we might have a supply of corn for his countrymen when they should come; for want might be a temptation to them to disagree, or not to think themselves deliver'd otherwise than out of one difficulty into another. "You know," said he, "the Children of Israel, tho' they rejoyc'd at first for their being deliver'd out of Egypt, yet rebell'd even against God himself that deliver'd them, when they came to want bread in the wilderness."

His caution was so seasonable, and his advice so good, that I could not but be very well pleas'd with his proposal, as well as I was satisfy'd with his fidelity. So we fell to digging, all four of us, as well as the wooden tools we were furnish'd with permitted. In about a month's time, by the end of which it was seed-time, we had gotten as much land cur'd and trimm'd up, as we sowed twenty-two bushels of barley on and sixteen jarrs of rice, which was, in short, all the seed we had to spare; nor indeed did we leave ourselves barley sufficient for our own food, for the six months that we had to expect our crop, that is to say, reckoning from the time we set our seed a-side for sowing, for it is not to be supposed it is six months in the ground in the country.

Having now society enough, and our number being sufficient to put us out of fear of the savages, if they had come, unless their number had been very great, we went freely all over the island, where ever we found occasion. Here we had our escape or deliverance upon our thoughts, and it was impossible, at least for me, to have the means of it out of mine. To this purpose, I mark'd out several trees which I thought fit for our work, and I set Friday and his father to cutting them down. Then I caus'd the Spaniard, to whom I imparted my thoughts on that affair, to oversee and direct their work. I shew'd them with what indefatigable pains I had hew'd a large tree into single planks, and I caus'd them to do the like, till they had made about a dozen large planks of good oak, near two foot broad, thirty-five foot long, and from two inches to four inches thick. What prodigious labour this took up, any one may imagine.

At the same time I contriv'd to encrease my little flock of tame goats as much as I could; and to this purpose, I made Friday and the Spaniard go out one day, and myself with Friday the next day; for we took our turns. By this means we got above twenty young kids to breed up with the rest; for whenever we shot the dam, we sav'd the kids and added them to our flock. But above all, the season for curing the grapes coming on, I caus'd such a prodigious quantity to be hung up in the sun that I believe, had we been at Alicant, where the raisins of the sun are cur'd, we could have fill'd sixty or eighty barrels; and these with our bread was a great part of our food, and very good living too, I assure you, for it is an exceeding nourishing food.

It was now harvest, and our crop was in good order. It was not the most plentiful encrease I had seen in the island, but it was enough to answer our end; for from our twenty-two bushels of barley, we brought in and thrash'd out above two hundred and twenty bushels; and the like in proportion of the rice, which was store enough for our food to the next harvest, tho' all the sixteen Spaniards had been on shore with me. If we had been ready for a voyage, it would very plentifully have victual'd our ship to have carry'd us to any part of the world, that is to say, of America.

When we had thus hous'd and secur'd our magazine of corn, we fell to work to make more wicker-ware, viz., great baskets in which we kept it; and the Spaniard was very handy and dextrous at this part and often blam'd me that

I did not make some things, for defence, of this kind of work, but I saw no need of it.

Now having a full supply of food for all the guests I expected, I gave the Spaniard leave to go over to the main to see what he could do with those he had left behind him there. I gave him a strict charge in writing not to bring any man with him who would not first swear, in the presence of himself and of the old savage, that he would no way injure, fight with, or attack the person he should find on the island, who was so kind to send for them in order to their deliverance; but that they would stand by and defend him against any such attempts and, where ever they went, would be entirely under and subjected to his commands; and that this should be put in writing and signed with their hands. How we were to have this done, when I knew they had neither pen or ink, that indeed was a question which we never ask'd.

Under these instructions, the Spaniard and the old savage (the father of Friday) went away in one of the canoes, which they might be said to come in, or rather were brought in, when they came as prisoners to be devour'd by the savages.

I gave each of them a musquet with a fire-lock on it, and about eight charges of powder and ball, charging them to be very good husbands of both and not to use either of them but upon urgent occasion.

This was a cheerful work, being the first measure used by me in view of my deliverance for now twenty-seven years and some days. I gave them provisions of bread, and of dry'd grapes, sufficient for all their countrymen for about eight days' time; and wishing them a good voyage, I saw them go, agreeing with them about a signal they should hang out at their return, by which I should know them again when they came back, at a distance, before they came on shore.

They went away with a fair gale on the day that the moon was at full by my account, in the month of October. But as for an exact reckoning of days, after I had once lost it, I could never recover it again; nor had I kept even the number of years so punctually, as to be sure that I was right, tho' as it prov'd, when I afterwards examin'd my account, I found I had kept a true reckoning of years.

It was no less than eight days I had waited for them, when a strange and unforeseen accident interven'd, of which the like has not perhaps been heard of in history. I was fast asleep in my hutch one morning, when my man Friday came running in to me, and call'd aloud, "Master, Master, they are come, they are come."

I jump'd up and, regardless of danger, I went out as soon as I could get my cloaths on, thro' my little grove, which by the way was by this time grown to be a very thick wood; I say, regardless of danger, I went without my arms, which was not my custom to do. But I was surpriz'd, when turning my eyes to the sea, I presently saw a boat at about a league and a half's distance, standing in for the shore, with a shoulder-of-mutton sail, as they call it, and the wind blowing pretty fair to bring them in. Also, I observ'd presently that they did not come from that side which the shore lay on, but from the southernmost end of the island. Upon this I call'd Friday in, and bade him lie close, for these were not the people we look'd for, and that we might not know yet whether they were friends or enemies.

In the next place, I went in to fetch my perspective-glass, to see what I could make of them; and having taken the ladder out, I climb'd up to the top of the hill, as I used to do when I was apprehensive of any thing, and to take my view the plainer without being discover'd.

I had scarce set my foot on the hill when my eye plainly discover'd a ship lying at anchor, at about two leagues and a half's distance from me SSE, but not above a league and a half from the shore. By my observation it appear'd plainly to be an English ship, and the boat appear'd to be an English longboat.

I cannot express the confusion I was in, tho' the joy of seeing a ship, and one who I had reason to believe was mann'd by my own countrymen, and consequently friends, was such as I cannot describe. Yet some secret doubts hung about me, I cannot tell whence they came, bidding me keep upon my guard. In the first place, it occurr'd to me to consider what business an English ship could have in that part of the world, since it was not the way to or from any part of the world where the English had any traffick. I knew there had been no storms to drive them in there, as in distress; that if they were English really, it was most probable that they were here upon no good design; and that I had better continue as I was than fall into the hands of thieves and murtherers.

Let no man despise the secret hints and notices of danger, which sometimes are given him, when he may think there is no possibility of its being real. That such hints and notices are given us, I believe few that have made any observations of things, can deny; that there are certain discoveries of an invisible world, and a converse of spirits, we cannot doubt; and if the tendency of them seems to be to warn us of danger, why should we not suppose they are from some friendly agent, whether supreme, or inferior and subordinate, is not the question, but that they are given for our good.

The present question abundantly confirms me in the justice of this reasoning, for had I not been made cautious by this secret admonition, come it from whence it will, I had been undone inevitably and in a far worse condition than before, as you will see presently.

I had not kept myself long in this posture, but I saw the boat draw near the shore, as if they look'd for a creek to thrust in at for the convenience of landing; however, as they did not come quite far enough, they did not see the little inlet where I formerly landed my rafts; but ran their boat on shore upon the beach, at about half a mile from me, which was very happy for me. Otherwise they would have landed just as I may say at my door and would soon have beaten me out of my castle and perhaps have plunder'd me of all I had.

When they were on shore, I was fully satisfy'd that they were Englishmen; at least, most of them; one or two I thought were Dutch; but it did not prove so. There were in all eleven men, whereof three of them I found were unarm'd and, as I thought, bound; and when the first four or five of them were jump'd on shore, they took those three out of the boat as prisoners. One of the three I could perceive using the most passionate gestures of entreaty, affliction and despair, even to a kind of extravagance; the other two I could perceive lifted up their hands sometimes and appear'd concern'd indeed, but not to such a degree as the first.

I was perfectly confounded at the sight and knew not what the meaning of it should be. Friday call'd out to me in English, as well as he could, "O Master! You see English mans eat prisoner as well as savage mans!" "Why," said I, "Friday, do you think they are a-going to eat them then!" "Yes," said Friday, "they will eat them!" "No, no," said I, "Friday, I am afraid they will murther them indeed, but you may be sure they will not eat them."

All this while I had no thought of what the matter really was, but stood trembling with the horror of the sight, expecting every moment that the three prisoners should be kill'd; nay, once I saw one of the villains lift up his arm with a great cutlash, as the seamen call it, or sword, to strike one of the poor men; and I expected to see him fall every moment, at which all the blood in my body seem'd to run chill in my veins.

I wish'd heartily now for my Spaniard and the old savage that was gone with him; or that I had any way to have come undiscover'd within shot of them, that I might have rescu'd the three men, for I saw no fire-arms they had among them. But this fell out of my mind another way.

After I had observ'd the outrageous usage of the three men by the insolent seamen, I observ'd the fellows run scattering about the land, as if they wanted to see the country. I observ'd that the three other men had liberty to go also where they pleas'd, but they sat down all three upon the ground, very pensive, and look'd like men in despair.

This put me in mind of the first time when I came on shore and began to look about me. How I gave myself over for lost; how wildly I look'd round me; what dreadful apprehensions I had; and how I lodg'd in the tree all night for fear of being devour'd by wild beasts. As I knew nothing that night of the supply I was to receive by the providential driving of the ship nearer the land, by the storms and tide, by which I had since been so long nourish'd and supported; so these three poor desolate men knew nothing how certain of deliverance and supply they were, how near it was to them, and how effectually and really they were in a condition of safety, at the same time that they thought themselves lost and their case desperate.

So little do we see before us in the world, and so much reason have we to depend cheerfully upon the great Maker of the world, that He does not leave His creatures so absolutely destitute, but that in the worst circumstances they have always some thing to be thankful for, and sometimes are nearer their deliverance than they imagine; nay, are even brought to their deliverance by the means by which they seem to be brought to their destruction.

It was just at the top of high-water when these people came on shore, and while partly they stood parlaying with the prisoners they brought, and partly while they rambled about to see what kind of a place they were in, they had carelessly stay'd till the tide was spent and the water was ebb'd considerably away, leaving their boat a-ground.

They had left two men in the boat, who as I found afterwards, having drank a little too much brandy, fell a-sleep. However, one of them waking sooner than the other, and finding the boat too fast a-ground for him to stir it, hollow'd for the rest who were straggling about, upon which they all soon came to the boat; but it was past all their strength to launch her, the boat being very heavy, and the shore on that side being a soft oozey sand, almost like a quicksand.

In this condition, like true seamen who are perhaps the least of all mankind given to fore-thought, they gave it over, and away they stroll'd about the country again. I heard one of them say aloud to another, calling them off from the boat, "Why let her alone, Jack, can't ye, she will float next tide"; by which I was fully confirm'd in the main enquiry of what countrymen they were.

All this while I kept myself very close, not once daring to stir out of my castle, any farther than to my place of observation, near the top of the hill; and very glad I was, to think how well it was fortify'd. I knew it was no less than ten hours before the boat could be on float again, and by that time it would be dark, and I might be at more liberty to see their motions and to hear their discourse, if they had any.

In the meantime, I fitted myself up for a battle as before, though with more caution, knowing I had to do with another kind of enemy than I had at first. I order'd Friday also, who I had made an excellent marks-man with his gun, to load himself with arms. I took myself two fowling-pieces, and I gave him three musquets. My figure indeed was very fierce; I had my formidable goat-skin coat on, with the great cap I have mention'd, a naked sword by my side, two pistols in my belt, and a gun upon each shoulder.

It was my design, as I said above, not to have made any attempt till it was dark. But about two a-clock, being the heat of the day, I found that in short they were all gone straggling into the woods, and as I thought were lay'd down to sleep. The three poor distress'd men, too anxious for their condition to get any sleep, were however set down under the shelter of a great tree, at about a quarter of a mile from me, and as I thought out of sight of any of the rest.

Upon this I resolv'd to discover myself to them and learn some thing of their condition. Immediately, I march'd in the figure as above; my man Friday at a good distance behind me, as formidable for his arms as I, but not making quite so staring a spectre-like figure as I did.

I came as near them undiscover'd as I could, and then before any of them saw me, I call'd aloud to them in Spanish, "What are ye gentlemen?"

They started up at the noise, but were ten times more confounded when they saw me and the uncouth figure that I made. They made no answer at all, but I thought I perceiv'd them just going to fly from me, when I spoke to them in English. "Gentlemen," said I, "do not be surpriz'd at me; perhaps you may have a friend near you when you did not expect it." "You must be sent directly from Heaven then," said one of them very gravely to me, and pulling off his hat at the same time to me, "for our condition is past the help of man." "All help is from Heaven, sir," said I. "But can you put a stranger in the way how to help you, for you seem to me to be in some great distress? I saw you when you landed, and when you seem'd to make applications to the brutes that came with you; I saw one of them lift up his sword to kill you."

The poor man with tears running down his face, and trembling, looking like one astonish'd, return'd. "Am I talking to God or man? Is it a real man or an angel?" "Be in no fear about that, sir," said I, "if God had sent an angel to relieve you, he would have come better cloath'd, and arm'd after another manner than you see me in; pray lay aside your fears; I am a man, an Englishman, and dispos'd to assist you. You see, I have one servant only. We have arms and ammunition. Tell us freely, can we serve you? What is your case?"

"Our case," said he, "sir, is too long to tell you, while

our murtherers are so near; but in short, sir, I was commander of that ship; my men have mutiny'd against me; they have been hardly prevail'd on not to murther me, and at last have set me on shore in this desolate place, with these two men with me. One is my mate, the other a passenger, where we expected to perish, believing the place to be uninhabited and knowing not yet what to think of it."

"Where are these brutes, your enemies," said I. "Do you know where they are gone?" "There they lie, sir," said he, pointing to a thicket of trees. "My heart trembles, for fear they have seen us, and heard you speak, if they have, they will certainly murther us all."

"Have they any fire-arms?" said I. He answer'd they had only two pieces, and one which they left in the boat. "Well then," said I, "leave the rest to me. I see they are all a-sleep. It is an easy thing to kill them all, but shall we rather take them prisoners?" He told me there were two desperate villains among them, that it was scarce safe to shew any mercy to; but if they were secur'd, he believ'd all the rest would return to their duty. I ask'd him, which they were? He told me he could not at that distance describe them, but he would obey my orders in any thing I would direct. "Well," said I, "let us retreat out of their view or hearing, lest they awake, and we will resolve further." So they willingly went back with me, till the woods cover'd us from them.

"Look you, sir," said I, "if I venture upon your deliverance, are you willing to make two conditions with me?" He anticipated my proposals by telling me that both he and the ship, if recover'd, should be wholly directed and commanded by me in every thing; and if the ship was not recover'd, he would live and die with me in what part of the world soever I would send him; and the two other men said the same.

"Well," said I, "my conditions are but two. 1. That while you stay on this island with me, you will not pretend to any authority here. If I put arms into your hands, you will upon all occasions give them up to me, and do no prejudice to me or mine, upon this island, and in the meantime be govern'd by my orders. 2. That if the ship is, or may be recover'd, you will carry me and my man to England passage free."

He gave me all the assurances that the invention and faith of man could devize; that he would comply with these most reasonable demands, and besides would owe his life to me, and acknowledge it upon all occasions as long as he liv'd.

"Well then," said I, "here are three musquets for you, with powder and ball; tell me next what you think is proper to be done." He shew'd all the testimony of his gratitude that he was able, but offer'd to be wholly guided by me. I told him I thought it was hard venturing any thing; but the best method I could think of was to fire upon them at once, as they lay. If any was not kill'd at the first volley, and offer'd to submit, we might save them and so put it wholly upon God's providence to direct the shot.

He said, very modestly, that he was loath to kill them if he could help it, but that those two were incorrigible villains and had been the authors of all the mutiny in the ship, and if they escap'd, we should be undone still, for they would go on board and bring the whole ship's company and destroy us all. "Well then," said I, "necessity legitimates my advice, for it is the only way to save our lives." However, seeing him still cautious of shedding blood, I told him they should go themselves and manage as they found convenient.

In the middle of this discourse, we heard some of them awake, and soon after we saw two of them on their feet. I ask'd him if either of them were of the men who he had said were the heads of the mutiny? He said, "No." "Well then," said I, "you may let them escape, and Providence seems to have waken'd them on purpose to save themselves." "Now," said I, "if the rest escape you, it is your fault."

Animated with this, he took the musquet I had given him in his hand, and a pistol in his belt, and his two comrades with him, with each man a piece in his hand. The two men who were with him going first, made some noise, at which one of the seamen who was awake, turn'd about, and seeing them coming, cry'd out to the rest. But it was too late then, for the moment he cry'd out, they fir'd. I mean the two men, the captain wisely reserving his own piece. They had so well aim'd their shot at the men they knew, that one of them was kill'd on the spot, and the other very much wounded, but not being dead, he started up upon his feet and call'd eagerly for help to the other; but the captain, stepping to him, told him 'twas too late to cry for help, he should call upon God to forgive his villiany, and with that word knock'd him down with the stock of his musquet, so that he never spoke more. There were three more in the company, and one of them was also slightly wounded. By this time I was come, and, when they saw their danger and that it was in vain to resist, they begg'd for mercy. The captain told them he would spare their lives, if they would give him any assurance of their abhorrence of the treachery they had been guilty of and would swear to be faithful to him in recovering the ship and afterwards in carrying her back to Jamaica, from whence they came. They gave him all the protestations of their sincerity that could be desir'd, and he was willing to believe them and spare their lives, which I was not against, only that I oblig'd him to keep them bound hand and foot while they were upon the island.

While this was doing, I sent Friday with the captain's mate to the boat, with orders to secure her and bring away the oars and sail, which they did. By and by, three straggling men that were (happily for them) parted from the rest, came back upon hearing the guns fir'd, and seeing their captain, who before was their prisoner, now their conqueror, they submitted to be bound also; and so our victory was compleat.

It now remain'd that the captain and I should enquire into one another's circumstances. I began first, and told him my whole history, which he heard with an attention even to amazement, and particularly, at the wonderful manner of my being furnish'd with provisions and ammunition; and indeed, as my story is a whole collection of wonders, it affected him deeply. But when he reflected thence upon himself, and how I seem'd to have been preserv'd there, on purpose to save his life, the tears ran down his face, and he could not speak a word more.

After this communication was at an end, I carry'd him and his two men into my appartment, leading them in, just where I came out, viz., at the top of the house, where I refresh'd them with such provisions as I had and shew'd them all the contrivances I had made during my long, long, inhabiting that place.

All I shew'd them, all I said to them, was perfectly

*I presently saw a boat at about a league and a half's distance,
standing in for the shore, with a shoulder-of-mutton sail.*
(*page 288*)

amazing; but above all, the captain admir'd my fortification and how perfectly I had conceal'd my retreat with a grove of trees, which having been now planted near twenty years, and the trees growing much faster than in England, was become a little wood and so thick that it was unpassable in any part of it, but at that one side where I had reserv'd my little winding passage into it. I told him this was my castle and my residence, but that I had a seat in the country, as most princes have, whither I could retreat upon occasion, and I would shew him that too another time, but at present, our business was to consider how to recover the ship. He agreed with me as to that, but told me he was perfectly at a loss what measures to take; for that there were still six-and-twenty hands on board, who having enter'd into a curs'd conspiracy, by which they had all forfeited their lives to the law, would be harden'd in it now by desperation and would carry it on, knowing that if they were reduc'd they should be brought to the gallows as soon as they came to England or to any of the English colonies; and that therefore there would be no attacking them with so small a number as we were.

I mus'd for some time upon what he had said and found it was a very rational conclusion. Therefore some thing was to be resolv'd on very speedily, as well to draw the men on board into some snare for their surprize, as to prevent their landing upon us and destroying us. Upon this it presently occurr'd to me that in a little while the ship's crew, wond'ring what was become of their comrades and of the boat, would certainly come on shore in their other boat to see for them, and that then perhaps they might come arm'd and be too strong for us. This he allow'd was rational.

Upon this, I told him the first thing we had to do was to stave the boat, which lay upon the beach, so that they might not carry her off and, taking every thing out of her, leave her so far useless as not to be fit to swim. Accordingly, we went on board, took the arms which were left on board out of her, and whatever else we found there, which was a bottle of brandy, and another of rum, a few bisket-cakes, a horn of powder, and a great lump of sugar, in a piece of canvass. The sugar was five or six pounds, all of which was very welcome to me, especially the brandy and sugar, of which I had had none left for many years.

When we had carry'd all these things on shore (the oars, mast, sail, and rudder of the boat were carry'd away before, as above), we knock'd a great hole in her bottom, that if they had come strong enough to master us, yet they could not carry off the boat.

Indeed, it was not much in my thoughts that we could be able to recover the ship; but my view was that if they went away without the boat, I did not much question to make her fit again, to carry us away to the Leeward Islands, and call upon our friends, the Spaniards, in my way, for I had them still in my thoughts.

While we were thus preparing our designs and had first, by main strength, heav'd the boat up upon the beach so high that the tide would not fleet her off at high-water-mark; and besides, had broke a hole in her bottom, too big to be quickly stopp'd, and were sat down musing what we should do; we heard the ship fire a gun and saw her make a waft with her antient, as a signal for the boat to come on board. But no boat stirr'd, and they fir'd several times, making other signals for the boat.

At last, when all their signals and firing prov'd fruitless, and they found the boat did not stir, we saw them, by the help of my glasses, hoist another boat out and row towards the shore. We found as they approach'd that there was no less than ten men in her and that they had fire-arms with them.

As the ship lay almost two leagues from the shore, we had a full view of them as they came and a plain sight of the men, even of their faces, because the tide having set them a little to the east of the other boat, they row'd up under shore to come to the same place where the others had landed and where the boat lay.

By this means, I say, we had a full view of them, and the captain knew the persons and the characters of all the men in the boat, of whom he said that there were three very honest fellows, who he was sure were led into this conspiracy by the rest, being over-power'd and frighted.

But as for the boat-swain, who it seems was the chief officer among them, and all the rest, they were as outrageous as any of the ship's crew, and were no doubt made desperate in their new enterprize, and terribly apprehensive he was, that they would be too powerful for us.

I smil'd at him and told him that men in our circumstances were past the operation of fear. That seeing almost every condition that could be was better than that which we were suppos'd to be in, we ought to expect that the consequence, whether death or life, would be sure to be a deliverance. I ask'd him what he thought of the circumstances of my life and whether a deliverance were not worth venturing for. "And where, sir," said I, "is your belief of my being preserv'd here on purpose to save your life, which elevated you a little while ago? For my part," said I, "there seems to be but one thing amiss in all the prospect of it." "What's that?" said he. "Why," said I, " 'tis that, as you say, there are three or four honest fellows among them who should be spar'd; had they been all of the wicked part of the crew, I should have thought God's providence had singl'd them out to deliver them into your hands; for depend upon it, every man of them that comes a-shore are our own, and shall die or live, as they behave to us."

As I spoke this with a rais'd voice and cheerful countenance, I found it greatly encourag'd him, so we set vigorously to our business. We had, upon the first appearance of the boat's coming from the ship, consider'd of separating our prisoners and had indeed secur'd them effectually.

Two of them, of whom the captain was less assur'd than ordinary, I sent with Friday, and one of the three (deliver'd men) to my cave, where they were remote enough and out of danger of being heard or discover'd or of finding their way out of the woods, if they could have deliver'd themselves. Here we left them bound, but gave them provisions and promis'd them, if they continu'd there quietly, to give them their liberty in a day or two; but that if they attempted their escape, they should be put to death without mercy. They promis'd faithfully to bear their confinement with patience and were very thankful that they had such good usage as to have provisions and a light left them; for Friday gave them candles (such as we made ourselves) for their comfort, and they did not know but that he stood sentinel over them at the entrance.

The other prisoners had better usage. Two of them were kept pinion'd indeed, because the captain was not free to trust them, but the other two were taken into my service upon their captain's recommendation and upon their solemnly engaging to live and die with us. So with them and the three honest men we were seven men, well arm'd; and I made no doubt we should be able to deal well enough with the ten that were a-coming, considering that the captain had said there were three or four honest men among them.

As soon as they got to the place where their other boat lay, they ran their boat in to the beach and came all on shore, haling the boat up after them, which I was glad to see, for I was afraid they would rather have left the boat at anchor some distance from the shore with some hands on her to guard her, and so we should not be able to seize the boat.

Being on shore, the first thing they did, they ran all to their other boat, and it was easy to see that they were under a great surprize to find her stripp'd as above, of all that was in her and a great hole in her bottom.

After they had mus'd awhile upon this, they set up two or three great shouts, hollowing with all their might, to try if they could make their companions hear; but all was to no purpose. Then they came all close in a ring and fir'd a volley of their small arms, which indeed we heard, and the echoes made the woods ring. But it was all one; those in the cave we were sure could not hear, and those in our keeping, though they heard it well enough, durst give no answer to them.

They were so astonish'd at the surprize of this that, as they told us afterwards, they resolv'd to go all on board again to their ship and let them know that the men were all murther'd and the longboat stav'd. Accordingly, they immediately launch'd their boat again and got all of them on board.

The captain was terribly amaz'd and even confounded at this, believing they would go on board the ship again and set sail, giving up their comrades for lost, and so he should still lose the ship, which he was in hopes we should have recover'd. But he was quickly as much frighted the other way.

They had not been long put off with the boat but we perceiv'd them all coming on shore again, but with this new measure in their conduct, which it seems they consulted together upon, viz., to leave three men in the boat, and the rest to go on shore, and go up into the country to look for their fellows.

This was a great disappointment to us, for now we were at a loss what to do; seizing those seven men on shore would be no advantage to us if we let the boat escape, because they would then row away to the ship and then the rest of them would be sure to weigh and set sail, and so our recovering the ship would be lost.

However, we had no remedy but to wait and see what the issue of things might present. The seven men came on shore, and the three who remain'd in the boat put her off to a good distance from the shore and came to anchor to wait for them; so that it was impossible for us to come at them in the boat.

Those that came on shore kept close together, marching towards the top of the little hill, under which my habitation lay. We could see them plainly, tho' they could not perceive us. We could have been very glad they would have come nearer to us, so that we might have fir'd at them, or that they would have gone farther off, that we might have come on board.

But when they were come to the brow of the hill, where they could see a great way into the valleys and woods which lay towards the north-east part and where the island lay lowest, they shouted and hollow'd till they were weary; and not caring it seems to venture far from the shore, nor far from one another, they sat down together under a tree to consider of it. Had they thought fit to have gone to sleep there, as the other party of them had done, they had done the jobb for us; but they were too full of apprehensions of danger to venture to go to sleep, tho' they could not tell what the danger was they had to fear neither.

The captain made a very just proposal to me upon this consultation of theirs, *viz.*, that perhaps they would all fire a volley again, to endeavour to make their fellows hear, and that we should all sally upon them, just at the juncture when their pieces were all discharg'd, and they would certainly yield, and we should have them without bloodshed. I lik'd the proposal, provided it was done while we were near enough to come up to them, before they could load their pieces again.

But this event did not happen, and we lay still a long time, very irresolute what course to take. At length I told them there would be nothing to be done in my opinion till night, and then if they did not return to the boat, perhaps we might find a way to get between them and the shore, and so might use some stratagem with them in the boat to get them on shore.

We waited a great while, tho' very impatient for their removing, and were very uneasy, when after long consultations, we saw them start all up, and march down

towards the sea. It seems they had such dreadful apprehensions upon them of the danger of the place that they
resolv'd to go on board the ship again, give their companions over for lost, and so go on with their intended
voyage with the ship.

As soon as I perceiv'd them go towards the shore, I
imagin'd it to be as it really was, that they had given over
their search and were for going back again. The captain, as
soon as I told him my thoughts, was ready to sink at the
apprehensions of it, but I presently thought of a stratagem
to fetch them back again which answer'd my end to a tittle.

I order'd Friday and the captain's mate to go over to
the little creek westward, towards the place where the
savages came on shore when Friday was rescu'd; and as
soon as they came to a little rizing ground, at about half
a mile distance, I bade them hollow as loud as they could
and wait till they found the seamen heard them; that as
soon as ever they heard the seamen answer them, they
should return it again and then, keeping out of sight, take
a round, always answering when the other hollow'd, to
draw them as far into the island and among the woods, as
possible, and then wheel about again to me, by such
ways as I directed them.

The seamen were just going into the boat when Friday
and the mate hollow'd, and they presently heard them.
Answering, they ran along the shore westward, towards
the voice they heard, where they were presently stopp'd
by the creek where, the water being up, they could not get
over, and call'd for the boat to come up and set them over,
as indeed I expected.

When they had set themselves over, I observ'd that the
boat being gone up a good way into the creek and, as it

were, in a harbour within the land, they took one of the three men out of her to go along with them, and left only two in the boat, having fasten'd her to the stump of a little tree on the shore.

This was what I wish'd for and, immediately leaving Friday and the captain's mate to their business, I took the rest with me and, crossing the creek out of their sight, we surpriz'd the two men before they were aware, one of them lying on shore, and the other being in the boat. The fellow on shore was between sleeping and waking, and going to start up; the captain, who was foremost, ran in upon him and knock'd him down, and then call'd out to him in the boat, to yield, or he was a dead man.

There needed very few arguments to persuade a single man to yield when he saw five men upon him and his comrade knock'd down; besides, this was, it seems, one of the three who were not so hearty in the mutiny as the rest of the crew, and therefore was easily persuaded, not only to yield, but afterwards to join very sincere with us.

In the meantime, Friday and the captain's mate so well manag'd their business with the rest, that they drew them by hollowing and answering from one hill to another, and from one wood to another, till they not only heartily tyr'd them, but left them where they were very sure they could not reach back to the boat before it was dark; and indeed they were heartily tyr'd themselves also by the time they came back to us.

We had nothing now to do but to watch for them, in the dark, and to fall upon them, so as to make sure work with them.

It was several hours, after Friday came back to me, before they came back to their boat; and we could hear the foremost of them long before they came quite up, calling to those behind to come along, and could also hear them answer and complain how lame and tyr'd they were, and not able to come any faster, which was very welcome news to us.

At length they came up to the boat, but 'tis impossible to express their confusion when they found the boat fast a-ground in the creek, the tide ebb'd out, and their two men gone. We could hear them call to one another in a most lamentable manner, telling one another they were gotten into an enchanted island; that either there were inhabitants in it, and they should all be murther'd, or else there were devils and spirits in it, and they should be all carry'd away and devour'd.

They hollow'd again, and call'd their two comrades by their names a great many times; but no answer. After some time, we could see them wringing their hands like men in despair, and that sometimes they would go and sit down in the boat to rest themselves, then come ashore again, and walk about again, and so over the same thing again.

My men would fain have me given them leave to fall upon them at once in the dark, but I was willing to take them at some advantage, so to spare them, and kill as few of them as I could; and especially I was unwilling to hazard the killing of any of our own men, knowing the others were very well arm'd. I resolv'd to wait to see if they did not separate; and therefore, to make sure of them, I drew my ambuscade nearer and order'd Friday and the captain to creep upon their hands and feet as close to the ground as they could, that they might not be discover'd, and get as near them as they could possibly before they offer'd to fire.

They had not been long in that posture, but that the boat-swain, who was the principal ringleader of the mutiny, and had now shew'd himself the most dejected and dispirited of all the rest, came walking towards them with two more of their crew. The captain was so eager, having this principal rogue so much in his power, that he could hardly have patience to let him come so near as to be sure of him, for they only heard his tongue before. But when they came nearer, the captain and Friday, starting up on their feet, let fly at them.

The boat-swain was kill'd upon the spot, the next man was shot into the body, and fell just by him, tho' he did not die till an hour or two after; and the third ran for it.

At the noise of the fire, I immediately advanc'd with my whole army, which was now eight men, viz., myself generalissimo, Friday my lieutenant-general, the captain and his two men, and the three prisoners of war who we had trusted with arms.

We came upon them indeed in the dark, so that they could not see our number. I made the man we had left in the boat, who was now one of us, call to them by name, to try if I could bring them to a parley, and so might perhaps reduce them to terms, which fell out just as we desir'd. Indeed, it was easy to think, as their condition then was, they would be very willing to capitulate. So he call'd out as loud as he could, to one of them, "Tom Smith, Tom Smith"; Tom Smith answer'd immediately, "Who's that, Robinson?" for it seems he knew his voice. T'other answered, "Aye, aye; for God's sake, Tom Smith, throw down your arms and yield, or you are all dead men this moment."

"Who must we yield to? Where are they?" said Smith again. "Here they are," said he, "here's our captain, and fifty men with him, have been hunting you this two hours; the boat-swain is kill'd, Will Frye is wounded, and I am a prisoner; and if you do not yield, you are all lost."

"Will they give us quarter then," said Tom Smith, "and we will yield?" "I'll go and ask, if you promise to yield," said Robinson. So he ask'd the captain, and the captain then call'd himself out, "You, Smith, you know my voice; if you lay down your arms immediately and submit, you shall have your lives, all but Will Atkins."

Upon this, Will Atkins cry'd out, "For God's sake, captain, give me quarter, what have I done? They have been all as bad as I." This, by the way was not true neither; for it seems this Will Atkins was the first man that lay'd hold of the captain, when they first mutiny'd, and used him barbarously, in tying his hands and giving him injurious language. However, the captain told him he must lay down his arms at discretion and trust to the governour's mercy, by which he meant me; for they all call'd me governour.

In a word, they all lay'd down their arms and begg'd their lives; and I sent the man that had parley'd with them, and two more, who bound them all. Then my great army of fifty men, which particularly with those three, were all but eight, came up and seiz'd upon them all, and upon their boat, only that I kept myself and one more out of sight, for reasons of state.

Our next work was to repair the boat and think of seizing the ship; and as for the captain, now he had leisure to parley with them. He expostulated with them upon the villiany of their practises with him and at length upon the further wickedness of their design, and how certainly it must bring them to misery and distress in the end, and perhaps to the gallows.

They all appear'd very penitent and begg'd hard for their lives. As for that, he told them they were none of his prisoners, but the commander of the island; that they thought they had set him on shore in a barren uninhabited island, but it had pleas'd God so to direct them that the island was inhabited; that the governour was an Englishman; that he might hang them all there, if he pleas'd; but as he had given them all quarter, he suppos'd he would send them to England to be dealt with there, as justice requir'd, except Atkins, who he was commanded by the governour to advise to prepare for death, for that he would be hang'd in the morning.

Tho' this was all a fiction of his own, yet it had its desir'd effect. Atkins fell upon his knees to beg the captain to interceed with the governour for his life; and all the rest begg'd of him for God's sake, that they might not be sent to England.

It now occurr'd to me that the time of our deliverance was come and that it would be a most easy thing to bring these fellows in to be hearty in getting possession of the ship. So I retir'd in the dark from them, that they might not see what kind of a governour they had, and call'd the captain to me. When I call'd, as at a good distance, one of the men was order'd to speak again and say to the captain, "Captain, the commander calls for you"; and presently the captain reply'd, "Tell his Excellency, I am just a-coming." This more perfectly amus'd them, and they all believ'd that the commander was just by with his fifty men.

Upon the captain's coming to me, I told him my project for seizing the ship, which he lik'd of wonderfully well, and resolv'd to put it in execution the next morning.

But in order to execute it with more art, and secure of success, I told him we must divide the prisoners, and that he should go and take Atkins, and two more of the worst of them, and send them pinion'd to the cave where the others lay. This was committed to Friday and the two men who came on shore with the captain.

They convey'd them to the cave, as to a prison; and it was indeed a dismal place, especially to men in their condition.

The other I order'd to my bower, as I call'd it, of which I have given a full description; and, as it was fenc'd in and they pinion'd, the place was secure enough, considering they were upon their behaviour.

To these in the morning I sent the captain, who was to enter into a parley with them; in a word to try them, and tell me whether he thought they might be trusted or no to go on board and surprize the ship. He talk'd to them of the injury done him; of the condition they were brought to; and that tho' the governour had given them quarter for their lives, as to the present action, yet that if they were sent to England, they would all be hang'd in chains, to be sure; but that if they would join in so just an attempt as to recover the ship, he would have the governour's engagement for their pardon.

Any one may guess how readily such a proposal would be accepted by men in their condition. They fell down on their knees to the captain and promis'd with the deepest imprecations that they would be faithful to him to the last drop; that they should owe their lives to him and would go with him all over the world; and that they would own him for a father to them as long as they liv'd.

"Well," said the captain, "I must go and tell the governour what you say and see what I can do to bring him to consent to it." So he brought me an account of the temper he found them in, and that he verily believ'd they would be faithful.

However, that we might be very secure, I told him he should go back again, and choose out five of them, and tell them they might see that he did not want men; that he would take out five of them to be his assistants, and that the governour could keep the other two and the three that were sent prisoners to the castle (my cave) as hostages for the fidelity of those five; and that if they prov'd unfaithful in the execution, the five hostages should be hang'd in chains alive upon the shore.

This look'd severe and convinc'd them that the governour was in earnest; however they had no way left them but to accept it; and it was now the business of the prisoners, as much as of the captain, to persuade the other five to do their duty.

Our strength was now thus order'd for the expedition: 1. The captain, his mate, and passenger. 2. The two prisoners of the first gang, to whom having their characters from the captain, I had given their liberty and trusted with arms. 3. The other two who I had kept till now in my appartment, pinion'd; but upon the captain's motion, had now releas'd. 4. The single man taken in the boat. 5.

These five releas'd at last. So that they were thirteen in all, besides five we kept prisoners in the cave and the two hostages.

I ask'd the captain if he was willing to venture with these hands on board the ship, for as for me and my man Friday, I did not think it was proper for us to stir, having seven men left behind; and it was employment enough for us to keep them asunder and supply them with victuals.

As to the five in the cave, I resolv'd to keep them fast, but Friday went in twice a day to them to supply them with necessaries; and I made the other two carry provisions to a certain distance, where Friday was to take it.

When I shew'd myself to the two hostages, it was with the captain, who told them I was the person the governour had order'd to look after them and that it was the governour's pleasure they should not stir anywhere but by my direction; that if they did, they should be fetch'd into the castle and be lay'd in irons; so that as we never suffer'd them to see me as governour, so I now appear'd as another person and spoke of the governour, the garrison, the castle, and the like, upon all occasions.

The captain now had no difficulty before him but to furnish his two boats, stop the breach of one, and man them. He made his passenger captain to one, with four other men; and himself and his mate and six more, went in the other. They contriv'd their business very well, for they came up to the ship about midnight. As soon as they came within call of the ship, he made "Robinson" hale them, and tell them they had brought off the men and the boat, but that it was a long time before they had found them, and the like; holding them in a chat till they came to the ship's side; when the captain and the mate ent'ring first with their arms immediately knock'd down the second mate and carpenter, with the butt-end of their musquets, being very faithfully seconded by their men, they secur'd all the rest that were upon the main and quarter decks, and began to fasten the hatches to keep them down who were below, when the other boat and their men ent'ring at the forechains, secur'd the forecastle of the ship, and the scuttle which went down into the cook room, making the three men they found there prisoners.

When this was done, and all safe upon deck, the captain order'd the mate with three men to break into the round-house where the new rebel captain lay, and having taken the alarm, was gotten up, and with two men and a boy had gotten fire-arms in their hands, and when the mate with a crow split open the door, the new captain and his men fir'd boldly among them, and wounded the mate with a musquet ball, which broke his arm, and wounded two more of the men, but kill'd no body.

The mate, calling for help, rush'd however into the round-house, wounded as he was, and with his pistol shot the new captain thro' the head, the bullet ent'ring at his mouth, and came out again behind one of his ears; so that he never spoke a word; upon which the rest yielded, and the ship was taken effectually, without any more lives lost.

As soon as the ship was thus secur'd, the captain order'd seven guns to be fir'd, which was the signal agreed upon with me, to give me notice of his success, which you may be sure I was very glad to hear, having sat watching upon the shore for it till near two a-clock in the morning.

Having thus heard the signal plainly, I lay'd me down, and, it having been a day of great fatigue to me, I slept very sound, till I was something surpriz'd with the noise of a gun; and presently starting up, I heard a man call me by the name of "Governour, governour," and presently I knew the captain's voice; when climbing up to the top of the hill, there he stood and, pointing to the ship, he embrac'd me in his arms. "My dear friend and deliverer," said he, "there's your ship, for she is all yours, and so are we and all that belong to her." I cast my eyes to the ship, and there she rode within little more than half a mile of the shore, for they had weighed her anchor as soon as they were masters of her; and the weather being fair, had brought her to anchor just against the mouth of the little creek; and the tide being up, the captain had brought the pinnace in near the place where I at first landed my rafts, and so landed just at my door.

I was at first ready to sink down with the surprize. For I saw my deliverance indeed visibly put into my hands, all things easy, and a large ship just ready to carry me away whither I pleas'd to go. At first, for some time, I was not able to answer him one word; but, as he had taken me in his arms, I held fast by him, or I should have fallen to the ground.

He perceiv'd the surprize and immediately pull'd a bottle out of his pocket and gave me a dram of cordial, which he had brought on purpose for me. After I had drank it, I sat down upon the ground and, though it brought me to myself, yet it was a good while before I could speak a word to him.

All this while the poor man was in as great an extasie as I, only not under any surprize, as I was. He said a thousand kind tender things to me, to compose me and bring me to myself; but such was the flood of joy in my breast that it put all my spirits into confusion, at last it broke out into tears, and in a little while after I recovered my speech.

Then I took my turn and embrac'd him as my deliverer, and we rejoyc'd together. I told him I look'd upon him as a man sent from Heaven to deliver me and that the whole transaction seemed to be a chain of wonders; that such things as these were the testimonies we had of a secret hand of Providence governing the world and an evidence that the eyes of an infinite Power could search into the remotest corner of the world and send help to the miserable whenever He pleased.

I forgot not to lift up my heart in thankfulness to Heaven, and what heart could forbear to bless Him who had not only in a miraculous manner provided for one in such a wilderness, and in such a desolate condition, but from whom every deliverance must always be acknowledg'd to proceed.

When we had talk'd awhile, the captain told me he had brought me some little refreshment, such as the ship afforded, and such as the wretches that had been so long his master had not plunder'd him of. Upon this he call'd aloud to the boat and bid his men bring the things ashore that were for the governour; and indeed it was a present, as if I had been one not that was to be carry'd away along with them, but as if I had been to dwell upon the island still, and they were to go without me.

First he had brought me a case of bottles full of excellent cordial waters, six large bottles of Madera wine; the bottles held two quarts a-piece; two pounds of excellent good tobacco, twelve good pieces of the ship's beef, and six pieces of pork, with a bag of pease, and about a hundredweight of bisket.

He brought me also a box of sugar, a box of flour, a bagful of lemons, and two bottles of lime juice, and an abundance of other things. But besides these, and what was a thousand times more useful to me, he brought me six clean new shirts, six very good neckcloaths, two pair of gloves, one pair of shoes, a hat, and one pair of stockings, and a very good suit of cloaths of his own, which had been worn but very little; in a word, he cloathed me from head to foot.

It was a very kind and agreeable present, as any one may imagine to one of my circumstances. But never was any thing in the world of that kind so unpleasant, awkward, and uneasy, as it was to me to wear such cloaths at their first putting on.

After these ceremonies past, and after all his good things were brought into my little appartment, we began to consult what was to be done with the prisoners we had; for it was worth considering whether we might venture to take them away with us or no, especially two of them, who we knew to be incorrigible and refractory to the last degree. The captain said he knew they were such rogues that there was no obliging them, and if he did carry them away it must be in irons, as malefactors to be deliver'd over to justice at the first English colony he could come at; and I found that the captain himself was very anxious about it.

Upon this, I told him that if he desir'd it, I durst undertake to bring the two men he spoke of, to make it their own request that he should leave them upon the island.

"I should be very glad of that," said the captain, "with all my heart."

"Well," said I, "I will send for them up, and talk with them for you." So I caus'd Friday and the two hostages, for they were now discharg'd, their comrades having perform'd their promise; I say, I caus'd them to go to the cave and bring up the five men pinion'd, as they were, to the bower, and keep them there till I came.

After some time, I came thither dress'd in my new habit, and now I was call'd governour again. Being all met, and the captain with me, I caus'd the men to be brought before me, and I told them I had had a full account of their villianous behaviour to the captain, and how they had run away with the ship and were preparing to commit further robberies, but that Providence had ensnar'd them in their own ways and that they were fallen into the pit which they had digg'd for others.

I let them know that by my direction the ship had been seiz'd, that she lay now in the road, and they might see by and by that their new captain had receiv'd the reward of his villiany, for that they might see him hanging at the yard-arm.

That as to them, I wanted to know what they had to say, why I should not execute them as pirates taken in the fact, as by my commission they could not doubt I had authority to do.

One of them answer'd in the name of the rest that they had nothing to say but this; that when they were taken the captain promis'd them their lives, and they humbly implor'd my mercy. But I told them I knew not what mercy to shew them, for as for myself, I had resolv'd to quit the island with all my men and had taken passage with the captain to go for England. As for the captain, he could not carry them to England, other than as prisoners in irons to be try'd for mutiny and running away with the ship; the consequence of which, they must needs know, would be the gallows; so that I could not tell which was best for them, unless they had a mind to take their fate on the island; if they desir'd, that I did not care, as I had liberty to leave it; I had some inclination to give them their lives, if they thought they could shift on shore.

They seem'd very thankful for it and said they would much rather venture to stay there than to be carry'd to England to be hang'd. So I left it on that issue.

However, the captain seem'd to make some difficulty of it, as if he durst not leave them there. Upon this I seem'd a little angry with the captain and told him that they were my prisoners, not his; and that seeing I had offer'd them so much favour, I would be as good as my word; and that if he did not think fit to consent to it, I would set them at liberty, as I found them; and if he did not like it, he might take them again if he could catch them.

Upon this they appear'd very thankful, and I accordingly set them at liberty and bade them retire into the woods to the place whence they came, and I would leave them some fire-arms, some ammunition, and some directions how they should live very well if they thought fit.

Upon this I prepar'd to go on board the ship, but told the captain that I would stay that night to prepare my things, and desir'd him to go on board in the meantime and keep all right in the ship, and send the boat on shore the next day for me, ordering him in the meantime to cause the new captain who was kill'd to be hang'd at the yard-arm that these men might see him.

When the captain was gone, I sent for the men up to me to my appartment and enter'd seriously into discourse with them of their circumstances. I told them I thought they had made a right choice; that if the captain carry'd them away, they would certainly be hang'd. I shew'd them the new captain, hanging at the yard-arm of the ship, and told them they had nothing less to expect.

When they had all declar'd their willingness to stay, I then told them I would let them into the story of my living there, and put them into the way of making it easy to them. Accordingly, I gave them the whole history of the place, and of my coming to it; shew'd them my fortifications, the way I made my bread, planted my corn, cur'd my grapes; in a word, all that was necessary to make them easy. I told them the story also of the sixteen Spaniards that were to be expected, for whom I left a letter and made them promise to treat them in common with themselves.

I left them my fire-arms, viz., five musquets, three fowling-pieces, and three swords. I had above a barrel and a half of powder left, for after the first year or two I used but little and wasted none. I gave them a description of the way I manag'd the goats, and directions to milk and fatten them and to make both butter and cheese.

In a word, I gave them every part of my own story; and I told them I would prevail with the captain to leave them two barrels of gun-powder more, and some garden-seeds, which I told them I would have been very glad of; also I gave them the bag of pease which the captain had brought me to eat, and bade them be sure to sow and encrease them.

Having done all this, I left them the next day and went on board the ship. We prepar'd immediately to sail, but did not weigh that night. The next morning early, two of the five men came swimming to the ship's side, and making a most lamentable complaint of the other three, begg'd to be taken into the ship, for God's sake, for they should be murther'd, and begg'd the captain to take them on board, tho' he hang'd them immediately.

Upon this the captain pretended to have no power without me; but after some difficulty, and after their solemn promises of amendment, they were taken, and were some time after soundly whipp'd and pickl'd, after which, they prov'd very honest and quiet fellows.

Some time after this, the boat was order'd on shore, the tide being up, with the things promis'd to the men; to which the captain at my intercession caus'd their chests and cloaths to be added, which they took, and were very thankful for. I also encourag'd them, by telling them that if it lay in my way to send any vessel to take them in, I would not forget them.

When I took leave of this island, I carry'd on board for reliques, the great goat-skin cap I had made, my umbrella, and my parrot; also I forgot not to take the money I formerly mention'd, which had lain by me so long useless that it was grown rusty, or tarnish'd, and could hardly pass for silver, till it had been a little rubb'd and handl'd, as also the money I found in the wreck of the Spanish ship.

And thus I left the island, the 19th of December, as I found by the ship's account, in the year 1686, after I had been upon it eight-and-twenty years, two months and nineteen days; being deliver'd from this second captivity, the same day of the month that I first made my escape in the longboat, from among the Moors of Sallee.

In this vessel, after a long voyage, I arriv'd in England, the 11th of June, in the year 1687, having been thirty-and-five years absent.

When I came to England, I was as perfect a stranger to all the world as if I had never been known there. My benefactor and faithful steward, who I had left in trust with my money, was alive, but had had great misfortunes in the world; was become a widow the second time and very low in the world. I made her easy as to what she ow'd me, assuring her, I would give her no trouble; but on the contrary, in gratitude to her former care and faithfulness to me, I reliev'd her as my little stock would afford, which at that time would indeed allow me to do but little for her; but I assur'd her, I would never forget her former kindness to me. Nor did I forget her, when I had sufficient to help her, as shall be observ'd in its place.

I went down afterwards into Yorkshire; but my father was dead, and my mother and all the family extinct, except that I found two sisters and two of the children of one of my brothers. As I had been long ago given over for dead, there had been no provision made for me, so that in a word, I found nothing to relieve, or assist me; and what little money I had would not do much for me, as to settling in the world.

I met with one piece of gratitude indeed, which I did not expect; and this was that the master of the ship, who I had so happily deliver'd, and by the same means sav'd the ship and cargo, having given a very handsome account to the owners of the manner how I had sav'd the lives of the men and the ship, they invited me to meet them, and some other merchants concern'd, and altogether made me a very handsome compliment upon the subject, and a present of almost 200 pounds sterling.

But after making several reflections upon the circumstances of my life, and how little way this would go towards settling me in the world, I resolv'd to go to Lisbon and see if I might not come by some information of the state of my plantation in the Brasils, and of what was become of my partner, who I had reason to suppose had some years now given me over for dead.

With this view I took shipping for Lisbon, where I arriv'd in April following; my man Friday accompanying me very honestly in all these ramblings and proving a most faithful servant upon all occasions.

When I came to Lisbon, I found out by enquiry, and to my particular satisfaction, my old friend the captain of the ship, who first took me up at sea, off of the shore of Africa. He was now grown old and had left off the sea, having put his son, who was far from a young man, into his ship, and who still used the Brasils trade. The old man did not know me, and indeed, I hardly knew him. But I soon brought him to my remembrance, and as soon brought myself to his remembrance, when I told him who I was.

After some passionate expressions of the old acquaintance, I enquir'd, you may be sure, after my plantation and my partner. The old man told me he had not been in the Brasils for about nine years; but that he could assure me, that when he came away, my partner was living, but the trustees, who I had join'd with him to take cognizance of my part, were both dead. However, he believ'd that I would have a very good account of the improvement of the plantation, for that upon the general belief of my being cast away and drown'd, my trustees had given in the account of the produce of my part of the plantation to the procurator fiscal, who had appropriated it, in case I never came to claim it: one third to the king, and two thirds to the monastery of St. Augustine, to be expended for the benefit of the poor and for the conversion of the Indians to the Catholick faith; but that if I appear'd, or any one for me, to claim the inheritance, it should be restor'd; only that the improvement, or annual production, being distributed to charitable uses, could not be restor'd. But he assur'd me that the steward of the king's revenue (from lands) and the proviedor, or steward of the monastery, had taken great care all along, that the incumbent, that is to say my partner, gave every year a faithful account of the produce, of which they receiv'd duly my moiety.

I ask'd him if he knew to what height of improvement he had brought the plantation and whether he thought it might be worth looking after. Or whether on my going thither I should meet with no obstruction to my possessing my just right in the moiety.

He told me he could not tell exactly to what degree the plantation was improv'd; but this he knew, that my partner was grown exceeding rich upon the enjoying but one half of it; that to the best of his remembrance, he had heard that the king's third of my part, which was it seems granted away to some other monastery, or religious house, amounted to above 200 moidores a year; that as to my being restor'd to a quiet possession of it, there was no question to be made of that, my partner being alive to witness my title and my name being also enroll'd in the register of the country. Also, he told me that the survivors of my two trustees were very fair honest people, and very wealthy, and he believ'd I would not only have their assistance for putting me in possession, but would find a very considerable sum of money in their hands, for my account, being the produce of the farm while their fathers held the trust, and before it was given up as above, which as he remember'd, was for about twelve years.

I shew'd myself a little concern'd and uneasy at this account, and enquir'd of the old captain how it came to pass that the trustees should thus dispose my effects, when he knew that I had made my will, and had made him, the Portugueze captain, my universal heir, &c.

He told me that was true, but that as there was no proof of my being dead, he could not act as executor until some certain account should come of my death, and that besides, he was not willing to intermeddle with a thing so remote; that it was true he had registered my will and put in his claim; and could he have given any account of my being dead or alive, he would have acted by procuration and taken possession of the ingenio, so they call'd the sugar-house, and had given his son, who was now in the Brasils, order to do it.

"But," said the old man, "I have one piece of news to tell you, which perhaps may not be so acceptable to you as the rest, and that is that, believing you were lost, and all the world believing so also, your partner and trustees did offer to accompt to me in your name, for six or eight of the first years of profits, which I receiv'd; but there being at the time great disbursements for encreasing the works, building an ingenio, and buying slaves, it did not amount to near so much as afterwards it produced. However," continu'd the old man, "I shall give you a true account of what I have receiv'd in all, and how I have dispos'd of it."

After a few days further conference with this antient friend, he brought me an account of the six first years' income of my plantation, sign'd by my partner and the merchant trustees, being always deliver'd in goods, viz., tobacco in roll and sugar in chests, besides rum, molossus, &c. which is the consequence of a sugar-work. I found by this account that every year the income considerably encreas'd; but, as above, the disbursement being large, the sum at first was small. However, the old man let me see that he was debtor to me 470 moidores of gold, besides sixty chests of sugar, and fifteen double rolls of tobacco which were lost in his ship; he having been shipwreck'd coming home to Lisbon about eleven years after my leaving the place.

The good man then began to complain of his misfortunes and how he had been oblig'd to make use of my money to recover his losses and buy him a share in a new ship. "However, my old friend," said he, "you shall not want a supply in your necessity; and as soon as my son returns, you shall be fully satisfy'd."

Upon this, he pull'd out an old pouch, and gave me 160 Portugueze moidores in gold; and giving me the writing of his title to the ship, which his son was gone to the Brasils in, of which he was quarter part owner, and his son another, he put them both into my hands for security of the rest.

I was too much mov'd with the honesty and kindness of the poor man to be able to bear this; and rememb'ring what he had done for me, how he had taken me up at sea, and how generously he had used me on all occasions, and particularly, how sincere a friend he was now to me, I could hardly refrain weeping at what he said to me. Therefore, first I ask'd him if his circumstances admitted him to spare so much money at that time and if it would not straiten him. He told me he could not say but it might straiten him a little, but it was my money, and I might want it more than he.

Every thing the good man said was full of affection, and I could hardly refrain from tears while he spoke. In short, I took 100 of the moidores, and call'd for a pen and ink to give him a receipt for them; then I return'd him the rest, and told him if ever I had possession of the plantation, I would return the other to him also, as indeed I afterwards did; that as to the bill of sale of his part in his son's ship, I would not take it by any means; but that if I wanted the money, I found he was honest enough to pay me; and if I did not, but came to receive what he gave me reason to expect, I would never have a penny more from him.

When this was pass'd, the old man began to ask me if he should put me into a method to make my claim to my plantation. I told him I thought to go over to it myself. He said I might do so if I pleas'd, but that if I did not, there were ways enough to secure my right, and immediately to appropriate the profits to my use; and as there were ships in the river of Lisbon, just ready to go away to the Brasils, he made me enter my name in a publick register, with his affidavit, affirming upon oath that I was alive and that I was the same person who took up the land for the planting the said plantation at first.

This being regularly attested by a notary, and a procuration affix'd, he directed me to send it with a letter of his

And thus I left the island, the 19th of December, after I had been upon it eight-and-twenty years, two months, and nineteen days. (page 322)

writing to a merchant of his acquaintance at the place and then propos'd my staying with him till an account came of the return.

Never was any thing more honourable than the proceedings upon this procuration; for in less than seven months, I receiv'd a large packet from the survivors of my trustees the merchants, for whose account I went to sea, in which were the following particular letters and papers enclos'd.

First, there was the account current of the produce of my farm, or plantation, from the year when their fathers had balanc'd with my old Portugueze captain, being for six years; the balance appear'd to be 1,174 moidores in my favour.

Secondly, there was the account of four years more while they kept the effects in their hands, before the government claim'd the administration, as being the effects of a person not to be found, which they call'd civil death; and the balance of this, the value of the plantation encreasing, amounted to 38,892 cruzeiros, which made 3,241 moidores.

Thirdly, there was the prior of St. Augustine's account, who had receiv'd the profits for about fourteen years, but not being able to account for what was dispos'd to the hospital, very honestly declar'd he had 872 moidores not distributed, which he acknowledg'd to my account; as to the king's part, that refunded nothing.

There was a letter of my partner's congratulating me very affectionately upon my being alive, giving me an account how the estate was improv'd and what it produc'd a year, with a particular of the number of squares or acres that it contain'd; how planted, how many slaves there were upon it, and making two-and-twenty crosses for blessings, told me he had said so many *Ave Marias* to thank the Blessed Virgin that I was alive; inviting me very passionately to come over and take possession of my own; and in the meantime to give him orders to whom he should deliver my effects if I did not come myself; concluding with a hearty tender of his friendship and that of his family, and sent me, as a present, seven fine leopard-skins, which he had it seems receiv'd from Africa, by some other ship which he had sent thither, and who it seems had made a better voyage than I. He sent me also five chests of excellent sweetmeats, and 100 pieces of gold uncoin'd, not quite so large as moidores.

By the same fleet, my two merchant trustees shipp'd me 1,200 chests of sugar, 800 rolls of tobacco, and the rest of the whole accompt in gold.

I might well say, now indeed, that the latter end of Job was better than the beginning. It is impossible to express here the flutterings of my very heart, when I look'd over these letters, and especially when I found all my wealth about me; for as the Brasils ships come all in fleets, the same ships which brought my letters, brought my goods; and the effects were safe in the river before the letters came to my hand. In a word, I turned pale and grew sick; and had not the old man run and fetch'd me a cordial, I believe the sudden surprize of joy had overset nature and I had dy'd upon the spot.

Nay, after that I continu'd very ill and was so some hours till, a physician being sent for and some thing of the real cause of my illness being known, he order'd me to be let blood, after which, I had relief and grew well. But I verily believe, if it had not been eas'd by a vent given in that manner, to the spirits, I should have dy'd.

I was now master, all on a sudden, of above 5,000 pounds sterling in money, and had an estate, as I might well call it, in the Brasils, of above 1,000 pounds a year, as sure as an estate of lands in England. In a word, I was in a condition which I scarce knew how to understand, or how to compose myself, for the enjoyment of it.

The first thing I did was to recompense my original benefactor, my good old captain, who had been first charitable to me in my distress, kind to me in my beginning, and honest to me at the end. I shew'd him all that was sent me; I told him that next to the providence of Heaven, which disposes all things, it was owing to him; and that it now lay on me to reward him, which I would do an hundredfold. So I first return'd to him the 100 moidores I had receiv'd of him, then I sent for a notary and caus'd him to draw up a general release or discharge for the 470 moidores, which he had acknowledg'd he ow'd me in the fullest and firmest manner possible. After which, I caus'd a procuration to be drawn, empowering him to be my receiver of the annual profits of my plantation and appointing my partner to accompt to him and make the returns by the usual fleets to him in my name; and a clause in the end, being a grant of 100 moidores a year to him, during his life, out of the effects, and 50 moidores a year to his son after him, for his life. And thus I requited my old man.

I was now to consider which way to steer my course next and what to do with the estate that Providence had thus put into my hands. Indeed, I had more care upon my head now than I had in my silent state of life on the island, where I wanted nothing but what I had and had nothing but what I wanted. Whereas I had now a great charge upon me, and my business was how to secure it.

I had ne'er a cave now to hide my money in, or a place where it might lie without lock or key, till it grew mouldy and tarnish'd, before any body would meddle with it. On the contrary, I knew not where to put it or who to trust with it. My old patron, the captain, indeed was honest, and that was the only refuge I had.

In the next place, my interest in the Brasils seem'd to summon me thither; but now I could not tell how to think of going thither, till I had settled my affairs and left my effects in some safe hands behind me. At first I thought of my old friend the widow, who I knew was honest and would be just to me; but then she was in years, and but poor, and for ought I knew might be in debt. So in a word, I had no way but to go back to England myself and take my effects with me.

It was some months however before I resolv'd upon this; and therefore, as I had rewarded the old captain fully, and to his satisfaction, who had been my former benefactor, so I began to think of my poor widow, whose husband had been my first benefactor, and she, while it was in her power, my faithful steward and instructor. So the first thing I did, I got a merchant in Lisbon to write to his correspondent in London, not only to pay a bill, but to go find her out and carry her in money 100 pounds from me, and to talk with her and comfort her in her poverty, by telling her she should, if I liv'd, have a further supply. At the same time I sent my two sisters in the country, each of them, 100 pounds; they being, though not in want, yet not in very good circumstances, one having been marry'd and left a widow, and the other having a husband not so kind to her as he should be.

But among all my relations, or acquaintances, I could

not yet pitch upon one to whom I durst commit the gross of my stock, that I might go away to the Brasils and leave things safe behind me; and this greatly perplex'd me.

I had once a mind to have gone to the Brasils and have settled myself there; for I was, as it were, naturaliz'd to the place; but I had some little scruple in my mind about religion, which insensibly drew me back, of which I shall say more presently. However, it was not religion that kept me from going there for the present; and as I had made no scruple of being openly of the religion of the country, all the while I was among them, so neither did I yet; only that now and then having of late thought more of it (than formerly), when I began to think of living and dying among them, I began to regret my having profess'd myself a Papist and thought it might not be the best religion to die with.

But, as I have said, this was not the main thing that kept me from going to the Brasils, but that really I did not know with whom to leave my effects behind me. So I resolv'd at last to go to England with it, where, if I arriv'd, I concluded I should make some acquaintance or find some relations that would be faithful to me; and according I prepar'd to go for England with all my wealth.

In order to prepare things for my going home, I first (the Brasils fleet being just going away) resolv'd to give answers suitable to the just and faithful account of things I had thence. First, to the prior of St. Augustine I wrote a letter full of thanks for their just dealings, and the offer of the 872 moidores, which was indispos'd of, which I desir'd might be given 500 to the monastery and 372 to the poor, as the prior should direct, desiring the good padre's prayers for me, and the like.

I wrote next a letter of thanks to my two trustees, with all the acknowledgment that so much justice and honesty call'd for; as for sending them any present, they were far above having any occasion of it.

Lastly, I wrote to my partner, acknowledging his industry in the improving the plantation and his integrity in encreasing the stock of the works, giving him instructions for his future government of my part, according to the powers I had left with my old patron, to whom I desir'd him to send whatever became due to me till he should hear from me more particularly; assuring him that it was my intention, not only to come to him, but to settle myself there for the remainder of my life. To this I added a very handsome present of some Italian silks for his wife and two daughters, for such the captain's son inform'd me he had; with two pieces of fine English broad-cloath, the best I could get in Lisbon, five pieces of black bays, and some Flanders lace of a good value.

Having thus settl'd my affairs, sold my cargo, and turn'd all my effects into good bills of exchange, my next difficulty was which way to go to England. I had been accustom'd enough to the sea, and yet I had a strange aversion to going to England by sea at that time. Tho' I could give no reason for it, yet the difficulty encreas'd upon me so much, that tho' I had once shipp'd my baggage in order to go, yet I alter'd my mind, and that not once, but two or three times.

It is true, I had been very unfortunate by sea, and this might be some of the reason. But let no man slight the strong impulses of his own thoughts in cases of such moment. Two of the ships which I had singl'd out to go in, I mean, more particularly singl'd out than any other, that is to say, so as in one of them to put my things on board, and in the other to have agreed with the captain; I say, two of these ships miscarry'd, viz., one was taken by the Algerines, and the other was cast away on the start near Torbay, and all the people drown'd except three; so that in either of those vessels I had been made miserable, and in which most, it was hard to say.

Having been thus harass'd in my thoughts, my old pilot, to whom I communicated everything, press'd me earnestly not to go by sea, but either to go by land to the Groyne and cross over the bay of Biscay to Rochell, whence it was but an easy and safe journey by land to Paris and so to Calais and Dover; or to go up to Madrid, and so all the way by land thro' France.

In a word, I was so prepossess'd against my going by sea at all, except from Calais to Dover, that I resolv'd to travel all the way by land, which as I was not in haste, and did not value the charge, was by much the pleasanter way. And to make it more so, my old captain brought an English gentleman, the son of a merchant in Lisbon, who was willing to travel with me. After which, we pick'd up two more English merchants also, and two young Portugueze gentlemen, the last going to Paris only; so that we were in all six of us, and five servants; the two merchants and the two Portugueze, contenting themselves with one servant, between the two, to save the charge. As for me, I got an English sailor to travel with me as a servant, besides my man Friday, who was too much a stranger to be capable of supplying the place of a servant on the road.

In this manner I set out from Lisbon; and our company being all very well mounted and arm'd, we made a little troop, whereof they did me the honour to call me captain, as well because I was the oldest man, as because I had two servants and indeed was the original of the whole journey.

As I have troubl'd you with none of my sea-journals, so I shall trouble you now with none of my land-journal; but some adventures that happen'd to us in this tedious and difficult journey, I must not omit.

When we came to Madrid we, being all of us strangers to Spain, were willing to stay some time to see the court of Spain and to see what was worth observing; but it being the latter part of the summer, we hasten'd away and set out from Madrid about the middle of October. When we came to the edge of Navarre, we were alarm'd at several towns on the way with an account that so much snow was fallen on the French side of the mountains that several travellers were oblig'd to come back to Pampeluna, after having attempted, at an extreme hazard, to pass on.

When we came to Pampeluna itself, we found it so indeed; and to me that had been always used to a hot climate, and indeed to countries where we could scarce bear any cloaths on, the cold was insufferable; nor indeed was it more painful than it was surprizing, to come but ten days before out of the old Castile where the weather was not only warm but very hot, and immediately to feel a wind from the Pyrenean Mountains, so very keen, so severely cold, as to be intolerable, and to endanger benumbing and perishing of our fingers and toes.

Poor Friday was really frighted when he saw the mountains all cover'd with snow, and felt cold weather, which he had never seen or felt before in his life.

To mend the matter, when we came to Pampeluna, it continu'd snowing with so much violence, and so long, that the people said winter was come before its time; and the roads, which were difficult before, were now quite impass-able. For in a word, the snow lay in some places too thick for us to travel; and being not hard frozen, as is the case in northern countries, there was no going without being in danger of being bury'd alive every step. We stay'd no less than twenty days in Pampeluna, when seeing the winter coming on, and no likelihood of its being better (for it was the severest winter all over Europe that had been known in the memory of man), I propos'd that we should all go away to Fonterabia and there take shipping for Bourdeaux, which was a very little voyage.

But while we were considering this, there came in four French gentlemen who, having been stopp'd on the French side of the passes, as we were on the Spanish, had found out a guide who, traversing the country near the head of Languedoc, had brought them over the mountains by such ways that they were not much incommoded with the snow; and where they met with snow in any quantity, they said it was frozen hard enough to bear them and their horses.

We sent for this guide, who told us he would undertake to carry us the same way with no hazard from the snow, provided we were arm'd sufficiently to protect ourselves from wild beasts; for he said upon these great snows it was frequent for wolves to shew themselves at the foot of the mountains, being made ravenous for want of food, the ground being cover'd with snow. We told him we were well enough prepar'd for such creatures as they were, if he would ensure us from a kind of two-legg'd wolves, which we were told we were in most danger from, especially on the French side of the mountains.

He satisfy'd us there was no danger of that kind in the way that we were to go; so we readily agre'd to follow him, as did also twelve other gentlemen, with their servants, some French, some Spanish; who, as I said, had attempted to go, and were oblig'd to come back again.

Accordingly, we all set out from Pampeluna, with our guide, on the 15th of November; and indeed, I was sur-priz'd, when instead of going forward, he came directly back with us, on the same road that we came from Madrid, above twenty miles; when being pass'd two rivers and come into the plain country, we found ourselves in a warm cli-mate again, where the country was pleasant and no snow to be seen. But on a sudden, turning to his left, he ap-proach'd the mountains another way; and tho' it is true the hills and precipices look'd dreadful, yet he made so many tours, such meanders, and led us by such winding ways, that we were insensibly past the heights of the mountains, without being much encumber'd with the snow; and all on a sudden, he shew'd up the pleasant fruit-ful provinces of Languedoc and Gascoign, all green and flourishing, tho' indeed it was at a great distance and we had some rough way to pass yet.

We were a little uneasy however when we found it snow'd one whole day and a night, so fast that we could not travel; but he bid us be easy, we should soon be past it all. We found indeed that we began to descend every day and to come more north than before; and so depending upon our guide, we went on.

It was about two hours before night, when our guide being something before us, and not just in sight, out rushed three monstrous wolves, and after them a bear, out of a hollow way, adjoining to a thick wood. Two of the wolves flew upon the guide, and had he been half a mile before us, he had been devour'd indeed before we could have help'd him. One of them fasten'd upon his horse, and the other attack'd the man with that violence, that he had not time or not presence of mind enough to draw his pistol, but hollow'd and cry'd out to us most lustily. My man Friday being next me, I bid him ride up and see what was the matter; as soon as Friday came in sight of the man, he hollow'd as loud as t'other, "O Master! O Master!" but like a bold fellow, rode directly up to the poor man and with his pistol shot the wolf that attack'd him into the head.

It was happy for the poor man that it was my man Friday, for he having been used to that kind of creature in his country had no fear upon him, but went close up to him and shot him as above; whereas any of us would have fir'd at a farther distance and have perhaps either miss'd the wolf or endanger'd shooting the man.

But it was enough to have terrify'd a bolder man than I, and indeed it alarm'd all our company when, with the noise of Friday's pistol, we heard on both sides the dismallest howling of wolves, and the noise redoubl'd by the echo of the mountains, that it was to us as if there had been a prodigious multitude of them; and perhaps indeed there was not such a few as that we had no cause of apprehensions.

However, as Friday had kill'd this wolf, the other that had fasten'd upon the horse left him immediately and fled; having happily fasten'd upon his head, where the bosses of the bridle had stuck in his teeth, so that he had not done him much hurt. The man indeed was most hurt, for the raging creature had bit him twice, once on the arm, and the other time a little above his knee; and he was just as it were tumbling down by the disorder of his horse, when Friday came up and shot the wolf.

It is easy to suppose that at the noise of Friday's pistol we all mended our pace and rid up as fast as the way (which was very difficult) would give us leave to see what was the matter. As soon as we came clear of the trees, which blinded us before, we saw clearly what had been the case and how Friday had disengag'd the poor guide, tho' we did not presently discern what kind of creature it was he had kill'd.

But never was a fight manag'd so hardily and in such a surprizing manner, as that which follow'd between Friday and the bear, which gave us all (tho' at first we were surpriz'd and afraid for him) the greatest diversion imaginable. As the bear is a heavy, clumsy creature, and does not gallop as the wolf does, who is swift and light, so he has two particular qualities, which generally are the rule of his actions. First, as to men, who are not his proper prey; I say, not his proper prey because tho' I cannot say what excessive hunger might do, which was now their case, the ground being all cover'd with snow; but as to men, he does not usually attempt them, unless they first attack him. On the contrary, if you meet him in the woods, if you don't meddle with him, he won't meddle with you; but then you must take care to be very civil to him and give him the road; for he is a very nice gentleman, he won't go a step out of his way for a prince; nay, if you are really afraid, your best way is to look another way, and keep going on, for sometimes if you stop and stand still, and look steadily at him, he takes it for an affront; and if you throw or toss any thing at him, and it hits him, tho' it were but a bit of a stick as big as your finger, he takes it for an affront and sets all his other business aside to pursue his revenge; for he will have satisfaction in point of honour; that is his first quality. The next is, that if he be once affronted, he will never leave you, night or day, till he has his revenge, but follows at a good round rate till he overtakes you.

My man Friday had deliver'd our guide, and when we came up to him he was helping him off from his horse, for the man was both hurt and frighted, and indeed, the last more than the first; when on the sudden, we spy'd the bear come out of the wood, and a vast monstrous one it was, the biggest by far that ever I saw. We were all a little surpriz'd when we saw him; but when Friday saw him, it was easy to see joy and courage in the fellow's countenance. "O! O! O!" said Friday, three times, pointing to him, "O Master! You give me to leave! Me shakee te hand with him! Me make you good laugh!"

I was surpriz'd to see the fellow so pleas'd; "You fool you," said I, "he will eat you up!" "Eatee me up! Eatee me up!" said Friday, twice over again. "Me eatee him up! Me make you good laugh! You all stay here, me show you good laugh!" So down he sat, and got his boots off in a moment, and put on a pair of pumps (as we call the flat shoes they wear) and which he had in his pocket, and gave my other servant his horse, and with his gun away he flew swift like the wind.

The bear was walking softly on and offer'd to meddle with no body, till Friday, coming pretty near, call'd to him, as if the bear could understand him. "Hark ye, hark ye," said Friday, "me speakee wit you!" We follow'd at a distance; for now being come down on the Gascoign side of the mountains, we were enter'd a vast great forest, where

the country was plain, and pretty open, tho' many trees
in it scatter'd here and there.

Friday, who had as we say, the heels of the bear, came
up with him quickly, and taking up a great stone, threw at
him and hit him just on the head, but did him no more
harm than if he had thrown it against a wall. But it answer'd Friday's end, for the rogue was so void of fear that
he did it purely to make the bear follow him and show us
some laugh as he call'd it.

As soon as the bear felt the stone and saw him, he turn'd
about, and came after him, taking devilish long strides and
shuffling along at a strange rate, so as would have put a
horse to a middling gallop; away ran Friday and took his
course, as if he ran towards us for help. So we all resolv'd
to fire at once upon the bear, and deliver my man, though
I was angry at him heartily for bringing the bear back upon
us, when he was going about his own business another way;
and especially I was angry that he had turn'd the bear
upon us and then run away. I call'd out, "You dog, is
this your making us laugh? Come away, and take your
horse, that we may shoot the creature." He heard me and
cry'd out, "No shoot, no shoot, stand still, you get much
laugh." And as the nimble creature ran two foot for the
beast's one, he turn'd on a sudden, on one side of us, and
seeing a great oak-tree fit for his purpose, he beckon'd to us
to follow, and doubling his pace, he got nimbly up the tree,
laying his gun down upon the ground at about five or six
yards from the bottom of the tree.

The bear soon came to the tree, and we follow'd at a
distance. The first thing he did, he stopp'd at the gun,
smelt to it, but let it lie, and up he scrambl'd into the tree,
climbing like a cat, tho' so monstrously heavy. I was

342

amaz'd at the folly, as I thought it, of my man, and could not for my life see any thing to laugh at yet, till seeing the bear get up the tree, we all rid nearer to him.

When we came to the tree, there was Friday got out to the small end of a large limb of the tree, and the bear got about half way to him. As soon as the bear got out to that part where the limb of the tree was weaker, "Ha," said he to us, "now you see me teachee the bear dance!" So he fell a-jumping and a-shaking the bough, at which the bear began to totter, but stood still, and began to look behind him, to see how he should get back; then indeed we did laugh heartily. But Friday had not done with him by a great deal; when he saw him stand still, he call'd out to him again, as if he had suppos'd the bear could speak English: "What you no come farther? Pray you come farther!" So he left jumping and shaking the tree, and the bear, just as if he had understood what he said, did come a little farther, then he fell a-jumping again, and the bear stopp'd again.

We thought now was a good time to knock him on the head, and I call'd to Friday to stand still, and we should shoot the bear; but he cry'd out earnestly, "O pray! O pray! No shoot, me shoot, by and then." He would have said, "By and by." However, to shorten the story, Friday danc'd so much, and the bear stood so ticklish, that we had laughing enough indeed, but still could not imagine what the fellow would do. First we thought he depended upon shaking the bear off, and we found the bear was too cunning for that too, for he would not go out far enough to be thrown down, but clung fast with his great broad claws and feet, so that we could not imagine what would be the end of it and where the jest would be at last.

But Friday put us out of doubt quickly, seeing the bear cling fast to the bough, and that he would not be persuaded to come any farther. "Well, well," said Friday, "you no come farther, me go, me go; you no come to me, me go come to you!" And upon this, he goes out to the smallest end of the bough, where it would bend with his weight, and gently lets himself down by it, sliding down the bough, till he comes near enough to jump down on his feet, and away he runs to his gun, takes it up, and stands still.

"Well," said I to him, "Friday, what will you do now? Why don't you shoot him?" "No shoot," said Friday, "no yet, me shoot now, me no kill; me stay, give you one more laugh!" And indeed so he did, as you will see presently; for when the bear saw his enemy gone, he came back from the bough where he stood; but did it mighty leisurely, looking behind him every step, and coming backward till he got into the body of the tree. Then with the same hinder end foremost, he came down the tree, grasping it with his claws and moving one foot at a time, very leisurely. At this juncture, and just before he could set his hind feet upon the ground, Friday stepp'd up close to him, clapp'd the muzzle of his piece into his ear, and shot him dead as a stone.

Then the rogue turn'd about, to see if we did not laugh, and when he saw we were pleas'd by our looks, he fell a-laughing himself very loud. "So we kill bear in my country," said Friday. "So you kill them," said I, "why have you no guns." "No," said he, "no gun, but shoot, great much long arrow!"

This was indeed a good diversion to us; but we were still in a wild place, and our guide very much hurt, and what to do we hardly knew. The howling of wolves ran much in my head, and indeed, except the noise I once heard on the shore of Africa, of which I have said something already, I never heard any thing that filled me with so much horror.

These things, and the approach of night, call'd us off, or else, as Friday would have had us, we should certainly have taken the skin of this monstrous creature off, which was worth saving. But we had three leagues to go, and our guide hasten'd us, so we left him and went forward on our journey.

The ground was still cover'd with snow, tho' not so deep and dangerous as on the mountains, and the ravenous creatures, as we heard afterwards, were come down into the forest and plain country, press'd by hunger to seek for food, and had done a great deal of mischief in the villages, where they surpriz'd the country people, kill'd a great many of their sheep and horses, and some people too.

We had one dangerous place to pass, which our guide told us if there were any more wolves in the country, we should find them there; and this was in a small plain, surrounded with woods on every side, and a long narrow defile or lane, which we were to pass to get thro' the wood, and then we should come to the village where we were to lodge.

It was within half an hour of sun-set when we enter'd the first wood; and a little after sun-set when we came into the plain. We met with nothing in the first wood, except, that in a little plain within the wood, which was not above two furlongs over, we saw five great wolves cross the road, full speed one after another, as if they had been in chase of some prey, and had it in view. They took no notice of us, and were gone and out of our sight in a few moments.

Upon this our guide, who by the way was a wretched

faint-hearted fellow, bid us keep in a ready posture, for he believ'd there were more wolves a-coming.

We kept our arms ready, and our eyes about us, but we saw no more wolves till we came thro' that wood, which was near half a league, and enter'd the plain. As soon as we came into the plain we had occasion enough to look about us. The first object we met with was a dead horse; that is to say, a poor horse which the wolves had kill'd, and at least a dozen of them at work; we could not say eating of him, but picking of his bones rather, for they had eaten up all the flesh before.

We did not think fit to disturb them at their feast, neither did they take much notice of us. Friday would have let fly at them, but I would not suffer him by any means, for I found we were like to have more business upon our hands than we were aware of. We were not gone half over the plain, but we began to hear the wolves howl in the wood on our left, in a frightful manner, and presently after we saw about a hundred coming on directly towards us, all in a body, and most of them in a line, as regularly as an army drawn up by experienc'd officers. I scarce knew in what manner to receive them, but found to draw ourselves in a close line was the only way. So we form'd in a moment. But that we might not have too much interval, I order'd that only every other man should fire, and that the others who had not fir'd should stand ready to give them a second volley immediately, if they continu'd to advance upon us, and that then those who had fir'd at first, should not pretend to load their fuzees again, but stand ready with every one a pistol, for we were all arm'd with a fuzee, and a pair of pistols each man. We were by this method able to fire six volleys, half of us at a time; however, at present we had no necessity, for upon firing the first volley, the enemy made a full stop, being terrify'd as well with the noise, as with the fire; four of them being shot into the head, dropp'd, several others were wounded, and went bleeding off, as we could see by the snow. I found they stopp'd, but did not immediately retreat; whereupon rememb'ring that I had been told, that the fiercest creatures were terrify'd at the voice of a man, I caus'd all our company to hollow as loud as we could, and I found the notion not altogether mistaken; for upon our shout, they began to retire and turn about. Then I order'd a second volley to be fir'd in their rear, which put them to the gallop, and away they went to the woods.

, This gave us leisure to charge our pieces again, and that we might lose no time, we kept going; but we had but little more than loaded our fuzees and put ourselves into a readiness, when we heard a terrible noise in the same wood, on our left, only that it was farther onward the same way we were to go.

The night was coming on, and the light began to be dusky, which made it worse on our side. The noise encreasing, we could easily perceive that it was the howling and yelling of those hellish creatures, and on a sudden, we perceiv'd two or three troops of wolves, one on our left, one behind us, and one on our front; so that we seem'd to be surrounded with them. However, as they did not fall upon us, we kept our way forward, as fast as we could make our horses go, which the way being very rough, was only a good large trot; and in this manner we came in view of the entrance of a wood, thro' which we were to pass, at the farther side of the plain; but we were greatly surpriz'd, when coming nearer the lane, or pass, we saw a confus'd number of wolves standing just at the entrance.

On a sudden, at another opening of the wood, we heard

the noise of a gun; and looking that way, out rush'd a horse, with a saddle and a bridle on him, flying like the wind, and sixteen or seventeen wolves after him, full speed. Indeed, the horse had the heels of them, but as we suppos'd that he could not hold it at that rate, we doubted not but they would get up with him at last, and no question but they did.

But here we had a most horrible sight; for riding up to the entrance where the horse came out, we found the carcass of another horse, and of two men, devour'd by the ravenous creatures, and one of the men was no doubt the same who we heard fir'd the gun, for there lay a gun just by him, fir'd off, but as to the man, his head and the upper part of his body was eaten up.

This fill'd us with horror, and we knew not what course to take, but the creatures resolv'd us soon; for they gather'd about us presently, in hopes of prey, and I verily believe there were three hundred of them. It happen'd very much to our advantage that at the entrance into the wood, but a little way from it, there lay some large timber trees, which had been cut down the summer before, and I suppose lay there for carriage; I drew my little troop in among those trees, and placing ourselves in a line, behind one long tree, I advis'd them all to light, and keeping that tree before us, for a breast work, to stand in a triangle, or three fronts, enclosing our horses in the center.

We did so, and it was well we did, for never was a more furious charge than the creatures made upon us in the place; they came on us with a growling kind of a noise (and mounted the piece of timber, which as I said, was our breast work) as if they were only rushing upon their prey; and this fury of theirs it seems was principally occasion'd by their seeing our horses behind us, which was the prey they aim'd at. I order'd our men to fire as before, every other man; and they took their aim so sure, that indeed they kill'd several of the wolves at the first volley. But there was a necessity to keep a continual firing, for they came on like devils, those behind pushing on those before.

When we had fir'd our second volley of our fuzees, we thought they stopp'd a little, and I hop'd they would have gone off; but it was but a moment, for others came forward again. So we fir'd two volleys of our pistols, and I believe in these four firings we had kill'd seventeen or eighteen of them, and lam'd twice as many; yet they came on again.

I was loath to spend our last shot too hastily, so I call'd my servant, not my man Friday, for he was better employ'd; with the greatest dexterity imaginable, he had charg'd my fuzee, and his own, while we were engag'd. But as I said, I call'd my other man, and giving him a horn of powder, I bade him lay a train, all along the piece of timber, and let it be a large train; he did so and had but just time to get away when the wolves came up to it, and some were got up upon it, when I snapping an uncharg'd pistol, close to the powder, set it on fire; those that were upon the timber were scorch'd with it, and six or seven of them fell, or rather jump'd in among us; with the force and fright of the fire, we dispatch'd these in an instant, and the rest were so frighted with the light, which the night, for it was now very near dark, made more terrible, that they drew back a little.

Upon which I order'd our last pistol to be fir'd off in one volley, and after that we gave a shout; upon this, the wolves turn'd tail, and we sally'd immediately upon near twenty lame ones, who we found struggling on the ground, and fell a-cutting them with our swords, which answer'd our expectation; for the crying and howling they made was better understood by their fellows, so that they all fled and left us.

We had, first and last, kill'd about three score of them, and had it been day-light, we had kill'd many more. The field of battle being thus clear'd, we made forward again, for we had still near a league to go. We heard the ravenous creatures howl and yell in the woods as we went, several times, and sometimes we fancy'd we saw some of them, but the snow dazzling our eyes, we were not certain. So in about an hour more, we came to the town where we were to lodge, which we found in a terrible fright and all in arms; for it seems that the night before, the wolves and some bears had broke into the village in the night and put them in a terrible fright, and they were oblig'd to keep guard night and day, but especially in the night, to preserve their cattle, and indeed their people.

The next morning our guide was so ill, and his limbs swell'd with the rankling of his two wounds, that he could go no farther; so we were oblig'd to take a new guide there and go to Tholouse, where we found a warm climate, a fruitful pleasant country, and no snow, no wolves, or any thing like them. But when we told our story at Tholouse, they told us it was nothing but what was ordinary in the great forest at the foot of the mountains, especially when the snow lay on the ground. They enquir'd much what kind of a guide we had gotten, that would venture to bring us that way in such a severe season, and told us it was very much we were not all devour'd. When we told them how we plac'd ourselves, and the horses in the middle, they blam'd us exceedingly, and told us it was fifty to one but we had been all destroy'd, for it was the sight of the horses which made the wolves so furious, seeing their prey; and that at other times they are really afraid of a gun. But they being excessive hungry, and raging on that account, the eagerness to come at the horses had made them senseless of danger; and that if we had not by the continu'd fire, and at last by the stratagem of the train of powder, master'd them, it had been great odds but that we had been torn to pieces; whereas had we been content to have sat still on horseback, and fir'd as horsemen, they would not have taken the horses for so much their own, when men were on their backs, as otherwise. Withal they told us, that at last, if we had stood altogether, and left our horses, they would have been so eager to have devour'd them, that we might have come off safe, especially having our fire-arms in our hands, and being so many in number.

For my part, I was never so sensible of danger in my life; for seeing above three hundred devils come roaring and open-mouth'd to devour us, and having nothing to shelter us, or retreat to, I gave myself over for lost. As it was, I believe, I shall never care to cross those mountains again; I think I would much rather go a thousand leagues by sea, tho' I were sure to meet with a storm once a week.

I have nothing uncommon to take notice of, in my passage thro' France; nothing but what other travellers have given an account of, with much more advantage than I can. I travell'd from Bourdeaux to Paris, and without any considerable stay, came to Calais, and landed safe at Dover, the 14th of January, after having had a severely cold season to travel in.

I was now come to the center of my travels, and had in a little time all my new discover'd estate safe about me, the bills of exchange which I brought with me having been very currently pay'd.

My principal guide, and privy councellor, was my good

antient widow, who in gratitude for the money I had sent her, thought no pains too much, or care too great, to employ for me. I trusted her so entirely with every thing, that I was perfectly easy as to the security of my effects, and indeed, I was very happy from my beginning, and now to the end, in the unspotted integrity of this good gentlewoman.

And now I began to think of leaving my effects with this woman, and setting out for Lisbon, and so to the Brasils. But now another scruple came in my way, and that was religion; for as I had entertain'd some doubts about the Roman religion, even while I was abroad, especially in my state of solitude, so I knew there was no going to the Brasils for me, much less going to settle there, unless I resolv'd to embrace the Roman Catholick religion, without any reserve; unless on the other hand, I resolv'd to be a sacrifice to my principles, be a martyr for religion, and die in the Inquisition. So I resolv'd to stay at home, and if I could find means for it, to dispose of my plantation.

To this purpose I wrote to my old friend at Lisbon, who in return gave me notice that he could easily dispose of it there. But that if I thought fit to give him leave to offer it in my name to the two merchants, the survivors of my trustees, who liv'd in the Brasils, who must fully understand the value of it, who liv'd just upon the spot, and who I knew were very rich, so that he believ'd they would be fond of buying it, he did not doubt, but I should make 4,000 or 5,000 pieces of eight, the more of it.

Accordingly I agre'd, gave him order to offer it to them, and he did so; and in about eight months more, the ship being then return'd, he sent me account that they had accepted the offer and had remitted 33,000 pieces of eight, to a correspondent of theirs at Lisbon, to pay for it.

In return, I sign'd the instrument of sale in the form which they sent from Lisbon and sent it to my old man, who sent me bills of exchange for 32,800 pieces of eight to me, for the estate; reserving the payment of 100 moidores a year to him, the old man, during his life, and 50 moidores afterwards to his son for his life, which I had promis'd them, which the plantation was to make good as a rent-charge. And thus I have given the first part of a life of fortune and adventure, a life of Providence's chequerwork, and of a variety which the world will seldom be able to show the like of. Beginning foolishly, but closing much more happily than any part of it ever gave me leave so much as to hope for.

Any one would think that in this state of complicated good fortune, I was past running any more hazards, and so indeed I had been, if other circumstances had concurr'd. But I was inur'd to a wand'ring life, had no family, not many relations, nor however rich had I contracted much acquaintance; and tho' I had sold my estate in the Brasils, yet I could not keep the country out of my head, and had a great mind to be upon the wing again, especially I could not resist the strong inclination I had to see my island and to know if the poor Spaniards were in being there and how the rogues I left there had used them.

My true friend, the widow, earnestly disuaded me from it, and so far prevail'd with me that for almost seven years she prevented my running abroad. During which time, I took my two nephews, the children of one of my sisters into my care. The eldest, having something of his own, I bred up as a gentleman, and gave him a settlement of some addition to his estate, after my decease; the other I put out to a captain of a ship; and after five years, finding him a sensible, bold, enterprizing young fellow, I put him into a good ship and sent him to sea. And this young fellow afterwards drew me in, as old as I was, to further adventures myself.

In the meantime, I in part settl'd myself here; for first of all I marry'd, and that not either to my disadvantage or dissatisfaction, and had three children, two sons and one daughter. But my wife dying, and my nephew coming home with good success from a voyage to Spain, my inclination to go abroad, and his importunity prevail'd and engag'd me to go in his ship, as a private trader to the East Indies. This was in the year 1694.

In this voyage I visited my new colony in the island, saw my successors the Spaniards, had the whole story of their lives, and of the villains I left there; how at first they insulted the poor Spaniards, how they afterwards agre'd, disagre'd, united, separated, and how at last the Spaniards were oblig'd to use violence with them. How they were subjected to the Spaniards, how honestly the Spaniards used them; a history, if it were enter'd into, as full of variety and wonderful accidents, as my own part, particularly also as to their battles with the Carribees, who landed several times upon the island; and as to the improvement they made upon the island itself, and how five of them made an attempt upon the main-land, and brought away eleven men and five women prisoners, by which, at my coming, I found about twenty young children on the island.

Here I stay'd about twenty days, left them supplies of all necessary things, and particularly of arms, powder, shot, cloaths, tools, and two workmen, which I brought from England with me, viz., a carpenter and a smith.

Besides this, I shar'd the island into parts with them, reserv'd to myself the property of the whole, but gave them such parts respectively as they agre'd on. Having settl'd all things with them and engag'd them not to leave the place, I left them there.

From thence I touch'd at the Brasils from whence I sent a bark, which I bought there, with more people to the island, and in it, besides other supplies, I sent seven women, being such as I found proper for service, or for wives to such as would take them. As to the Englishmen, I promis'd them to send them some women from England, with a good cargo of necessaries, if they would apply themselves to planting, which I afterwards perform'd. And the fellows prov'd very honest and diligent after they were master'd, and had their properties set apart for them. I sent them also from the Brasils five cows, three of them being big with calf, some sheep, and some hogs, which, when I came again, were considerably encreas'd.

But all these things, with an account how three hundred Caribees came and invaded them, and ruin'd their plantations, and how they fought with that whole number twice, and were at first defeated, and three of them kill'd; but at last a storm destroying their enemies' canoes, they famish'd or destroy'd almost all the rest, and renew'd and recover'd the possessions of their plantation, and still liv'd upon the island.

All these things, with some very surprizing incidents in some new adventures of my own, for ten years more, I may perhaps give a further account of hereafter.